'Rare and very refreshing... a n̶o̶v̶e̶l̶ ̶w̶h̶e̶r̶e̶ middle-aged women are represented in all their wise, sensual, flawed complexity. I enjoyed it SO much'                    **Marian Keyes**

'A psychological thriller in the truest sense of the word: a thoughtful examination of the psyche of three credible women with baggage and flaws. So much will resonate, not least Hall's exploration of gender politics and motherhood. At points I was folding pages repeatedly. Deeply unsettling. Recommended'
**Sarah Vaughan**

'Not only a deeply satisfying psychological thriller but an insightful and sometimes disquieting exploration of relation-ships, families and the challenges and pressures confronting women today'                    **Cara Hunter**

'A brilliant exploration of the secrets and hidden lives women create for themselves as they try to navigate their way through life. The friendships are real and touching, the relationships are consuming and passionate. I read this in no time and really enjoyed the pace, flow and insights Araminta writes about. A fabulous novel of modern love, life and people, with an excellent twist'                    **Dorothy Koomson**

'A dark, delicious thriller which holds the complexity of female friendship at its heart. I loved it'                    **Louise O'Neill**

'A stunning, dark novel about who women want to be and the reality of who they are. Beautifully written, thought-provoking and should not be missed'                    **Samantha Downing**

'*Perfect Strangers* is a painfully honest, haunting portrait of friendship, betrayal, marriage and disappointment. While Hall is able to keep you on the edge of your seat (and awake much later than you should be) she can also make you weep, such is her insight and lack of judgement of the human condition. A beautiful book that will stay with me for a very long time'

**Dolly Wells**

'Beautifully written and expertly structured – a masterclass in psychological thriller writing'  **Simon Lelic**

'A slow-burning, tense build to a furious conclusion. Female friendships and the compromises women make are explored in stark detail, and through three different perspectives the story develops to a pleasing and very just ending. It's great'

**Harriet Tyce**

'It's been clear from the start that Araminta Hall has a talent for telling unpalatable truths and *Perfect Strangers* is no exception. Expertly peels the layers from the everyday lies we tell each other, and ourselves'  **Sarah Hilary**

'Dark, visceral, proper psychological thriller with a powerful feminist agenda'  **Laura Wilkinson**

'An immersive, intelligent and gripping exploration of the deep wells of female friendship and what it means to be a woman in a world made by and for men. Hall gives us three flawed female characters and shows how their expectations of life are thwarted in different ways, exploring their relationships and enticingly messy behaviour with compassion, even in the darkest of deeds'

**S.E. Lynes**

**Araminta Hall** has worked as a writer, journalist and teacher. Her first novel, *Everything and Nothing*, was published in 2011 and became a Richard & Judy read that year. Her second, *Dot*, was published in 2013, and her third, *Our Kind of Cruelty*, in 2018.

She has taught creative writing for many years at a variety of places, including New Writing South in Brighton, where she lives with her husband and three children.

Follow Araminta on Twitter @aramintahall to find out more.

*Also by Araminta Hall*

Everything and Nothing
Dot
Our Kind of Cruelty

'A stunning example of the new breed of "psychological thriller" with a deep dive into the conflicted worlds of three brilliantly drawn female characters, irradiated by a terrible crime. A pitch-perfect, meticulously-observed and utterly absorbing novel'

**Philippa East**

'A cracking read'                    **Steph McGovern**

'A dark take on friendship and festering secrets that had me turning pages well into the night'    **Caroline Hulse**

'A tense psychological story about female friendship and bad choices'                    **Julie Cohen**

'A perfect slow burning thriller that beautifully dissects the complexities of female friendship and the choices women make'

**Nikki Smith**

'A brilliantly unsettling exploration of secrets and lies'

**Jo Spain**

'A psychological page-turner of a story that deftly explores the dark and confronting dualities of womanhood. I read it hungrily in a day'                    **Laura Jane Williams**

'Toxic relationships, crushed hopes and rebuilding yourself from rock bottom ... a fabulous novel'    **Liv Matthews**

'The story of three female friends and the equally imperfect men in their lives. It's about deception, disappointment & murder. It's also about female friendship and platonic love, which cuts through the darkness. Gripping stuff!'    **Paul Burston**

# PERFECT STRANGERS

Araminta Hall

ORION

An Orion paperback

First published in Great Britain in 2020
by Orion Fiction,
This paperback edition published in 2021
by Orion Fiction,
an imprint of The Orion Publishing Group Ltd.,
Carmelite House, 50 Victoria Embankment
London EC4Y 0DZ

An Hachette UK Company

1 3 5 7 9 10 8 6 4 2

A CIP catalogue record for this book is
available from the British Library.

ISBN (Paperback) 978 1 4091 9610 5

Typeset at The Spartan Press Ltd,
Lymington, Hants

Printed and bound in Great Britain by Clays Ltd,
Elcograf S.p.A.

MIX
Paper from
responsible sources
FSC® C104740

www.orionbooks.co.uk

To my own wonderfully imperfect women,
Polly, Emily M, Dolly, Shami & Emily S

'The perfect human being is all human beings put together, it is a collective, it is all of us that makes perfection.'

*Socrates*

# ELEANOR

'Eleanor.'

She sat up because she hadn't even been aware of answering the phone and the night was still black and nothing made sense. Her head spun and she dropped it forward to make it stop, which allowed other things to fall into place.

'Robert?'

'I'm sorry to wake you.'

'What time is it?'

'Just after four.'

'My God, has something happened?'

'No. Well, I don't know. Nancy's not here. I must have fallen asleep when I was reading because I've just woken up and she's not back. And her phone's going straight to voicemail.'

The streetlights were seeping in through the cracks in Eleanor's curtains and she tried to focus on the strip of artificial light, as if it meant something.

'You don't know where she is, do you? I mean, she didn't by any chance come back to yours after dinner, did she?' His voice sounded like overstretched elastic.

'No, no, she didn't.' She swung her legs out of the bed and all the irritation she'd felt for Nancy the night before, for ages really, sloshed around her body. 'Look, I can be there in fifteen minutes.'

'Oh, God, you don't have to ...'

'It's fine, Robert. I'll throw on some clothes and get in the car.'

The elastic in his voice snapped. 'Oh God, do you think then ... I mean, should I call the police?'

'No, wait for me.' Eleanor pulled on her jeans as she spoke and her irritation mutated to anger. She wanted to pick up something and hurl it against the wall. She wanted to scream into Nancy's perfect face. She wouldn't let her get away with this. She would recount everything, every last painful second, she would spare her nothing.

As she drove the few miles between her small flat and Nancy's large house, Eleanor calibrated all the words she would say to her friend when she saw her next. How she would demand that Nancy stopped playing these stupid games with them all and just bloody own up to what she'd done so they could get on with their lives. Over the years Eleanor had watched Nancy constantly create little dramas in her life, culminating now in this big one, and she couldn't help wondering if it was to add interest to a life that wasn't nearly as full as it could have been. She wondered sometimes what it must be like to occupy Nancy's brilliant brain, but never put it to any tangible use. Nancy could really have been or done anything, and yet she had so often failed to commit to anything whole-heartedly. It sometimes felt like Nancy had written herself out of the story of her own life, and surely that was an act of sabotage.

She stopped at a red traffic light and three teenagers tripped across the road, their arms interlinked, their faces creased by laughter. And then she just felt sad because they seemed to have appeared like a message from her past, or a rip in the seam of time, because they could have been her, Nancy and Mary from thirty years before.

One of the girls turned as they passed the car and her gaze locked with Eleanor's so her smile faltered for a moment before she was pulled back into the conversation by her friend. They looked like the students Nancy, Mary and her had been when they'd met, on almost the first day of Freshers' week, amazed at their luck in finding each other so soon. Eleanor wondered if they were going back to a messy house in which they'd laugh about the night they'd just had, before talking about the people they were going to become, the loves they would experience, the lives waiting for them to step into.

As she started driving again she tried to remember what it was they'd felt so certain they'd accomplish. She supposed she'd not swerved too far from her path, although she'd imagined herself running Oxfam and sitting on committees by now, instead of the small aid charity she'd set up. Mary had wanted to stay in the world of Greek gods forever and had her eye on a life of academia. In actuality, Eleanor thought her life more closely resembled the punishment of a Greek god, with her terrible marriage that seemed to have sucked the life out of her, although she did undeniably adore her children, who were now not even children, and where the hell did time go. It was hard even to remember what Nancy had wanted to be. Eleanor thought it had to do with journalism, editing a newspaper she thought had been the ultimate goal, although it all seemed so unlikely now, as the idea of Nancy ever being satisfied enough by anything seemed implausible.

Nancy and Robert's house was lit up like a Christmas tree. Eleanor could tell from the road that Robert must have been into every room and now it shone out of the dark street as if ready for a party. Robert's face showed up in the rounded living-room window and he opened the front door as she came up the steps, where they hugged a greeting, him drawing her in as he always did.

'Shall I make some tea?' he asked as they went downstairs to the basement kitchen.

'I'll do it. Sit down,' Eleanor said.

He did as he was told, folding his already crumpled body into a chair and rubbing his hands into his eyes, creasing further his already rumpled skin. His blond hair was a mess, sleep ravaged, she thought, and it spiked her familiar tenderness for him.

They sat together and sipped their tea and neither of them said anything because neither of them wanted to be the one to say it, neither wanted to know or tell. For a second, Eleanor thought, they could have just been a couple, an early start at work beckoning, their comfortable house settled around them.

'Do you know where she is?' Robert asked finally.

'Not exactly.' Eleanor cupped her hands around her mug and tried to imagine how she was going to say what she knew.

'But there is someone else, isn't there?' He looked straight at her with his question.

'Oh God, Robert, I could kill Nancy.' She couldn't be the one to tell Robert, but then again she couldn't lie to his face.

'How long has it been going on?'

'You need to have this conversation with her.'

'But I can't, she's not here.'

Eleanor thought that Nancy had been putting her in impossible situations for most of their lives, but this was perhaps the worst. She might not forgive her this time. 'Oh, Robert, I'm so sorry.'

'Did she go to him last night?'

'After we met, she said she was going to meet him. I didn't know beforehand, I promise.'

'It's not your fault, Eleanor.' But his voice was harsher than she'd heard before. 'Do you think that's it then? Have they run away together?'

'I really don't think so. She's been trying to end things with him, but he hasn't been taking no for an answer.' For the first time, Eleanor felt a seam of fear in her belly because Nancy had been wanting to end the affair for a while now and she couldn't imagine what this other man could have said to make her change her mind like this. Nancy wasn't mean, she certainly wasn't the sort of person not to come home to her husband of over twenty years. She spoke again to allay her fears. 'She's hardly told me anything about him, beyond the fact of him. She was upset last night. She really has been trying to finish things.'

'Who is he?'

Eleanor felt nausea rise through her body with the warmth of the tea. 'Really, I don't know. All she's told me is that he's called David and she met him through a work thing.'

He flinched at the information as if she'd burnt him. 'But is it serious enough for her to do this, for her to leave?'

Eleanor thought of Nancy's pale face from the night before, from this same night really, which was an absurd thought. It was true that she'd wanted to end the affair, but she had also been visibly devastated and it was always so hard to tell with Nancy what was real or exaggerated. Eleanor comforted herself with the thought that Nancy was impetuous and daring. She wouldn't have run away, but it was possible that she could have done something this stupid. Eleanor looked back at Robert and his sharp blue eyes, his solid being, and she couldn't understand why he hadn't been enough. She'd gone to bed feeling guilty that she hadn't been nicer to her friend, but now she thought she hadn't been harsh enough.

'I don't know. It's been going on for about a year.' He rocked backwards with her words. 'But, really, she was in the process of ending it, or at least trying to. She wants to try to make it work with you.' God, Nancy deserved less than this.

'So this could just be one last...' His words trailed into the air, their sordidness sullying the perfection of the new kitchen Nancy had just put in.

'Oh, Robert, this is fucking ghastly. You don't deserve this. I am so sorry.' Eleanor thought of the times she'd sat round this table eating Robert's food and drinking his wine, of the weekends spent at their Sussex house, of the comfy beds and hot baths, of the fireside chats and the long walks. And it seemed shameful that she had betrayed his friendship.

'Anyone would have done the same in your position. I mean, Nancy's your friend.'

'But you're my friend too.' She reached over and put her hand over his as she spoke and his skin was surprisingly soft.

The smile he gave her was stretched and tight.

'If it makes it any better I've told her how much I disapprove of it all, since the beginning. I've never encouraged her.'

He checked the clock above the door and so Eleanor followed his gaze. 'I suppose I should be getting ready for work.'

'But it's only five-thirty.'

'We've got a big case on.'

'But, I mean, surely today. Are you really going in?'

'I can't sit around here moping. And I'd rather not make any decisions before I've spoken to Nancy. It would be better to keep busy.'

'So you're going to forgive her?' Eleanor's voice sounded shrill to her ears. 'Without knowing any of the facts?' The charm of Nancy's life reverberated around her and for a moment she couldn't bear it, couldn't bear that she would get away with this as well. But she pushed that thought away because she needed to stop letting the last year sour her feelings about Nancy. Nancy was also a woman she loved and cherished, who made her laugh, who was always at the other end of the phone, who often took care of her.

'I didn't say that.' Eleanor heard the pureness of the anger in his voice. His hand was gripping the side of the table, the veins standing out of his skin. 'But we've been together for a very long time. And there's Zara. I mean, you don't just throw away over twenty years.'

The moment felt unreal, maybe because it was so early and still dark as night outside. Eleanor swallowed down her tears along with her shame – of course she didn't know what it was like to consider those sorts of things, other people, long-time loving. But then Robert stood and so Eleanor did the same because he clearly wanted her to leave.

'Thanks for coming,' Robert said as they made their way back up the stairs.

They stopped at the front door. 'How did you know she was having an affair?'

Robert shrugged and his eyes refused to rest on hers. 'Something's obviously been up for a while. I suppose it's just one of the things you consider.'

Eleanor rubbed Robert's arm through his jersey. 'I think you'll sort it out. I hope you do.'

He opened the front door and the chill of the early morning was penetrating. 'If you hear from her today let me know, she might not call me.'

'Of course I will. And you me.' She was shivering with the cold, but Robert hadn't seemed to notice. 'Anyway.' She turned to go but as she did a white car pulled up outside the house. She looked back at Robert and his face told her that she wasn't wrong. They both watched in the silent, thick stillness of the beginning of a day as two policemen got out of the car and turned towards the house.

'Oh God,' Robert said behind her.

As they came up the steps, their uniforms blended into the dark.

'Mr Hennessy?' one asked.

'Yes,' Robert said.

'Can we come in, please, sir?'

Robert stepped backwards and Eleanor remembered how you had to invite vampires into your house, they couldn't just walk in.

They went back into the hall and Eleanor wanted to shake them all, to ask the policemen why it wasn't strange to find them standing on the doorstep before dawn. She didn't want to be part of their world in which everything and anything was probable.

'Is there somewhere we can sit down?' the policeman asked, so Robert opened the door to the drawing room, painted in the bright yellow Nancy had always loved. *One room in every house should be sunny*, Eleanor heard her say as she sat on the sofa, like they were a group of friends who happened to be meeting before most people were awake.

'Sorry, and you are?' the policeman said to her.

'Oh, sorry, this is Eleanor Meakins. She's a good friend of my wife's.' The statement hung terrifyingly in the air when it should have needed explanation.

'Please, Mr Hennessy, sit down,' the policeman said.

'No,' replied Robert, 'I'd rather stand.'

The policeman removed his hat and his colleague copied. 'I'm very sorry. The body of a woman in her late forties was found just over an hour ago and we have reason to believe it is your wife, Nancy Hennessy.'

Robert sat at that, right next to Eleanor; she felt the sofa compress and his body sink against hers. She concentrated on that for as long as she could as the rest of the world spun around her.

'What makes you think it's Nancy?' Robert asked finally.

'Her bag was found with her and her driving licence was in her purse.' The second policeman still hadn't spoken and Eleanor wondered if he was on some sort of training exercise.

'Oh my God. What happened to her?' Eleanor's mind was filled with the thought of Nancy spending the night out in this freezing cold.

'At the moment we're not entirely sure. But it looks like she suffered a head trauma.'

Eleanor tried to make sense of the words that were being said. They had called Nancy a body and now they were talking about a head trauma. Surely someone hadn't hurt her in some way, surely there was some mistake? She felt a sickening anger at that thought, and a desperate desire to rush to her friend and soothe away her pain.

'Where is she?' Eleanor asked. 'I mean, is she dead?'

Both policemen and Robert turned to look at her as if she was stupid. 'Yes,' the speaking policeman said finally. 'I'm sorry, I thought you understood . . .' He blushed a deep crimson. 'She's in a mortuary now.'

'Where was she found?' Robert asked.

'By the river, near Hammersmith. I'm sorry to ask but have you got a recent photo of your wife?'

Robert didn't seem like he was going to move so Eleanor stood and fetched a photo from the mantelpiece. She picked a recent one of Nancy with her arm round Zara. Bad photos of Nancy didn't exist, but this one was particularly luminous because the sun was behind her and accentuating her perfection, almost giving her an outline. She handed it to the policeman and he nodded when he looked at it.

'We're going to have to ask you to come and identify the body, Mr Hennessy. Or if there's someone who can do it for you?'

Robert groaned, a low bear-like sound.

'I can do it,' Eleanor said.

'No,' Robert said. 'It should be me.'

Their eyes met as he spoke and Eleanor felt a jolt of terror pass through her as she realised that everything about Nancy's death was worse than any other death anywhere. They would all suffer and nothing would ever be the same again.

As she waited for Robert on the cold plastic chairs outside the viewing room she couldn't remember how they'd arrived at the mortuary. She tried to reassemble the journey in her mind, to give it some cohesion, but nothing came. Robert reappeared relatively quickly, but his eyes were unfocused and his body appeared to be trembling.

'Do you mind if I go in?' Eleanor surprised herself by saying, but he waved her in, so then she felt like she should.

The room was artificially dark, or at least subdued, with fake flowers dusty in vases and a navy velvet chair in one corner. The outline of a body, which Eleanor supposed to be Nancy, lay on the bed, covered by a sheet. A woman was standing next to the shape and she nodded, so Eleanor nodded back. The woman leant forward and folded the white sheet back, so Eleanor only realised what she was doing when it was too late and she didn't have any time to prepare herself for what she was going to see. And then there was nothing more to do than step closer and look at her friend. She momentarily felt a pang of relief because they'd clearly got it wrong, it wasn't really her. It was just a facsimile of Nancy, a waxwork, a cardboard cut-out. Eleanor wanted to reach out and feel her skin, which already looked devoid of anything meaningful. Her beauty, which had been so present in life, had vanished, as if it knew what was to come, as if it couldn't bear to let itself mush and decay and be eaten by worms. Eleanor gasped at her own thoughts, but the woman holding the sheet averted her gaze and besides, she must have seen everything in this terrible room. What a job. It seemed impossible that anyone would want a job like this.

Eleanor stepped closer because there was something wrong, or missing perhaps, that she couldn't work out. Nancy's left cheekbone was swollen and a yellow bruise had crept up under the strange turban-like thing she was wearing. Her jaw looked strange as well, almost as if she'd been to the dentist and left in the wodge of cotton wool they used. She wanted to turn away because it all spoke of something very ugly that had happened to her friend and she couldn't bear to think of the violence that must have produced those marks. Her last moments had been painful, that much was blindingly clear.

But in fact the strangest thing was that Nancy didn't have any hair, or at least that her hair had been completely covered by this odd turban. Nancy was always surrounded by her golden hair, long and straight in university, rising upwards, curling, now a flouncy bob that stopped just above her shoulders. That was as far as her hair would go, Eleanor realised with a jolt, Nancy would never have another haircut.

But mixed in with all of that, was the knowledge that Eleanor had known Nancy had been going to meet her lover, and what if he was the person who had done this? What if Eleanor could have said the right words to stop her going and didn't? She hadn't even tried, she realised. Sickness rose through her and her anger at this woman she had shared so much of her life with pooled in a mess by her feet, so she was just left with shame at herself. Eleanor had loved this woman and had let this happen to her.

'Why has she got that round her head?' Eleanor pointed at the turban, as if it mattered.

'The wound on the back of the head was quite substantial, this is so we contain it,' the woman answered.

'Will there be a post-mortem?'

'I would imagine so.'

'So they'll cut her up? She won't ever look like this again?' Eleanor couldn't understand why any of this mattered, but it was fuelling a building desperation inside her. She wanted very much to lean down and kiss Nancy's alabaster cheek, but she didn't dare, not just because she was being watched, but because of what it might make her feel.

'They're very good at their job. And it really is essential in cases like this, it helps us recover all the evidence.'

Eleanor nodded, because what else was there. She heard the woman replacing the sheet as she left.

A policeman drove them home, or at least to Nancy's home, which already felt vacuous without her in it, or the knowledge of her return. It was filled with other police, both inside and out, the rooms busy and crowded. There were also a few people loitering outside, a couple with cameras slung about their necks, one of whom rushed up to them and asked Robert if he wanted to make any comment, before being pushed aside. Once inside, a policewoman asked Robert if he wanted them to inform Zara, she said a family liaison officer could be sent to her university halls and she would be taken care of. But Robert said no, he had to do it, which was not something he looked capable of. He considered driving up to tell her in person, but Eleanor persuaded him against that and they compromised by dispatching the family liaison to be there after Zara had taken the phone call. Eleanor left him alone and went to the kitchen with a different policeman where she started to make tea, aware that there was nothing really useful she could do and that from now on all tasks might seem pointless.

It was absurd that nothing was different: that you still had to get a teabag from its box in the cupboard, drop it into a mug, fill the kettle and flick the switch, listen to the sing of the boil, pour the water over, fish out the bag, add milk. She watched herself perform these actions but they were as unconnected to her as the used brown bag that she dropped into the bin.

They sat and had their tea in the kitchen and Eleanor thought it was just another moment, that was all. And she had had plenty of terrible moments in her life. Probably none quite as terrible or unreal as this, but nonetheless, another moment to be lived through, like all the others. What was important was for her to remember this wasn't about her, it was about Nancy, Robert and Zara. She mustn't think about her dinner with Nancy the night before, or what had been said, or not said. She couldn't fall apart, not yet.

'Do you mind if I ask you a few questions?' the policeman said, breaking into her thoughts. The sky had lightened to a dead grey outside and, when she looked up through the window, she could see the trees on the street stripped and bare, tiny specks of rain pattering the glass. 'My name is DS Daniels and we find if we get these cases started quickly we have much better outcomes.'

'What do you mean? What cases?' Momentarily, Eleanor was lost in what he meant.

'Suspicious deaths.' The policeman looked exasperated and it made Eleanor realise that this had now officially become something else.

'Do you, I mean, do you think she was murdered, then? I mean, isn't it possible that she fell or something?' Except she had seen Nancy and her face sort of put paid to that thought, but she clung on stubbornly because it had to be the best option in a series of terrible ones.

'Everything is possible at this stage,' DS Daniels said, calmly. 'But there are certain indications that are pointing us towards the thought that this wasn't an accidental death.'

'Oh God.' It felt like things were slipping away and they were entering a new realm.

'We know you had dinner with Mrs Hennessy last night.'

'Yes.'

'It makes what you tell us extremely important.'

'I suppose it does.' She could hear herself speaking, but it all seemed unlikely.

'How did Mrs Hennessy seem? Do you know where she went after dinner? What time did you leave the restaurant?'

Eleanor drew in her breath because now, she knew, was the moment that she would make everything change. 'We left around ten and Nancy went to meet her lover.'

DS Daniels sat forward, unable to check his excitement. 'Her lover? Who is that?'

'I don't know.' Eleanor suddenly felt so weary she worried she might simply fall asleep. There was too much to tell and too little time.

'Does Mr Hennessy know about the lover?'

'Yes. At least he does now. He rang me at four this morning, because Nancy hadn't come home, and I came round and told him. But he'd guessed already.'

'How had he guessed?'

She looked at the eager man writing in his book and it struck her again that this was no more than a job to him, possibly a promotion if all went well. 'I'm not sure. He said they'd been getting on badly and it's one of the things you consider.'

'And you say you don't know the lover's identity?'

'That's right. Nancy was very ashamed about it all. She'd only spoken to me about it because she felt so guilty, but she never told me any details.' Eleanor remembered what it had been like in the early days of the affair, when she'd practically had to peel Nancy off the ceiling to have a conversation, but she also wanted to protect Nancy from what she knew everyone would think because that wasn't the truth about her friend. 'The only thing she ever told me was that he was called David and she met him through work.'

'Nothing else? No surname?'

'Of course I'd tell you if I knew his surname.'

'But you're sure he was called David?'

'Yes, it was the only specific piece of information she ever told me about him. And only because I asked so many times. She said I didn't know him so there was no point in telling me any details.' But then Eleanor remembered something from the night before, which seemed like a thousand years ago. 'Oh, actually, I asked Nancy last night if he was married and had children and she said yes.'

'That's all she said? She didn't tell you the name of his wife, or how many children?'

'No.' Eleanor focused on a line of red spots at the side of the policeman's chin, which could be a shaving rash.

'Do you know how long had it been going on?'

'A bit over a year, that I know of.'

'So possibly longer?'

'Possibly, yes.' Although Nancy was bad at keeping things to herself, so Eleanor thought it unlikely.

'And did Nancy talk to anyone else about this?'

'I don't know. I don't think so. Maybe our friend Mary, but I think I'd know if she had.' She thought of Mary going about her life and it seemed impossible that it hadn't yet been shattered.

'She was really scared about Robert finding out, so I can't imagine she spoke to anyone else about it.'

DS Daniels wrote in his pad. 'And she said she met him through work?'

'Yes. I think she said at a party.'

'Where did Mrs Hennessy work?'

'Well, actually, mainly at home. She translates books. She speaks fluent French, so if a publisher buys a French book she would translate it into English.'

Eleanor thought the policeman looked depressed at the number of paths that answer could lead him down.

'And when you left the restaurant last night did Nancy tell you where she was meeting this David? Or did you see which direction she went in?'

Eleanor felt her face flush with the memory of their parting. 'Actually, Nancy left before me. I stayed on to pay, so no, I didn't see where she went.' Eleanor wondered if the policeman understood what a terrible friend she was.

'Did you pay because Nancy had no money on her?'

'No, I mean, I didn't ask, I just offered to pay.' At least that made Eleanor feel a bit better. 'But Nancy always had money on her.'

'Would she have been carrying cash, do you think?'

'I don't know. Why are you asking this?'

He looked like he didn't want to tell her why, but then said, 'When she was found her purse was lying open next to her body and there was no cash or cards in it.'

'She definitely would have had a card at least on her.'

'And did she have a phone?'

'Yes, of course. Was that gone as well?'

'We didn't find one. Did you see her use her phone last night?'

Eleanor searched through her memory but all she could see

was Nancy's pleading face. 'No, sorry. But I'm completely sure she would have had it on her.'

'Yes, most people do.'

'But surely the man she was meeting wouldn't have robbed her?' It was definitely better if she hadn't been killed by the lover, as if it made Eleanor less responsible.

The policeman nodded, but then ruined it by saying, 'Robbery isn't the only reason someone might take those things.'

'Oh God, because there could be messages from him on her phone? Can't you trace it somehow, or read the messages anyway?'

'We've got a team working on that now, but it's not quite as easy as TV shows would have you believe.' He leant back and stopped himself from stretching. 'Anyway, you've been very helpful, Miss Meakins.'

Eleanor stayed until Zara got home and then she left them to it – a weeping bundle of misery, which made her feel like an intruder. Also Nancy's mother, Pearl, was on her way and the thought of seeing her was too much right then. She promised to come back in the morning, not sure if she was needed or wanted, except Robert looked so grateful that she thought she should. It was dark again by the time Eleanor left and this time nothing stopped her; it could have been a replay of the morning and Nancy might not be dead and time could have unravelled and any way you looked at it nothing was ever going to be the same again.

She sat with her hands on the steering wheel and her body felt shredded, as if a car had run her over and then reversed back again and again. Her mouth was dry and her heart jarred against her ribs, the sweat lining her armpits so her own odour rose to greet her. Mary still didn't know. It wasn't something she had felt capable of telling her over the phone, but the policeman had warned her it would be all over the news that night and it was coming up for six o'clock and she doubted Mary watched it that early, but who knew. She started the car and turned in the direction of Kilburn, inching along with the rush-hour traffic, men and women locked in their own private lives, nothing out of the ordinary.

Mary's gate was still hanging off its hinges as it had done for years. Her front garden was still a mess of weeds and the broken pane of glass in the door was still held together with Sellotape. She rang the bell and Maisie answered, which meant she had to smile.

'Hi, Ellie.' Maisie smiled, her newly acquired teenage spots heartbreaking. 'I didn't know you were coming round.'

'I'm not. At least, I am, but nobody knew.'

'Mum,' Maisie shouted, 'Ellie's here.'

Mary came out of the kitchen, wiping her hands down her skirt, her hair hanging by her face in long strands and Eleanor found herself thinking she should cut it, as if that would resolve something.

'Ellie, what a lovely surprise.' She stepped forward. 'Is everything OK? You don't look well.'

Eleanor found something had lodged in her throat so even though she opened her mouth all that happened was she cried. 'Mimi,' Mary shouted up the stairs, 'come here.'

There was a thud and then Mimi was there, staring at Ellie along with her little sister and Eleanor knew it was all wrong, she was doing it all wrong.

'Take Maisie and go and watch some telly or something,' Mary said. 'Don't come into the kitchen.' Then she took Eleanor by the elbow and led her through to the hot, steamy room, which smelt of mince. 'Sit down,' she instructed and Eleanor did because otherwise she was going to faint anyway. 'Do you want anything?'

'Some wine. Or whisky. Or anything.'

Mary opened the fridge. 'Howard's got a beer in here?'

'That'll do.'

Mary handed her the cold black can and sat next to her. 'What the hell's happened, Els?'

She tried to think of a good way of saying what she knew, but there was none. 'Nancy's dead. The police seem to think she was murdered.' The beer tasted yeasty and reminded her why she didn't like it, but at least it stopped her crying.

'What on earth do you mean?' Mary's eyes were wide behind her glasses so she looked like a cartoon character.

'Oh my God, Mary, she's dead.'

Mary sank into a chair and started crying in a way Eleanor wished she could, in a pure and complete way, with noise and tears and snot. She moved her chair closer and put her arms around her old friend and they sat together while Mary heaved and moaned.

Eventually Mary's sobs subsided and when she pulled away her eyes were swollen and her cheeks blotchy. 'But how? I mean, why? When?'

'They found her really early this morning, on a path by the river in Hammersmith, right next to the bridge. She died from a large wound on the back of her head.'

Mary cupped her hand to her mouth as if she might be sick. 'Oh my God. But I mean, who did it? Do they know why?'

'No.' Eleanor felt the weight of all the conversations she'd had that day.

'Was she raped?'

The question felt like a jolt. 'God, I don't know. I don't think so. I mean, surely they'd have told us that.' Although maybe they'd said something to Robert and the thought churned her stomach.

'Was it a mugging that went wrong or something then?'

'It could be. Her bag was next to her, but her cash and phone are missing.'

'Oh God, she can't be dead over an iPhone.'

Eleanor took her friend's hand. 'Did you know she was having an affair?'

'No. My God, did she tell you?'

And Eleanor thought it was always there in friendships, even this far down the line, that possibility of jealousy. 'Yes, but I think only because she was desperate.'

'So they think he did it?'

'Yes, maybe. I saw Nancy last night and she was going to meet him afterwards. She's been trying to end it for a couple of months, but he's been making it very hard for her.'

'Who is he?'

'I don't know. She never told me.'

'How long have you known?'

'About a year.'

'Is that how long it's been going on?'

'I don't know. I think so, pretty much.'

Mary looked at her like everyone else had that day. A year of knowing that about one of your best friends and you don't make them tell you who it is? What sort of friend does that make you? What sort of person? She felt like she might float away soon.

'She must have told you something.'

'She didn't talk about it much. I know he was called David and she met him through work, but that hardly narrows it down.'

'God, poor Robert,' Mary said finally. 'How is he? And Zara?'

'Terrible, as you'd expect.'

Mary's face folded in on itself and the tears came again. 'Oh, I can't bear to think about them.'

Eleanor gulped from the metal can again, forcing the thick liquid down her throat.

'I can't get my head around any of it,' Mary said.

'Mary Mary Mary.' There was no pause between the words. They simply rolled down the stairs and through the door of the kitchen.

'What's Howard doing home?' Eleanor didn't bother to keep the harshness out of her voice.

'He's been here all day. Some sort of sick bug.'

Mary's name continued to bang on the door and Eleanor watched her friend stand automatically. 'For God's sake, tell him to shut up,' she said, so unlike herself that Mary paused on her way to the door. But at least she sat back down. 'You should have done that years ago.'

'What?'

'Not answered him.'

'But he's ill.'

'Well, yes, today he's ill. I'm talking generally.'

Mary leant forwards onto the table, her greasy hair pooled across her arms. 'Oh God, Ellie, not now please. We've got to get through this first.'

In the end Eleanor arrived home relatively early, just after half past eight, although she felt so ungrounded that time didn't seem entirely real. She had found herself unable to stay at Mary's, finding something grotesque about how even in the depth of misery, Mary still had to pull herself forward and consider other things. The full house made it impossible not to acknowledge that life was going to continue and much would stay the same. And Howard went on needing things, which Mary provided too easily in Eleanor's opinion, although her friend was right, it was not the time to go back down that well-trodden path. Besides, her dislike of Howard was insignificant compared to her misery at what had happened to Nancy.

So, Eleanor had made her excuses and left, promising to call in the morning. But, as she let herself into her house from the street and stepped into the bland hallway she shared with her downstairs neighbour, Irena, she felt a crushing dread at the thought of opening her own front door and being confronted with all the empty space in her flat. She'd seen the light on in Irena's front room as she'd walked up the path and she stood outside the door now, her hand raised, unsure whether or not to knock.

Eleanor's flat was the top floor of a house which had once belonged entirely to Irena, a house in which the woman had lived for over fifty years, since she'd arrived from Poland with her new husband all that time ago, bringing up her children and creating a life. A life which had involved its own share of terrible losses and hardships – her parents were murdered in the war and she nursed her husband through a fatal illness when their two children were very young. It made Eleanor hesitate to impose her own sadness on her, but she was also desperate for the woman's understanding.

As she stood outside Irena's door she thought back to when she'd made an offer on her flat, fifteen years before, and the estate agent had embarrassedly told her that she had to meet Irena before her offer could be accepted. It had put other people off, he'd said, but Eleanor had been charmed by the idea and agreed immediately, going round the next day to sit in Irena's warm, cinnamon-scented kitchen where they'd talked and laughed, so that afterwards she'd waited by her phone like an excited schoolgirl, desperate to know if the object of her affections returned her feelings.

They'd always been more than just neighbours, her and Irena, more than just people who exchanged polite chit-chat when they bumped into each other. They'd sat in each other's kitchens and learnt things about each other, they'd helped each other out of bad situations, they'd carried milk and medicine to front doors, they'd included each other at times of festivities. Then, a few years ago Irena's daughter, Sarah, had rung Eleanor and said she had begun to worry about her mother living alone, with both Sarah and her brother living over an hour away in different directions, but that Irena was refusing move. Eleanor had totally understood her reluctance to move, and had also been appalled at the idea of her not being there, so she'd said Sarah could call her anytime if she was worried about her mother, and that she would make sure she went to see Irena at least once a week. So now she had supper with Irena every Thursday, unless she was away or tied up with work, and it had become a little oasis in her week, which she sometimes thought she needed more than Irena did.

It wasn't Thursday, in fact it was Tuesday, but Eleanor longed for Irena as she stood outside her door and the hall light clicked itself off. She longed for her in a way she'd used to long for her mother, who had finally lost her grip on a sanity that had been tenuous for a while, five years before, and now wouldn't recognise her, even if she'd been able to speak. Eleanor knocked and tried not to cry. But as soon as Irena opened the door, leaning on her walking stick, and the sweet fog of her flat hit her she couldn't stop herself, her mouth simply pulling towards the ground and her tears spouting from her sore eyes.

'Eleanor, Eleanor,' Irena said in her accent that still retained its Polish roots, 'child, what is the matter?'

But Eleanor couldn't stop crying or form words into sentences, so Irena pulled at her elbow and she allowed herself to be led by this tiny woman, who hobbled in front of her to the little kitchen at the back of the house.

'Sit,' Irena said, pointing at a chair with her stick and so Eleanor sunk gratefully. 'Do you need tea? Or vodka?'

Eleanor laughed briefly. 'Vodka.'

Irena reached down to a low cupboard and produced a dusty bottle and two grimy shot glasses, which she placed on the table, before sitting herself. 'Now, you tell me what has happened.'

Eleanor accepted the little glass, greasy with fingerprints and age, downing the warm liquid that rushed through her blood. 'You know my friend Nancy?'

'The one with the big house and lots of complaints?'

Eleanor felt ashamed that her descriptions of Nancy had resulted in Irena seeing her this way. 'Yes. She died last night.'

'Oh my God.' Irena crossed her bony fingers over her pigeon chest and it made Eleanor think of her heart and how much sadness it had had to endure and she wondered how it had been possible. 'I am so sorry. How did it happen?'

'I think, maybe, I mean, they seem to think she was murdered.' The concept still didn't feel real to Eleanor; surely murder was something that happened to other people.

'The lady by the river? I heard about it on the news this evening.'

'Yes.' Eleanor's tears had now dried but her body had developed an internal shake. She poured them both more vodka and they both downed the shot. 'I don't know what to do, Irena.'

'Nothing tonight but weep. And then you get up tomorrow and you start doing.' She placed her hand over Eleanor's and it felt like wax paper.

'No, but you don't understand. I saw her last night and I wasn't nice to her.' The words felt sharp in Eleanor's chest.

'You argued?'

'Not really, no. It was an argument we'd been having for a while. I suppose I sort of disapproved of how she was living and I was angry with her that she couldn't seem to sort it out.'

'Ah.' Eleanor forced herself to look into Irena's eyes and tried to find the judgement she felt should be there, but if anything they looked worried, kindly even. 'We only bother to argue with the people we love, you know.' Eleanor tried to smile, but her face hurt too much. 'When my children were little and told me I was mean because I had shouted at them about their manners or told them they couldn't eat sweets for breakfast or all the other things that make mothers cross, I used to tell them that it takes so much more effort to be stern than it does just to say yes, that if I wanted an easy life I would let them do all they asked. But I also told them I loved them too much to always say yes, that I took the time to scold them and argue with them so they would learn what was right or wrong. Anger is often not cruelty, Eleanor, it is more often love.'

'But the last things I said to her were so unkind. I feel terrible.'

Irena shook her head. 'I don't think I have ever told you, Eleanor. But when my husband died I felt guilty for months afterwards. I was forever going over and over in my head how I could have made him more comfortable, or told him I loved him more, or hidden my sadness better. Anything I could find to torture myself with I did. Until one day I realised all I was doing was hiding from my grief. That the guilt allowed me to make it about me, not about losing him.'

Eleanor tried to let Irena's words penetrate her but she felt hollowed out by grief, as if it was eating away at her and she had to grab hold of something, anything to pull her back upwards.

'I'm not sure how I can go on.' She hated herself for saying those words to Irena, a woman who had experienced such hardships, but also couldn't stop herself.

Irena reached her hand up and cupped Eleanor's face so she was forced to meet her eyes. 'You will go on because you have to.'

'How did you do it, Irena?' Eleanor's voice was no more than a whisper and it felt like the whole world had contracted around them. She stared at Irena's creased face as if precious secrets were held within its pendulous folds.

'I remember that I am nothing special. I have this picture in my head of the world and all these bright lights shining out of it. All that goodness everywhere. And it reminds me that what feels like a great tragedy to me is nothing more than a small sorrow in the big scheme of things.'

'What do you mean?' Eleanor couldn't make sense of the idea of a smallness at this moment.

Irena's red, mouse-like eyes were watering, as they so often did. 'Sorrow is a bit like sacrifice. We, as women, absorb it so others don't have to. But then one day we stand back and we say, enough, I have done my bit, let another person take this. So we pass it on and the next woman steps forward and it all begins again. All our sorrows and sacrifices are small, ultimately, and that is a good thing. That is the way of the world.'

Eleanor's alarm sounded as it always did to the news at 7 a.m. the next day. But the stories didn't wash over her, or irritate her, or niggle at her conscience like they usually did. They instead lifted her out of her bed in pure terror, her heart hammering against her chest as the newsreader relayed the details that she already knew about her friend, details made so much more certain by the fact that they were coming out of a radio. She dressed quickly and went to the Co-op near her house, where she was greeted by Nancy's face on the cover of most editions, her smile looming out as if she didn't have a care in the world. They seemed to already know all the details and Eleanor wondered how it was possible that nothing stayed quiet or personal any more. Her phone vibrated in her pocket as she left empty handed, because she didn't want or need a souvenir of this terrible day.

'It's all over the news,' Mary said.

'Yes, I know.'

'How on earth do they know about the lover already? And how did they get a photograph of her?'

'The photo's her Facebook profile picture and the house was swarming with police yesterday, and there were already press outside, so I guess someone said something.' Whole sections of life that she had never before considered now seemed like a new order.

'Are you going there again today?'

'Yes, I'm on my way now.'

'Oh, God,' Mary said, which was precisely how Eleanor felt.

The numbers of young men and women in ill-fitting suits standing outside Nancy's house had at least doubled since the day before. A few shouted questions at her as she climbed the steps to the front door and a flashlight even went off behind her back. But inside it was like the house had been held in aspic. Nothing was different, it was all still awful, all still bitingly terrible. Nancy's mother, Pearl, had arrived and was apparently in Nancy's study, so Eleanor went to find her, even though she was scared by what she would find. The last time she'd seen Pearl had been at Nancy's father's funeral, and that had been about ten years before.

As Eleanor climbed the stairs to the study, she remembered being annoyed at the ease with which Nancy had found work after taking nearly a decade off after Zara was born. She'd bristled when Nancy had shown her the cosy room with duck-egg blue walls and a pale wooden desk, thinking of her own drab grey office in a municipal building where she actually employed people, or how if she worked from home it was at the kitchen table because her flat was so small. But she remembered also how Nancy had always been so aware of her ability to irritate. How, as they'd walked back downstairs, she'd said, 'I feel like a fraud with an office all set up when I've only got a couple of jobs.'

Eleanor also remembered how she'd replied and how much she'd meant the warm words, 'Well you shouldn't, it's lovely.'

'I'm so glad I'm doing it though,' Nancy said from behind her. 'It's taken me way too long. I've wanted to go back to work for ages, but I felt guilty when Zara was young. And then I lost my confidence and I didn't think anyone would want to employ me. I mean, they still might not, but at least I'm giving it a go now. And, you know, sometimes I find myself wandering around the house and think I might go mad with the fact that I don't really have anything to do. Or nothing that seems like it means anything much.' They'd reached the bottom of the stairs and Eleanor turned to see that Nancy had flushed red. 'God, I feel embarrassed admitting that to you, with your wonderful career.'

'What do you mean?' Eleanor thought it was strange how she could think damning things about Nancy, but when those same thoughts came out of Nancy's mouth she wanted to protect her from them. 'Are you talking about being a mum and making a home?'

'Yes.'

'But of course that's important.'

Nancy looked like she was close to tears. 'I know, but do you know how hard it is to hang on to that when you're actually doing it? When you're bombarded with women "having it all", as they like to say, rushing to a meeting in a smart suit with a baby on their hip. Domesticity has never been valued.'

It was hard not to think about Mary as Nancy spoke, so trapped under the weight of domesticity that Eleanor could sometimes go for weeks without seeing her and, when she finally did, she was either being climbed over by a child or distracted by someone else's problem. 'It's funny, but lots of the countries I've worked in, which we consider third world, value domesticity very highly. It's true that unmarried, young women are usually at the bottom of the social scale, but mothers are almost worshipped.'

'Yes, but here we worship money, so of course those who earn it are prized above those who don't.'

Eleanor had felt a rush of shame then as she realised she too could think like that about both Mary and Nancy, although she was less inclined with Mary because she had three young children and no money, which made everything seem more worthy. It was very confusing because they had all seemed like complete equals at university, but now, it was true, they had assumed positions that had nothing to do with who they were. Nothing was ever simple when you were a woman and she tried to think of a way to tell Nancy this. 'You know, I'm getting to that age where everybody asks me if I have kids and, when I say I don't, actually ask me why not, or if I want them, which they would never, ever do to a man. And there's this kind of judgement behind the question that I'm not fulfilling my womanly duties by becoming a mother. And then I work with lots of women who have children and they're constantly feeling guilty about not being with them, and definitely being judged by the same people who judge me for not having them, or you for not working.'

'How did we let this happen?' Nancy said and Eleanor thought she saw real fear in her eyes, which made her want to pull her into a hug and tell her it was all going to be all right.

She stepped forward and put her hand on to Nancy's arm. 'You know, Nance, you're amazing and the rest is bullshit. Really, you could do anything you want. And you mustn't feel bad about any of the choices you've made.'

But Nancy shook her head so abruptly that Eleanor remembered feeling such a deep pang of love for her it almost knocked her over. Nancy's vulnerability was so close to the surface it was like it shimmered off her, like it existed intrinsically within her friend, like it was never going to let her go.

Pearl was sitting very still with her hands on Nancy's desk and her gaze firmly centred out of the window, into the garden. The room smelt profoundly of Nancy, like a bed of roses warmed by the sun. She turned as Eleanor came in and her skin was slack and pale, her eyes red and rheumy. She held out her hands and Eleanor took them, sitting as she did on the little armchair next to the desk.

'I'm so sorry,' Eleanor said. 'This is just so dreadful.'

Pearl nodded, her namesakes at her ears and neck bobbing in agreement. 'I can't quite take it in.' Her voice was quiet, but even in her desolation it was as clear as it always had been to see where Nancy had inherited her beauty. 'Did you know about this other man?'

'Yes. A bit. She never really told me anything about him.'

'Just that he was called David?'

'Yes.'

'And you have no idea who he is?'

'I'm so sorry, really, I don't.'

Pearl sat back and took her hands with her. 'What was she doing anyway, the silly girl?' Eleanor tried to hear the admonition in Pearl's words, but they weren't there. She was beginning to feel infected by Nancy's secret, as if she'd been the one betraying them all. 'Did Mary know?'

'No.' Eleanor wound her silver ring against her finger. She had bought it for herself in Jaipur, fifteen years before, and the movement was comforting. 'She was trying to end it, you know.'

'They think that's why he did it, don't they?' Pearl said. 'A fit of jealousy or something.'

'Are they saying that now, that it was definitely him?' There were lots of questions Eleanor wanted to ask, but she knew she had to save them for the police.

'Well, they're not saying anything definite, but it seems obvious to me.'

'She did say he wasn't taking the idea of it ending very well.' The police had called that morning saying they needed to interview her properly. She had to get the story straight in her head.

'I just can't believe she'd do any of this. Poor Robert.'

'How is he this morning?'

'Awful. He's in with the police now. And of course Zara's inconsolable.'

Eleanor thought of all the people she'd seen over the years desolated by loss. Places where the earth had moved from under them or seas had risen up and devoured them. Women and men who had lost everything and everyone. She realised she'd always been rather sniffy about Western grief, as she thought of it. How she'd read stories about a murder or a teenager dying of an overdose and wonder at the extent of the reaction, wanting to take the writers of these articles to the places she knew, where you could legitimately use the word 'devastation'. But she hadn't known what it was like to inhabit moments like this, how no word seemed enough, how it really did feel like the end of the world.

'I'm so glad Hank died before all this,' Pearl said. 'If she could have waited a few more years I could have been gone as well.'

Eleanor looked at Pearl and the odd tenuousness of her words, which she barely understood. She thought of her own mother, unencumbered by sanity, in her care home in Devon and wondered if she'd even understand if one of her children died.

It was strange, the times she thought of her mother, and the shock of realising that she wasn't still the mother she'd known, always struck her as a fresh blow. Eleanor imagined being able to ring her now to talk about Nancy and the comfort she would give. It had been such a talent her mother possessed, the giving of comfort, and the absoluteness of Eleanor's grief spun her back through time to her childhood home and her mother's exuberant, fizzing presence. She heard her mother's deep laugh as it echoed up the winding stairs of their draughty house, past her father's study, through their messy rooms, over unwashed dishes and dusty surfaces. *There are always better things to do than clean*, her mother would say as she rushed from one charity appointment to the other, pulling Eleanor and her sister along with her when they were too young to be left alone. Her mother had always liked Nancy, but she would have disapproved of the opulence of her life, something that Eleanor thought could have influenced how she saw her friend.

'We tried to have a baby for ten years before Nancy came,' Pearl said, and Eleanor wished she'd stop. 'And then she came and she really was the most perfect little thing we could have wished for. Except there's always been this side of her that I've never understood, this urge to always push things further than they should go, don't you find?'

'I suppose.'

'Even going to university. I can't remember why she went. Why did you go, Eleanor?'

'Because I ...' Eleanor looked again at her hands but they seemed smaller than she remembered. 'Because I wanted to go on with my studies. I don't know.'

'Sometimes I think it was easier when women just didn't.' But Pearl stopped herself and Eleanor thought she'd learnt to put away the age she'd been born in to and wear the present like an itchy jumper. She swiped at her eye, batting the tears in to submission. 'And actually, I do know where she got it from. Hank was just like that, always locking himself in his study and falling into what we used to call his moods. Except he was allowed to behave like that, we all thought it was part of his genius. I would make sure he had everything he needed and life was ready for him when he wanted to open the door. But, of course, Nancy was a woman so she didn't have that option.'

Eleanor felt slightly stunned by Pearl's outburst, so she said something totally benign that sounded irritating even to her own ears. 'Why don't we go downstairs, get some tea or something.'

Pearl rose with a sigh. 'I don't want any bloody tea ever again.'

Zara was in the kitchen, sitting cross-legged on the floor, with the dog on her lap, weeping into his fur. Her hair was matted on her head and her body was encased in what Eleanor supposed must be Robert's dressing gown. She howled when they walked in, propelling herself off the floor and throwing herself against Eleanor, making her stagger backwards. She smoothed Zara's hair and muttered something ineffectual and bland.

'I can't bear it, I can't bear it,' Zara was repeating over and over, like a bloody incantation. Eleanor manoeuvered her to a chair and sat her at the table, which she collapsed onto, her head banging against the wood. Pearl sat next to her but didn't seem able to make anything better. Eleanor boiled the kettle. It was like being in hell.

Pearl and Eleanor had drunk their tea by the time Robert

came back, but Zara's was cold in front of her. Her weeping had become a backdrop to Eleanor's thoughts, which whizzed and spun down endless memories. She had stood in a hole in the ground once and watched a digger dump countless broken bodies in to its centre. People who had to be buried to avoid the spread of disease but whose loved ones would never know where they'd ended up. She'd been fresh out of university then and was unhardened by tragedy. It is amazing what the mind can process. She'd written to her parents that evening, a letter which probably hadn't reached them until after her father had died anyway.

'They want to see you next,' Robert said to Eleanor, his mouth turned down and his eyes deep in his head.

'Me?' She stood up, not completely ready yet.

'They appear to have set up some sort of interview room in the drawing room. They're going to want to talk to all of us today.'

'Whatever for?' Pearl asked.

'To get a complete picture.' Robert said the words as if they were enclosed in speech marks, his anger and frustration bubbling so close to the surface, Eleanor fancied she could see it rippling through him. 'And while they do that the bastard who did it is probably getting on a plane to Acapulco.'

'I'm sure they know what they're doing,' Eleanor tried. At least Zara had stopped crying for a moment, her head was even lifted to look at her father.

He waved towards the stairs. 'They're waiting for you.' She left with the feeling that he was angry with her, maybe he had been too quick to relieve her of responsibility last night.

DS Daniels from the day before was waiting in the drawing room, but the one who hadn't spoken had vanished and in his place sat another much sterner man, dressed in a smart uniform instead of a suit.

'Ms Meakins,' DS Daniels said as she came in. 'Please sit down.'

It felt odd to be invited to sit in Nancy's drawing room. Eleanor perched on the edge of the chair facing them.

'So.' He looked down at his notes. 'You've known Nancy Hennessy for twenty-eight years, I believe.'

'Yes, we met at university.'

'And you've always been close?'

'Oh yes, since almost the first day, Nancy, Mary and me.'

'Mr Hennessy mentioned Mary.' He looked back down at his pad. 'Mary Smithson. We'll be contacting her today.'

'I was with her last night.' She could feel their eyes on her and nothing she said sounded right. 'She's very upset.'

He ignored this. 'Would you say the three of you are the closest of friends?'

Eleanor looked at the man in the uniform but his stare was impenetrable. 'Yes, absolutely.'

'Told each other everything?'

'Well, I suppose—'

'You see the thing is –' he sat forward '– when my missus gets going with her friends there's no stopping her. They yabber on for hours and I don't reckon there's a subject that's not discussed. If one of them was having an affair there is no way they'd keep it quiet.'

Eleanor felt her colour rise with her anger. 'Not all women are the same.' The other man coughed.

'No, of course not, my apologies, Ms Meakins. I do have a very chatty wife.' He tried to hide his embarrassment with a laugh, but it came out all wrong, like a school-boy's giggle. 'But I do find it hard to believe that the three of you were so close and Nancy told you next to nothing about the affair. Perhaps she told Mrs Smithson more details?'

'Mary knew nothing about it. And why would I be lying? I mean, if you knew who he was then you could arrest him, couldn't you, and all this would be over.' She hated him suddenly and the stupid man in the uniform, who was clearly playing some pathetic power game. She turned to him. 'Sorry, and who are you?'

He held out his hand. 'Detective Chief Inspector Farrelly. Forgive me, I'm just observing at the moment.' She took his hand and it was hot and limp.

'What does that mean?' She had the sensation again that this was being used as a training exercise.

'Well, this is DS Daniels' case, but as the Senior Investigating Officer I'm in charge of the operation, as it were. There are still quite a few unanswered questions surrounding this case, and at the moment it's a top priority for us.'

Eleanor thought he was making it sound like a sales conference.

'It's imperative we know the identity of the man Nancy was having an affair with,' DS Daniels said. 'Sometimes we think we're doing the right thing protecting people and that's completely understandable.'

'What on earth are you saying?' Eleanor stopped herself from shouting. 'Who would I be protecting?'

'How well would you say you know Mr Hennessy?'

'Robert?' His change of tack threw her off guard. 'I know him very well. I mean, I've known him nearly as long as I've known Nancy.'

'Of course, because you were all at university together, weren't you?' Eleanor thought she heard a sneer in his voice.

'Yes. But also we work in the same field, Robert and I, so...'

Eleanor felt herself trailing off. She had always thought of her relationship with Robert as special; she had in fact often felt a sense of ownership around him. Once, many years before, when Nancy had such a hard time after Zara's birth, Robert had called her and they'd spent over an hour discussing what might be wrong with Nancy. Eleanor had felt grubby afterwards, realising that she had been way too quick to agree with Robert's exasperated version of her friend, rather than allowing herself to tell him what it meant to be a woman. How for women it wasn't simply a question of wanting to be one thing and then going about doing it. How so much got in the way, how feelings could derail you, how often life felt like a knife scratching against your skin.

'What do you do, Ms Meakins?' DS Daniels asked, interrupting her thoughts.

'I run a charity that helps with overseas relief.'

He nodded. 'And because Mr Hennessy is a human rights lawyer, you see him through work, is that what you mean?'

'Yes, I've helped him with a couple of cases over the years. People trafficking and things like that.'

'So you must have all spent a lot of time together, you and Mr and Mrs Hennessy?'

'Well, I've travelled a lot. But yes, of course we have.'

'And you've never …?' He blushed with his words but Eleanor held her ground, refused to make it easier for him. She'd given up doing that for people a long time ago. 'I mean, have you ever had a husband?'

She almost laughed. 'No, I've never been married.'

'Career woman.' He smiled as he spoke and she thought he was actually trying to be nice because he felt sorry for her. Sorry that no man had ever risen her to that pedestal of wife. She refused to acknowledge his words, so he bumbled on. 'What sort of relationship would you say Mr and Mrs Hennessy had?'

She felt herself blush for reasons she couldn't place. How she answered seemed important, but it was also absurd because how on earth was she expected to sum up all she knew about Nancy and Robert in a few sentences. 'They've had their ups and downs, like any couple. But they've also always been pretty solid, which I know sounds unlikely because of the affair, but it is true. I don't think she'd ever have left him.'

'So why was she having an affair?'

'I don't know. Nancy was like that, impetuous. Cosy domesticity was never enough for her, even though she loved Robert and Zara.'

DS Daniels sat back and rubbed at a spot on the bridge of his nose; Eleanor thought it was all put on. 'I have to admit I'm finding this all very confusing. Mr Hennessy has said the same sort of things. It's hard to understand.' Eleanor sat still. 'Why do you think Mr Hennessy called you when he realised Nancy hadn't come home?'

'Because Nancy and I had been out to dinner that evening. He wondered if she'd come back with me.' The heat rose through her body.

'Had she ever done that before?'

'Not for about twenty-five years.'

'Yesterday you told me Nancy left the restaurant before you and you stayed on to pay the bill. Are you absolutely sure that happened and you didn't leave together?'

Eleanor laughed. 'What on earth are you implying?'

He shook his head. 'Nothing at all. It's just we find in very distressing situations people often forget things, or get muddled.'

'Well, I'm not doing either of those things. As I said, Nancy left the restaurant on her own at about quarter to ten, I stayed on to the pay the bill and left about ten minutes after her, by which time she'd gone.'

'You said yesterday that Mr Hennessy knew Nancy was having an affair?'

'Well, I didn't exactly…' She stammered over her words for reasons she couldn't place. 'I said he said that he'd suspected.'

'Had he ever discussed those suspicions with you before?'

'No.'

The policeman wrote something in his book. 'You also said yesterday that Mrs Hennessy was scared of her husband finding out about the affair. I wondered what you meant by that?'

Eleanor looked between the two men, but neither met her eye. 'I just meant that Nancy didn't want her marriage to end, so she didn't want Robert to find out. I suppose in case he couldn't forgive her.'

DS Daniels hesitated for a moment. 'But you used the word scared. Would you say Mr Hennessy is a jealous man?'

The room blurred round the edges. It didn't seem possible that they could be thinking this and yet it was also obvious that they would. She remembered some statistic she'd read ages ago about how something like 90 per cent of murders are committed by people close to us. 'No, I mean, I wouldn't have thought so.'

He looked back up and the atmosphere shifted. 'And finally, Ms Meakins, can you confirm the information you gave us about the man Mrs Hennessy was having an affair with?' He looked up, so she nodded. 'He was called David, she met him at a work party and he was married with children?'

'Yes.' They seemed like such flimsy pieces of information and she wished she had more to give them, especially Robert and Zara, locked in their grief in the room beneath her feet.

'You're absolutely sure that she didn't go in to any more details.

Like what his job was, or where he lives, or something about his family? Anything she said, however insignificant it might seem.'

Eleanor felt totally washed out. 'I'm sorry, really there was nothing else.'

'Thank you, Ms Meakins.' The detective shut his book as a signal that the interview was at an end, but Eleanor stayed sitting, weighted in place by the things she needed to know. 'You've been very helpful,' he said, clearly in the hope she'd leave.

Eleanor felt her face flush, but held her ground and willed herself to speak, because she felt lost in what was happening. There were so many possibilities and variables surrounding Nancy's death and she couldn't get a handle on it, couldn't work out what they were even dealing with. 'I was wondering if you could tell me, I mean, what happened to Nancy, exactly?'

'Do you mean, her injuries, how she died?' DS Daniels glanced over at the silent man, who nodded.

'Yes.' Eleanor felt like there was a wedge of bread stuck in her throat. She also wanted to clamp her hands against her ears and not hear.

She heard the dry click of his mouth as he opened it to speak. 'Mrs Hennessy died from a large wound to the back of her head. At the moment we can't say if this blow was inflicted by a weapon or if it happened as she fell. But it caused internal bleeding in her brain, which she would have been unable to recover from.'

'Did she die instantly?'

'She would have been unconscious in minutes.'

It was rare, Eleanor thought, ever to get a direct answer to any question. 'I saw marks on her face.'

DS Daniels stuttered when he spoke. 'There was evidence of a fight. She did have a couple of injuries to her face, as if she'd been hit. They weren't injuries that would have killed her on their own, but they do obviously indicate that this was not an accident.'

Eleanor wound her fingers together. 'And was she, I mean, was she raped, or anything like that?'

'No, I can assure you nothing like that.' He smiled as if at least that was something, which, she supposed, it was.

The days became clichés. If anyone had asked Eleanor how she felt she would have said that they were existing in a bubble, that her world was falling apart, that she couldn't catch her breath, that time had lost all meaning. But no one did ask Eleanor how she was; instead they asked her constantly how Robert and Zara were doing, which was almost impossible to answer. She didn't even know how she'd become their designated carer, how she'd somehow moved into the house, how she was the person shielding them from the reporters outside their front door. She longed for her small flat, with its crisp white walls and mismatched pottery and the chequered counterpane on her bed, which had once belonged to her grandmother. She longed to go back to the office and deal with those faraway emergencies that had always seemed more real to her than anything else. She longed to read the Doris Lessing she was halfway through, to lie in her wonderful deep bath, which had cost almost as much to install as to buy, to fall asleep at night in her soft bed, listening to Radio 4, with a cup of chamomile tea next to her.

She also longed for a time when Nancy hadn't occupied the national consciousness. It was strange, because in a way Nancy had been such a perfect candidate for celebrity that maybe life had simply conspired to make it happen, maybe fate had decreed that her beautiful face should be plastered across newspapers and television screens and that commentators should endlessly discuss her life. Eleanor remembered watching Nancy at the debating society at university, and her whole presence seemed to fill the room. She remembered how she stabbed at the air with her hands as she'd spoken, how her eyes had sparkled, how her body had vibrated with belief. How the room had felt suspended somehow, as if they were all holding their collective breath so they could hear every syllable, so they could agree with her emphatically. She'd felt so proud to be her friend that day, in fact, she'd often felt proud to be Nancy's friend.

Robert was already vaguely well known in rarefied highbrow circles and Eleanor thought she detected a certain glee in the press coverage, at something so sordid happening to people who seemed so unassailable. It was also such a good story, what with the affair and the scraping away of a perfect life.

Nancy Hennessy, she read in endless variations, had been 'brutally murdered in a frenzied attack on a dark towpath'. Her clothes had been ripped and she had been beaten around the face, in an attack police described as 'one of the most violent they had seen in years', a description that did not tally with the Nancy Eleanor had seen in the morgue. An insider said, 'it bears all the hallmarks of a crime of passion'. Women on midday chat shows discussed in detail the dangers of having affairs, and segued into discussions about internet dating and sites on which you could meet people for casual sex, as if Nancy had done those things. They wondered aloud if the lover had killed her when she'd tried to finish things, or if perhaps the husband had wanted to take revenge? It all felt like white noise, like a screech Eleanor couldn't stop hearing.

But they all had to keep listening because nothing could move on until the funeral had taken place and it took a while for the body to be released. Once it had been, Eleanor planned details with Zara, who had lost weight and now looked strikingly, sickeningly like Nancy. Zara had lots of opinions about what her mother would like, but Robert waved all her suggestions away and told her it didn't matter, whatever she chose would be great. She found Nancy's address book in a drawer in her desk and rang everyone in it, asking them to the funeral, thankful that the publicity meant they all knew about her death.

For Eleanor it was like being dropped into the burning hot centre of hell. She woke every morning with a tight chest and a dull headache, which rose and spread in intensity all day. And it wasn't just because one of the people she loved best in the world had been ripped away from her, but because she was in a state of permanently heightened emotions. There was no certainty any more, no structure to her days, no safety from feelings of desolation, which threatened to pull her under and suffocate her.

Eleanor had always thought that she kept her life unencumbered by relationships and children for precisely the reason that she wanted to be able to pack up and run into the unknown at a moment's notice. Except her past life hadn't ever felt like this, this strange sort of free falling, impossible to predict how she might feel from one hour to the next. She had stood her ground in countries in which lands shifted or cyclones raged or wars ravaged and had never felt like she might dissolve into the atmosphere in the way she did now.

For the first time in forever, Eleanor found herself thinking obsessively about her father's death, which had occurred twenty-five years before, just as she was starting out on life after university. They had watched him wither and die before their eyes, consumed by a horrible, relentless cancer. Eleanor could once again hear the hiss of the oxygen pump and the bleep of the machine that dispensed morphine like sweets, overlaid always by the sound of her mother's weeping, replacing forever her famous laugh. As Eleanor lay in her bed at night and cried, she sometimes forgot whom it was for.

It became easier simply to stay as busy as possible, which meant spending as much time as she could at Nancy's house, where she was always needed and there was always something to do.

Robert got himself a lawyer. He came back from a police interview and announced his intention, loudly and accusatorily, as if Eleanor was the one questioning him and not the police.

'They haven't said as much, but it's obvious I'm a suspect,' he said as they ate a desultory takeaway. 'They keep going over and over if I knew about the affair and how it made me feel.'

Eleanor felt her breath like a physical force inside her. 'What are they suggesting?'

'I suppose they're thinking that if I knew Nancy was having an affair and she wanted to leave me, then that would give me a motive to kill her.'

'But you didn't know. I told you about it the night it happened.' His demeanour was so strained that Eleanor felt a fluttering in her chest. He hadn't seemed himself for days now, but surely that was to be expected?

He rubbed at his bruised-looking eyes. 'I know. I'm not sure they believe me though.'

'But why wouldn't they?' They had gone down the rabbit hole and everything was different now. 'They can't be thinking you had anything to do with it.'

Robert hunched further over his plastic carton, spooning orange food into his mouth. 'I haven't got an alibi,' he said finally. 'I mean, no one saw me that night. By the time I got home from work Nancy had already gone to meet you and I didn't speak to anyone until I rang you at four in the morning.'

Just tell me you had nothing to do with this, Eleanor wanted to scream at him, in the hope that he'd allay her sense of unease, but there was a noise at her back, and she turned to see Zara standing in the doorway, her expression fixed and definite with her brow set in a deep frown.

It rained on the day of the funeral, the sky so dark and menacing it looked as if the world was in mourning. The turnout was large despite Robert deciding to hold the ceremony in Sussex, at their country home. Eleanor couldn't help thinking Nancy would have been very pleased at the sheer number of people there, at the extent of their grief. She looked around the rows and rows of sombre men and women, all dressed in black, all red eyed, and wondered how Nancy had known so many people. Eleanor couldn't help thinking of her own funeral and how sparse it would be and then she wondered why she had always been happy to keep herself at a remove.

Robert and Zara sat at the front of the church, their shoulders hunched and their misery visceral, but still people went up to them and patted them on the back or made them stand up to hug them, making Eleanor realise how much Nancy had existed within a community. And with that thought came the panic she thought she'd quelled, that rising feeling of weightlessness which always threatened to spin out of the top of her head and dissolve her into dust.

She felt a hand on her arm and turned to see Mary as she sat down next to her. Her friend kissed her on the cheek and the warmth of touch was enough to ground her for a while. She reached over and squeezed Mary's hand.

'Are you on your own?' Eleanor asked.

'No, the girls are sitting with Howard at the back. He's still really unwell so he might need to leave.'

Eleanor turned and saw Howard in a pew by the door. He

looked shockingly bad, a poor impression of the man she'd always known, gaunt and hunched. Even his beard had whitened, making him look decades older. 'My God. He looks awful. Has he been ill since that evening when I came round to tell you about Nancy?' Eleanor realised she hadn't asked after him once in all the times she'd spoken to Mary since.

Mary nodded. 'He just can't stop being sick. The doctors don't know what's wrong. They're even talking some form of cancer now. He's got to go for tests at the hospital next week.'

'Oh, Mary, I'm sorry. I had no idea you were coping with that as well.' It seemed very unfair that Mary couldn't be allowed to mourn Nancy properly, without yet another thing to worry about. Although that was a mean way to think as even Howard couldn't have planned an illness to coincide with this. Eleanor tried to muster up some sympathy for the man, but she knew too much about him for it to feel completely sincere.

She'd argued with Nancy a few times over the years about Howard, Nancy not able to comprehend why he irritated Eleanor so, which Eleanor in turn understood because he presented such a consummate face to the world. It would have been much easier for their friendships if Mary had confided in Nancy as well about how Howard had behaved in the past decade, although Eleanor also understood why she hadn't done that. It would be hard to sit in front of someone who appeared to have as much as Nancy and admit that everything had gone to shit.

Mary leant into her ear. 'I feel awful for him, he's so poorly.'

'Do you?' Eleanor instantly regretted her words. Maybe she should take a leaf out of Nancy's book and be more magnanimous about Howard, it was clearly the supportive thing to do. She looked back again and saw Mary and Howard's daughters flanking their father, but their son was nowhere in sight. 'Where's Marcus?'

'No idea.'

'But wasn't Nancy his godmother, like me?'

Tears darted into Mary's eyes. 'Yes. I don't know what's going on with him. You know how his behaviour has been deteriorating this last year? Well, it's suddenly got much worse. I reminded him about the funeral yesterday and he said he'd come, but he didn't come home last night and he's not been picking up his phone all morning.'

But then a collective hush descended and the vicar took his position at the front of the church and Eleanor could hear Zara's deep intake of breath, followed by her slow and steady sobbing.

'Nancy would have been so pleased to see so many of you here,' Robert said, and she couldn't believe they'd got to that part already. She must have sung the carefully chosen hymns, and yet she couldn't remember doing so. 'She always loved a party and she must be very annoyed to be missing this one.' Contained laughter rang out and Mary squeezed her hand. 'I met Nancy at a party actually. I'd spotted her months before and thought she was simply the most gorgeous girl I'd ever seen. I pursued her pathetically until I finally plucked up the courage to speak to her. But very quickly I realised there was so much more to Nancy than her startling physical presence.'

He looked down and swallowed, which made Eleanor want to go to him and wrap her arms around him. 'She was wise and funny and quick and so much fun to be around.' His eyes flickered towards his daughter and his mouth tried to smile. 'She was also a brilliant mother to Zara, something that I will always be immensely grateful for.' Eleanor could see Zara's bony shoulders shaking through Nancy's black velvet coat. 'When Zara followed in Nancy's footsteps and went to St Hilda's, I remember Nancy saying how proud she was of her.' He stopped and put his hand against his forehead. Eleanor had heard him pacing his room in the previous nights, his voice low and insistent through the wall, and she realised he must have been practising this. Except now he looked lost, almost as if he'd forgotten not just his words, but where he was, who he was even. He scanned the room and she caught his eye and smiled gently at him, although he could have been looking straight through her. 'Time is so strange, isn't it,' he said, his hands dropping to his side. 'It seems only a minute ago and yet now ... now it's over.' His voice caught and his expression turned. 'We'll all miss her terribly,' he said, stumbling back to his seat.

She couldn't watch the coffin descending, so she stood back slightly, behind a tall man who obscured her view. Nancy had been long gone even on that first day in the mortuary, but still it seemed impossible that her body was simply going to rot into the ground they stood on. Pearl was standing at the head of the grave, her arm interlinked with Zara's, and that sight was perhaps worse. Eleanor thought that everything about Nancy was like a stone thrown into a pond, reverberating away from her in concentric circles.

They walked like a gaggle of black swans up the path from the church to the house, with the wind buffeting them and mud splashing onto the backs of trousers and tights, so they looked like the members of a secret society. If anyone had been passing they would have stared, wondering at this strange procession, then they would have turned away, not wanting the grief to contaminate them.

The house was unbearably busy and hot, despite the freezing cold outside. Robert and Zara stood by the front door, accepting condolences and hugs, invitations and stories. They had both clearly had a drink because there was colour in their cheeks for the first time since it had happened. A few people were moist eyed, but the general feeling was one of release and the murmur of conversation was beginning to sound like a cocktail party.

Mary found her in the crush but she hadn't even taken off her coat. 'I'm not going to stay. I just wanted to speak to Robert and Zara.'

'I wish I could go,' Eleanor answered. 'But I don't think I can leave them.'

'How long are you going to stay?'

Eleanor had been wondering the same thing. 'I don't know.'

Mary put her hand on her arm. 'I've got to run. Howard's in the car and he's not in a good way. But let's talk tomorrow.' She leant over and brushed her lips against Eleanor's cheek. 'Love you.'

'Love you, too.'

It was Nancy who had started that tradition, Eleanor thought as she watched Mary squeeze her way between the groups of people. Neither of them would have been brave enough to say they loved each other and yet for Nancy it came naturally. *God, I sometimes think I love you two more than Robert*, Nancy would say.

How much longer to stay was a question that circled Eleanor in the days that followed. She did go back to work, but her days were short and her staff still had to pick up most of the slack. They assured her they didn't mind, but she thought they probably did because they all had lives and you can only take on someone else's grief for so long before it becomes irritating. She even spent the odd night at home and once went for dinner with a friend, although she felt guilty doing so. She met Mary for a walk one Sunday, but all she wanted to talk about was how Howard was getting worse, even though the hospital tests hadn't shown up anything bad yet, at least nothing that was going to kill him. Still though, more often than not, Eleanor found herself drawn back to Nancy's house, as she still thought of it, and the misery it contained, as if she owed them something, as if her silence about Nancy's affair had condemned her to be forever in their servitude. Not that they made her feel that way. They made her feel like one of the family, like she was the one person they could let their guard down with, like she mattered to them. And that feeling was intoxicating, dangerous even.

She let herself in nine nights after the funeral and the atmosphere was different. Zara came out of the drawing room and took her hand, pulling her forward before she had a chance to take off her coat. Robert was standing in the middle of the room, his arms folded across his chest as he stared at the television. It took Eleanor a moment to focus on what they were watching, which was the blurry pictures of a man being put into a police car as what seemed like a thousand bulbs flashed in his face. Then the shot switched to a young, stern-faced reporter, his hair plastered to his head by the driving rain.

'Fifty-five-year-old French author Davide Boyette was arrested at four o'clock this afternoon as part of the on-going investigation into the murder of Nancy Hennessy last month. Mrs Hennessy, who had been having an affair for the past year, was found on a path next to the Thames in London, beaten to death in an attack the police describe as sustained and violent. Mrs Hennessy worked translating French books into English, and it is believed she had translated some of Mr Boyette's novels. She was the daughter of Sir Hank Rivers, composer of the Queen's anthem, and is survived by her husband, Robert Hennessy, the human rights lawyer and their nineteen-year-old daughter, Zara. Davide Boyette is married to a British woman, Wendy Harper, and they live in Harrogate with their two daughters. The police have refused to comment.'

'What?' Eleanor felt her legs suddenly giving way so she had to sit on the sofa.

'They've found the man Mum was having an affair with,' Zara said, her eyes wide and feverish.

'But. I mean, who?' She looked over at Robert but he was still standing in the same position, his eyes now on the floor.

'You know,' Zara said. 'You must have heard of him, he writes under D. H. Boyette. That crime stuff.'

'Oh my God, yes, of course.'

Robert turned off the television, his face grey and drawn.

'Did you know about this?' Eleanor asked.

'The police came round this morning,' he answered. 'It appears they've been following up with all the authors she worked with. She'd translated four of his novels and had met him a couple of times through his publishers. Last year they both attended the same Christmas party at the publishers, which fits in with the timeline. And of course he's called David, well Davide, but she'd hardly have told you that, as it would have made it obvious who he was. And he's married with two children.'

She felt inexplicably hurt that Robert hadn't rung her earlier. 'And they're sure it's him?'

'God knows,' he said.

'But has he admitted it?' Eleanor thought she might faint.

'No, he's denying everything. Says he barely even knew her. Says they did meet at the publishers a couple of times, and he was at the party a year ago, but that he didn't even see her there, let alone speak to her. The police are questioning people to see if anyone saw them together, but so far nothing.'

'But then, how? I mean, what?'

'He's on a book tour at the moment,' Zara said, 'and he was in Richmond at a hotel the night it happened and no one saw him after nine. He was meant to go to a dinner but said he

53

had a headache and went to bed. And he's had affairs before, according to his wife.'

Eleanor looked past Zara at Robert and with each word he seemed to be sinking further into himself. 'Get your dad a drink,' she said, standing and taking him by the arm. She led him to a chair and made him sit, although it wasn't hard, he appeared easily malleable. Zara handed her two tumblers of whisky and they all drank in one easy gulp, the warm liquid rushing through them.

'He looks like such a fucking idiot,' Robert said.

The phone rang from the hall and Zara went to answer it. Eleanor stood with her empty glass looking at the top of Robert's head.

'Ellie,' Zara shouted, 'it's Mary.'

There wasn't enough evidence to charge Davide Boyette. Nor was there enough evidence to charge Robert. There were no fingerprints and no witnesses, which was hardly surprising as even the most amateur of criminals wore gloves and the night Nancy died had been so cold you had to have been either mad or bad to be outside. Nancy's phone records revealed deleted messages from her lover, which proved she'd been trying to end it and that he had been very angry. But the phone the lover had used was a pay as you go that had never been connected to the internet so couldn't be tracked and in her contacts he was simply listed as D. It also hadn't been used since the night of the murder and they'd never referred to each other by name on any text. As for Robert, there was no physical evidence linking him to the riverbank, and he maintained that he hadn't known about the affair for definite until Eleanor confirmed it, by which time Nancy was already dead. Quite apart from the fact that none of Robert's friends or colleagues thought he was capable of violence and there had never been the hint of a suggestion of it in their marriage.

But the police made it very clear to anyone who would listen that it was definitely the husband or the lover. And everyone wanted to listen because, by then, it had become something that everyone was talking about. Newspapers splashed pictures of everyone involved across their front pages for so many days it stopped being possible to say that soon everyone would forget about it. Their lives, or at least fragments of their lives, became public property. Reporters even followed Zara back to Oxford and she told Eleanor she felt like she was going to faint every time she went outside. Davide Boyette's wife went on television and said, even though she was sure he wasn't capable of murdering anyone, it had been hell living with a philanderer and she was going to do her best to make sure he didn't see their daughters again. People in the audience cheered, people who had never met either of them. Commentators started to question Robert's ability to make a woman as beautiful as Nancy happy, with all the intended innuendo, or to discuss the perceived anger behind his cold blue eyes. It seemed like it might never stop or go away and that nothing good was ever going to happen again. And all the while Eleanor simply missed her friend with a hollow grief that sometimes took her by surprise, even though it seemed always to be with her.

'Would you like to go to the opera tonight?' Robert asked when he rang her at work one day.

'I thought Zara was going with you.' She rubbed at the front of her head where a pain was building. Really she needed to stay late at work and finish the reports.

'She's just rung to cancel.' She heard him breathing down the line and imagined him shut in his office. 'She's not coming at all this weekend, in fact.'

'I'm sure she's just busy.'

'No, you know it's more than that. She's furious with me.'

'Well, she has no right to be.' Eleanor bent her chin towards her chest to try to ease the tension in her neck and across her shoulders.

'She blames me, and she's probably right. I mean, if I'd been more lovable Nancy wouldn't have needed to have an affair with that terrible man.' Eleanor shut her eyes against an image of Robert sitting at his desk, a large empty house to go home to. 'Or maybe she actually blames me. Enough people do. When I walk into meetings now most of the women look at me through these narrow eyes and I can tell they've passed judgement already.'

'Stop it, Robert. Of course Zara doesn't think that. Look, OK, I'll come, what time shall I meet you?'

'Seven-thirty outside Covent Garden tube station.'

'OK. See you there.'

'Thanks, Ellie,' he said, and her breath quickened because he'd never shortened her name before.

She nearly told Nancy that she'd met him first all those years ago, after a party the three of them had gone to at the end of their second year. She wondered now how life would have panned out if she had, because Nancy would never have stood in her way, in fact she'd have encouraged her to go for it.

She'd been fixing herself a drink in the kitchen, while Mary and Nancy danced in the sitting room, when Robert had wandered in. She'd noticed him earlier, his tall, clean blondness so at odds with the general scumminess of the party. He was wearing a light blue shirt and chinos with loafers and she couldn't help smiling, which he misinterpreted as an invitation to introduce himself. But he seemed a bit lost, so she asked him what course he was doing and when he said Law she snorted and raised her eyebrows.

'Not like that,' he said, waving his hands in front of his face.

She laughed, turning round and leaning back against the sink, taking a sip from her drink. 'I didn't know there were different ways of taking Law.'

His blush was endearing. 'Well, the degree's the same. I just mean, I'm not into the idea of becoming some sort of corporate hotshot defending another oil spill, or getting a celebrity off a rape charge. I want to do good with it.'

It was her turn to blush then, because his words sounded so close to what she held secretly in her heart. She tried to keep her voice casual. 'I know what you mean. I'm reading English but actually I want to work in overseas relief. I just can't shake the thought of all the need out there and then doing something that doesn't mean anything.'

His face broke in to a wide smile. 'Yeah, that's just how I feel. I look round when I'm in lectures sometimes and you can almost see the pound signs above everyone's head.' She had to stop herself from smiling at his words and her insides felt like she'd swallowed a packet of sherbet.

'Do you want some?' She tilted the bottle that she'd been about to take out to Mary and Nancy his way.

'Thanks, yes, please.' He held his plastic cup towards her and when she took it their fingers brushed and it felt like when you unplug something and there's a loose connection and it sparks into your hand. She made sure their eyes met when she handed the cup back to him and was sure he could feel it as well, sure it wasn't just her.

They'd stayed like that for a couple of hours, leaning against the kitchen cabinets, chatting and drinking the sticky bourbon, laughing into the sounds of decadent party coming from the other room. She'd only moved when Nancy came to find her to tell her they were leaving. She introduced them, but Nancy's eyes were hardly focusing, so they'd left in a rush, which meant no numbers were exchanged and then she hadn't even felt like saying anything about him to Nancy or Mary as they walked home, because it had seemed private and special.

All the next day she sat at her desk, thinking of the ways he might track down the phone number of their house, allowing herself to become too involved in the fantasy of where he might take her and what they might discuss. The phone had finally rung at about five and she'd held her breath as she heard Nancy run for it, but it took too long, so by the time Nancy came into her room she hadn't been prepared for what she was about to hear.

'That was that boy Robert, from last night,' Nancy said, falling on to Eleanor's bed. 'You know, you introduced us when I came to get you from the kitchen.'

Eleanor looked at her friend, her sleek body curled in on itself like a cat's as she bit at the side of her nail, her blonde hair falling in waves across her shoulders, and reminded herself that it wasn't Nancy's fault that she had been born so beautiful. 'What did he want?' She gave herself one more moment, because it could still have been about her.

'It was a bit odd actually. He asked me if I wanted to go for a drink. I mean, we hardly spoke. You were chatting to him. Was he nice?'

Eleanor's eyes felt suddenly sore. 'Yes, he was lovely.'

Nancy looked up. 'God, do you like him? Obviously I won't go if you do.'

'No, no. Don't be silly, of course not. He's not my type at all.'

Eleanor felt her body wash with heat. She did debate saying something, but she hadn't wanted to come second to Nancy, a ridiculous sentiment when she looked at the goddess lying on her bed. She bent her head back to her desk. 'You should go, he was nice.'

Eleanor stopped her thoughts by ringing Zara, who answered almost immediately. She could hear the blare of the television in the background. 'No lessons?' She regretted the question as she said it.

'Yes, but I can't be bothered. Anyway, I'm writing a book.'

Zara, Eleanor found, had the same capacity as Nancy to make her feel slightly dizzy. 'A book?'

'A novel.'

'Really?'

'It's the only thing that stops me crying at the moment.'

'Well, that's good. Your dad just called. He said you're not coming down any more.'

'No.' She could almost see Zara sticking out her bottom lip as she spoke.

'He's disappointed.'

'He'll get over it.'

'You're not being fair on your dad. He's a good man.'

'You weren't there. You didn't live with us.'

'What do you mean?' She felt cold and her guts ached, along with her head.

'He was always nitpicking at her. Always telling her she was doing things wrong. And he never wanted to do any of the fun things she liked. All he ever wanted to do was go to Sussex and read the paper.' Eleanor remembered this exact complaint from Nancy and it annoyed her that she should have spoken to Zara about it, it seemed totally disloyal.

'That's a bit unfair. He works very hard.'

Zara snorted and Eleanor had to hold the phone away from her ear for a second because it could have been Nancy she was talking to.

'You can't be angry with him for that anyway. Your mum did love him, you know.'

'What if it wasn't Davide? I mean, she did say he was called David.'

'Yes, but obviously she wouldn't have said Davide to me. It would have given so much away about him. But, you're right, maybe it wasn't him. It might be another David entirely.'

'Or not the lover at all.' There was a pause and Eleanor thought she heard Zara gulp down the line. 'Why do you think the police questioned Dad so much?'

'They wouldn't have been doing their job if they hadn't.'

'But he could get really angry. Mum and him argued quite a bit.' Zara's voice had withdrawn and she sounded about ten.

Eleanor had to shut her eyes for a moment against her spiralling thoughts, because not everything she knew could be shaken, or she might not survive. 'All married couples argue, Zara. And everyone gets angry. It doesn't mean anything.'

'Sometimes I can almost understand what Mum saw in Davide Boyette.' Neither of them spoke for a moment because it was such a terrible thing to say.

'Anyway,' Eleanor said finally, 'don't worry, I'm going to go with your father tonight.' After she had put the phone down though she found herself googling Davide Boyette, which she had spent weeks trying not to do. There were plenty of images of him online from slick author shots, to animated pictures of him talking at book festivals, to magazine profiles. He was rugged looking, with thick, unkempt, greying hair and a stylish beard cut close to his solid face. His eyes sparkled out of the photographs like he had just told a dirty joke. She could imagine Nancy finding him attractive, he was after all the exact opposite of Robert, and Nancy had spent most of her life looking for different things.

She hadn't been to the opera for years and had forgotten how the music could lift you up and transport you away. She glanced at Robert a few times but his expression was set, his jaw muscles clenched and his eyes glinting. She gave up trying to listen and simply let the sounds possess her, allowing herself to feel them in every part of her body, deep and sensual. They drank champagne in the interval, whilst people looked at them out of the corners of their eyes, and it went straight to her head, making the second half even more dreamy than the first.

'Why don't you come back to mine for a nightcap,' Robert said as they stood in the cold after it had finished. 'I can't bear the thought of going to a bar and someone asking me about Nancy.'

'That would be lovely,' Eleanor replied, tucking her neat bob behind her ears because her hands felt suddenly useless. *Oh, you're so stylish*, Nancy had said to her once as they'd jostled for space in front of the mirror before a party, and Eleanor had felt totally shocked that someone like Nancy could envy anything about anyone else, especially her. *But you're so beautiful,* she'd answered, *you don't have to be stylish. I have to work at myself, you can just be.* Nancy had frowned into the mirror. *Did you notice Professor Sutcliffe staring straight at me when he was talking about Keats today?* Eleanor hadn't. *Well, he was,* Nancy said, *because he knows beauty can be a curse as well as a blessing.*

The house was warm after the cold of the night but it still felt empty, as if a bomb had destroyed the upper floors. Robert poured them both drinks and they sat next to each other on the sofa.

'Lovely dress, by the way,' Robert said.

Eleanor looked down at the brown silk that she worried looked shapeless on her round, short frame. 'Thank you.' She wondered what Nancy used to wear to the opera, something perfect no doubt.

'It's been nearly two months,' Robert said. 'I was thinking the other day, I'm so glad it happened just after Christmas. Imagine if we'd had to get through that as well.'

'And the weather should turn soon. I think you'll feel better when you can get stuck in at Coombe Place again.'

He nodded and smiled. 'You know, Nancy and I had been talking about me retiring early and moving down there, maybe selling this place and getting a small flat?'

'No.' She couldn't place Nancy as the country wife.

'Maybe she was only saying it to placate me, but it seemed like she really meant it. Especially in the last month or so.'

Eleanor put her hand over the top of Robert's. 'She was always so complicated, Nancy. I expect she did mean it.'

He turned to her and his eyes were desperate. 'Had she really spoken to you about finishing things with . . .' He looked like he had a bad taste in his mouth. 'Well, with Davide? I'd rather know the truth.'

'You know it might not be Davide Boyette. I mean, the police couldn't pin anything on him at all.' He was like a little boy and she wanted to make it better for him.

'Oh I know. But, was she really talking about ending the affair?'

She would never tell Robert what Nancy had been like at the beginning. How she had radiated, how she'd seemed driven and compelled, how Eleanor had never seen her so happy. But it was also true that at the end something had totally switched and she'd seemed desperate to be rid of the man she had risked everything for. 'Yes, she really wanted to end it, but he wasn't letting her. I'm sure that's what happened that night. I'm sure she told him it was categorically over and they got into a fight.'

Robert hunched over himself and a fierce cry escaped before he clamped his hand over his mouth. Eleanor felt like she was looking at a drowning man, at someone who had to be physically pulled back to life. She enclosed him and he encircled her waist, clinging to her, his head against her breast, sobs wracking his body. She kissed the top of his head and stroked his back, as she would any wounded animal. And all at once her anger at Nancy was right there again, just underneath her skin, prickling and needling at her. He straightened himself so their heads were level and his lips were red and swollen against his gaunt, pale face.

She didn't know she was going to kiss him until she did, but as soon as she had she knew it wasn't chaste. His response was urgent, his tongue searching out every corner of her mouth. He put his hands under her buttocks and pulled her forward so she was lying underneath him, waiting and wanting. The silk of her dress rose easily, she heard the zip of his fly and then she felt him inside her and it was like coming home, like everything she had ever wanted, so she had to pinch the back of her hand to remind herself that she was fucking her dead best friend's husband and she could not take joy from the moment in any way.

'Oh God,' he shouted as he came, his eyes closed and his face so scrunched it was impossible to tell how he meant it.

'I'm sorry,' he said as they disentangled themselves from each other.

'Don't be,' she answered.

They sat next to each other on the sofa and Robert took her hand again, so she leant her head against his shoulder. They didn't speak but she wondered if he too was looking at the photos of Nancy on the mantelpiece.

This can't be anything, Eleanor said to herself a thousand times a day. This man is mourning your best friend. She sits on the end of your bed. She won't ever go away. You don't want her to go away. You cannot, cannot love him.

She made him laugh one day. Spontaneously and naturally so she knew he meant it, knew he found something funny, knew that for one second he had forgotten. They were walking in the woods near Coombe Place and she pointed at a blue tit that she said reminded her of Winston Churchill.

But other days she felt like she could barely reach him. As if he had positioned himself behind a tall wall and locked the gate. She would chat about the news or the weather or what vegetables he'd planted and his face would close and his answers would come in brief, staccato bursts.

She felt like she'd lost the right to talk about Nancy, almost as if the word was sullied when she spoke it. Zara naturally knew nothing about whatever it was that her and Robert were doing and wanted to talk all the time about her mother. She rang Eleanor most days, sometimes late at night, crying. Nancy had become deified, which Eleanor had noticed often happened with the dead, and surely more so when the dead person was your mother. But sometimes she wanted to shake Zara and remind her that Nancy had been far from perfect, far from blameless. Although she couldn't because that would mean betraying her friend even more than she was doing already.

*

She dreamt about Nancy all the time. Things they'd done, things they'd never done, things they'd talked about, things they'd never talked about. She found herself in impossible situations with her, shouted at her, was shouted at by her. They danced cheek to cheek, they scratched at each other's faces, they swapped bodies, Nancy stole her children, except they were hers in the first place. They sang and laughed and cried together. I'm sorry, she said out loud once on waking, but she got the impression that Nancy didn't care.

Then it was suddenly spring, as if they had all shut their eyes and wished and finally whatever it was that was out there had granted them a small reprieve. Talk of the case had died down in the media and the police hadn't been in touch for a while, not that the case was closed, they assured them, but there just wasn't any fresh evidence and they'd hit so many brick walls.

Eleanor felt like she'd been swept along by something outside of herself, this unfamiliar feeling in the centre of her chest that made it harder and harder to stay focused on her own life. She knew Mary needed her because Howard simply wasn't getting better – they had run endless tests on him and all they could say with any certainty was that he didn't have a terminal illness – but she also knew that she wasn't visiting as much as she should because the pull of Robert was always too strong.

About the only thing she did with any regularity was to make sure that she spent Thursday nights at home because that was when she visited Irena. So it perhaps wasn't a surprise when Irena's daughter, Sarah, pulled her back slightly into her life. She rang on a Monday afternoon to say that she'd just spoken to her mother and she sounded sick and would Eleanor mind looking in on her that evening. Eleanor had been due to have supper with Robert, and she itched for that meeting, so much that she considered making up a lie to Sarah. But she also knew that if Irena was ill she wouldn't admit it, and would need to be hustled into being looked after.

On the way home from work she bought some fresh soup and bread, as well as a ginger cake, some milk and eggs. She didn't bother going up to her own flat, knocking as soon as she came in the front door. It took Irena ages to answer, so long that Eleanor felt a sharp pang in her chest; she put her bags on the floor and was looking for her keys when Irena's door finally swung inwards. The woman appeared slightly shrunken, if that was possible, and her skin had taken on a yellowy, earthy pallor, her white hair hanging in thin wisps about her face when usually it was pinned back.

'Sarah rang,' Eleanor said by way of introduction. 'She said you sounded ill and so I've brought you some supper.'

'Oh, that girl,' Irena said, but Eleanor noticed Irena stepped back, which was unlike her, allowing herself to be taken care of.

She ignored the fear that sprung up at the thought of her old friend being ill and bustled through into the kitchen. The flat was uncomfortably hot, even though the day hadn't been cold, and Eleanor immediately felt a sticky sweat break out on her skin. 'Go and sit down. I'll just heat up the soup and bring it in to you.'

'There's no need.' But Irena was already making for the living room and so Eleanor went to the kitchen, where she took off her jacket and started putting away the shopping. The cupboards and fridge depressed her in their economy, as if Irena's life had shrunk to the smallest of offerings. Her kitchen would look like this one day, she thought, as she jangled a saucepan on to the stove top, and prayed silently for someone like herself to notice. She buttered bread while she waited for the soup to warm, made a cup of tea and cut a thick slice of cake, which she knew Irena would never eat. When it was ready she arranged it on a tray and carried it into the front room, where Irena was sitting in her tall wing-backed chair, looking out of the window.

'The lilac is flowering,' she said as Eleanor set down the tray.

Eleanor looked out at the frothy purple bush, with all the millions of tiny flowers that made up each outrageous head. It seemed amazing that nature made that much effort year after year. 'Would you like me to pick you some?'

Irena waved her away. 'Not now. Sit down.' Eleanor did as she was told as Irena began to take bird-like mouthfuls. Her face was swollen with cold, her nose pinked, with flashes of red across her cheekbones.

'I wish you would call me when you're feeling unwell. I can always cook you supper, or anything, you know.'

'I am fine. Sarah worries too much.'

'Have you taken your temperature?'

Irena tusked and so Eleanor shut up, instead looking back at the lilac as it swayed outside the window. It made her realise that the lilac would be coming out at Coombe Place, where she was going that weekend, and even though the thought was filled with the sadness from knowing Nancy would never see another lilac, it was overridden with the joy of spending time alone with Robert.

'Who is in your head?' Irena asked, making Eleanor jump her attention back to her.

She tried to laugh. 'No one.'

'You were smiling.'

Eleanor blushed. 'I was thinking about someone, actually.'

'But also trying not to?'

'How do you know?'

Irena shrugged. 'I have been alive for a very long time.'

'I don't know what I'm doing.' Eleanor looked back at the

lilac, so pure and easy in its existence. 'I think I might have fallen in love.'

'But that is something good, no?' Irena had only eaten a tiny bit of soup and a corner of bread. She was sipping at her tea now as if she'd finished.

'Can't you eat any more?'

'Tell me about your love, Eleanor, that will make me feel much better than any soup can.'

Irena had the sweetest smile, Eleanor thought, a desperate desire to speak about Robert always inside her. 'I seem to be, I don't know how you'd describe it, to be, I suppose, having a sort of relationship with Robert. Nancy's husband.'

Irena's smile fell like a landslide, her face wobbling and her eyes narrowing. It lurched Eleanor's heart and made her wish she hadn't said anything, made her even feel anger for this gentle woman who couldn't possibly understand what those words meant.

'I'm sorry, I've shocked you,' Eleanor said finally.

But Irena shook her head. 'You don't reach my age and feel shock. But you do know when something is wrong.'

'It's not wrong.' Her voice sounded harsher than she'd meant it. 'I'm sorry, it's just, I've known him for a very long time. Almost as long as I knew Nancy. It's not what it sounds like. It's not sordid.' She felt herself flushing and her heart was beating uncomfortably so she could feel it in her throat.

'It might not be sordid, but it is wrong.' Irena was speaking softly, but her eyes were like hard little pebbles. 'It is wrong for him and for Nancy, but most importantly it is wrong for you, Eleanor.'

She thought she might cry, but she forced her tears back inside. It had been stupid of her to think this old woman could understand, could possibly remember what it was like to be consumed by someone, to know that there was only one way of existing.

'I can see that he is very special to you,' Irena said, and Eleanor couldn't look up at her. 'But you are special to me, Eleanor, and I want you to be careful. I want you to look after yourself. Be kind to yourself.'

Eleanor guffawed, a harsh sound that jarred against Irena's sentiments. She stood, because otherwise she felt like she might faint. 'I think you should have a bath while I'm here. I'll get on with the washing up.'

'I don't need putting to bed like a baby,' Irena answered, but she stood and shuffled to the bathroom.

Eleanor washed up in a flurry of nerves, her blood jangling through her body, her mind refusing to settle on anything Irena had said. And by the time the flat and Irena were clean, a new calmness had settled around them like dust on furniture.

'I am sorry if I said too much,' Irena said as she resettled herself in her armchair by the window, refusing to go to bed, saying there was a programme on the television she wanted to watch later.

'You never say too much,' Eleanor replied, overtaken by a sudden surge of tenderness. 'I'll look in on you before I leave for work in the morning.'

'Eleanor.' Irena called her back from the door of the sitting room, making her turn around when all she wanted now was to be alone in her cool flat, with a glass of wine and thoughts of Robert in her head. 'Promise me one thing.'

'Anything.'

'Remember you are special.'

It was a preposterous concept, but to Irena she said, 'Anything you say,' which at least made the woman smile.

She hurried now, but as she did her foot snagged on something in the hall and she lost her balance, nearly falling. She knelt down and saw the carpet was actually two pieces joined together, one of which had come loose and stuck up above the other. She smoothed it back down, but made a mental note to fix it properly. Perhaps she should also speak to Sarah about getting Irena one of those necklace alarms she'd seen advertised on the telly.

Robert called first thing in the morning, shaken by a dream he'd had of Nancy in which she'd shouted words he couldn't remember with blood running down her face. Eleanor sat on the phone soothing him and then, when they'd finished, realised she was seriously late for her first meeting and that popping in on Irena was going to throw out her whole day. She kept her head down as she passed Irena's door, telling herself that she probably shouldn't knock anyway as the best thing for a cold was to get lots of sleep.

Robert called again in the afternoon and said he'd bought tickets to the theatre as he wanted to be around people. Eleanor knew she'd end up staying the night, but she'd left some papers at home she needed for the next day, so had to leave work a bit early. Irena was sitting in her chair in the window as Eleanor rushed up the path and she motioned for Eleanor to come in, which made her feel like she was getting heartburn.

Irena was at the door to her flat by the time Eleanor came in the front door and so she had no choice but to let herself be led in to the warm, stuffy air.

'Would you like a cup of tea?' Irena asked as they made their way past the kitchen towards the sitting room.

'I can't really stop. I'm going to the theatre.'

Irena sat in her chair and so Eleanor sat opposite her, perching on the edge for a quick getaway. 'Are you going with Robert?'

The question caught Eleanor off guard, it seemed so unlikely that Irena would even remember his name. 'I am actually.' She hated herself for blushing.

Irena's eyes were bright and her face slightly flushed, which Eleanor hoped was from her cold. 'I have been thinking about this since you told me.' Eleanor nodded, a terrible urge to cry blocking her throat. 'You really must not do this, Eleanor.'

'I don't think...' She stammered over her words, sucking down the impulse to shout at the woman. 'I mean, really, you don't know anything about the situation.'

'But I don't need to know anything about the situation. I care about you and I don't want to see you hurt.'

'Irena, please.' Eleanor could feel a sickness building in her stomach. 'I know it all seems too complicated and wrong, but I'm fine. Really, it's all fine.'

Irena shook her head. 'One of the only good things about getting old is that you can say exactly what you think. You are my friend, Eleanor, and so it is my job to sometimes tell you things you do not want to hear. I hate interfering in people's lives, but nothing good can come of this.'

Eleanor wanted to clamp her hands over her ears because Irena's words sounded like a curse. She looked instead at her watch. 'I have to go or I'll miss the start of the play.'

She made to stand but Irena put her hand on her arm. 'You know, Eleanor, most love is fantastic. Magical and fantastic. But sometimes love is dangerous. Sometimes it rips out the heart and tramples over your life. Sometimes it is just not worth it.'

Eleanor stood then, letting Irena's hand fall. 'I'm sorry, I'm going to go now.'

Irena nodded. 'I will see you for supper tomorrow, like usual?' But Eleanor couldn't even make herself turn around, a total and desperate need to be out of the flat all she could focus on. She didn't slam the door behind her but she would have liked to rip it off its hinges, would have liked to break it into tiny splinters.

Mary rang Eleanor at lunchtime the next day and asked if she'd like to pop round on her way home. She could tell by her friend's tone that she was feeling low, so she agreed, going straight to Mary's house as soon as she could get out the door of work. It was a balmy evening, which made Eleanor think that there was now no denying it was spring, which meant, miraculously, the world really had continued to turn.

'What's going on with you?' Mary asked once they were sitting in her garden, with a glass of wine in their hands.

'What? Nothing.' Eleanor realised she didn't need to sound so guilty. 'What do you mean?'

But Mary didn't have time to answer as Marcus walked through the back door into the garden. Eleanor turned in her chair and the sight of him was shocking. He looked like he'd given up, as if he was trying to escape reality as he shielded his eyes against the pale evening light. His skin was grey and angry red spots circled his mouth, contrasting with the deep black round his eyes. His clothes looked unwashed and his hair was greasy. 'D'you have any cash, Mum?'

'Hello, Marcus,' Eleanor said.

He glanced towards her. 'Oh yeah, hi.'

'How are you?' She felt Mary shift next to her.

'You know.'

'How's college going?'

'I'm dropping out.'

'Oh, I didn't know. How come?'

He looked back at his mother and she said, 'My purse is in the kitchen.'

A bell rang from inside the house and Mary started to get up.

'I'll do it, Mum,' Marcus said. 'I think he just wants a cup of tea.'

'OK, thanks, Marcus. Are you going out then?'

'Yeah, I'll make the tea then shoot.'

'When will you be home?'

'Dunno. See ya.'

Eleanor looked at Mary, waiting for her friend to speak, but she didn't. 'Is Marcus OK?' She tried in the end. Mary had been worried about her son for a while and Eleanor realised she hadn't taken enough interest in this, letting other things overtake something that clearly should be of great concern.

'How do you mean?' Mary sounded defensive.

'Well, I know you've been saying that you're worried about him. And he doesn't look great.'

'I know.' Mary sipped at her wine. 'I told you, I don't know what's going on with him. It began last summer. He started going out more and staying out late and I know he's smoking and drinking. But it seems to have escalated now and I don't really know what to do about it.'

'Have you spoken to his college?'

'Only insofar as they keep calling me about him missing lessons. All he has to do now is sit his bloody A-Levels, but he's adamant that he won't.'

'How about the doctor then?'

'I know I should, but I don't know what to say and it's all been really full on with Howard.'

'I don't think I've ever heard Marcus offering to help Howard before.'

Mary rubbed her toe into the patchy grass. 'He's been really good about all that, actually. It makes me feel like the lovely old Marcus must be in there somewhere. I think that's what's so hard, in fact. He's always been such a sweet, sensitive boy and suddenly he's become this sort of parody of a teenager.'

'Of course he's still sweet. It's bound to just be a phase or something.' Eleanor realised as she spoke that Marcus and Zara were both officially adults now and that made her feel skittish and strange, like she wanted to run a lap of the tiny garden or something.

Mary sniffed dramatically, making Eleanor look over at her, her beautiful skin had taken on a grey pallor, with purple patches around her eyes. Sometimes she wondered what had become of them all.

'Can your parents help with Howard?' She'd only visited Mary's parents' house once, apart from for Mary's wedding, and she remembered it as a happy place, filled with warmth and laughter. She remembered Mary's mother with her bright blonde perm and her Bangladeshi father who cooked curries that tasted like you were eating by an ocean. It made her long perversely for her own parents, dead or useless to her for so many years now it was an unfair trick of her brain to play on her.

'They call me a lot. But they're getting on and they're not that mobile. And Naomi's so busy with her kids and her job. If I get totally desperate they'd come, obviously, but it's not really practical.'

'Have you found out any more about what Howard's actually got?'

'No. They've just prescribed him with anti-depressants. I think it's a bit of a last-ditch attempt.'

'What's happening with his work?'

'He can take early retirement next year, so they're sort of seeing what happens until then. They've been really good about it.'

Eleanor often forgot that Howard was more than a decade

older than them. He'd certainly never seemed it before. She looked over at Mary tugging on a piece of her hair and wondered if she'd ever considered the possibility that he might get sick when she was still young, which was a stupid thing to think because of course she hadn't. Which made her wonder at all the things she hadn't considered about Robert, all the ways she could get hurt, all the ways she'd left herself horribly vulnerable for the first time in her life.

'How old is he again?'

'Fifty-nine. Although right now he looks about a hundred and fifty-nine.'

'God, I hate what you're having to go through.'

Mary was quiet for a while, and Eleanor was worried that she'd gone too far, but then Mary spoke again. 'You know, it's very strange, but his illness has given me a sort of silence and space that I've never had in our marriage before. And I've been filling that gap with memories, which hasn't been that great. It's made me feel very strange, as if I'm looking at myself from the outside.'

'But what are you going to do?' Eleanor wished she could help Mary in the way she helped other people. But the situation was like a maze and she couldn't see a way out.

'I don't know. It sounds really selfish, but if he's not going to get better, I don't think I can let this be my life.'

'It's not selfish at all. Even if Howard had been the perfect husband it wouldn't be selfish. But he hasn't exactly given you loads of reasons to want to look after him now. I mean, he's hardly been the best husband, has he?'

A tear escaped, which Mary batted away with such force it was like she wanted to hurt herself. 'He was wonderful at the beginning.'

Eleanor felt a tug of pure sadness for her friend. 'I know, sweetheart. But the last ten years or so really haven't been great.'

Mary half laughed. 'It's ironic that I should be feeling like this now, isn't it? I've even thought about whether it would be possible to leave him.'

'Maybe it's just what you said, it's the first time you've had a bit of space in this marriage.' She didn't really know how to give advice about this because she couldn't imagine what it must be like to share your life with someone for so long, which in turn made her think about Robert and Nancy. It felt as if all her nerve-endings were exposed, so even her teeth ached.

'I feel like I wasn't really there for Nancy at the end,' she tried, looking for a way to explain how she felt.

'I know what you mean. We didn't speak nearly as much as we used to in the last year or so.' Mary's finger was wrapped tightly into her hair and her eyes welled. 'Do you remember that stupid idea we had about her volunteering for a charity about a year ago, a bit longer, actually, as it was at our Christmas lunch, which we didn't have last year? So it must have been the Christmas before last.'

'Nancy cancelled our lunch last Christmas, didn't she?'

'Yes.'

'I think she did that because that was when she was trying to end the affair and she was in a mess.'

'Or maybe she was still annoyed at us. Because do you remember at the lunch the year before you told her about how you have supper with Irena every week and suggested she could visit someone elderly, but she took it quite badly?'

'Yes.' The memory made Eleanor cringe.

'I was thinking about it the other night and, you know, I don't think she really spoke to me after that lunch. I mean, not properly. Maybe that's why she didn't tell me about the affair. I think we offended her way more than we realised.'

Eleanor remembered how uncomfortable that conversation had been, but surely it couldn't have had that much of an effect. Nancy had, after all, confided in her about the affair after that, although it was also true that often it seemed like she wished she hadn't. 'I don't think it can have been that. I mean, we apologised and she must have known we meant it kindly.'

Mary nodded. 'I guess. You know, in a funny way I never really felt good enough for Nancy.'

'Good enough?' Although Eleanor knew what Mary meant.

'Yes, like I wasn't the sort of person Nancy should be friends with. Like it had only happened because we met on that first night at uni. None of us would ever have met any other way. Didn't you ever feel that?'

Eleanor reached for her glass by her feet and took a deep sip of wine. 'I suppose I did a bit.'

'If you'd stopped contacting me I'd have been at your flat banging your door down. But I think I always suspected that would happen with Nancy, one way or another.'

Eleanor looked up into the orange sky, streaked with hundreds of chemical trails, raining poison down on them all. 'I'm sleeping with Robert.'

'I thought you were.'

Mary's answer shocked her because maybe she had opened herself up more than she'd even realised. 'How?'

'It's obvious.'

'Oh God.'

'I don't mean to everyone, I just mean to me.'

A police siren raced down the road. 'I'm a terrible person.'

Mary rolled her head so she was looking straight at her. 'No, you're not. But it's impossible it'll end well.'

Her knowing gaze made Eleanor want to cry. 'I never would have done anything if Nancy were alive. Nor would he.' Except, my God, this feeling superseded so much she couldn't be sure she was telling the truth. Maybe Nancy had felt like that about her lover, and all Eleanor had done was judge like a prissy schoolgirl.

They were silent for a while and then Mary said, 'He loved her very much, Els. You know that, don't you?'

'Of course I do,' she replied too quickly, but really the words struck at her, forcing her to acknowledge something she was trying to forget.

'I just don't want you to get hurt. I mean, Els, tell the absolute truth. Do you completely never think it could have been him?'

'No, of course not. Why do you even ask that?'

The moonlight was dancing off Mary's glasses. 'Because he loved her so much, I don't think he could have borne losing her to another man.'

Slime slithered through Eleanor's guts. It was true, she had lain with him sometimes and looked at his strong hands wrapped around her body and wondered at all the things they could do and all the things she couldn't know about him. The ground rocked beneath her chair. 'But he didn't know about the affair.'

'He told you he suspected. And, trust me, you always know, even when you're in the stage of not admitting it to yourself.'

A bell rang from upstairs, out of the opened window of Howard and Mary's bedroom, as if on cue. 'Bloody hell,' Eleanor said. 'Doesn't it drive you mad?'

'Less mad than when I didn't know where he was or who he was with, or when I had to listen to those silent phone calls, or when one of his students turned up at the house and I'd have to pretend I hadn't heard her crying.'

'That's a bit sick, Mary.'

'Maybe, but I guess we all adjust to whatever becomes normal

78

for us. Seriously though, Els, you don't have to. Even the easiest of relationships are rocky, and I don't want you to get dashed against rocks.'

'I'm not in one of your Greek tragedies.' Eleanor tried to laugh, but the sound died on her lips.

'We're all in a bloody Greek tragedy,' Mary said.

The bell rang again through the window like a ghostly summons and this time Mary did get up. 'I'd better see what he wants.'

Eleanor watched her friend's tiny departing figure as she was swallowed into the darkness of her kitchen. Mary's reasons for staying with Howard had always seemed so confusing, but for the first time Eleanor felt the beginnings of an understanding. Robert was the worst person for her to have fallen in love with and yet it had happened and she would never be able to explain it to anyone, not even herself. She didn't even want to try, she just wanted to revel in it.

She remembered coming to visit Mary with Nancy after Maisie's birth thirteen years before, when all her freind seemed to do for so many years was grow babies in her distended stomach, squeeze them out at home because Howard didn't believe in hospitals, then have them continually attached to her body because Howard believed in separation anxiety.

The pregnancy had been hard for Mary, her body barely recovered from Mimi's birth, but still that had been the time Howard had chosen to start behaving badly. During those nine months Eleanor fielded plenty of late-night phone calls in which Mary was desperate because Howard either hadn't come home, or because he'd shouted at her or belittled her over something trivial. And then, just before she'd given birth, a girl, who Mary had claimed was no more than nineteen or twenty, turned up on their doorstop and, according to Mary, it had been obvious that something was going on between them.

Somehow none of it had massively surprised Eleanor. It wasn't that she'd disliked Howard before then, but she also hadn't entirely felt comfortable around him. She'd always put it down to the fact that he'd been married when Mary had met him and then, when she'd got pregnant with Marcus, there was a lot of toing and froing before he finally left his wife. And he did always have a slight air of superiority about him that rankled.

Nancy had brought a basket of fruit with her, which she remembered Howard exclaiming over. He had been holding Mimi in his arms and he made a play of bouncing her around and showing her the colours. He had the air of a busy and distracted man, trying desperately to hold everything together as best he could, a part Eleanor thought he played very well. He'd told them to go up and how much Mary was looking forward to seeing them, so they'd manoeuvered past the toys and papers and clothes on every step and found Mary looking frighteningly pale and worn out in the messy bed, with Maisie sucking at her giant, veined breasts. The room was too hot and suffocated by an earthy, iron smell, which made Eleanor look round the room until her eyes rested on a pile of bloodied sheets festering in the corner.

'Is that Marcus I can hear crying?' Mary had asked, her eyes looking past them out of the door.

'I don't know,' Eleanor said.

'Oh God, I can't bear it.' Her voice caught on the words and her eyes filled with tears.

'Do you want me to go and have a look?' Eleanor offered. 'Maybe make you a cup of tea? Shall I put those sheets in the wash?'

Mary flicked her attention back into the room and a livid red rose on her cheeks. 'Oh, I'm sorry, would you mind?'

Eleanor picked up the rancid sheets whilst Nancy went to sit on the bed next to their friend. Nancy would be good at soothing talk, she thought, as she left the room and made her way down to the kitchen, a hard anger building inside her. Marcus was sitting at the table and Howard was leaning over him with Mimi balanced on his hip.

'My God, Marcus,' he was saying. 'She's just had a baby, she doesn't want you bothering her every second of the day.' He looked up as Eleanor came in but his face remained neutral, like he was daring her to say something. Eleanor suspected that he knew Mary had confided in her about the girl, which had probably made him detest her, but she supposed they would both have to pretend otherwise, hiding their blood-red thoughts.

'Mary needs a cup of tea,' Eleanor said, refusing to look away. 'And these sheets need washing.'

They stared at each other for a few seconds in which anything seemed possible, even violence. But in the end Howard smiled and motioned to the machine. 'Leave them there, I'll do it.' He turned his back to her and raised the pitch of his voice, 'I don't know how Mary does it all. I barely know if I'm coming or going.'

She dropped the sheets on the floor and then rinsed three mugs and made three cups of tea. When she had them in her hands she said, 'Marcus, do you want to come up with me? I'd love to have a chat with you.'

Marcus looked up at his father, his bottom lip quivering, snot encrusted round his nose. Howard's smile was tight, but he nodded at his son, putting Mimi down and going towards the washing machine. Eleanor smiled at Marcus so he slithered off the chair, rushing before her up the stairs.

*

When Mary came back into the garden from tending to Howard, darkness had properly fallen and there was a slight chill in the air. She was carrying a new bottle of wine and poured more into Eleanor's glass as she sat.

'God, what time is it?' Eleanor asked.

'Just after eight.'

'Shit.'

'Somewhere you should be?'

She was due at Irena's, as she was every Thursday, except the idea of sitting again in that stuffy flat was too much to bear. Irena's words from the evening before had refused to leave her all day, as if they had implanted themselves into her flesh and were now travelling round her blood. She couldn't hear them again, mainly because she didn't think she'd be able to deny them a second time.

'Shall we be really decadent and get a takeaway?' Mary said.

'Yes,' Eleanor answered, relaxing into her decision.

There was a line of light coming from under Irena's door when she got home a few hours later, but she was tired and her head felt heavy from the wine and Robert. Halfway up she hesitated, because it was impossible to forget the night of Nancy's death and how Irena had enfolded her, how she'd stopped her from blowing away. But also, what if Irena was right and she was making the biggest mistake of her life? It didn't seem possible that she should lose Nancy and then her understanding of herself.

She went straight to bed when she got in, but then found she couldn't sleep. The shadows from the dancing trees outside her window were playing on her light curtains and something about them tugged at her, as if she had forgotten something important. She breathed deeply and the air flowed freely through her, which in turn made her realise how calm she felt, how without worry. And then she knew what it was she'd forgotten: she'd forgotten to feel anxious, forgotten that the whole of life is really terrifying.

Eleanor pulled herself up, her heart now racing as if making up for lost time. Robert, she realised, was as mesmerising as the swaying trees; he had lulled her into a false sense of security, in fact to a state of almost total languishment. But what if she had been right all along and love was a dangerous fallacy, hiding much deeper and darker truths? She thought of Nancy and Mary, her mother, herself, and wondered if this happened to all women in the end, this subjugation to a man, this total relinquishing of self, to the point at which you forgot what was important?

A panic wave, as she had come to think of them over the years, undulated through her, fizzing out of the top of her head. What if Zara was right and the lover, whoever he might have been, didn't have anything to do with Nancy's death? And Mary was definitely right, Robert had adored Nancy, maybe too much ever to let her go. Which, naturally, begged a question about what they were doing together, what the hell she hoped to get out of this bizarre mess. Or maybe, more pertinently, what he was getting out of the situation.

They had already decided to spend the weekend in Sussex and the truth was Eleanor still wanted to go when she woke the next morning. The situation might be wrong, it might even be dangerous, but it was also intoxicating. If this was love then it was more powerful than all the guilt or doubts she had. She heard a door slam in Irena's flat downstairs, a horrible reminder that she still needed to apologise for the missed supper the night before. But she also knew she would have to tell Irena she was going away and she would ask where, and when she told her it was with Robert her face would crease in a way that would make her feel ashamed. Eleanor decided to compromise, finding a walnut cake in her cupboard and writing a quick note on a bright postcard: *Am away for the weekend, thought you might like this. Will come and see you on Sunday evening. Much love, E x.* She left them outside Irena's door, trying to ignore the grubby coating slathering her skin. Nothing would stop her going round when she got back on Sunday evening, when they could have a proper conversation and Eleanor could explain why it wasn't wrong with Robert, as soon as she'd worked out the answer for herself.

Robert picked her up from her office after work and they sped down the sleek motorways towards the house she had always loved, but never considered properly before. Now Coombe Place occupied her thoughts too much and her considerations were becoming dangerous. Eleanor thought the kitchen was designed badly and she would never have used the shades Nancy had, they verged on twee when the house was large and broad, like an old friend. The walls, she thought, cried out for greys and whites and the floors shouldn't be carpeted. She started to imagine her possessions within its framework, saw some of her photographs hanging on its walls.

It was the first time they had been there for two weeks when they arrived at nine that evening, and the house smelt dusty and unloved, almost as if it was admonishing them for their absence. Or maybe, she thought, as she walked in behind Robert, the house hated her for not being Nancy, for thinking she knew what it would like more than its real mistress.

The muffled ring of her phone sounded from her bag before she'd even taken off her coat. It was Irena's daughter, Sarah.

'Oh, hi, Eleanor. I'm really sorry to be a pain and call again, but I can't get hold of Mum and I just wondered if you'd seen her this evening. Or if you could pop down?'

Eleanor tried to keep her voice light. 'I haven't been home, actually. I've come away straight from work.'

'Are you away for the weekend?'

'Yes.' She should have got up early and knocked on Irena's door, or made the effort to go home after work and pop in, it had even occurred to her, but she knew Robert liked to try to miss the traffic.

'Oh, don't worry.' Sarah's voice sounded false. 'I'm sure it's fine. She often doesn't answer the phone. I'm just being silly because she was ill in the week.'

'She really did seem much better.' Although Eleanor thought of their last meeting and how she hadn't even asked her how she was feeling, only focusing on what Irena had made her feel.

'Did you see her yesterday evening like usual, then?'

'Yes.' Eleanor almost gasped with the audacity of the lie. She didn't even know what she was trying to achieve, why she always needed to be seen as the good one. 'She was fine.'

'Oh well, I'm sure I'm worrying about nothing then. Thank you so much, by the way, for you know, seeing her on Thursdays. She does love your visits.'

Something acidic sunk deep into Eleanor's stomach. 'I love them as well.'

'OK, well, thanks anyway.'

'We should have stopped to get some food,' Eleanor said as she dropped her phone back in her bag, because the wide hall made her feel suddenly starving.

Robert had been flicking through the mail on the hall table, but he came towards her now and pulled her into him, crushing the air between their bodies. She looked up at him and he pushed her fringe off her face, looking into her eyes in a way she didn't really understand. 'Come on,' he said, leading her up the stairs.

They had only ever stayed in one of the guest bedrooms before, but this time he led her into the room he had shared with Nancy.

'Oh, I can't.' She stopped at the doorway.

'It's only a room. I hate that other mattress. This one has all my dents in it.' She smiled but didn't move. She couldn't lie on Nancy's side of the bed. 'It doesn't mean anything.' He came closer and unbuttoned her silk shirt, slipping his hand inside, underneath her bra, so that she actually groaned.

Their love making always felt urgent, almost feral. Eleanor heard herself make sounds she never had before and her body felt alive with him. She wanted him inside her all the time, she didn't care about foreplay, she just wanted to feel him in every part of her, to rip herself in two, turn herself inside out, anything and everything. And Robert also seemed filled with the same desperation. His movements were jagged and needy, he bit the side of her neck and pulled her into strange positions.

Afterwards they both lay entangled in the bedsheets and Eleanor wondered if Robert had changed them since Nancy died. She sat up and pulled at her clothes, straightening herself out, not really sure what she was doing. *Irish linen*, she heard Nancy say, *and I have them decadently laundered.* She worried that if she turned her head Nancy would be standing right there, looking down on them.

She felt Robert's hand on her back. 'Are you OK?'

'Don't you ever feel guilty?' She didn't dare look around. The room smelt of roses.

'I feel lots of things.'

'Is this a way of paying her back?' Eleanor hadn't even realised she thought that until she said it.

He pulled her down so they were lying on the bed, facing each other. 'Of course not.'

'No, but really, I mean...' She wanted to ask him things worthy only of a schoolgirl. Am I better than her? I know I might not be as beautiful, but am I kinder, cleverer? She rolled onto her back and wanted to scream.

'Ellie, you know this isn't about that.'

She dug her fists into her eyes so she saw flashes of light. 'I don't know anything. I have no idea what we're doing. I mean, imagine if Zara ever found out.'

'She won't.'

And that was almost the worst thing he could say. 'But then what is this?'

'I don't know what you're asking me? I lost my wife five months ago and I feel shredded, if you want to know the truth. You know I think you're amazing, I always have. But if you're asking me if this would have happened if Nancy were alive, then no, it wouldn't.'

'Of course I'm not asking that.'

She took her hands away from her face and rolled back onto her side so their noses were almost touching. 'Would you have forgiven her, do you think?'

'I don't know. That's one of the worst things, not knowing the details, not knowing if she wanted to leave or not.'

'Do you remember when we first met?'

He screwed up his face and Eleanor knew she should remember this moment, because it told her what she needed to know. 'I guess through Nancy. I mean, obviously I remember you at university.'

She laughed as lightly as she could. 'I'm glad you remember me.'

'No, you know what I mean. In fact, I was thinking about it the other day and it made me feel happy.'

'What did?'

'I was thinking about how I didn't really properly consider you before. I mean, I liked you and I looked forward to seeing you and everything, but you were Nancy's friend and so I guess there was always a remove.'

'Right.' It was almost impossible to believe that he didn't remember the party, or how their hands had brushed, or the things they had said. She had carried that memory around with her for so long, but without his corresponding memory, it might as well not be real. She knew she had to remember this moment, in which he was either lying or really had forgotten because she had never meant anything to him.

'No, but I mean, that's wonderful in a way, isn't it?'

'What is?'

'How you can just be another person to each other and then suddenly you're so much more. It sort of gives you hope for the future.'

What future, she wanted to ask. But she knew how pathetic the words would sound out in the open. It felt like someone was squeezing her heart, making it drip down the centre of her chest.

The next day Robert had to go to lunch with one of his so-called neighbours, a couple that actually lived a fifteen-minute drive away. This always happened when they were in Sussex, people rallying round the lonely widower. Eleanor understood that it was too soon and too complicated for Robert to take her to these lunches, which she didn't even want to go to, but she suspected that soon there might be a single woman sat next to him.

She sat on one of the wicker sun loungers on the terrace after he'd gone, breathing in the grassy air and letting the warm sun heat her bones as she attempted and failed to read a book. The garden was close to what she imagined paradise must look like, but it wasn't enough, and the hours ahead seemed endless. A knowing loneliness wound itself into her gut, which made her unhinged enough to consider texting and asking when he might be home. All of which was pathetic as she'd spent most weekends of her adult life alone in one way or another, always able to entertain herself with trips to galleries and lunches with friends, walks in parks and films seen in the middle of rainy afternoons. Men had come and gone, but never stuck, no one had ever really seemed right, not before Robert.

And that in turn made her feel awful because she didn't think she'd spent the past nearly thirty years lusting after her friend's husband. Except now she couldn't be so sure, couldn't swear to herself that she hadn't fostered a connection, at times let her gaze rest on him a second too long, made too much of their first meeting. She supposed she had never let herself think like that because she loved Nancy, but the strength of feeling she now had for Robert also could not have come totally out of the blue. And if that was true, then what sort of person was she, deep down?

Eleanor let the book drop from her lap onto the stones and didn't even bother to pick it up. She had been crazy to think she could compete within this world she had watched for so many years, a world in which Nancy and Robert sat across the top like a pair of golden-haired titans. They were like perfect mirror reflections of each other, with their beauty and their brains, their money, their power, their friends, their influences. It was Nancy who had always included her, she saw now, Nancy who had loved her, and Robert had gone along with it because he too was fond of her and enjoyed her company, but mainly because he loved Nancy too much ever to deny her anything. It was suddenly obvious that he didn't remember that he had met her first, because Nancy had eclipsed everything else for him.

Eleanor stood, her body jangling with her thoughts in an uncomfortably familiar way. Tall, elegant poplars swayed at the bottom of the garden and beyond that she could see the steeple of the church where they'd buried Nancy only five months before. She was nothing but a fraud in this perfect place, an intruder in the life that Nancy and Robert had created. She turned and stepped back into the cool of the house, but nowhere seemed like the right place for her to be as she wandered through the rooms, choking on her tears. Eventually there was only one room she hadn't gone in and that was perhaps the room she'd been heading towards all this time: Robert's study.

She opened the door gently, pushing through the mustiness of the space, which felt unused and unloved. The walls were lined with messy bookshelves, files and folders and books stuffed onto them seemingly at random. The old wooden desk with its leather top sat in the window, covered in papers and mugs, some of which had grown a white line of fur. There were more papers on the floor and a pair of women's brogues kicked into the corner. She sat at the desk and immediately saw a silver-framed photo of Nancy smiling out at her. It wasn't the image that arrested her, the house was after all filled with such images, but more the quaintness of Robert having it on his desk, when surely he would have only had to walk into the next room to see her in actuality. Unless he had put it there since she died, although that seemed unlikely. Eleanor couldn't remember him ever coming into this room in all the times they'd been to Sussex together.

There was an armchair in the corner, next to a bookcase, positioned so that whoever sat in it could chat to the person sitting at the desk. The seat was indented and a half-read book was lying across the arm. Eleanor reached forward and turned it round so she could see what it was – *Deep Water* by Patricia Highsmith. She couldn't imagine Robert reading that, but she knew anyway it was Nancy who had sat in that chair and read that book. She knew immediately why Robert never came in here, why the door stayed shut. With a sick jolt she realised that this had been, more than their bedroom, their place. It was too easy to see Nancy curled in to the chair, her legs pulled up underneath her, her brow furrowed as she read, Robert sighing over some detail of a case. They would look up now and then and smile at each other, a little acknowledgment all they needed.

She felt trapped then, almost as if Nancy and Robert were laughing at her together. She wanted to break something, tear the book in half and throw the photograph through the window. But instead she opened the drawers of the desk, trespassing through Robert's papers, in the only reckless act she could find at that moment.

There was a card at the bottom of one of the drawers with a piece of paper folded inside it. She pulled it out with shaking hands, her breath high in her throat. On the front was a watercolour of the church at the bottom of the garden and inside Nancy had written: I am sorry, Robert darling, forever and completely sorry. I don't mean to make you so sad and angry. I know I must try harder and I know how frustrating I am. I think I forgot back there all we are, all we always have been. Please be kind to me.

Eleanor read the words again, but still they didn't sound right. The image of Nancy as supplicant was not one she had ever before considered. She wanted to scratch at the words, as if there was a secret code hidden underneath them, but they remained stubbornly solid. Undated, it was impossible to tell when it had been written – it could have been from twenty years before, or only a few months. Except, either way it didn't make sense as there was not one moment in Nancy's relationship with Robert that Eleanor could ever remember her expressing contrition or even worry.

She unfolded the letter to read Robert's reply to Nancy's apology. But even in the first few lines it seemed off, it was written on an old-fashioned typewriter, which was not something she could imagine Robert using, and there certainly wasn't one in the study.

Oh my love, there were so many things I wanted to say to you after you left today. Sometimes I feel like you don't listen to me properly and run away with your own thoughts. So please read this carefully and think about what I have to say.

I love you for how strongly you feel your guilt, but when all is said and done, it is a pedestrian emotion. Some things exist outside the normal moral parameters because they are perfect. We, however, live in an imperfect world, which needs petty rules and codes because most people are stupid and lacking in any form of understanding. You and I are above those feelings, which is what drew us together and made it impossible that we could do anything other than fall in love. What we are doing cannot be wrong by virtue of the fact that it is so right.

Eleanor came up for air, looking down the view of the garden, a sudden realisation dawning: there was no way these words could have come from Robert. She was in fact reading a letter from Nancy's lover, a letter Robert must have found, a letter Nancy must have been apologising for him having to read.

I understand it is hard to rid yourself of guilt, especially when
you think about our families. But what if us shaking things up will
actually be good for them in the long run? You talk constantly of
your fear of Zara finding out, but I think it could be just what she
needs. She is lazy and spoilt, as are my children, when all is said
and done. They all need a dose of reality, a moment of looking up
from the small things they think important.

When they find out about us they will shout and scream
because they don't understand. But they will do in time. We just
have to hold our nerve. We could teach the world how to love. We
could end wars and cure diseases with our love.

Be brave and strong, my perfect lady, my heroine, my one and
only, because you are.

Eleanor sat very still for a long while after she finished reading, staring at the photo of Nancy in front of her. At first she
simply felt surprised that Nancy could have ever been involved
with anyone who used words in the way this man did, like
a landmine disguised in a war-torn earth. But then another
thought emerged: Robert had clearly read this letter before
Nancy died, for her to have apologised for it.

She stood up, but her head spun so she had to lean over
Robert's desk. The indented chair spoke of an unimaginable
closeness and the room suddenly seemed stuffed with secrets
that stifled the air. God, they must have rowed; they must have
screamed and shouted and raged. But they also must have loved
each other, so intently and passionately that they had clung together even when confronted with this letter and all the betrayal
contained within it. Eleanor might not know much about love,
but she did know that passion like that couldn't exist very far
from hate.

Her mind was racing, but she knew she had to calm herself to work out what was going on. Certain things were now obvious. Robert had clearly known about the affair before Nancy's death, which meant that when he had called her round on the night she was killed and got her to tell him, he had been playing a game. But Nancy also had lied to her; towards the end of the affair when the lover had been harassing her, Eleanor had begged her to go to the police, but Nancy always said she couldn't because she didn't want to risk Robert finding out. Why also was Robert withholding this letter, which might contain clues or even DNA evidence? What was he gaining by keeping Davide Boyette as a suspect unless it was that it kept the attention off him? She fished her phone out of her pocket and took a photo of the letter, not really sure why, sure she'd never show it to anyone, but needing access to it to prove something to herself, if nothing else.

By the time Robert got home Eleanor was back on the sun lounger and the book was back on her lap. He looked tired as he sat heavily on a chair next to her. She kept her sunglasses over her eyes. 'Good lunch?'

He rubbed his eyebrows. 'They were very nice.' He stood up again, almost immediately, and she recognised the need to keep moving. 'God, I need a drink. D'you want one?'

'Yes, please.'

He went into the dark sitting room and she could hear the fizz of opening bottles and the chink of ice against glass. He emerged back into the sunlight with two tall gins and the tannin fizzed up her nose with her first sip.

'What did you do with yourself?' he asked.

'Oh, nothing much. Read a bit, you know.'

Robert walked to the end of the terrace and stood with his back to her. 'I'm sorry, Ellie,' he said finally.

Her heart skipped. 'What for?'

He turned back and came and sat on the end of her lounger, taking her bare feet in his hands, making little sparks of desire shoot up through her legs. 'Oh, everything really. It's shit, isn't it.'

'I don't know, not everything.'

'But it's all such a mess. Us sneaking around and Nancy dead and Zara hating me. It's like I'm in freefall and I don't know what's happening.'

She sat forward so their bodies were closer and she could put her hand on his cheek. She had been thinking such damning things about him, but now he was here she felt them falling away. She had to have got it wrong in some way, there had to be something she wasn't seeing.

'It hasn't been long enough for you to be thinking straight yet. Give yourself a break.' But then she saw he was crying, his tears falling off the end of his nose and landing like summer rain on the hot stones at his feet. 'Oh, Robert.' She pulled herself onto her knees so she could enfold his body in her arms.

He turned his face against her shoulder and she felt his tears soak through her t-shirt and land in the dip of her collarbone.

'I just miss her so much. So fucking much.'

Eleanor had to shut her eyes because she felt like she was standing on a tiny ledge, a thousand feet off the ground, with the air rushing past her ears.

They ate supper in bed, after fucking. They went to the kitchen like teenagers and made cheese sandwiches which they ate with a bottle of wine, not caring about crumbs in the already dirty bedsheets. The window was open and the air was heavy with the smell of tobacco. Nancy had planted stocks round the house for the very purpose of scenting the summer evenings. The sun had dipped away, but there was still light in the sky, the horizon a lingering salmon pink.

'You know, you don't have to hide what you're feeling from

me,' Eleanor said. 'You're not going to hurt me by talking about Nancy.'

'It's such a fucked-up situation.'

'You wouldn't have left her, would you?' Eleanor put her sandwich on the bedside table because it had begun to taste of chalk.

'No, probably not.'

'Did you talk to her about the affair? I mean, about your suspicions?' She couldn't look at him and longed for the gathering dusk to envelope them like a crowd of people.

'No.'

His lie was painful. 'Why not?'

'Because I was scared of what she might say.'

Birds were singing to each other in the trees outside, a final goodbye to the day. 'What made you think she was having an affair, though?' She held her breath, giving him another chance, willing him to tell her and prove her wrong.

'Oh, it was just a feeling really. When you've known someone for as long as Nancy and I knew each other you can tell things. It's almost like a sort of telepathy.'

She wound the linen sheet around her finger and felt something heavy in her head. 'So you never had any proof then?'

He turned his head to her and half laughed, so convincingly it made her stomach clench. 'No. What do you mean?'

His lie pushed her heart high into her chest. 'I don't know. I can't get my head round it. If I'd been married to someone for nearly thirty years and I thought they were having an affair I'd confront them, I couldn't bear not to.'

'Yes, but you're like that, Eleanor.' The air was heavy with the implication of his unsaid words. He sighed. 'Nancy and I didn't really do full-on confrontation. We sort of said things without actually saying them.'

'You wouldn't have let her leave either, would you?' Eleanor said eventually.

Robert slipped down the bed, so his head was lying on the pillow, his blond hair mixed with the white sheets. The room was suddenly almost dark and she could see the newly risen moon glinting off his proud profile. 'I guess not,' he said, as he rolled onto his side so she was left only with the sharp ridges of his spine.

On the way back to London the next day, Sarah rang again, but Eleanor let it click onto message and then didn't even listen when the little red 1 appeared by the sign for the phone. She had a thick headache that was pulsating upwards from the tightness in her jaw, but she was looking forward to seeing Irena, which she would do as soon as she got home. Maybe she could talk to her about Robert again. Maybe she could even tell her about the letter, because Irena was about the only person she could think of who might be able to tell her what it all really meant.

Robert drove too fast so the scrubland on the side of the motorway blurred and it was only just after four when they reached the top of her road. The whole day had felt ominously like a countdown and she wondered if Sunday's in Sussex had felt like that for Nancy as well.

'Just drop me here,' she said. 'There's no point in you having to turn at the end.'

'What's going on?' He was looking across her, so she followed his eyes and saw flashing lights at the end of the street. 'Isn't that outside your place?'

'No,' she lied.

'Do you want me to come down with you? Check everything's OK.'

'No, don't worry. It won't be anything.' Except even as she

spoke her heart was twisting and she could feel sweat slicking her hands.

'Well, if you're sure. Call me and let me know what it is.'

She opened the door and stepped out. 'Of course. Thanks for a lovely weekend.'

He smiled as she shut the door, out of relief Eleanor thought. But she couldn't dwell on that for too long because, the closer she got to home, the more obvious it became that the police were outside her house. She turned up her path and saw two policewomen standing in the hallway, one on the radio attached to her shoulder, the other with an arm around a sobbing woman.

'Excuse me,' said a voice behind her so she turned to see another policewoman. 'Can I help you?'

'I live here.'

The sobbing woman turned at that and she saw it was Sarah, her face rumpled and made ugly by tears and grief. It was obvious what had happened and the knowledge seeped in like poison.

Sarah broke away from the policewoman and came towards Eleanor. 'I tried calling you a couple of hours ago. I couldn't get hold of Mum all weekend and then when she still wasn't answering this morning I drove up. And then when I got here, oh God...' Her words were all running into each other.

'Is she all right?'

Sarah shook her head. 'No. She's dead.'

It felt like a physical blow, across Eleanor's cheek. 'Oh God.' She felt her body tilt and thought for a second she was going to fall. 'What happened?'

'They think a stroke. She was lying in her hallway when I found her. It looks like she tripped on a loose bit of carpet, but they don't think the fall killed her. They think she had a stroke sometime after that.'

The world did a complete spin that sent a wave of nausea right through Eleanor. 'Oh, Sarah, I'm so sorry. Do they know when it happened?'

Sarah blew her nose. 'The paramedics said probably in the last few days. There was a cake from you outside her front door, which meant she can't have left the house all weekend, I'm presuming. When did you leave it?'

'Friday morning, before I left for work.' Something cold was rushing through Eleanor's head.

'She went to her social group on Thursday morning and you saw her on Thursday evening, so it must have happened that night or Friday morning, I suppose, as I tried ringing her on Friday afternoon.' Sarah's face crumpled again. 'Oh God. I don't know why I didn't come yesterday. Or even Friday. She might have been lying there for hours, maybe even days. I just can't bear it.'

Eleanor reached out and touched Sarah's arm, which was folded around her waist as if she were hugging herself. 'It wouldn't have made any difference. I mean, when you'd come.'

Sarah wiped her nose on the back of her hand. 'But it might have. I just can't bear to think of her dying alone like that.'

'She probably wouldn't have known anything about it.' Although, Eleanor knew, she might have known all about it. She might have had to lie for hours waiting for death to take her, knowing what was coming. It was shameful to think that a woman as wonderful as Irena should have such an end.

'I hope not. God, I hope not. She looked so strange lying on the floor. I mean, I knew she was dead immediately. She looked completely departed.' Eleanor nodded, remembering Nancy. 'I'm so glad she saw you on Thursday though. She really did love you living above her. We all did. It's made us feel so much better about Mum being alone.'

'I loved it as well. Your mother was an amazing woman. I'll miss her.' Which was horribly, irreversibly true. And also so much worse than Sarah could possibly imagine. Eleanor remembered the banging door she'd heard from Irena's flat on Friday morning. It couldn't possibly have been Irena falling, surely, surely not.

Eleanor felt suddenly dizzy, as if she had been outside too long in a strong sun. 'Will you let me know when the funeral is?' She wanted so desperately now to be in her flat it was as if a stone was pressing down on the top of her head. She kept her smile fixed, but inside she was already thrashing, so she feared she might soon fall to the ground and weep on the unswept path of her home.

'Of course I will.'

Eleanor nodded and stepped past her. Her flat smelt musty and enclosed, almost like an ancient relic, and it reminded her so much of herself she thought she might be sick. She knew all at once that she couldn't bear to watch Irena's son and daughter sell the flat, as they no doubt eventually would. She couldn't bear to see life move on and over, new people move in, as if nothing was real or concrete.

She stood for a while in the centre of her sitting room, watching the maple tree outside the window undulate in the breeze. The sky behind was an azure blue, with little wispy clouds lying across its surface. She didn't believe in God, or heaven or hell for that matter, but it seemed impossible that Nancy wasn't somewhere. That she didn't sit on a cloud and entertain the angels, that she didn't know everything.

She walked to the window to look at the sky that had to contain Nancy, but her attention was drawn to the noise outside her front door. Irena was there, looking upwards as she always had when she came in, waving if she caught sight of Eleanor at her window. Except this time all Eleanor could see was the form of Irena, shrouded by a black body bag, as two sweating men manoeuvered her out of the doorway and down the path to a discreet private ambulance. She wondered if that was how Nancy had left the riverbank.

Eleanor's legs felt as if her bones had shattered within them and nothing was supporting her. She turned from the window and walked over to the sofa, sitting down just before she fell. Everything seemed very far away and her thoughts skittered across her brain, refusing to settle. She felt her muscles harden and knew that movement would soon feel jagged and clumsy. Her heart knocked uncomfortably against her chest, like a bad horror film, and her eyes stung. She had the odd sensation that a gauze sheet was being drawn between her and the world and that it was going to take a lot of effort to remove it again.

She had told Sarah that Irena's death wasn't her fault and that was true, but it was impossible to absolve herself of responsibility. Which, of course, if she were being honest, was the same as Nancy's death. It seemed in fact entirely possible that she was responsible for both these deaths. Too wrapped up in her own problems or judgements or preconceptions to stop and try to help two women whom she had loved deeply, who had loved her in return, who had needed her help.

'I'll call you tomorrow and let you know how it goes,' had been Nancy's last words to her and Eleanor knew that she'd kept her head down as she'd heard them spoken, pretending to look for something in her bag. She had physically felt Nancy's need vibrating through the air like a piece of string and still she hadn't looked up, still she had let her perceived irritation at her friend be the thing that mattered.

'Oh my God,' she said, but then clamped her hand tight over her mouth so she couldn't betray herself any more.

But the thoughts had her already, they had set up home inside her while she'd been fucking Nancy's husband, and now they burrowed out of her, piercing her skin with their jagged edges. You wanted this to happen, they said to her, you jumped at the opportunity it gave you with Robert. You were stupid and vain enough to believe he would fall in love with you, to actually think that he had loved Nancy but you could erase that memory. You wanted to take her place, didn't you? You wilfully didn't help her so you could swap your sad, sorry life for her glorious one. Except that life doesn't fit you; you're no better than the ugly sisters trying to squeeze their feet into the glass slipper, trying to take what isn't yours, you sad, stupid fuck. Then when Irena saw the truth of the situation, instead of listening to her, you turned away, so desperate not to hear words you knew to be true, that you were willing to sacrifice her for your pretend happiness.

The chair felt too high and so Eleanor lay on the floor, hoping her back would crick against the hard wood. As the day lengthened and the sky darkened she didn't draw the curtains or allow herself to go to the loo, even though her bladder ached. Her body began to protest, but it was nothing compared to the tidal wave building in her mind. If she moved she feared she might break into so many pieces it would be impossible to glue herself back together.

Eleanor could not shake the image of Irena lying scared and alone on the floor just beneath where she was now herself lying. Except she could move if she wanted to, could relieve the pressure in her body, if not the fear in her mind. Irena would have been helpless, probably in pain, her bones cracked and her flesh bruised. Perhaps she called out for Eleanor, maybe she even heard her come down the stairs and leave the stupid cake outside her door. All it would have taken was a simple knock on the door, a turn of the key, a moment of time. Even if she hadn't been able to save Irena's life she could have perhaps been with her when she died. Could have cradled her fragile head, kissed that wrinkled brow, whispered warm words to a wise and dignified woman who had deserved so much more than the death she had.

Eleanor let herself weep for a while, but even that felt too self-indulgent, so she swallowed her tears back down and lay staring up at her cracked ceiling, forcing herself to acknowledge how much she had fucked up. It was suddenly obvious how right Irena had been about Robert – how she had jumped into him so totally and completely she hadn't stopped to consider how insane she was being, or even who he really was. She thought about the card and the letter in his desk and her stomach flipped. She had to stop this madness and yet, without Robert, the world seemed terrifying and huge. She couldn't believe she had operated for so long on her own, that she had kidded herself into thinking her life was full and worthwhile. Black chasms opened inside her head, each one threatening to pull her inwards and turn her inside out. She groped for someone to call, even though she knew the act of doing so was way beyond her powers. She couldn't really even remember who she was exactly, because from the ground looking up it appeared as if she had constructed an outward version of herself that bore no relation to the reality.

Her job made it look like she was a caring person, but that suddenly seemed like an abstract kind of caring. Helping thousands all at once so that no one got close enough to say thank you, or she never got close enough to see it through to the end. She hadn't helped Nancy at the end of her affair, she hadn't helped Mary as her marriage crumbled, she hadn't helped her mother when she slipped away from sanity, she hadn't helped her sister when her husband walked out, leaving her alone with two young sons, she hadn't helped Irena when she had simply needed a carpet mending and more soup buying. And now she wasn't helping Robert or even herself, just dragging them deeper into the dark waters of fear and uncertainty. She couldn't even be sure any more if Robert needed help, or if she'd got everything catastrophically wrong.

Morning came inevitably and she found that it was in fact possible to drag her tired, stiff body upright, to even shower and dress in clean clothes and force down half a piece of toast and a cup of tea. But she did everything as if observing, as if movement was a hard-gained act, as if her brain lagged behind her body. She rang in to work to say she thought she was coming down with something so wouldn't be in, but then realised she could not spend all day alone in her flat, so rang Mary who told her to come round.

Within the hour Eleanor was in Mary's full, messy house, which she had grown to see as an extension of her friend, almost like the massive shell of a snail. Today though the house felt very quiet with the girls at school, Marcus asleep and Howard catatonic in his chair. Eleanor almost wanted to leave as soon as she stepped into the choked atmosphere, but she saw the loneliness she was feeling reflected back in Mary's eyes, so she went through to the kitchen and accepted a cup of tea.

'You OK?' Eleanor asked, when they were sitting opposite each other at the table piled high with magazines, books, pens and various random items that didn't belong in a kitchen.

'I don't even know any more.' Mary rubbed at the back of her neck with her knuckles.

She didn't feel ready yet to talk about Robert, so it was good that she had other questions to ask. 'How's Howard? Have the anti-depressants worked?'

Mary shook her head. 'They're talking now about him having

had a nervous breakdown. Or maybe even something called Random Bi-polar.'

'What's that?'

'Bi-polar which comes on suddenly in middle age. But it's bizarre, it attacks you physically as much as mentally. It can be brought on by an overload of stress, and running that politics department was so stressful, I mean, maybe it's caught up with him.'

'Maybe.'

'He's always been so volatile as well, hasn't he? I always thought that I annoyed him or put him into bad moods, but I've been wondering recently if actually he's very highly strung? Some people would look back on how he's been behaving this past ten years or so and say he's spent a decade on the verge of a breakdown.'

'Oh God, Mary.'

'I know.' The corners of Mary's mouth twitched downwards and Eleanor could see the jut of her collarbone under her shirt. 'But I'm more worried about Marcus, to be honest. He's high most of the time now.'

'Still? What do you think's going on?'

'I don't know. But he seems intent on annihilating himself at the moment.' Mary swallowed hard and Eleanor knew she was trying not to cry; could suddenly imagine her friend weeping on her own at this very table. 'Being alone this much isn't good. I've been thinking way too much, about our life and everything. I should have taken Marcus away from Howard when he was younger. I should have taken them all away.'

'There's no point in thinking like that now.'

'I can't think about anything else. I think Howard's brand of disdain, or whatever it is, is almost worse than if he'd hit them or something. And Marcus always got the brunt of it. I'm starting to think he never actually liked him and Marcus must have known, deep down.'

'But that can't be true.'

'Oh, I don't know. We didn't plan to have children, did we? Maybe Howard never really wanted them? Because when I think about it now I'm starting to realise how selfish he is and you can't be selfish when you have children. When things started to go wrong between us he often used to say that the kids had held him back.'

Families made Eleanor feel vertiginous; how they clung and melded. She'd wondered over the years if she would have ever ended up doing what she did if her mother hadn't been so involved with charities when she was young, and that thought made her feel insubstantial. She'd been right to keep herself distant and it was no wonder that everything should be falling apart since she'd fallen for Robert. 'You can't blame yourself.'

'Of course I can.'

There was a spurt of red across the wall behind the cooker that looked like blood, but was probably tomato sauce. 'How about if he did some volunteering for me?' She spoke before she'd really thought it through, but it didn't sound like a bad idea out in the open.

'Marcus?' Mary shook her head. 'He's not that reliable.'

'We could start him slowly. We've got a few projects going in London at the moment. It might be just what he needs.'

Mary's eyes flashed and Eleanor saw what it meant to her friend. 'Oh, Els, that would be amazing. I mean, really?'

'Of course. I don't know why I didn't think of it before.' The words struck at Eleanor and before she knew it she was crying.

'God, what's wrong?' The concern was deep in Mary's voice.

'I am so fucking selfish,' Eleanor said. 'I never think about anyone other than myself.'

'What are you talking about?'

'Irena died yesterday.' She felt her heart catch on the words.

'Irena your neighbour? I'm sorry. But I don't ...'

'It was my fault.'

'Your fault she died?' Mary sounded incredulous.

'You remember I was here last Thursday?' Mary nodded. 'I go to see Irena every Thursday, but I stayed later here because we were talking about Robert. And I couldn't be bothered when I got home and I didn't even check on her on Friday morning, even though I was going to Coombe Place for the weekend. And I'd known she was ill in the week. And I lied to her daughter when she rang on Friday night cos she couldn't get hold of her, I lied and said I'd seen her the night before. So she didn't come over till Sunday, by which time Irena was dead.'

'That's sad and awful, but it isn't your fault.'

Eleanor's tears intensified, in a messy, histrionic way that embarrassed her. 'It is. I've been so wrapped up in Robert I've lost all sense of everything. It's made me realise I'm a very selfish person.'

'You're the least selfish person I know.'

'No, you only think that. I'm not really.'

Mary rubbed her bony hands across her face, shutting her eyes for a moment. 'What's this really about, Els?'

'It is about that.'

'And Robert?'

'I don't know what I'm doing with him. It's like a form of madness.'

'Isn't all romantic love?'

'I don't know.'

'It sounds like you're giving yourself a very hard time.'

Eleanor burned to tell Mary about the letter she'd found in Robert's study, but there was something so incriminating about it she couldn't force the words out of her mouth, so she told a half-truth instead. 'When I was with Robert at the weekend I found a card Nancy had written him. She sounded so different in it. The tone was apologetic, like she'd made him really angry or something. Almost like she was scared of him.'

'Their life can't have been as perfect as it looked.'

'Of course I know that. But this was . . . it just didn't sound like Nancy at all.'

'Marriage is very strange. It's as full of hate as it is love. We can't possibly speculate at what happens between any couple when all the doors are shut and all the curtains are drawn.'

Eleanor wondered if she was partly talking about herself and Howard. It seemed impossible to imagine tenderness between them and yet there had to have been, otherwise surely there wouldn't be three children and she wouldn't still be sitting here.

'That's not to say though that I think you should keep seeing him,' Mary said. 'You're only going to get hurt.'

'I'm hurt already.'

'Bloody men.' She puffed out her cheeks. 'They always get what they want. We're always the ones who have to go away.'

'It's not Robert's fault. I think he's delirious with grief. He's going to wake up one day soon and be disgusted to see me lying next to him.'

'Oh, Els.'

There was still time to tell Mary about the letter, but what would it do? It didn't prove anything and there were lots of reasons why Robert hadn't told anyone he had it; he could have even forgotten it was there, she thought desperately. No, she had to try to find other ways of making things better, and Marcus was a good start, although surely there was more she could do for Mary and even Nancy as well.

Mary pulled her chair over so she was sitting right by Eleanor's side, then put her arm around her shoulders. She was tiny, skin and bone really, but still it felt good and Eleanor laid her head against her friend's shoulder, letting her tears silently fall.

When Eleanor got home later on she rang Zara and asked her if she wanted to meet for lunch the next day. She lied and said she had a meeting in Oxford as she didn't want it to sound like she was making the trip especially to see her, but Zara was so pleased with the idea it just made her feel worse, because she was another person she'd been neglecting for Robert.

They met in a restaurant of Zara's suggestion, which was crowded and noisy, with lots of mirrors that made Eleanor feel slightly off balance. Zara was already sitting in a booth, made to look like a grand 1940s Russian hotel. She was sipping on a glass of wine and running a finger up and down her phone.

'You're looking good,' Eleanor said as she sat, which was never a lie with Zara.

'I think I've lost weight with all the stress.' Zara tried to smile, but the corners of her mouth twitched downwards.

'I hope you're taking care of yourself.'

Zara shrugged. 'Sometimes I don't see the point.'

'Oh, Zara, that's silly. There's every point. How are your studies going?'

Zara poured out some wine for Eleanor and topped up her own glass. 'Fine. What do think of my book?'

Eleanor thought of all the documents on her computer, the most recent of which she hadn't been able to make herself open. All the words she'd read had sounded alternately like a howl of misery and a catalogue of parental failures. 'I can understand why you're writing it. Is it finished?'

'You don't like it because I'm not nice about Dad?'

'It's not that. I just think you should be careful. You could really hurt your father.'

Zara sighed. 'It's all always about him, isn't it? Have you seen him recently?'

She shook her head. 'He'd be very hurt by some of the things I've read.'

Zara looked up and her eyes were so full of Nancy, Eleanor had to look down. 'I still believe a lot of the things I wrote,' she said, defiantly.

'You're so like her,' Eleanor said before she could stop herself. But Zara smiled. 'Am I?'

'Yes, you must know that.' Eleanor shook her head. 'But maybe none of us know our mothers until we get older. And even then some of us never do. God, Zara, you know, out of everyone I've ever known, Nancy was probably the most ridiculous person to die young.' Although even as she spoke she wondered if that were true. Nancy could have ended up as so many different versions of herself, as she supposed they all still could do. It was just that they existed within a solid reality, whereas Nancy was created by all of them, new and exciting, every time they spoke about her. And, in the same way that it's easier to love your partner when they are away, so it's easier to think well of the dead.

A waiter brought over their food, but Zara didn't even pick up her fork. 'I don't know what I'm going to do with myself.'

'Come on,' Eleanor said coaxingly, struggling against the bleakness of the conversation. 'You've got a wonderful life ahead of you. You're at Oxford, you're writing a book. And you'll meet someone and fall in love and have your own children.'

Zara shrugged. 'I think I'm incapable of sustaining a relationship.'

Eleanor felt the same fluttering anxiety Nancy used to produce in her, making her desperate to please without understanding how. 'Come on, that's not true.'

'I wish she was still here.' Zara's eyes were nearly overflowing.

Eleanor had to pull a breath deep inside to be able to speak. 'Of course you do. We all do.'

'I know this sounds horrid, Ellie, but I'm really angry with her. And Dad.'

'Angry how?'

'I'm angry at her for getting herself killed and I'm angry at Dad for either killing her, or not loving her well enough.' Zara spluttered with the awfulness of what she was saying.

'You don't really think your father could have killed her, do you?' The letter bobbed in her brain.

Zara leant forward. 'I don't know, not really, I suppose. But it's like my ability to judge character has been ruined by those two. I don't trust anyone. And how is that going to play out for me in relationships? You know, what if the whole fucked-up cycle just keeps on going?' She stopped and a tear rolled down her cheek.

Eleanor looked across the table at the young woman sitting opposite her, the daughter of a woman she had loved, struggling and searching. 'Talk to me, Zara,' she said, as she should have done to Nancy on that last night, as she wished with all her heart she had done, because she was suddenly washed through with a deep love for her friend, a love that seemed to stretch back through time, pulling everything important with it.

Zara flushed. 'And really, Mum was as bad as Dad. I mean, she sacrificed all of us for that bloody Davide, or whoever it was.'

Eleanor leant across the table, over their uneaten food, and took Zara's hand, which was slick with sweat. The desire to defend Nancy was very strong inside her, almost as if she was understanding her properly for the first time, as if all the years between suddenly meant something more than she'd even realised. 'You know, your mother was very complicated. We're all complicated really, Zara, none of us gets a free pass. Nancy was clever but she got lots of things wrong and she didn't know how to properly structure her life, and it drove her mad with frustration. I don't think the affair meant anything, I think it was just a way of her trying something different.'

Zara looked like a child, like she still had too much to learn, so Eleanor went on. 'I know I haven't had children, but I don't think you get a magic answer to life when you do. I think you still go on fucking up. And that doesn't mean you don't love them with everything you have. It just means you don't love yourself.'

A sob heaved from Zara, like an explosion in her chest and Eleanor felt scared for what she'd said. 'I remember all those times I'd come home from school and rush up to my room or not speak to her at dinner and roll my eyes. She must have been so lonely and that's the worst feeling in the world.'

'I think a lot of women feel like that,' Eleanor admitted, wondering if you should burden young women before they'd worked it out for themselves.

'But surely you don't, I mean, you've got a fabulous career.' Zara looked at her and Eleanor was transported back to a dinner what, maybe ten or more years before, when Nancy had said almost the same thing to her. Her vision narrowed and darkened and the face before her swam and swayed. She hadn't known what to say at the time, but now she thought she might.

'Of course I feel like that. Sometimes I think that women are too involved with life, we dissect it and poke around, shine light into dark corners. And sometimes that's wonderful, but sometimes it's awful. And we shouldn't hate men for not doing it, just like they shouldn't hate us for doing it. It's really, really hard to make sense of it all and to feel like anything means anything at all. But if I can give you one piece of advice it's to not feel guilty for the things you feel. We waste so much energy that way.'

It felt almost like she was playing the part of the grown-up, but maybe that was all being grown-up was, the ability to pretend better. Because the words she had spoken were not ones which she applied to her own life, or her own feelings. Zara wiped frantically at the tears on her cheeks, her nose pinking. Eleanor felt the beginnings of an understanding start to form. What she was thinking still felt far away, as if, however hard she reached, she couldn't yet grab on to it, but it made her know what she needed to say next.

'What your mum did and what happened to her had nothing to do with you or your father, Zara. She loved you both completely. But the truth is she didn't love herself and that made her do some really stupid things. I know I'm not your mother. Nowhere near, but I love you and I'll always be here for you. Please always remember that.'

Tears prickled against her eyes and she remembered something Robert had said to her not long before about how the wonderful thing about love was that it could always expand to include more people. And that was true, she thought, as she held Zara's hand across the table, it really was infinite, it really could be generous.

Robert rang as she was making breakfast the next morning and asked if she wanted to go out for dinner that evening. He didn't ask her what the police had been doing on her road when he'd dropped her on Sunday.

'I can't,' she said. 'My downstairs neighbour, Irena, died on Sunday.'

'I'm sorry, were you close?'

'Yes.'

'Maybe going out for dinner would do you good?'

She half laughed. 'I can't, Robert. Really, I don't feel up to it. I should have taken better care of her and it's made me feel very strange.'

'What do you mean?'

'I looked in on her a bit and I knew she had a cold and the carpet in her hall had snagged and I should have done something about it, or called her daughter, or something. I'm just feeling really guilty about it all.'

He snorted. 'Why would you feel guilty? It wasn't your responsibility.'

She opened her mouth to explain, but then realised there was no point. Women, Eleanor thought, carry guilt and responsibility like a second skin, so much so it weighs them down and stops them ever achieving quite everything they should. She knew also that a man faced with the true extent of a woman's guilt only ever really thinks that she is mad, she could hear it already in Robert's tone. Madness, neurosis, heightened emotions are all such easy monikers to apply to women but, as Eleanor was beginning to see after only a few months of love, really they're just men failing to take into account the simple fact that women are different from them.

'Look, I'll call you in a few days,' she said instead.

Sometimes, she thought, there are answers out there, all you have to do is ask. And what she wanted now, more than anything, were some real, concrete answers. Davide Boyette's agent was easy to find and she agreed to pass on the email Eleanor wrote him. His reply popped up on her screen only a few hours later: he would be happy to meet her, as long as she was prepared to come to him. The last six months had been pretty hard and he still wasn't up to making long journeys.

*

She thought she should turn around many times, but she didn't. Once you had decided things like this, she had learnt, you had to see them through. The motorway was almost deserted, grey and straight, with a light rain falling, which smeared Eleanor's windscreen. Soon she would be turning off and then, he had told her, there was a good hour's driving through the Yorkshire Moors. Some people turn back when they first come to visit, he'd said in the scant few emails they'd exchanged only the day before. They think that I can't possibly live out here in the middle of nowhere and they're scared of getting lost. You don't need the moors to lose yourself, Eleanor had thought but obviously not said.

She thought about Howard as the miles turned beneath her tyres, and what it meant to lose your mind. Where it went and what replaced it? And even when minds stayed intact, often bodies didn't, hearts especially. She thought of Robert and it felt razor sharp, making her heart beat against her chest like a caged bird. A wave of heat prickled through her veins, making her hands slippery on the wheel.

Something, no more than an impression, caught her eye and she couldn't stop herself turning to look. What she saw was like an ancient painting – the old, satanic hills topped by a swirling, violet sky pierced by a bright shaft of light which reached through the clouds in a perfect circle, beaming through the air like a searchlight right the way to the ground. As irreligious as she was, it felt like a divine offering, like a sign, like a meaning. Although a sign of what, she had no idea.

A horn blared into her thoughts and she looked back just in time to see she was drifting over into the fast lane, a sleek car speeding up behind her. She righted her car just in time, slowing down and breathing deep in to her stomach. So much was decided in split seconds when you were looking elsewhere, your mind already around the corner. It was all so arbitrary and the thought was terrifying.

Davide hadn't been lying when he'd said his house was in the middle of nowhere, but finally she arrived at an open gate and a small path which led, like a fairy tale, to a tiny house, made of grey stone, with smoke leaking from the chimney and a battered Fiat in front of the door and she wondered all over again, what the hell she was doing there.

She sat for a while still in her seat as she took in the dour scene, and was gripped by a tight fear that made her want to turn around and drive straight home. But then the front door opened and a man stepped out, who looked more like a ship-wrecked sailor than the sleek author she'd seen on the internet. He'd let his hair and beard grow much longer, his eyes no longer sparkled and his skin was loose and sallow. He came towards the car so she had to open the door and step out into his air, had to confront a face that might have been the last one Nancy ever saw.

Inside the house was far neater than the impression created by the outside, and far cosier, although it was stiflingly hot, with a lit fire, even though the temperature outside was balmy. Davide was also wearing a jumper and Eleanor wondered if it was pos-sible he was still in shock, and what that might mean. Was it shock at losing Nancy, or what he'd done to her, or of being accused of something he hadn't done? The big old Labrador nestled next to Eleanor's legs as she sat down and the clock kept up a steady tick.

'It's good of you to agree to see me, Davide,' she said finally, when all the formalities had been dealt with.

He smiled and Eleanor thought his eyes were warm. 'It's no bother. As you can imagine I don't get many visitors.' His voice was still tinged with a French accent, but overlaid also by a slight Yorkshire burr, which made him sound as if he existed nowhere.

'I live alone as well.' She wasn't really sure why she'd said that.

'Do you like it?'

She shrugged. 'Yes, I do, I suppose. Do you?'

He shook his head vigorously. 'Oh no. Not at all.'

Eleanor instinctively looked out of the window, at the expanse of moors beyond them. 'But, I mean, why here then? Why not in a city?'

Davide leant down to the dog who had migrated back to him and rubbed behind her ears. 'Oh, I'm not really fond of any people, just people I like.'

'Am I right in remembering you have children?'

'Yes, two girls, they're twelve and fourteen.' He smiled again. 'They live in Harrogate, with their mother. It's not far, I see them a couple of times a week.'

The thought cheered Eleanor. 'Well, that's good.'

He nodded. 'But it'd be better if they all lived here with me.'

Eleanor sipped at her tea. A lot could be better for everyone everywhere she supposed. 'I'm sorry.'

'Oh, don't be sorry,' he said in a rather irritating way, as if he had wanted to lead her down one emotional path only to shy away from it. 'It's my own stupid fault, I expect.' He reached for a packet of cigarettes on the table next to him. 'Do you mind?'

'Of course not.' She shook her head when he offered her one.

Davide spoke as he lit his cigarette. 'It was good to get your email. I've even been thinking about contacting Nancy's husband recently.'

'He's a very nice man. But I'm not sure.'

He half laughed. 'Are you sure he didn't do it?'

'Oh, absolutely. Robert wouldn't hurt a fly. And he loved Nancy, you know.' Her response sounded so certain, even though the letter still loomed large in her head. Her deceit made her realise that Davide could just as easily be lying to her.

Davide leant forward and threw his half-smoked cigarette into the fire. 'What did you want to ask me, Eleanor? I mean, why drive two hundred miles to sit opposite me after all this time?'

It felt like all the moments between then and now had been squashed and compressed to nothing. 'I'm not sure,' she admitted. Davide stood up and went to a table under the window where he poured them both a whisky, which she accepted gratefully. 'Recently I've started to feel very discombobulated. Like we've all just accepted that Nancy's dead and we'll never know what happened to her.'

'I'm not going to be much help with that.' Davide poked at the fire with a copper rod.

It was easier to ask the question when he was looking at the flames. 'I suppose I just wanted to sit opposite you and hear you say that you never had an affair with her.' He could take that rod, she thought, and beat it against my head.

Davide grunted. 'Christ, you sound like my wife.'

Eleanor looked up and saw his eyes had narrowed and sunk, and she was struck by how far Nancy's reach had penetrated, how even in death she still had more influence than most people did when they lived. 'I'm sorry.'

'It's just if you follow that thought to its logical conclusion you're basically asking if I killed her.'

'Not necessarily.'

Davide sat back down. 'Well yes, you are. Very few people are killed by random strangers and the police always said it bore all the marks of a crime of passion. And if her husband didn't kill her when he found out about the affair, then the lover must have done because she was leaving him. You're the one who told the police that she was trying to break it off, weren't you?'

'Yes.'

'And you're the one who told them her lover was called David and they met through work?'

Eleanor looked at the amber liquid vibrating in her glass; it was probably foolish that she was sitting with this man at all. 'Yes, that's what she told me.'

Davide sat back and the air shifted. 'I'm not blaming you. In fact, I'm not blaming anyone really. It's simply one of those unfortunate yet life-changing coincidences that I'm called Davide, that our work paths had crossed and I didn't have a rock-solid alibi for that night.'

'Tell me your alibi again.'

'I was on a book tour. I did a gig and went back to the hotel and to bed. Usually we went out for dinner, but I had a headache and was tired. Sod's bloody law. I didn't even call Wendy, my wife, because we'd spoken earlier and she'd said that Holly, our eldest, had a temperature so I didn't want to risk the phone waking her. So, the last person to see me was the hotel receptionist and of course there was a record of the time and it was nine-thirty. And of course Richmond is just down the road from Hammersmith so I had ample time to slip out, beat Nancy about the head and have breakfast with my publicist in the morning.'

Eleanor was shocked by the brutality of his words, but they made her brave. 'But you didn't.'

'Of course I bloody didn't. I barely even knew her. We were introduced once when we happened to be at my publishers at the same time. And then I saw her a couple of times at various functions. If she hadn't been so pretty I don't think I'd have even remembered that.'

Eleanor nodded. 'I wonder what made her pick your name?'

He squinted at her like she was stupid. 'I'm sure it had nothing to do with me. David is hardly an unusual name. More likely when you asked her what her lover was called she'd just read about a David in a newspaper or the waiter had a name badge with David on it. Or maybe she wasn't lying and he really was called David. Who the fuck knows.'

They sat quietly for a while; it looked like a mist was rolling in, making her feel as if nothing she did or said in this room would matter. 'But how come your wife wondered?'

'She never thought I'd killed her. But she did think I could have been the person she was having an affair with, especially when she saw photos of her in all the papers. I'm sure you've read what a shit husband I was and most of what Wendy said was true. But I loved her and the girls so much, none of the other women ever meant anything.'

Eleanor nearly laughed because she could imagine Davide saying that to poor Wendy, dragging up an excuse so pallid and well worn she must have wanted to stab him with a sharp kitchen knife. 'But Nancy wasn't one of your women?' Her tone held too much bitterness.

He winced. 'Don't disguise what you think of me.'

'I'm sorry.'

He smiled. 'You apologise an awful lot, you know.'

Eleanor knew she was about to cry. 'It's just that ...' But the tears came and she had to wipe them away with the back of her hand. She wanted to say something that had nothing really to do with the conversation but knew she was going to say it because she was never going to sit opposite Davide in this little room again. 'It's just that I wasn't very nice to her the last time we met.' She could hardly believe she was admitting this to a stranger, although it felt easier than when she'd told Irena.

'I see.'

The tears were dripping off her face. She was going to carry on, she realised, could feel the words as if they existed physically inside her. 'Over the years I've thought some terrible things about her. And since she died I've almost blamed her for her own death.' Eleanor took a deep breath, but still felt dizzy with the confession. 'But really I was the one to blame. A good friend would have told her not to go and meet David, or whatever his bloody name was, that night. But she'd irritated me. She often irritated me, if I'm honest, even though I also loved her very much. That night I almost wanted her to get hurt. Not literally, of course, but I wanted someone to shout at her and tell her how selfish she was. So I watched her go off into the night and sat and finished my wine and thought I'd call her in the morning.' Eleanor was gulping at her words, like they might drown her if she let them.

Davide's voice was calm and kind when he spoke. 'I'm sure she'd understand. I'm never convinced about all these death-bed scenes, I think really they're dreamt up by people like me. Most of the time people die unexpectedly and it can't be possible that the last thing their loved ones said to them was kind or meaningful. I don't think it matters what you said to her last, more how much you loved her while she was alive.'

Eleanor blushed because of course it was so much worse than Davide could ever imagine and then she felt sick because what she had done with Robert suddenly seemed totally shameful, as if it exposed a naked truth about her she didn't want to confront.

Davide leaned his elbows onto his knees and clasped his hands in front of him. 'There is a certain irony in me being a suspect in Nancy's death, you have to agree?'

'Because of the books you write?'

'Yes. All through this nightmare I kept thinking, if I were guilty it would make for such a bloody good story. But I couldn't help but realise something else. We make so much out of the deaths of people like Nancy. Look at the attention her case has received, but is it any more tragic than the teenager knifed on an estate, or twenty people blown up at a checkpoint, or a little old man whose heart suddenly gives out?'

Eleanor felt a spinning through her body, as if something was trying to land in her brain, as if there was an understanding to be had if only she could grab hold of it. She knew it was about more than just Nancy, but it was as if she couldn't see past her. 'My downstairs neighbour, who was incredibly special to me, died about a week ago. It was a very different death from Nancy's, I mean she was in her late eighties and had a stroke at home. But the whole thing has made me feel like a fraud because her death doesn't feel as tragic as Nancy's death. Or maybe they both weren't tragic. I can't work it out.'

'That's what I'm saying. We think of something and Google tells us the answer, but death isn't always like that.'

'Nor is love,' Eleanor said, thinking of Robert.

'That's true.' He smiled.

'Are you telling me not to care so much about Nancy's death?'

Davide sighed and sat back. 'No. But only because she was your good friend so of course you care. I suppose I'm just talking in a more general sense. Maybe what I'm saying is don't beat yourself up about it so much. Don't feel like there was something you could have done to stop it, or that you have to extract a meaning out of it. Sometimes life is just shitty and we have to move on.'

'But it's so bleak to think there's no meaning. Or that we can't change things.' Eleanor felt a desperation in her gut, her eyes drawn to the window where the mist was creating an impression of timelessness.

'I think change is always possible, but we have to understand what it is we want to change. Or at least that's what the last six months has taught me.' Davide looked at his watch. 'Sorry, I've gone on for too long and made you maudlin.'

It was true, she did feel maudlin, but it wasn't because of anything Davide had said. Both Nancy and Irena were dead and maybe there was something she could learn from that, or maybe there wasn't. Maybe everything was random, or maybe there was a meaning to be found if you just tried hard enough, if you dug for long enough.

By the time Eleanor arrived back at her flat the next day, she felt consumed by a bone-chilling coldness that made her wrap herself in blankets, even though sweat then leaked from every pore. Her muscles felt weak and she shivered like a small child, her teeth actually chattering. She didn't have the strength to make food or the stomach to eat, and crawled into bed, where she slept fitfully, watching the time pass in the shadows outside her window, the emptiness from the flat below seeping up like it wanted to devour her. Her phone rang a few times and she knew it would be Robert or Mary, but didn't have the energy to answer because her mind by then was awash with Nancy and consumed by an all-powerful guilt.

She finally fell asleep, knowing as she did that she had to be better by morning, because that was the day of Irena's funeral and she was not going to let her down again. But daylight brought little change to her mood, even though the weather was bright and sparkling. Her fever had subsided though, so she was able to pull herself out of bed and under the shower, where she revived enough to get dressed and walk to the tube.

The service took place at a local crematorium, a municipal building in a cemetery in north London she hadn't even known existed. There was a sparsity of mourners compared to the throng that had attended Nancy's, but Eleanor reminded herself Irena had been nearly double Nancy's age. She cried when Irena's coffin went through the open doors to the flames, but she didn't feel the gut-wrenching devastation she'd experienced at the side of Nancy's grave, even though she had loved Irena and felt a crushing weight of guilt whenever she thought of her.

The wake was held in Sarah's small house in a distant suburb in which people spoke about a life that had been filled with its own share of sadness but had still been well lived, so the general feeling was of warmth and jollity, with no regrets. Eleanor had a strange moment as she stood on her own holding a cup of tea and slice of cake in which she could hardly marry the idea of Nancy and Irena's funerals being about the same event. There appeared to be an acceptance amongst Irena's family and the few friends she had left that this was a natural progression, sad of course, but also something to be celebrated. For a moment, Eleanor wondered, unfairly, if maybe Irena had been less loved than Nancy, or maybe because her death had been less dramatic, it was less important.

As Eleanor was getting her coat in the hall, Sarah came out of the chatter of the sitting room, her face flushed and her eyes fresh and bright from all the crying she'd done. 'I wanted to catch you, Eleanor,' she said. 'Mum left you something and I wanted to give it to you.'

'Me?' Eleanor felt a genuine dread at what it could be.

'It's nothing really,' Sarah said as she ran up the stairs. She was back in a moment with a small wooden box in her hands. 'It was something my father made for Mum when they first met. It was always very special to her.'

'Oh, I couldn't possibly...' Eleanor held her hands up in front of her, wanting to push the box back to Sarah. 'I mean, it belongs to you and your brother.'

'Mum left us lots of things. And she really wanted you to have this. She told me loads of times over the last few years not to forget to give it to you. She even had it written into her will.'

Eleanor held out her hand then because there never had been any arguing with Irena. Sarah placed a tiny wooden box into it, no bigger than a matchbox, made from wood the colour of honey, the sides planed and smoothed, but the top engraved with words Eleanor presumed must be Polish. 'What do they mean?' she asked as she traced her fingers across the foreign letters.

'You are loved.'

'Oh.' The surprise of the answer was almost enough to make her drop the box, but then she just felt filled with sadness, like she had been packed full of it. She wanted to tell Sarah that she didn't deserve this box and all the goodness it must contain. That she wasn't particularly loved or lovable. 'It's so beautiful.'

'Mum always said those words to us.' Eleanor looked up and saw Sarah's eyes had refilled with tears. 'She said they meant more than I love you, she said they gave you ownership of what it means to be loved, it reminds you of the responsibility that comes with loving and being loved. She used to say if anyone loves you then you have to be kind to yourself so as not to damage their investment.' She laughed lightly. 'Typical Mum. But, you know, she's right. I say the same thing to my children now.'

'I loved your mother,' Eleanor said, very simply, because what else was there.

'She loved you as well,' Sarah replied.

That night Eleanor slept what her mother used to call the sleep of the dead, so when she woke she couldn't remember who or where she was, wondered at what her purpose could possibly be. But the sensation only lasted a moment before recognition crashed around her. She felt stiff and off-balance when she threw her legs over the side of her bed, so she got straight into the shower.

Sarah had told her that if you are loved you have to be kind to yourself, but she didn't see how that was possible when she couldn't even be kind to the people she loved. She turned her face to the jets, a desire to totally cleanse herself beating inside her. What she needed in fact was an atonement, a reckoning of who she was. And then she knew: she had to apologise to Nancy. She would stand in front of Nancy's grave and reveal herself to her friend, ask for her forgiveness. And as it was Saturday she saw no reason why she shouldn't just get in her car and drive there. She turned off the shower and dried herself, dressing quickly and then collecting the few things she would need for the journey, her head buzzing at the thought of making the trip, her mind already working on what it was she wanted to say.

It was too warm for a coat, but as she went to pick her keys off the little table in the hall, she saw Irena's box where she had left it the night before and it looked like a talisman, like something that could protect her. She was wearing a stripy skirt with buttons all down the front, which she knew made her look round, but she somehow enjoyed the fact. It had two deep pockets on the front and she dropped the box into one of them, where it nestled quietly against her leg.

As she walked to her car Eleanor thought it was true that Nancy had been self-centred at times and irritatingly self-absorbed, but she'd also been kind and generous and non-judgmental. She felt sure that the things she'd told Zara over lunch had been right; Nancy's behaviour stemmed more from her own self-hatred than it did from a character flaw. Eleanor needed to apologise to her friend not just for all the things she had done in the past six months, but also for all the things she'd thought about her. It had taken death for her to understand Nancy, one of her oldest and dearest friends.

On the way she stopped at a flower stall by the local tube. The stall was bright and heady, but nothing looked quite right for Nancy, lilies were too funereal and roses too close to what a lover might give. She settled instead on a bunch of bright yellow tulips. She remembered a moment with Nancy once, looking out of the kitchen window in Sussex at the beginning of a different year. Eleanor had exclaimed at the tulips popping up in all the flowerbeds and Nancy had said she'd planted them that way, wild and free. She'd joined Eleanor at the window and they'd looked together, until Nancy had said, 'I think the reason I love tulips so much is because they give me such hope, the way they pop up so bright out of the ground just at the time when you've almost given up on the idea of seeing anything pretty ever again.'

Eleanor paid hurriedly for the flowers and took them back to her car, where she unwrapped them from their paper coating. She selected the brightest, most-open three and laid them carefully on the passenger seat next to her. She would lay them on Nancy's grave, one for each of them, her, Mary and Nancy, three small tulips, bright and cheery, sparking against the greyness of life.

The roads were surprisingly clear so it was still relatively early when she stepped out of her car with her flowers, into a sharp wind that had risen out of nowhere and made her wonder if Nancy was angry. And really, why shouldn't she be? She had to lie in this cold ground whilst her life moved on above her, whilst her friends forgot to visit, whilst people talked about her, whilst no one bothered to find out what had really happened, whilst her husband fucked her best friend.

Eleanor followed the path round to the back of the church, making for a spot at the edge of the cemetery. Robert had once told her that he was going to be buried on top of Nancy, but she wondered if that would actually ever happen. It was possible, she realised, that Robert could re-marry one day and that marriage might last for longer than his to Nancy had. If they all lived another forty years, Nancy would become nothing more than a section of his life; a phase. And if that was true of Nancy then what was she: a mere blip, probably one day even forgotten.

She stopped for a moment just before she crossed the sea of graves to Nancy's at the back because it looked like Robert had added something to its top. But as she got closer she saw that it was moving and then, in a few more steps, she saw it was actually three magpies, jostling on top of the headstone, squawking and pecking at each other, their wings flapping as they nearly lost their balance.

'Hello,' she said as she drew level with the birds, a laugh in her voice, because as they turned their black eyes on her, they reminded her so much of her, Nancy and Mary. The birds stayed stubbornly in their place and the old nursery rhyme she always chanted in her head whenever she saw magpies started up. She bowed to the birds, as her mother had taught her to do if she saw a solitary magpie to ward off the bad luck he brought on his monochrome wings, but still they didn't move. 'Not one then, but three for sorrow,' she said to them and that seemed to do the trick because they rose into the sky, understanding that there was no pleasure to be found in adding to her pain.

She looked then at the words on Nancy's stone, which she had thought so perfect when Robert chose them but now seemed like a heavy weight to Eleanor, as if no one should have to support that amount of responsibility.

## NANCY LOUISE HENNESSY

### Beloved mother, wife, daughter, friend

*'She walks in beauty like the night of*
*cloudless climes and starry skies'*

No date, because apparently Nancy had hated dates on grave-stones. Eleanor had presumed this was because she didn't want anyone knowing her age, but Robert had corrected her; no, it was because she always calculated people's ages when they walked through graveyards and it made her sad when someone had died young. She'd have hated to be responsible for making someone sad in this graveyard, Robert had said, his hand reaching out to brush the top of her headstone.

Eleanor reached out her own hand now and traced her finger across the markings, feeling the groove they left. Life seemed suddenly unbearably short and simple and unlikely that it could ever mean much. Her legs felt heavy and she let them buckle, falling forward onto her knees and then turning so she could lean her back against Nancy's headstone. She stretched her legs out in front of her and the clouds, which the wind must have churned, parted, so a streak of sun made her shut her eyes. The tulips fell next to her and it was true, they did look bright against the dark green of the grass, but they also looked impossibly small as well, and something about that caught at her heart.

She thought of Nancy beneath her, enclosed in the moist earth, unable to feel the sun or the rain or the wind or the touch of another. She couldn't remember how far down people were buried, maybe six feet, yes, she thought that was right. Nancy was no more than the length of Robert away, if she dug she could reach her in a day. She slid her body further down the tombstone until her head reached the ground and her back was flat and she was lying on top of Nancy. She rested her hands against the earth and kicked off her shoes so the wind cut at her ankles. Her hair mingled with the grass and the smell of the damp, fecund earth rose through her nostrils. The sky above was cobalt blue again with wispy clouds scudding across its surface, whilst birds she didn't recognise were shrieking sharply.

Her tears were hot against her cheeks and they ran into the earth on either side of her face. She imagined them dripping slowly downwards until they reached Nancy. She imagined touching her one more time.

'I'm so sorry,' she said in to the air. 'I am so very sorry.'

'Ellie.'

She snapped her eyes open and saw Robert looming over her, which made her scramble to her feet too quickly so the blood rushed to her head and little white spots danced before her eyes.

'I didn't know you were coming to Sussex,' he said. 'You said you were going to call me and I've been waiting. I was worried about you.'

'I'm sorry.' She had to look away from him, at the ground where the grass was flat from her body. 'I've been trying to sort my head out. It's all got a bit much for me.'

'Has something happened?' He took a step towards her and they were both aware of her taking one back.

'No. I mean, yes. I just want to know what happened.'

She dared herself to look at him, but he just shrugged. 'I'm not sure it matters who killed her. That's something this last six months have taught me. We all want to know who is responsible all the time, who is guilty, but it won't bring her back, it doesn't in the end make any difference.'

Eleanor knew she could just ask him about the letter, but

they were alone in a graveyard and his presence felt suddenly powerful. 'I can't do this any more, Robert,' she said instead.

Tears flashed to his eyes, but he stopped them from falling by clenching his jaw. 'What do you mean?'

'You're nowhere near over Nancy.'

'I don't suppose I ever will be.' He shook his head, his gaze now travelling over her head. 'You're right, you deserve more than that, Ellie. You deserve to be loved totally and completely.'

She couldn't hold her tears back any longer and they fell quietly and methodically, because she knew she loved him, whatever he'd done, because love was like that.

'I am so scared of being alone,' he said, finally.

'Being alone isn't so bad.'

'Oh, it isn't for someone as strong as you.' Eleanor was shocked he thought that about her, surprised to see herself cast in such an unfamiliar light. 'But it just wouldn't be feasible for me. It's not how I'm made. And I don't mean that in a practical sense, I mean fundamentally.' She nodded, but he went on, like a stuck tap. 'I worry so much about what's going to happen to Zara, without Nancy, I don't want her to feel alone.'

'She'll be fine. I've already told her I'll help her as much as I can.'

He searched out her eyes then and held her gaze. 'God, you've always said the right things, haven't you, Ellie.'

She felt about twenty years fall from her. 'Have I?'

He paused and blew out his breath so she felt it brush her cheeks. 'You've been so amazing to me and Zara. I never told you how much it meant to me.'

She heard the harshness in her voice as she spoke. 'You don't have to be grateful.'

'There, you see, that's why I haven't said it. I don't get things right.'

Eleanor had no choice than to say what she thought. 'I didn't do it because I felt sorry for you. I did it because I fell in love with you.'

Neither of them spoke for a minute, but then Robert did. 'I've handled everything very badly. I know I've hurt you and that's the last thing I wanted.' Her heart felt constricted and her throat clogged. 'I didn't expect to feel this way about anyone ever again, especially not now, so soon.' Robert kicked at something on the ground. 'What I'm trying to say is that I love you as well, but I also still love Nancy and I know those two things are impossible.'

She met Robert's gaze and knew she looked desperate. 'I'm not worth loving, Robert.'

He stepped forward and grabbed her arm, so hard it hurt. 'What? Don't ever say that, Ellie.'

'But it's true.' Her tears felt like they might never stop. 'I'm not a good person. I cause bad things to happen to people. I'm not good at love.' It felt raw to say it, but also good, like she could admit to all that had been revealed about her and then seal herself up.

Robert reached up and wiped the tears off her face with his thumb, making her stumble slightly and Irena's box, which she had so impulsively put into the pocket of her skirt at the start of the day, knocked against her leg. It felt strangely warm, filled with the goodness she knew it contained. You are loved, she thought, you are loved, but the words felt as unlikely as snow in her mind.

'I'm not a good person either,' he said. 'And I don't think I'm good at love.' She tried to search his face for his meaning, but it looked suddenly sealed, as if coated in wax.

He motioned to Nancy's grave behind her, where she'd been lying. 'I've done the same, many times.' He waited and the noise of the birds washed over them. 'She loved you, Ellie.'

Eleanor wanted to scoop up his words and put them in a jar by her bed. 'And I loved her.'

'And that's enough. It's probably time for us all to start moving on.'

They looked at each other and in the looking Eleanor felt seen in a way that made her shiver. 'I have to go.'

He raised his hand, but then dropped it back again. The air felt charged, as if there were so many possible outcomes to this moment. She could barely make her legs work, but she managed to move, taking steps away from him down a rutted path. She could feel him watching her as if his eyes were knives until she turned the corner past the church.

She could still feel Irena's box against her leg as she walked and she wanted so desperately to believe in its words. But the idea seemed only like yet another thing she was going to fail at. She felt instead as if she was falling from a great height without a parachute, as if everything had been whipped from beneath her feet.

Robert rounded the corner of the church, his face set hard and his hands clenched by his side. She fumbled with the keys, dropping them by her feet so she had to scramble to get them, willing strength into her trembling legs, praying she would be able to drive away.

# NANCY

Her phone rang again, and this time Nancy answered because the sound was drilling through her head and, besides, if she spoke to him then maybe he'd stop, although she'd been thinking that for too many weeks and nothing ever seemed to be enough for him.

'Why haven't you been picking up?' His voice was gruff, like his throat hurt.

'I didn't want to. I haven't got anything more to say.'

'I haven't got anything more to say.' He mimicked her voice rather well. 'Well, I still fundamentally disagree with everything you said in your letter and I don't think you've given me a proper explanation.'

'But we've been over everything a million times.'

His voice cracked then, the harshness evaporating. 'You're not thinking straight.'

Nancy looked at her pale, taut reflection in the tall mirror that hung in their hall and wondered if he was right, if in fact she had ever thought straight about anything.

'I know you love me.'

'I don't. I love Robert.'

'No, that can't be true. If you loved Robert you wouldn't have spent the last year risking it all to be with me.'

She closed her eyes against the year, against her desperation, against the terrible humiliations she had suffered. 'I thought I loved you, that's true. Maybe I even did at the beginning.' She could feel the tears building and tried to swallow them, but it was no good, they spilled down her cheeks and into her voice, which she hated herself for. 'But it was like a kind of madness, I can't believe I ever let it get this far.'

Her tears seemed to dry his and he softened his tone. 'You're just feeling scared, my love, which is understandable. But now's the perfect time for us to start a new life together. Zara's at university and my kids are a bit older.'

'Please. Please, don't mention Zara, or your children.' Her tears dried and a steely anger took their place. 'Your children are all still at home and there is no way you could leave, even if I wanted you to.'

'She'd hardly be the first single mother in the world and I wouldn't abandon them. Anyway, she's so obsessed with them she'd hardly notice if I was there or not.'

Nancy felt like she might be sick. 'Nothing you ever say will make me believe that she's anything like the person you describe.'

'You don't know the half of it.'

'If you go on talking like that I'll put the phone down.'

'Don't do that.' He spoke before he could check himself and Nancy heard a whine in his tone that reeked of desperation.

She decided to play to the advantage. 'Look, it's none of your business, but Robert's going to pull back on work next year and we've decided to move to Sussex and just get a flat in London, so all this would have had to end anyway.' She tried to keep her voice level and calm, because if she didn't she would tell him the truth, that she found him physically and emotionally disgusting.

But as soon as he spoke Nancy realised she'd misjudged – his voice was hard and brittle. 'So that's what it's all been about then? You've had your fun, but really when the chips are down, you'd rather money than an orgasm every night.'

'Fuck you.'

'You've always loved the life he's bought you, even though he's a chinless wonder with zero conscience or ethics. But that's not what love is. What we have is love. That feeling like you can't live without the other person.'

Nancy felt like she might faint. She had tried everything but nothing seemed to work and, more than that, she was very tired, had been worn to a shadow of herself by these constant arguments, which she had to endure in secret. So even when she'd had a full day of phone calls like this she still had to make dinner and smile and listen to Robert or maybe take a call from Zara. Sometimes it felt too much to bear, but she had no one to blame except herself.

'Please, I can't live like this any more.'

'So stop fooling yourself then. Just accept that we have to be together.'

'I'm not trying to fool you or me.' Her voice sounded pathetic, even inside her body. 'I'm telling the truth. I hate myself for all of this, hate and despise, and I have no idea why you'd want anything to do with me. I'm going to try to salvage what's left of my marriage and I wish you would do the same.' She put the phone down after that, shivering, even though the heating was turned right up.

Her phone rang immediately, as it so often did, so she swiped without looking at it, 'Yes, what now!'

'Nancy.' Robert sounded perplexed.

Her knees buckled slightly, so she could feel the cold tension of her muscles. 'Oh God, sorry.'

'What on earth's going on?'

She wanted him home with her so much at that moment she

was prepared to say anything, even if it meant telling him what had been going on since she'd ended the affair, or at least most of what had been going on. 'I can't do it any more.'

'What do you mean?'

'He's been calling me. Non-stop. I can't take it any more.'

'But you said it was over?'

'It is, Robert, I promise. He just won't leave me alone.' She gasped against the sourness of the air.

'Bloody hell.' She imagined him in his office, her just one more pathetic person he had to help. 'You're going to have to tell me who he is. I need to deal with this.'

'I can't. You have to trust me on that.' A fluttering panic took hold of her stomach, she had once again been stupid. 'I can handle it really.'

'I'm getting in a cab. I'll be home in half an hour.'

Nancy walked into the sitting room and hugged her arms around her body, which had started to repulse her. She had lost so much weight over the last couple of months that she could feel all her bones and her skin sat stretched across them. She couldn't stop crying and yet it seemed so pathetically self-indulgent that it made her want to bang her head against the wall. Her body was too jangled to sit, so she stood in the centre of the room, her skin itching and her insides shaking and nothing seemed real or likely to happen ever again.

Maybe if she saw him one more time he would get the message? Maybe she needed to stand in front of him and speak calmly and coherently? Of course she'd done that before, but maybe this time would be different? Except she couldn't tell Robert she was going to do that because he would insist on coming, or follow her, or try to stop her. And if he did and found out the truth then he wouldn't be able to forgive her, and then everyone would find out and they would all hate her, and then there would be nothing left for her but to jump off a bridge.

But then Nancy remembered she was meeting Eleanor for dinner the next evening and it seemed like the only chance she might have to meet him without anyone knowing. She'd been ignoring his texts but now she had to look at them to send one to him. She read them despite knowing she shouldn't, clicking down the list of capital-lettered explosions. It was nearly enough to stop her, but she knew how it would end if she didn't see him again. He would eventually turn up at her front door, because ultimately his desire for revenge would outweigh everything. And as she thought that, she wondered if it could ever be any different, or if she would spend the rest of her life worried at what he might say or do, even years down the line. But she had to try, because what else was there, so she typed out words she didn't mean: **Meet me tomorrow 10pm, under the bridge**. He texted back almost immediately: **See you there**.

She went into the hall then and opened the front door because she could hear a taxi idling outside and knew it would be Robert. He bounded up the steps to her and her stomach contracted at the sight of his lithe body encased in its blue suit, his blond hair flopping over his eyes, the bloom of pink on his cheeks, the fullness of his mouth. They went into the hall and he pulled her towards him; she wrapped her arms around his waist, under his jacket, to feel the warmth from his body.

'I've only got an hour,' he said.

She turned at that and led him up the stairs because their desire was rampant, had been for weeks now, since she'd told him about the affair. They had been sleeping together for nearly thirty years, but neither of them had ever wanted the other more. It was an odd reaction, Nancy knew, and yet maybe it was also explainable – because they had faced her betrayal head on and both decided that they still wanted each other. And maybe that made them feel powerful or united or desirable, she couldn't quite pin it down, knew only that she wanted to feel her husband's body pressed against and inside hers as often as possible. Knew also that if she'd felt this before none of this would have happened because it seemed like an answer to a question she hadn't even been aware of asking.

Nancy caught sight of them in the long mirror on the wardrobe as they lay diagonally across the bed, Robert glorious between her legs, which were wrapped around him, her body arching upwards and her arms outstretched at her sides, as if he had pinned her to the bed. She thought they were more beautiful and perfect at that moment than they ever had been. That their bodies, worn and battered by nearly fifty years of life, were more wonderful than they'd ever been when they met in their twenties.

Robert lay on his back afterwards and Nancy rested her head on his chest, feeling his arm wrap around her shoulders.

'I love you, Robert,' she said. 'I am so sorry.'

'You've said sorry enough. How much does he call?'

She'd lied so much over the past year it wasn't even hard to do any more, almost as if her brain had rewired itself. 'Oh, not much, a couple of times a week. He just wasn't very nice this morning and then you called straight after.'

'But what's he saying? Is he threatening you?'

'God, no.'

'I really think I should speak to him. You have to tell me who he is.'

'No, seriously, Robert. I don't want you to have to have anything to do with him. I'm worried if you see him or speak to him you won't be able to forgive me.' Which was dangerously close to the truth.

'Why? What's wrong with him? Do I know him?'

'No, don't be silly. Just that it would make it too real for you.'

'It's fucking real enough.'

She was aware of the time ticking down and the fact that he would need to shower and get dressed again soon because there were lots of other people who wanted something from him and she wanted to say something of importance, but couldn't think what that might be.

'What do you love about me?' she asked, in the end.

Robert laughed so his chest bobbed her head up and down. 'You haven't asked me a question like that for years. I've missed them.'

'Have you? I always thought they irritated you.'

'No, they make me feel like you care.' He pulled her slightly closer. 'I guess out of all the many things, I'd have to say your optimism.'

She spluttered. 'My optimism? But I don't have any.'

'Yes, you do. So much worries you, but you always battle on through. That's optimism.'

Nancy couldn't reply because she thought she might cry, because how could Robert still say things that surprised her after all these years? And how had she nearly thrown it all away?

'See, I've said the wrong thing.' He kissed the top of her head.

'No, the opposite, you've said just the right thing.' She remembered an afternoon a few months before when she'd asked the man she called David the same question, in almost the same moment, lying in his arms on a bed in the flat they met in, which she'd come to hate because of the ferns which trailed everywhere, even from the ceiling. I love what every man has always loved about you, he'd said, your perfection. She thought now maybe that had been the beginning of the end for her, it had certainly felt like a falling away, as if some mist she'd been existing within had suddenly cleared.

'Would you have told me if I hadn't found the letter?' Robert asked.

'No.' Except Nancy wasn't sure that she hadn't left the letter in her bag out of some subconscious desire for him to know and help her, just as he had. 'But that's only because I couldn't bear the thought of you finding out because I didn't want to hurt you and I didn't want you to leave me.'

'I don't think I could leave you.' His voice sounded strangely small.

She sat up on to her elbow so she was looking down at him. 'Robert, please will you promise me something?'

'What?'

'Don't ever tell anyone about this affair. I couldn't bear for Zara to find out and think even less of me than she does already.'

He reached up and tucked some stray hair behind her ear. 'Zara doesn't think badly of you. It's just her age.'

'But, please. She'd hate me if she knew what I'd done. My God, if she ever read that letter it would just be so awful. I mean the things he said about her.' She shivered involuntarily which seemed hammy even to her, but wasn't something she could control.

He looked at her quizzically. 'I wouldn't anyway.'

But it struck her that the possibility that one day the knowledge of the affair could be public, depending on the level of his vindictiveness. 'It's really, really important to me. No one must ever see that letter,' she re-iterated. 'I mean, whatever happens. Even if Zara finds out somehow, one day, you have to absolutely promise me that she never sees that letter. I just couldn't bear for her to think that I was ever with a man who thought that about her.'

'I can't bear that either,' Robert said in such a sad voice that she stroked her hand down his face.

'Robert, I am so sorry. But I'd almost rather she thought anything than that I ever agreed with what he said. You have to promise me, please.'

'We can burn it next time we're in Sussex.' Robert started to move, but she held him back with her hand on his arm.

'Ellie's the only person I've said anything to and I've barely told her anything anyway.'

She felt his body fall back against his movement. 'I wish you'd tell me who he is.'

Nancy's body washed with heat. 'I can't, Robert. He's nothing, nobody. He's totally harmless really,' she lied. 'He'll get the message soon and stop calling, really, I can feel him giving up already.'

It was the only way that she could live with herself, this keeping of David and everyone else in her life separate, except she was beginning to feel the artifice crumbling. She worried that when she let her two worlds combine in the proper way it would all be over. Keeping up the façade she had created was becoming harder and harder, as if reality was beating against her skull. The first time he introduced himself to her she had found the way he used his name romantic, now she saw it had been a necessity, a manipulation, a clever ploy which he had clearly used with intent and she had been stupid enough to believe in.

Robert pulled away from her, standing and walking towards their bathroom, and she knew he had every right to hate her, but still she couldn't bear that he didn't love her with every atom of his being.

It was strange because what had first attracted Nancy to Robert had become the thing that irritated her about him, and now was the thing she valued most about him. Robert was as steady and dependable as his strong walk, unlikely ever to let you down. She had needed that so much when they'd met, after the flamboyance of her youth, for want of a better word. Living with her father had made her believe that men were tricky, unstable and unreliable, one moment he could be drinking champagne and laughing loudly, the next locking his door against the world and not eating for days. She hadn't ever wanted to end up like her mother, a glamorous carer to a brilliant man, however fun he could be, however many parties you got invited to. It had made her keep herself at a remove with men, until she met Robert and realised she couldn't find any cracks in him, couldn't ever imagine him locking a door between them. She wondered now how this had ever mutated into feeling bored by him, or wishing for the spontaneity that had so scared her in her father. It seemed insane that she had forgotten all that, that she had had to meet another man like her father to remind her that she didn't actually like extremes, didn't actually like danger.

She heard the shower turning on and felt cold, so got into their bed, pulling the covers up under her chin like her mother had done when she was small. She'd started to feel like she didn't deserve Robert with his grace and calm kindness. He hadn't even shouted when he'd found the letter, but instead seemed so deeply saddened she'd worried that she might have done him irretrievable damage. He'd never threatened to leave her, as she would have done had the roles been reversed. He'd simply sat with her in front of the fire in Sussex and talked to her, trying to understand what had gone wrong, why she'd felt the need for someone else. And in the words they'd spoken to each other Robert had re-emerged to Nancy as the man she had fallen in love with all those years ago.

It had naturally been a blessing that the letter showed she wanted out of the relationship, even though she felt sick that

Robert had had to read the terrible, clichéd words. She shuddered at the thought of Robert finding one of the earlier ones, one of the ones they'd written to each other with such naked abandon, in which they'd detailed all the things they'd done to each other, all the ways they turned each other inside out. She'd burnt all those letters on the days she'd received them, devouring and memorising each word before doing so. But now she worried the ones she'd sent still existed. The man for whom she had risked everything was careless and might have left them somewhere they might one day be found. Or perhaps he would produce them and show them to everyone if she continued to refuse him, displaying them like trophies no one would ever want. She imagined the people she loved quite rightfully walking away from her and it felt like someone had shot her in the stomach and her guts were spilling onto the white sheets.

'Are you OK?'

She hadn't heard Robert come back into the room, but there he was, re-dressing in his crumpled clothes, and she wondered at all the things she didn't know. 'Have you ever slept with anyone else? I mean, since we've been married?'

'No,' he said, tucking his shirt in to his trousers.

'I hate myself.'

He bent down and picked his jacket up off the floor, shaking out the creases, before putting it on. 'Don't do this, Nancy.' He looked her straight in the eyes. 'Do me the decency of not making this all about you, for once. Don't ask me to prop you up over this.' She looked at him over the covers and knew he was right, but still she wanted to ask impossible things of him. But then she saw him soften. He came towards the bed and sat on the end, his shoulders drooping. 'It's not all your fault,' he said in whispers. 'I've been thinking about things a lot and I can see that I haven't been the best husband.'

'Don't say that, Robert...'

'No, listen. I'm not saying you were right to have an affair, or I was a complete shit, or anything. I'm just saying I think I got you wrong a bit. You and I are quite different and I think that scared me in some way I didn't even realise. In my head I made your difference something bad, when really it was just that, different. I didn't consciously want to make you feel that way, but I think maybe that's what happened somehow. And that must have made you feel terrible, worse perhaps than you needed to. And I'm sorry for that.'

They looked at each other and Nancy felt like it was the first proper conversation they'd ever had. Or maybe, the first time he'd truly understood her. It was almost more than she could bear, this tenuous hold on a life that promised so much, but was so precarious with David hovering in the background. He stood up and Nancy felt like she'd lost the opportunity to reply. 'Look, I've got to go. I'll see you tonight.'

Nancy turned onto her side as she heard the front door shut, pulling her legs up and into her constricted chest. Her head felt bloated and stuffy and she pressed the heels of her hands into her temples because she didn't want the bad thoughts to come. *But we've been with you all your life, why would we desert you now?* they laughed at her, which was a fair point.

She was amazed at how much they could still terrify her, the way they weighed down on her so it felt as if someone had laid a blanket over her mind and she couldn't think straight, magnifying outwards until they seemed larger than the sum of their parts. Even as a child she'd sometimes been overtaken by this feeling; she could be doing something totally ordinary like playing with her dolls or eating dinner or reading a book and a sensation of utter desolation would envelop her, wrapping around her and sucking her under until she felt sure she would suffocate. She would look up and out, she would try windows or familiar scenes, but it was as if a veil had been drawn between her and the world so nothing was clear and she was convinced she was existing outside her accepted reality.

Robert had pursued her so totally when they'd first met, at a party in some dingy student house where she'd drunk and smoked way too much. When he'd rung the next day he'd had to remind her who he was and then she'd presumed he wanted Ellie because they'd spent the night chatting in the kitchen. No, he'd said too loudly, then stumbled over his words when he told her that he'd only gone to the party because he'd known she was going to be there, but hadn't had the courage to speak to her, hoping that if he spoke to her friend she might join the conversation. Eleanor's great, he'd said, but not in that way. Then Ellie had strangely persuaded her to go for the drink, even though Nancy wondered if she liked him, because it would be just like Ellie to graciously step aside like that. But even after the first evening in the pub she'd been glad that it was her he liked. He'd seemed so smart and proper, his voice catching on his words and his hand shaking when he lit a cigarette. He called when he said he would, he told her he loved her, he spoke about a definite future and, within it all, made her feel like there was so much out there, so much waiting for her, so many corners to be turned.

Until last year he had also been the only man she'd ever slept with, which seemed unreal now as Nancy lay in her marital bed in the middle of the afternoon. It barely seemed plausible that the woman she was now had been the same young girl lying in the spare room of Robert's parents' house nearly thirty years before, her body encased in a clichéd silken nightdress, her legs inoffensively smooth and her hair clean and sweet smelling. She remembered how, as she'd waited for him to come and relieve her of her virginity, she'd thought about the last lecture they'd had on Keats, and how Professor Sutcliffe had looked straight at her when he'd spoken. It had made her suddenly fearful that Robert could only really be interested in her beauty and was actually far better suited to Eleanor. And if that was true, then Keats was right, her beauty would fade and die just like everything else and then where would that leave them? She wished momentarily for a disfiguring accident, but then regretted the thought instantly, which was worse as it made her realise that her beauty could be the thing she too liked best about herself, when really it was nothing more than a deception.

But then the door had inched open and Robert was reflected in the light from the hall, the actuality of him shockingly real and obliterating everything else. He tiptoed over to the bed and pulled back the covers, jumping in beside her. His feet were freezing but he kissed the side of her shoulder.

'You OK?' he whispered. 'We don't have to, you know.'

But, she remembered thinking, if I don't do it now, when will I? She was lying in a comfy bed in a beautiful house next to the man she loved and they had time and power and beauty on their side. Being with Robert in those strange days between Christmas and New Year had felt very much like stepping into her future. A future that was rightfully hers, a future that befitted her. To turn away from it would have been a sort of madness, certainly an act of sabotage. It would, in fact, have been like embracing the madness of her father, of giving in to the feelings that always threatened to pull her under. So Nancy had rolled onto her side and her lips were so close to Robert's she could feel his breath on them. He stroked his hand down her body and told her she was beautiful and that he loved her.

He'd kissed her and his tongue had tasted minty in her mouth, making her close her eyes. It felt like she was lying in a deep sea being turned round and round by the tide. She moved closer to him and pressed her hips against his, not wanting to lose the solid reality of him, not wanting to find that she could really slip away into a bottomless ocean. It had hurt and she bled, but she'd rightly presumed it wouldn't always feel like that.

And all of that had led her here, to this moment, this tasteful room, this sleek house, this life that shimmered around her. It seemed preposterous now that it hadn't been enough, making her kick and complain her way through so many decades. Because Nancy knew herself well enough to at least recognise that nothing had ever been enough for her, that the hollow taste always present on her tongue was her constant enemy.

Her therapist had a theory that her parents had put too much pressure on her, as a beloved and special only child, not helped by her father's high achievements and manic nature. She'd spent her childhood surrounded by brilliant adults and had always found it hard to make friends until she'd met Eleanor and Mary and realised some people of her generation also liked quick minds. But there was something more, some depth her therapist wasn't quite reaching, which she could feel rising to the surface. She had been remembering more recently how many times people had told her that life was hers for the taking, something she knew she'd always subconsciously believed to be true. You could not surely be as beautiful, well-connected, rich and adored as she was and not have wonderful things happen to you. But what constitutes wonderful, who arbitrates what is enough, who is the judge?

Sometimes Nancy's mind felt like it could swallow her whole, like there was a place inside her into which she could disappear forever. The only thing that drew her away from the edge at those moments was her friends, and she reached for her phone now, as the darkness pushed against her skin.

Eleanor answered in a few rings, but her tone was harried and Nancy imagined she'd disturbed something important. 'Sorry, can you talk?'

'Are you OK?' There was a brusqueness to her friend's voice she didn't like.

'I don't know. I just feel a bit scared.'

'Scared? Has something happened?'

'It's just—'

She heard Eleanor sigh down the line. 'Oh, Nance, I've tried so hard to help you over the last couple of months, but I don't really know where to go from here.'

'I know, I'm sorry.'

'You know you sort of have to make the decision to start helping yourself, even if it means telling Robert, or calling the police. I don't know what else I can say any more.'

Nancy felt a rush of fear at the thought of Eleanor knowing Robert knew, or of Robert finding out all he still didn't know, or of the police making sure everyone knew. The new fear mixed with the fear already swimming in her veins, so she momentarily wondered if she was going to scream. But she swallowed it all down and controlled her voice when she spoke. 'Sorry, I'm being silly. I'm fine, really.'

'Are you sure?' Eleanor hesitated for a moment. 'I mean, I've got a meeting in a minute, but we could chat after that, or I could come over later if something's up?'

'No, no, honestly. Just having a bad moment. I feel better now.'

'But has he done anything specific, I mean, anything else?'

'Look, I'll talk to you about it when we have dinner tomorrow.'

'If you're sure.'

'Yes, get back to work.'

Nancy had to hold her hands against the side of her head for a moment after she put down the phone. She understood why

Eleanor would feel exasperated at her, after months of support in which everything she suggested Nancy had to knock down. But also, surely Eleanor could remember what it felt like to be irrational, as if you couldn't support yourself any more, as if the worst version of you was waiting to break out. And surely she remembered that it was Nancy who had been the one to coax her out of those feelings when she'd come back from overseas work seven years before and found her old life too frightening.

Nancy had cocooned her, taken her to Sussex, listened to late-night phone calls and never once had she made Ellie feel stupid or as if they had run out of options.

'What if I haven't made the right decisions,' Eleanor used to say, over and over. 'What if I've missed the chance to have children and I'll wake up one day and regret it. Or I'll end up an old spinster that no one comes to visit and when I die my body won't be found until someone reports the smell.'

'That's just what women are told to think,' Nancy would answer, often adding, 'You're buying into a stupid myth that women have to be mothers.' Sometimes, 'It's not even what you think.'

Finally, one day, Eleanor had smiled, her tears glistening on her lashes. 'You're right. I never really wanted them. Or at least I didn't want them enough. I wanted the other things more. I'd never have been able to do the things I've done if I'd had children.'

'And you don't have to worry about dying alone,' Nancy replied, a rush of love for her friend running through her. 'You can come and live with me when you're too old to care any more.'

Eleanor laughed. 'I bet Robert would love that.'

'Oh, he'll either be dead or senile by then. We can move to Sussex and be like two batty old ladies, reading books to each other by the fire and drinking gin for breakfast. Maybe Mary will come as well. People will start to call us eccentric and one day some bright young thing will write a play about us.'

It still seemed to Nancy like a wonderful future, but she doubted it would be possible to get there with all she had done, doubted that Eleanor or Mary would want to go with her if they knew who she really was.

It took almost all Nancy's energy to force herself up and into clothes by the time Robert got home that evening. She'd brushed her hair and put on a bit of make-up and was satisfied that he wouldn't think she'd spent the afternoon crying in bed, or that her head was filled with terrible thoughts which made her want to scream into a darkened corner. The second glass of wine was helping; she'd made a simple pasta sauce and salad and they ate it with a candle between them at the kitchen table.

Robert looked tired, but he still asked after her afternoon and she lied and said she'd got a bit more work done on the tricky translation she was working on. He said he'd had a small argument with Dido about how to handle the case of the group of Syrian refugees they were representing. He complained about what a stickler she could be on small points of law, but Nancy barely listened because Robert always complained about Dido, but she knew he admired her as well and nothing ever came of the complaints. If someone was looking into their basement kitchen on the way home from work it would look cosy, enviable even.

'I'm going up,' Robert said. 'Long day again tomorrow.'

'OK. I'll be up in a bit.' Nancy knew her mind was too wired for sleep yet; if she was on her own she could finish the bottle and get to sleep that way. Robert stood up. 'Oh, by the way, I'm having supper with Ellie tomorrow.'

He turned and she saw the doubt in his eyes. 'Are you? Where?'

She tried to keep her tone light. 'That Greek place near her work, you know.'

'OK. I might have to work late anyway.'

'She seems a bit down, so I might be a bit late, but not too much, elevenish I would think.' After all this was done Nancy vowed to herself never to lie to Robert again.

He shrugged as he turned and left the room. 'Right.'

It might always be like this, Nancy thought as she loaded their plates into the dishwasher. Robert might never truly believe her and the thought was like a stab. She'd planned to take the bottle of wine to the sitting room and watch something on the telly, but even that seemed like too much of an effort now, so instead she sat back at the table and poured herself another glass. The people looking into the kitchen now might not find the scene so enviable, a woman on her own with a half-finished bottle of wine and a flickering candle in front of her. She reached out and put her finger to the warm wax in the pool of the flame, enjoying the pain from the heat as it spread through her hand.

Lots of people in her life had envied her, she thought as the hot pain numbed her, through school and university, and out into the world. Except what they'd envied had barely been worth the emotion: what she looked like, who she was married to, how she decorated her houses, where she holidayed, what she wore. Nothing that went beyond her surface, although she worried that was probably because nothing did go on below surface level.

She remembered laughing once with Ellie and Mary about the women at Zara's school gates. 'We should all have our husband's payslips tattooed on our foreheads, save the underhand competition,' she'd said and her friends had laughed, but she'd realised that they had no idea what she was talking about. And then she'd felt ashamed because it felt like she'd exposed an ugly side of herself to the only two women whom she cared about, so she worried that after she left they would wonder at the banality of her life. She'd wanted to call Ellie and Mary that evening and promise them that she wasn't really like that, that she was still the young woman who had sat up until dawn talking about what they would be, even if she hadn't achieved anything yet.

It was possible, she supposed, that Zara was having her version of those conversations now, plotting her future like a line on a map that you just had to follow to make true. The thought was enough to make her feel dizzy, as if time was a rollercoaster she couldn't get off. She should have been a better mother, should have warned Zara that ambition can get lost down the back of a sofa, or not to always think there was something bigger or better over the next hill, or to make choices and not regret them. Or, or... she really had no right to give her daughter any advice.

Nancy stood and got what she thought of as her emergency cigarettes from a drawer in the dresser. She opened a window and sat on a work surface to at least attempt to blow the smoke away, although she knew it was pointless and that even in the morning there would still be a stale stench in the air, which would make Robert tut. She shivered against the penetrating cold of the air coming in through the window, but knew that her shiver was really internal, as if her body was trying to rid itself of all memory of the last year.

She'd said that the past year had been a form of a madness and that is exactly what it now seemed. Almost as if her mind had been kidnapped by an idea, although Nancy couldn't remember what it might have been, wasn't sure she had ever known in the first place. She flicked the cigarette, smoked down to the filter, out of the open window and then immediately lit another, pulling the lethal fibres deep into her lungs.

After the second fag she felt woozy so she slipped off the worktop and reached for her wineglass, downing it in one go. But that just made her feel worse and she had to lean over the sink, worried she was going to be sick. But she deserved to be sick – she deserved pestilence and plague, eternal damnation. She deserved everything she feared and worse.

The sharpness of her betrayal wedged itself between her ribs like an arrow, its poison spreading through her blood. It felt in fact as if she was losing her mind, something that she thought was possible considering the amount of dislocation she'd had to participate in simply to function over the past year. David had existed for her as a separate entity because it had made what she was doing unreal, but that would not be possible any more. As she sat at her kitchen table she realised that she had seen him almost as a fantasy creation, ignoring the fact that he was not only made up of flesh and blood, but also emotions and desires. She had to face up not just to who he was, but also to what he made her.

It had been going on for a little over a year because it was now January and it had started at a publishing Christmas party the year before. It was true that she had been trying to extricate herself for a couple of months, but that was still a long time when she hadn't cared one iota about anyone other than herself and her own disgusting desire.

The party had been ostensibly to celebrate the unlikely mega success of a non-fiction book called *The Politics of Crime*. Nancy hadn't worked on the actual book, but they published lots of French crime writers whom she translated and who had contributed to the book. She hadn't been sure if any of them were going to be there and hadn't actually even met most of them, but she was always bored in December, when Robert's diary became full and she sat alone night after night wondering why it had taken her so long to create anything real for herself. The invitation had sparked a moment of pride that someone thought enough of her professionally to invite her and the feeling had buoyed her for days before the event.

Nancy, Ellie and Mary had a tradition to have a decadent lunch sometime in the weeks leading up to Christmas and, by luck, it had fallen on the same day as the party. She'd gone to the lunch so full of hope and excitement, but in fact it had put her in a terrible mood because, the more they'd chatted, the more she had realised how much thicker and fuller her friends' lives were than hers. And instead of this pleasing her, like it would a normal person, it had curdled deep in her stomach, sending a rot up into her brain.

As the bill came, Ellie had leant over and said, 'I was thinking about you earlier.'

'Were you?' Nancy asked, feeling warmed by the thought of occupying a little part of her friend's day.

'Yes, I was buying some food for Irena, you know, my downstairs neighbour. I have supper with her every Thursday.'

'Oh right.'

'Yes, and I just thought, maybe that would be a good thing for you to do. Visit someone elderly, I mean. There are loads of organisations I could put you in touch with. It's such a great thing to do. You get just as much out of it as they do.'

Nancy looked between Ellie and Mary and saw they were both blushing slightly and defiantly not looking at each other. Of course virtuous bloody Eleanor visited her elderly neighbour, but to Nancy it sounded like a ghastly thing to do. She didn't want to hear any more stories of woe, didn't want to be reminded that everything crumbles in the end. But most of all, she didn't want to think of her friends trying to think up ways for her to fill her fucking days.

'Have you been talking about me?' she asked.

'No, of course not.' But Eleanor spoke too quickly and Mary couldn't meet her eye.

'Just what is it you think I've become?' But as she asked the question she realised she would quite like one of them to tell her.

'I'm sorry,' Eleanor said. 'Really, I just thought you'd enjoy it.'

'We love you,' Mary said. 'Just sometimes, you don't seem all that happy.'

Nancy looked between her two friends and barely knew what to say. 'Are you both happy?'

Mary shrugged. 'Mostly, I suppose.'

She saw Eleanor shift before she spoke. 'Of course I'm not always happy. But when I'm not I hope you two would help me. I mean, you both have in the past.'

Nancy felt suddenly as if the carefully constructed veneer of her life had worn away and really everyone always knew how hard she found things. Or, maybe, more frighteningly, she was more pathetic and sad than even she had realised. Maybe her friends could see things in her that she didn't even know were there, which made her feel like she was losing her grip and in fact anything was possible. 'I should probably get going,' Nancy said, gathering her bag from the back of her seat. 'I'm going to a work party this evening and I need to do a few things beforehand.'

Eleanor put her hand on to her arm. 'I'm sorry, Nance, really. That was misjudged of me. I didn't mean to make you feel bad.'

'It's fine.' She made herself smile.

'Yes, sorry, Nancy,' Mary said.

She felt a desperate desire to leave then. 'Honestly, neither of you have to apologise.' She hurried away, completely sure that Eleanor and Mary would order another cup of coffee over which they would discuss all her problems, even the ones she didn't know she had.

Her whole afternoon went downhill after that, so it felt as if her failures were coating her skin and dragging her down to somewhere she hadn't even known existed. She contemplated just not going to the party, but knew that would make her feel worse. Instead she tried on and discarded countless outfits, mucked up her make-up and failed to make her hair sit properly, so all in all she felt disgusting when she walked into the glassed-in atrium of the publishing house.

The book had clearly done extremely well because the place was heaving. Young people with taut buns and serious cheek-bones were handing round champagne and everyone had already sequestered themselves into tight, jovial groups. Nancy drank a glass of champagne too quickly and then circled the room, trying to find a conversation to join. A few people were kind enough to chat to her, but she felt like she was intruding and uninteresting which, coupled with the lunch, made her feel as if she'd spent the previous week labouring under delusions of grandeur.

She decided to go to the loo and then home, so made her way to the back of the room to a long corridor, which she followed until she found the ladies. She nearly cried once she'd locked the cubicle door because she felt such a failure; people in their late forties either did or didn't have glittering careers and she didn't, even though she definitely could have done. She sat heavily on the loo, feeling a patch of wet on her thigh, and peed noisily.

She banged the door as she left, hoping she'd left a mark on the pristine white walls, wanting now only to get in a cab and go home, where she'd open a bottle of wine and find something on Netflix.

'I thought it was you. I wasn't sure.'

She turned, and seeing him so out of place knocked her slightly off balance. 'Oh hello, I didn't realise you'd be here.'

'I contributed to the book.'

She felt wrong-footed. 'Sorry, I didn't realise. Of course you would have. Makes sense.'

He stepped towards her and Nancy thought he wore his age well, like a creased shirt, in fact much like the creased blue shirt he was actually wearing. His shoes were scuffed and his beard had grown slightly longer than she'd seen before, which gave him a wolfish air.

'Nice dress, by the way.'

She looked down at the red woollen dress she was wearing and felt herself blush. 'Thanks.'

'But then you could probably wear a bin liner and make it look good.'

She felt the heat rise through her body, unsure what was happening because their friendship, if you could even call it that, had never included flirting. He was staring straight at her so she returned his gaze and his eyes were very bright and fathomless, so it felt more like he was dissecting her than just looking.

He took the three steps that were separating them through the electric atmosphere and then was so close she could smell his smoky breath. He held out his hand. 'David. Nice to meet you.'

'David?' She tried to laugh, but the sound came out striated. 'What are you talking about, Howard?' Because this was one of her best friend's husbands standing in front of her saying things that he shouldn't be saying, in ways that she knew she should walk away from. But an image of Mary and Eleanor flashed into her head from earlier that day, their pained expressions, their fucking condescension. She would stop in a minute anyway.

He fixed her with his stare. 'David's my middle name.' He bit his lip, as if he was unsure whether or not to speak and she couldn't decide if she desperately wanted him to or not. 'It was strange seeing you in there.' He motioned towards the sound of the party. 'It wrong-footed me because I hadn't expected it. I'm not used to seeing you that way.'

'What way?'

He moved infinitesimally closer, so she could feel the heat of his body. 'Vulnerable, I suppose. You looked a little lost, when I've always had you down as so self-assured.'

She felt absurdly as if she was going to cry, except it was like he'd looked deep into her soul, right down to who she really was. She had a preposterous feeling that he knew everything there was to know about her in a way no one else would. 'I've never been self-assured,' she said, but the words came out almost as a whisper.

'It made me feel very strange, if I'm honest, seeing you like that, so raw.' He paused and made her flittering eyes catch his gaze before he spoke again, 'So, as I said, my name is David, are you going to tell me yours?'

Nancy looked at Howard and knew that how she answered would determine something huge, and it made her whole body feel alive, as if it was thrumming with energy, like a memory of excitement or promise, something she'd forgotten. She took his hot hand and there was still time to tell him to go home to her best friend, to preserve the person she'd always thought herself to be. Except that person filled Nancy with disgust. She thought of her empty house and the bottle of wine, of the caverns inside her head. It was only a word after all, a simple puff of air; she deserved a moment of madness, because that was all it would be.

'Louise.'

He cocked his head to one side. 'Suits you.'

He reached down and ran his hand up her leg, from the knee where the split of her dress started, right to her crotch.

The feeling of existing outside of herself that always seemed to surround her snapped so she felt fully returned to herself in a way she wasn't sure she had ever been before. She gasped before she could stop herself and knew, at that moment, she would do anything he asked, if it meant always remaining so present.

He moved his hand round her back to pull her closer, but she could still feel it on her leg, as if he had awakened nerves she hadn't even known she possessed. Then his face was on hers and his tongue was in her mouth, the strangeness of his beard rubbing against her skin, but not unpleasantly. His other hand was groping her breast and all she could imagine was his lips on her nipple and his penis inside her. She wanted to lay down on the floor right there and then. To say fuck it to everyone and everything. But he pulled away.

'Not here,' he said. 'I'll call you tomorrow.' And then he turned and walked away and she had to lean against the wall because her whole body was shaking and she wasn't even sure it had happened.

She'd woken the next morning with a dull headache and a memory that seemed more like a bad dream. It clung to her like cheap perfume even after she got up, showered and drank a strong cup of coffee. She avoided looking directly at herself in the mirror, flashbacks jarring at her brain. She supposed he could quite easily get hold of her number, but she doubted he'd bother. Anyway, she didn't want him to call. It would be awkward next time they saw each other, but she would find a quiet moment to apologise and tell him she'd been very drunk. Except she didn't go to her usual Friday-morning exercise class and, even when she put out the bin bags, she tucked her mobile into the back pocket of her jeans.

He called just before twelve, when she'd veered from embarrassment to anger to desire and right the way round again. But when she saw the unidentified number flash up on her screen, her skin tingled from where he had run his hand up her leg and all she could imagine was his whole body right there, pressed against her, inside her.

'Can you meet me in an hour?' he asked.

'Really?' She was thrown off guard by his directness.

'I've got the keys to a friend's flat. He's in America. I could meet you there in an hour.' The furtiveness was almost more of an admission of what this was than anything else.

'Where's the flat?' Nancy almost giggled with the absurdity of it all, as if she was existing entirely outside of herself.

'Baron's Court. That big mansion block by the station.'

She put her fingers to her lips and felt his tongue again. 'Yes, I could get there in an hour.'

'Flat C, 14 Palliser Court.' He hung up before she even had a chance to write it down and then she had to sit herself, with her head in her hands, as her vision jarred. She shut her eyes but all she could see was Mary, Mary, Mary.

But she'd shaved her legs in the shower that morning and put on matching underwear. She retched into the air as she admitted this to herself.

They fucked before they spoke. Like animals, panting and sweating. And she had never felt anything like it before. Never felt those undulating ripples vibrate through her body. Never tasted desire, empty and scary, at the back of her throat. Never swallowed the salty semen she usually spat down the loo. Never wanted anyone to turn her over and pull her hips upwards. Never shut her eyes and forgotten where she was, who she was even. Never been so completely within herself.

It was only afterwards, as they shared a cigarette, lying on a strange round bed with ferns in macramé pots hanging above their heads, that pure shame engulfed her like a consuming fire.

'Wow, you're warm,' he said, and she wondered if she was actually getting sick.

'Oh my God, what have we done?' she asked, as if he would know.

He was quiet for a moment and she felt her fear that he was regretting it like a rock in her chest. 'I think we've done something inevitable.'

Despite herself she thrilled at his words.

'I feel scared as well,' he said. 'I mean, this is mad, I know. But you make me feel crazy.'

She cried then, with her head on his chest, so her tears mingled with his hairs. He wrapped his arms around her and kissed the top of her head and she felt a deep, intense calmness.

'It must never happen again,' Nancy said, sucking in his warm scent, tinged with the tang of his sweat. She wanted desperately to know that what she had said was true, that she would stop it from happening again, but she already doubted her resolve.

His finger traced her spine and it was like he left electric currents on her skin. Then his lips were where his fingers had been and she had to arch her back because it was too nice. He turned her around and his lips were on hers and she could taste herself on his tongue.

He pulled away. 'I've always wanted this. Since the first moment I met you.'

'Don't be silly.'

'No, it's true.' He leant back in and kissed her mouth and she felt as if her bones were being dissolved by his touch.

But she pulled back this time. 'I can't, I mean...' She found she couldn't speak either Robert or Mary's name, so settled on, 'Our families.'

'There's no point in talking about them. This is something different.'

He was making her feel desperate and she wanted to extract fairy-tale promises from him. 'Have you done this before?'

'I expect you've heard rumours?'

'No.' Except she wondered suddenly if that was why Eleanor hated him and she felt jealous at the thought of Mary confiding in Ellie and not her, so a bolt of anger shot through her. They had both always slightly looked down on her, she thought, as if they knew things about life she never could, when it wasn't her fault she was born into privilege, although maybe it was her fault she hadn't done anything with it.

He lay back and put his arms behind his head, so momentarily she felt compelled to look at the curve of his biceps and the dip of his collarbone. 'If you want to know the truth, we haven't had the easiest marriage. In fact, sometimes I think it's been unnecessarily hard.' He paused, as if choosing his words carefully. 'She's obsessed with our children, which leaves me on the edge of things, if that makes sense. It's not her fault. I just don't think we appreciated how different we were and how hard that is.' Nancy was relieved that he too hadn't spoken Mary's name out loud. 'Also, she gets insanely jealous. She's always convinced that I'm sleeping with someone else, which is very tiring.'

'But has she got a reason to think that?' Nancy held her breath because she couldn't be one of many.

'God, no, of course not.' He reached out and ran his finger down her arm, leaving little bumps like a trail of where he'd been. 'I hope you don't think this is something I would do lightly. I mean, I'm not in the habit of risking everything. And we might have grown apart, but that doesn't mean that I don't care for her, or respect her.'

Nancy's heart fluttered like it couldn't catch the next beat. The sheer awfulness of what they were doing sort of cancelling out all rational thought. 'I love her too,' she said. But also he was describing a version of Mary that Nancy recognised and she thought he did so with care and consideration.

'How about you? Do you really have a wonderful marriage?'

The question caught her off guard and she didn't know how to answer. 'I guess we've had a hard marriage as well. I know what you mean about being different, although in my case I think it's more like wanting different things. But it's not wonderful, no, not at all.'

Nancy couldn't stop herself lying closer to him, her chin on his chest, so she was looking up at him. She felt possessive of him already, angry almost at how he'd been marginalised, desperate to make it better for him.

He smiled down at her. 'Over the years, you've often seemed misunderstood to me, if that's the right word. Like Robert only sees one side of you. That vulnerability I saw in you last night, I bet he's never noticed it.'

She shivered at his words, but also couldn't let herself agree with them out loud. 'He does try. He's a good man. I think it's more that he doesn't understand vulnerability because he never feels it.'

'Yes, and long marriages are so bloody hard. I suppose I haven't been the best husband either. I suspect I've blamed Mary for her insecurities when maybe I've contributed to them in some way I don't understand. I think I've used work as a bit of a distraction. Although when I get too involved with that side of life she gets angry and accuses me of having an affair and the whole shitty cycle starts up again.'

'I'm sorry.' Nancy suddenly couldn't understand how Mary could ever have doubted this man, who seemed to understand life in a way that surely made things better.

'The irony of course being that I was married when I met her, so she is actually the only person I've ever had an affair with.'

'Maybe that's why she worries.' It was too strange a conversation to have as Nancy realised she was already taking Howard's side over Mary, and that simply couldn't happen. And yet, what he was saying sounded so reasonable.

'God, you're beautiful,' he said, looking down at her. 'I don't want to talk about all that stuff with you. You know what we said last night, when we introduced ourselves?' She nodded. 'From now on you will only ever be Louise to me. That's all I'll ever call you. And I can only be David to you. We can exist like that, just the two of us, outside all the other stuff. We can make each other happy, so, so happy.'

The idea was preposterous, but also undeniably wonderful. He was offering her a tiny island in the sea of shit that surrounded her and no one had ever done that before. She knew everything about what they were doing was wrong, so wrong, and yet nothing had ever felt so necessary to her very existence before. She looked straight at him when she spoke. 'OK, David.' And he was right, it did make it better, this separation, this disconnect. She knew immediately that it was the only way this thing, whatever it was, could exist. They had to not just pretend, but convince themselves, at all times, that they were not who they really were.

They continued looking at each other, like love-struck teenagers unable to break contact, and there was something so intense about the stare he returned to her that Nancy felt totally subjugated by it. Almost as if his eyes were magic, drawing her down to somewhere she both feared and desired. She had the same vertiginous feeling she'd had the night before when he'd kissed her. A feeling that he knew something about her no one else did; something he would reveal to her and in the revelation she would understand herself and life would become easier and her feelings of dread might just go away.

\*

Nancy pushed herself off the sink and turned round. She let out a low moan and let her tears fall then because it seemed impossible that it had happened, or that she was fundamentally this terrible person. Still her brain scrabbled to comfort herself and, even though she knew it didn't make it any better, she told herself that in a funny way she had barely known Howard before he had become David. It wasn't as if her, Mary and Eleanor had ever been that involved with each other's partners, almost as if they were enough for each other and they didn't want outsiders getting in the way. It was true that Ellie had spent a fair bit of time with her and Robert over the years, but they almost never saw Mary and Howard as a couple.

About the only time she could remember them all together was at a dinner from over a decade before, in which they had all sat around the kitchen table she was sitting at now. Ellie had just returned from one of her year-long trips and Nancy had invited them all over, thinking how nice it would be to have them all together, like old times, except with partners.

On the night, Robert had been late home, which she thought he must have done on purpose because he'd groaned when she'd told him about the dinner. 'I just bloody forgot,' he said as he raced up the stairs to get changed and Nancy knew that was just as bad.

Zara appeared at the top of the stairs as she stood at the bottom fuming. 'Can I get a drink?' she asked.

'Quick,' Nancy said. 'They'll be here in a minute.' But actually, she thought, it would be nice for Eleanor and Mary to see Zara, who must have been about eight or nine and had suddenly grown so tall and beautiful, a mini version of herself. 'Why don't you wait and say hello,' she said, to which Zara shrugged.

Nancy was sure she was right in remembering that Frederich

was the man Eleanor had brought with her that night. It was hard to place all the different men Eleanor returned from her trips with, but she was sure it had been Frederich, because he'd lasted a bit longer than most. They'd been the first to arrive with the remnants of a row still lingering on their pinched features. Frederich had been clearly impressed by the house, which made Nancy feel slightly pathetic, considering what he did. Eleanor exclaimed over Zara and started asking her a hundred questions, some of which Nancy realised she'd never asked, and when she saw Zara relax, she hated herself. Robert came downstairs and drinks were poured and Frederich seemed nice and she thought it might all go well after all.

Then Zara went upstairs and she checked on the duck because she didn't want it to dry out, and noticed it was quarter to nine, which meant that Mary and Howard were verging on being rudely late.

'Can I do anything?' Eleanor asked from behind her, making Nancy jump slightly so she burnt her hand on the oven door as she stood up.

'No.' She turned to her friend. 'You look amazing, by the way. You've lost weight and your skin is so brown.'

Eleanor laughed. 'Perks of the job.'

'He seems very nice, Frederich,' Nancy said, sucking on the burnt patch of skin.

'He is.' But Eleanor looked down and she thought she caught something in the movement.

'Everything OK?'

When Eleanor spoke again she sounded cheery. 'Yes, fine. I'm just slightly dreading spending a whole week with his daughter. We've met before, but only briefly and, well, you know.'

'Is it serious then, with Frederich?'

Eleanor shrugged. 'Not really, I suppose.'

Nancy wanted to ask Ellie how she managed to keep herself so aloof, but there was a ring at the door. 'Ah, that must be Mary, finally.'

Both women went to the door and opened it to what seemed like a gaggle of refugees, all dressed in flowing clothes that looked like they'd been dragged through mud. Marcus and Mimi were both crying and Nancy found herself thinking that Marcus was too old to be doing that and his nose was disgustingly snotty. The baby, if you could still call a nearly three year old a baby, which Nancy didn't think you could, was attached to Mary by a piece of material, which had been knotted about her like they didn't live in a wealthy Western country.

'Sorry we're late,' Mary said as they exploded into the hall. Her hair, which was the longest Nancy had ever seen it, looked like it needed a wash and her glasses were so dirty it was hard to catch her eye. Eleanor was already on her knees, helping Marcus and Mimi out of their coats.

Howard stepped forward from the back of the bunch, his smile broad, brandishing a bottle of good wine. 'I'm so sorry we're late,' he said with a look of patient resignation. 'It was all just in chaos when I got home and it's taken a while.' He half laughed and Nancy remembered smiling at him over Mary's head because she'd noticed as well how distracted she'd become since Maisie's birth and it must be hard for Howard, trying to hold everything together. Perhaps that had been her first betrayal, although it hadn't felt like that at the time, certainly she hadn't meant it that way, or she was sure she hadn't.

'I didn't realise you were bringing them all,' she said as brightly as she could.

'Well, we could hardly leave them behind,' said Mary, who had clearly never heard of a babysitter.

'Why don't you go in,' Nancy said to Howard, motioning to the sitting room. 'Robert will get you a drink.'

Then it took ages to get the older kids upstairs and comfy on her bed. Maisie simply refused to be left and clung to Mary like a limpet, which slightly disgusted Nancy, and made her think that all the bloody attachment parenting Mary did was actually ridiculous and probably even harmful. She was sure everything would have burnt and taste disgusting, but actually by the time she'd put the meal onto serving plates and called everyone into the kitchen it was fine.

As soon as they sat down Maisie started grappling with Mary's top and Nancy felt the revulsion from before build again. Surely Mary wasn't going to feed the child, Nancy thought, but then Mary simply got out her breast and Maisie started to feed. Nancy looked around the table but nobody else, apart from Robert, seemed bothered, or even to have noticed. He raised his eyes at her across the table, but she looked away because otherwise she worried she might laugh.

'What a room,' Howard said, casting his eyes round the space, which suddenly seemed embarrassing to Nancy.

'Tell me about your work,' Eleanor said to Howard, and Nancy wanted to kiss her.

Nancy had put Frederich on her other side and she turned to him now, in time for him to ask, 'And what do you do, Nancy?'

She felt her face heating up and stuttered. 'Oh, well, nothing really.'

'Nonsense,' said Robert. 'She looks after us all. Which is not as easy as it sounds.'

Nancy smiled over at her husband. 'Yes, but it's not actual work, is it?'

'If you mean because you don't get paid for it,' Eleanor said from the other side of Howard, 'then that's absurd. I've been working with a group of women in Sri Lanka helping them form a cooperative and they're all mothers and I tell you I have never seen people work as hard.' But, Nancy noticed, she directed her next statement at Mary. 'I honestly don't know how you do it with your three so young.'

The thought of a group of ill-educated, flood-ravaged Sri Lankan women forming a cooperative, whilst she sat in one of her large, smart houses, trying to fill her days, struck hard at Nancy.

'I don't think I do anything particularly well,' Mary answered.

'Oh, come on,' Howard said, 'you can't beat yourself up about the house and stuff like that. I keep telling her to stop fixating on all those pointless little things. She's bringing up three little humans very well and that would exhaust anyone.'

'That's a lovely thing to say,' Nancy said, not wanting to look at Robert, who she didn't think had ever said anything as nice to her.

'So, Howard,' Robert said from across the table, 'what's your latest cause, or big idea we should all know about?'

'Howard's got very into organic,' Mary said. 'And it does make a lot of sense when you read about it. Did you know all the big farms that supply our supermarkets use synthetic nitrogen in their fertilisers?'

Nancy noticed most people had stopped eating.

'It's already like that in New York,' Frederich said. 'I was there a few months ago and everyone was asking where the food was from and how it was farmed.'

'The Soil Association think that in twenty years we'll look back and see eating non-organic food in the same way we think about smoking now,' said Howard. 'Mark my words, it will be the next big thing, all over our supermarkets.'

'What you're saying doesn't make much sense,' Robert said, and Nancy could see he was a bit drunk and quite angry.

'In what way?' Howard's smile looked thin and she wanted to apologise for her brutish husband. She looked down and saw their legs were so close they were nearly touching, his thighs tight against the cotton of his trousers.

'Well, you cannot have an organic farm by definition,' Robert said. 'Unless you enclose it in a bubble or live on a very remote island or something. You do know how farming works?'

'A bit,' Howard answered.

'I only ask because then you would understand that if you have one farmer using pesticides and fertilisers and one who doesn't, seed from both farms will find their way to the other, which will result in cross-pollination and a mixture of the crops.'

'I bow to your superior knowledge,' Howard said with a little nod of his head. 'But I suppose I'm of the opinion that you might as well try to make things better, rather than just accepting the dullness of the status quo.'

Robert and Howard glared at each other and Nancy could imagine them leaping the table and fighting, because we are always only a few steps from the animal world. She stood up. 'Anyone for any more?'

There was much shaking of heads and murmurs of deliciousness, but at least the sound of collecting the plates disrupted the tension and by the time she came back in, carrying the ubiquitous chocolate mousse, there were lots of separate conversations going on and the gentle hum of party had resumed. Nancy, however, found it hard to shake her annoyance at Robert and a steady drip of irritation made her not even able to meet his eye as she handed over his pudding. His head was no doubt still full of some case, there was never much room for anything else, which often made him boorish. Howard was chatting animatedly to

Frederich about aid work, but Nancy felt like she could hear his thoughts. He must be disgusted by her and Robert, probably thinking they were catastrophically wedded to money and status. Which was too close to what Nancy worried really was wrong with them.

She poured herself another glass of wine as she sat with her own portion of chocolate mousse in front of her and thought she couldn't stomach it anyway. Really she should have organised seeing her friends on her own, because now she wouldn't get a proper conversation with them and God knew when they'd all next be in the same country again. It had just seemed like such a nice idea, to have not just the two women she loved most in the world around her table, but also the people they had chosen to love too.

She looked over at Mary, who was still battling with Maisie, batting her hand away from the buttons on her top, and wondered what had happened to her. Mary who used to read Virgil until the early hours of the morning. Who, at every fancy-dress party they ever went to, wrapped white sheets around her beautiful skin, which had always reminded Nancy of a particular reddish brown earth she'd only ever seen in Australia, and twisted bright flowers into her jet black hair. Mary, who had pulled herself out of an ordinary life because she loved the extraordinary, only to let herself become this person who seemed to exist only for others.

She found herself feeling sorry for Howard again, which she knew was all wrong because Mary was wonderful and it was circumstance, not choice, that was making her so harried. She leant across Howard towards Eleanor, desperate for something to take her out of this mood. 'Please tell me more about your amazing success,' she said. 'I feel like I've missed it all.'

Mary caught the conversation. 'Oh God, please do, Ellie.'

Eleanor blushed. 'It's not that much of a promotion. I just got lucky, that's all.'

'It can't just be that,' Nancy replied, not sure why it mattered to her so much that Eleanor admit to her success.

Eleanor rubbed at her eyes as if she was tired. 'It's all smoke and mirrors. I'm sure there were twenty other people as qualified as me, who'd do as good a job.'

'You wouldn't say that if you were a man,' Mary said.

Eleanor laughed. 'Possibly not.'

'And you've got to think it's fantastic, I mean, somehow, part of it at least,' said Nancy, feeling like she couldn't bear for Eleanor not to take some pleasure from it all.

Eleanor smiled. 'No, of course, it's great, yes.'

'I'm always amazed by what people class as success,' Howard said.

Eleanor turned to him. 'Yes, I agree.'

'It's baffling to me why actors are asked for their opinions or put on the covers of magazines. I mean, wouldn't it be better to have teachers on there, or doctors? Or even aid workers like you, Eleanor.'

'Maybe it's not even about jobs,' Eleanor replied. 'Maybe we should define success through relationships. I mean, why not ask mothers their opinions, or couples who've spent fifty years together.'

Nancy was surprised to see Eleanor blush with her words. 'That's a lovely idea,' she said as kindly as she could to her old friend.

'It is all that matters,' Frederich said in his clipped accent and they all turned to look at him. 'If you are successful in your relationships, everything else falls in to place.'

Nancy was aware of an uncomfortable shifting round the table, which made her want to giggle. But Robert started re-filling glasses and the atmosphere broke and swayed like a rocking light.

'Well, I still think that you need to have done something outside yourself to be truly successful,' Howard said.

'I don't know,' said Mary, yawning as she spoke, the baby still clamped to her. 'You're not going to look back on your death bed and think of much else than your kids are you?'

Nancy couldn't help flicking a look at Eleanor, who was looking into her wineglass. She'd never been brave enough to actively ask her friend if she minded not having children. The presumption had always been that she was too busy saving the world, but maybe that was wrong, maybe she hadn't made a decision at all, maybe it was just what had happened to her. It wasn't that Nancy thought women were only fulfilled when they had pushed another human out of their vagina, but more just that she couldn't imagine anyone making a total decision about anything so comprehensive. She, after all, had barely made the decision to have a child, so it seemed unlikely that many people made the decision not to.

'I suppose the best is to have both,' Nancy said. 'I mean, successful relationships and jobs.' She snorted and realised she was a bit drunk. 'It's just that seems bloody hard to achieve. At least for women.'

'You're right,' Mary said. 'I don't know who came up with the idea of having it all, but I bet it was a man. I mean, God knows when I'll be able to get back to work. And, you know, I want to be the best mother I can be, but I also really do miss the university.'

'It's all up to you though,' said Howard. 'Which is not something our mothers could have said, which has to be seen as real progress.'

'What do you mean, it's all up to her?' Eleanor asked. 'Or are you talking about women in general? As in, it's up to us to sort out going back to work and raising children?'

Howard flushed slightly and Nancy hoped Eleanor wasn't about to start an argument. 'I think it's all about putting the right systems in place for the home and really getting organised. And also you have to look at the finances, you know, see who earns more and what childcare costs.'

Mary laughed, but it sounded strained. 'Howard mistakes child-rearing with lecturing and babies with tax returns.'

Howard sat back and shrugged. 'I just don't understand what's more important than raising our children.'

Nancy thought that was the sort of thing people said when they didn't have to do it, but she still applauded the sentiment and thought again how Robert would never say anything like that to her.

Mary had red flashes across her cheeks. 'It's not quite that simple though, is it, Howard. I think it's fair to expect that maybe you can do both.'

'Well, you have to be capable of both,' Howard answered. 'You find all the domestics hard enough and I wouldn't want you totally stressing yourself out with a job as well.'

The table had fallen quiet and it felt like they were listening to one of those well-worn marital arguments. Nancy tried to think of something to say, but found she simply didn't know what she thought. In the end Eleanor spoke, her voice falsely jolly. 'I know I don't have kids, so I can't really talk, but all my friends with children say going to work's the easy bit. I think it'd do you good to go back, Mary.'

Howard laughed in a tight way. 'Like I said though, child-care is extremely expensive. The second salary has to justify the expense.'

'Or maybe,' Eleanor said, 'you have to make a judgement on

what's better for the happiness and health of everyone concerned. Maybe the burden of domesticity shouldn't rest on one person's shoulders.'

None of them, Nancy realised, had really become what they had imagined for themselves when they used to sit up into early mornings discussing what they would do with their lives. She saw them almost as if she were watching a film or looking at a stylised photograph; they all appeared young and fresh and beautiful in her mind, even the lighting was clear and bright. She had met these women at university, when they had been at the height of their powers, or at least at the beginning of what they had thought would lead to powers. And now look at them, her especially. She wondered, suddenly and horribly, if they spoke about her ever, if they wondered at the nothing her life had become and the tedium of her days.

Robert stood, which disrupted the tension and allowed smaller conversations to start up. He came back with the cheese, somehow his job, although their roles at dinner parties had never been discussed. Although then again, what had been discussed? She wondered what he would have said if she'd suggested he stayed at home when Zara was younger, whilst she went out to work. She hoped things would be different for Zara, Mimi and baby Maisie. Time seemed to be free-wheeling around her so she felt as if the years were spinning by and soon there would be nothing left of any of them. She turned her head, trying to find a conversation to join, desperate for something to ground her in the present. But the only person who caught her eye was Howard, who was speaking to Eleanor.

'It's an important article,' he was saying. 'I think we have to totally re-evaluate our relationship with the ruling class. They have to be more accountable just by virtue of the fact that we can see so much more of them now.'

Eleanor was barely answering, nodding in a tight fashion, which seemed rude. Howard turned to Nancy and smiled, but when he did Eleanor stood and exclaimed at the time. Mary looked relieved and Nancy remembered they still had to get the children into a taxi and then the hell of getting them to bed at the other end, although she also imagined Howard helping Mary and something like envy contracted around her because Robert had barely ever made it home for bedtime when Zara was small.

It seemed to take hours and the goodbyes became almost unbearable. Nancy had a desperate desire to cling to both of the women as they left and to extract promises from them like she would a lover. When would they see each other again? Please could everyone call more frequently? Why couldn't they all live in the same city? They kissed and hugged and went into the cold night, back to plans and lives and destinations which she never could be part of. And of course that was all right, and of course she had her own path anyway. But still it felt desolate after the door shut for the last time and she found herself sitting on the bottom of the stairs and weeping uncontrollably so her shoulders shook and her breath came in gasps.

'It wasn't that bad,' Robert said jokingly. 'Although I would happily never see that prick Howard again.'

Nancy knew she should answer but she felt unable to pull herself together. Robert sat next to her on the narrow stair.

'Hey, what's up?' He spoke much more tenderly.

'I don't know,' she answered, looking up as she felt he wanted. 'It just seems so sad.'

'Sad?'

She groped for what she wanted to say and knew she'd never be able to articulate it. 'I used to spend every day with those women.'

Robert put his arm round her. 'Growing up can be hard to do.'

She was surprised. 'You don't feel that though, do you?'

'Occasionally. It's not much fun sitting in an office filled with men in suits every day.'

'Really? I thought you loved it.'

'I don't mind it. I just don't think about it too much.'

And she suspected that was the fundamental difference between men and women. She leant her head against his broad shoulder and he kissed her forehead. It was all so bloody confusing.

Nancy shook herself out of her reveries. The wine was finished and the clock told her it was nearly 2 a.m. She was aware suddenly of the pain in her head and how scratched her throat felt. Nancy stood and her memories fell in waves about her, breaking whatever spell they had, so the clarity of the situation was laid bare. She had spent the past year having an affair with the husband of one of her best friends, an act which made her more repulsive than she could fathom. She wondered desperately if there was any way back and how you lived with knowledge like this about yourself.

As she stood, the small of her back tugged in the way it had started to do when she sat on hard chairs for too long and she tried not to let the despondency of aging smother her. But at least the wine had worked its magic and she felt tired as she made her way up to bed, simply letting her clothes fall to the floor and then climbing in next to the sleeping body of her husband.

She woke with Robert's 6 a.m. alarm the next morning and rolled into his warm, sleep-filled body. They made love slowly and delicately and when Robert got out of the bed she lay where he had been all night and felt the indentations his body had made in the mattress.

'I wish you didn't have to go in today,' she said as he dressed.

'Me too.' Although she thought he seemed distracted.

'I can't stand how life gets in the way.' She felt an aching desperation for something she couldn't put her finger on, which felt as scary as a monster under the bed.

He laughed. 'God, it's complex inside your head, isn't it?'

After Robert had gone Nancy got up and made herself coffee, which she took to her desk and switched on her computer. She was translating a very beautiful book by a female writer she admired and it worried her she wouldn't ever be able to get the nuance of the words correct. She was agonising over almost every sentence and her deadline was drawing near and she was finding it too easy to be distracted. She shut the door of her study and turned on the heater by her desk, even though the radiators were pumping, making the room soon warm up cosily, as it always did. She loved her study out of all proportion to what it was because it represented something to her, some moment where she had taken at least partial control of her own destiny and done something positive.

After two hours her back ached so she stood, without anything really to do, her head filled with the lyrical sentences that had wrapped themselves around her brain. Her study was next to Zara's bedroom so she went and sat on her daughter's bed. She'd only returned to university from the Christmas break a week before and the air was still heavy with her. Nancy lay back on the striped pillows, inhaling the scent of Zara's peachy shampoo. Her eyes teared and her belly ached as if it was empty and she hated life for making everything so complex. She would, she realised, never not miss her daughter, and yet their relationship had always been so fraught and complex and Nancy knew she hadn't been the mother she should have been. She had never, if the truth be told, enjoyed Zara enough. But now she was leaving, in dribs and drabs, and it was like someone was ripping the heart out of her chest, which was not how she'd expected to feel.

Her feelings towards Zara had always been complicated; total immersive love on the one hand and a suffocating weight of responsibility on the other. Taking pride in moments and then losing days to nothing. Shutting doors, opening others, always feeling left behind, never catching up. And on top of it all, like a bow round a present, a deep, searing guilt that nothing she'd ever done was enough.

When Zara was a baby and Robert left in the mornings she always wanted to fall at his feet and beg him to stay, in fact she did a few times. What is wrong with you? he would say. Why do you find it so hard? in a way which did little to hide how much he hated her at those times, almost as much as she hated herself. And why had she found it so hard? So all consumingly impossible, so that sometimes when she was pushing Zara in her pram she would feel as if she was shrinking and disappearing and that soon she would fall through the cracks in the pavement.

Every single little thing became hard, from the moment she opened her eyes to the moment she slept again at night. She was so tired it felt like an illness; all her muscles ached, her mouth was dry and her head pounded, constantly, incessantly. All day alone with Zara she felt sure she was going to pass out and that when she did Zara would scream for hours, or fall over, or get stuck, or drink bleach, or a million other deadly scenarios.

In the end her head buzzed all day and she cried all night and Robert sent her to a health farm. He drove her there himself and she felt like the car was so alive with anger she didn't dare speak. Then when they got there she was sure the place was more of a loony bin than a health farm and was sure there were secret doctors behind secret doors. She screamed at Robert in the room they'd given her overlooking the garden, accusing him of lying to her and trying to get her committed. He had stood at the window with his hands in his hair and said, 'I just don't think I can do this for much longer. You are mad. Totally fucking crazy.'

Yes, she remembered now, lying on Zara's bed – Zara who had somehow grown and prospered despite having her as a mother – those were the last words he'd said to her before she'd spent two weeks in a dressing gown with other similarly unhinged people. She'd always worried about going mad, but it had been an abstract worry, which was somehow confirmed by those fourteen days. Certainly, whilst at the health farm, the more Nancy thought about it the more likely it seemed that Robert must be right – she didn't appear to use her mind in the same way as other people and that must mean it was defective. Which meant that it was imperative she control it, otherwise bad things could happen to Zara, she could even be taken away from them.

Nancy scanned the walls of Zara's bedroom, covered with photographs, concert tickets, foreign train tickets and dog-eared posters and wondered if it might have been better for Zara if she had been taken away. If she hadn't had to witness her mother's volatility and dissatisfaction, instead of just being happy with a lot so much better than most other people's. Robert might have been right all those years ago because surely only someone mad would have spent the last year as she had?

Except she didn't think that was the whole story and another memory from the health farm worried at her brain: how, during her stay, she'd worked out that all she needed to do was go back to work. Maybe not full time, but she was sure the magazine she'd been working on would let her do three days a week. She had to get back into the world and speak to other adults on a regular basis, buy sandwiches for lunch, sit in parks in the sun on her own, visit galleries, meet friends for drinks. It was not possible to exist only as the servant of a small, tyrannical being, however much you adored them. It had seemed like a fantastically simple solution to Nancy, sitting by the side of a swimming pool that stunk of too much chlorine, but it had calmed the buzzing in her brain, so she slept through the nights and the days ticking down to her departure stopped being scary, even something to look forward to.

Robert had employed some sort of nanny while she'd been away and, on the drive home, he told her Zara was now sleeping through the night, which made her feel odd. Putting her to bed that night Nancy had felt her infant daughter almost turn away from her and there had been something unnerving about leaving the room while she was still awake and not hearing her cry. She loitered outside Zara's room for a while until Robert walked past and asked what she was doing.

'I can't believe she doesn't need me to rock her to sleep,' Nancy said, her voice a bit choked.

Robert arched an eyebrow. 'But that's good, isn't it? You were always complaining about the wasted time before.'

'Oh, I know. It just feels weird as well. Like she's breaking away from me or something.'

'I thought that's what you wanted.'

'Not exactly.' Although what she had wanted, what she did want, suddenly wasn't entirely clear to herself either.

Robert shook his head. 'God, you're complicated. Can't you just be happy that she's finally sleeping?'

Nancy followed Robert to the kitchen to eat the supper he'd prepared, which made her feel like a visitor in her own life. He'd cooked cod with rice, a bizarre offering that looked totally anaemic on her plate and stuck in her throat when she tried to swallow.

'You do look better,' he said. 'You've put on a bit of weight. You don't have that haunted look any more.'

'Thanks.'

'Oh, you know what I mean.'

Nancy pushed the over-cooked fish around her plate with her fork. It was true she'd eaten better at the health farm, because she'd felt hungry, but now the familiar sickness had settled itself back in her stomach and she couldn't imagine finishing a plate of food again. 'I did a lot of thinking while I was away.'

'That sounds ominous.'

Nancy looked up to see if Robert was joking but he didn't appear to be. 'I think I should go back to work.'

He returned her gaze then, his fork halfway to his mouth. 'Why on earth would you do that?'

Her stomach felt cold. 'Because I want to.'

'But we don't need the money.'

'Do you work just for the money?'

He ate his forkful. 'Well, no, but that's different.'

'Different how?'

'In that I have to work to pay the mortgage and everything, so it would be pretty shit if I didn't enjoy it. Unless that's what you'd like. Me to go to a job I hated every day so I could feel your pain.'

It was like he'd slapped her. 'Why would I want that? You can't honestly think I'd want that.'

Robert pushed his plate away from him and sat back in his chair. 'I don't know what you want, Nancy. I don't think you know what you want.'

'But I've just told you.' She felt like they were speaking different languages and that understanding was too far away.

He snorted. 'Oh for fuck's sake. You want to pay someone to

look after our child so you can what, go and feel good about yourself?'

She felt like she was losing the thread of the argument. 'Not entirely. But would that be so bad anyway? I mean, I'm not talking full time.'

They looked at each other across the kitchen table and Nancy felt the air shift. Sometimes she thought their hatred was enough for one to stab the other with a kitchen knife.

'So I take it the last two weeks haven't changed anything,' Robert said. 'I mean, you're still just as dissatisfied as before.'

'Oh God, Robert.' She felt a fizzing sense of desperation. 'I wish you could do a week of my life. Then perhaps you wouldn't be so fucking sanctimonious about me wanting to work.'

'I do get it. I couldn't do what you do.'

'Men always say that, as if women have some innate capacity to become a domestic drudge. We find it as hard as you would, you know.'

'I'd hardly call your life a domestic drudge.'

There was little she could do to stop her voice rising this time. 'Christ, are you talking about the very occasional times I meet my friends or have my hair done or something? We all have to have something that isn't work. What would you call your dinners or meeting friends in the pub?'

He looked tired round the eyes. 'So Zara's work?'

It was like there was an explosion building in her chest. 'Are you being deliberately obtuse? Of course she's fucking work. But that doesn't mean I don't love her completely.'

He rubbed his hands over his face. 'I don't understand why you find it so hard.'

'As opposed to whom?' The anger was swelling but Nancy kept her voice calm because she knew the last two weeks would give Robert license to always call her mad and she couldn't let him do that now. 'I honestly think you have some fantasy that those boring dinner parties we go to are real life. That all those women chatting and laughing and seemingly effortlessly producing coq au vin and Pavlova are like that all the time. Don't you realise that most of the men who come to our house probably go home wishing their wives were like me? None of us shows our real selves, Robert. Please tell me you know that.'

He sat back and held up his hands and Nancy knew what he said next would be designed to throw her off balance and question herself in some way. 'You know what, Nance, I don't need a lecture on women's lib. I'm not some Neanderthal like my father. Are you sure you're feeling OK?'

Her hand tightened against the stem of her wineglass with the effort it took not to throw it into his face. She spoke evenly, knowing if she shouted now he would have won. 'Don't do that, Robert. Don't ever question my mental health because I am disagreeing with you.'

'I wasn't.' But he looked sheepish. 'What about when we have another baby?'

She was sipping her wine as he spoke and she nearly choked. 'What?'

'I mean, if you're working, when we have the next one, won't that be really hard?'

'Another baby?' She looked at her husband and wondered if he knew anything about her at all. Or her him. Or if they were just two bodies existing within the same space. 'Robert, I am never having another baby.'

'Well, not now. But, I mean, in the next couple of years.'

She couldn't help a laugh blaring out of her. 'No, no, never.'

'But why?' He looked crestfallen, like a little boy.

'Because it is far and away the hardest, most terrifying thing

I have ever done. I never knew it was possible to love someone so much and that love like that is actually the scariest feeling in the world, because you spend all the time worrying about it being taken away.'

'What?'

But she was on a roll now and the anger balloon in her chest had burst. 'And, by the way, I'd want another baby if I were you. Because quite apart from the love shit, which you clearly don't feel, you don't have to get so fat you can't go up the stairs without getting out of breath, you don't have to develop piles and then push the damn thing out of your fanny. You don't have to spend the following year in a state of constant exhaustion because it won't sleep. You don't have to contemplate four years hard labour after that in parks and playgroups, or mashing food that gets thrown across the room.'

'Christ, Nancy.'

'And it's not even just about Zara and what I feel for her, but what I feel for me as well. I look back at my life sometimes and think I've never made any real choices. You know, I went to university because I was clever enough and that's what you did, then I did nothing with my degree, then I married a man who was always going to become rich and successful, then we had a child.'

'You talk like you've been sent down a coal mine.' She wanted desperately to slap him but knew he would have somehow won then.

Nancy sucked in some air. 'I'm not saying I have it so bad. I just want something different. And I don't even know what that thing is yet. I just know it's not this.' And that had been the truth; there was something else out there, that still encompassed everything she had, but somehow included more. It wasn't that she thought that something would be better than what she had now, but by including it in her life, everything would be better. She just didn't know what that something was, even though she could feel it like a presence on her skin.

Nancy's phone buzzed, returning her to the present, so she hauled herself off Zara's bed and went into her study where she was rewarded with a text from Howard: **Can't wait to see you tonight. I feel like I hardly exist when you're not with me.** She deleted it immediately and then had to sit because she felt like she might fall if she didn't. The naked trees in her garden looked menacing, clawing against the granite grey of the freezing sky. She hadn't known a winter as harsh as this in years, which felt right and was almost comforting, as the seasons seemed to have vanished over the past few years, which spoke to Nancy of an erosion of meaning. She hoped for snow, snow that would pile and flatten and deaden, so that everything appeared fresh and silent. Although of course snow like that didn't exist any more, especially not in London, where it was always insipid and grey and slushy.

The phone in her hand rang, making her jump, but it was Zara's name on the screen, so she swiped gratefully. 'Hello, darling,' she said brightly. 'How are you?'

'I don't feel very well, Mum. How can you tell if you're coming down with flu or if it's just a cold?'

'Well, have you got a temperature?' Nancy involuntarily put her hand to her own forehead as she spoke. Zara had been offered a meningitis jab last year and now she couldn't remember if she'd had it, but didn't want to worry her by asking.

'I do feel a bit clammy.'

'What about a headache? Do you feel sick?'

'Not really. My head hurts a bit.'

'Where are you?'

'Just in my room. But I've got this essay I have to finish and a tutorial in an hour.'

I love you, Nancy wanted to say, but found she couldn't get the words out. I have been lying on your bed because I miss you so much.

'It won't matter if you miss one tutorial, especially if you ring and explain.'

'Yes, but the essay.'

'The best cure for a cold is lots of rest, drink lots of water and stay warm. Maybe you can write in bed?' Somehow, Nancy thought, she'd become a mother without realising it.

'Yeah.'

'Is everything else OK?'

'Uh huh. What are you doing?'

'Oh, just a bit of work. I'm having dinner with Ellie later.' The house is so quiet without you, she wanted to add, I feel you everywhere, sometimes I hear you call my name, but something like embarrassment stopped her. Or maybe it was subtler than that, maybe it was not wanting to put any pressure on Zara to call or come home if she didn't want to.

'Give her my love.'

'I will. And call me back if you feel worse. I can always drive up, it's not far.'

Zara laughed. 'I don't think it's that serious.'

She felt disappointed, because there was nothing she would like more than to see Zara at that moment. She could cancel everything tonight and even Howard would understand. 'OK, well, I'll call you tomorrow to see how you're feeling.'

'OK. Thanks, Mum.'

'Bye, love.'

'Yeah, bye.'

Nancy held the silent phone in her hand and wondered if

saying goodbye to Zara was always going to feel like this, even when she was grown and permanently away from them, with a life of her own. She thought tomorrow when she called she would tell Zara she loved her at least. And she can't have been what she continually feared, that bad a mother, if Zara was still calling her with little worries.

She rang Robert because the house was too silent then, but he sounded irritated when he picked up. 'Are you OK?'

'Yes, I just spoke to Zara. She's got a cold.'

'Oh.' Nancy knew he was doing something else. 'He hasn't called again then?'

'No.'

'Right. Are you still going out for dinner?'

'Yes.'

'To that Greek place?'

'Yes.'

Robert hesitated, but then. 'You would tell me if you were seeing him, wouldn't you?'

Nancy's heart caught in her throat. 'Yes, of course. I'm not. I don't want to.' At least the last part was true.

She could hear how his breathing had quickened down the line and she realised, suddenly, just how angry he was. How in fact his calmness was because he couldn't let himself get angry, it would be too dangerous. And for the first time she felt scared, of what Robert could do.

'I'll see you later,' he said, and then put the phone down before she could reply.

She sat very still at her desk then, with the day lengthening and darkening and thought how Robert's calm anger had often stopped her without her realising. How that was the real reason she hadn't got a job until Zara was ten, long after she'd needed to be around all the time. It had been nothing to do with buying

Coombe Place and all the years she spent distracting herself with paint charts and antique shops. Nothing to do with her father being ill and helping her mother. Nothing to do with the charity boards she'd sat on or the dinner parties she'd given or whatever else she'd used to paper over the cracks in her life.

The accepted wisdom about her and Robert was that he loved her very much, that he adored her in fact, which on many levels Nancy knew to be true. He had proved this to her so many times over their marriage, meaning good even when he was getting it wrong. He had always tried to include her in his life, always tried to pull her out of her thoughts, always looking for ways to make her laugh. She knew what they looked like as a couple, why hundreds of people had turned up for their wedding, why they were invited to dinner parties, why even Eleanor could look misty eyed when she spoke about them. But she knew also that many compromises had kept them in this space, compromises that mainly she had been required to make.

They had lived, she realised, by Robert's version of the truth, which wasn't necessarily bad, but it was different to her version. He made her feel wrong, he made her doubt choices and thoughts that differed from his. And for the first time she understood part of why she had embarked on this crazy affair.

It had simply been the wrongest thing she could do and that had been thrilling and amazing for a while. It had been like a mind-bending drug, a euphoria beyond compare, a true ecstasy. Looking back, it had been nothing to do with desiring another person, simply the danger of the whole thing. Nancy thought she should find a way to tell this to Robert. Maybe they could start their relationship over, not entirely, but just those fundamental things that grated and tore at them until they both felt bloodied and bruised.

They had spent the past month being properly kind to each

other and it had reminded her that they did love each other very much. They had been able to stop the sniping and griping because they had confronted the ugliest version of themselves and still clung on. They needed each other because their differences were what made each of them understand themselves. But life without Robert, she now saw, would be impossible, just as life without her would be impossible for him. It filled her with a kind of warmth, the thought that everyone had been right and they actually held a grand passion for each other, like all the best love stories.

But that realisation also made her sad, because it made her see that she'd probably possessed the missing part of herself all along. She remembered one of the first times that she'd slept with Howard and how he'd kissed the entire length of her body, before saying to her 'you're my heroine'. The words had driven into her, as if he'd drilled holes into her body and shone warm light into all her dark places. Although now that seemed like such a pathetic thing to want to be, a heroine, and maybe she'd already been one anyway. Or maybe being someone else's heroine was never going to be anyone's answer?

The day, which had never achieved what you might call lightness, had almost folded over itself back into darkness, so Nancy went down to the kitchen to make herself tea. Her stomach felt cavernous, but she couldn't be bothered to make anything, so she picked at some pieces of ham and cheese as she stood by the open fridge. She would take better care of herself after all this was over, she thought – when they got to the country, perhaps she could grow vegetables and make jams, although the thought made her laugh out loud.

The other thing she was going to do was rekindle her friendships with Mary and Eleanor. She knew that now she really just irritated Eleanor and, because she hadn't told Mary anything about the past year for obvious reasons, they had drifted. But she longed for her friends with a strange passion. She longed to make Eleanor laugh again, her kind face cracking like it used to and her infectious laugh bubbling out of her. And she longed for all Mary's idiosyncrasies, her encyclopaedic knowledge of the classics, her deep thinking, her passion for her children.

She wished in fact that they could forget all about men and live together again, like they had at university when they shared a draughty house that smelt of cats and damp. The first winter they spent there had been freezing, as cold as it was now, she was sure it had even snowed. The heating had naturally broken and, to keep warm, they'd dragged their mattresses into the sitting room so they could sleep in front of the fire. She remembered all their lean, long limbs splayed out before her, how she'd woken many nights to find an arm slung across her chest, or to the sounds of Ellie whispering in her sleep. She remembered how they all smelt of the same coconut body cream Mary used, how their breath fogged the windows in the mornings, how they borrowed make-up and clothes until nothing belonged truly to anyone. She remembered The Carpenters washing over everything they said, hot toddies drunk out of cheap glasses, chips eaten out of vinegar-soaked paper.

She also remembered a conversation between Mary and Eleanor very late one night about the Bangladeshi Liberation War in which they'd discussed how women had been raped as an act of war. They'd bandied figures around; impossible, stupid figures – over three million dead, up to four hundred thousand raped – figures that didn't make sense. As Nancy listened to them she realised she hadn't even heard of the war, which seemed impossible and shameful. Mary's father hadn't had anything to do with the war but, she realised now, still Mary had always occupied this place of death in her mind, ever since that conversation. Nancy realised that she had always seen her friend in this context, even all these many years down the line. She'd always seen her as a survivor, as someone who got away. But what if she couldn't survive this betrayal, what if Nancy was the person to bring her down?

Nancy stuck her finger into a jar of mayonnaise to stop her thoughts, licking off the cloying goo as the cold of the fridge pulsated outwards. Then she made some tea and took it back to her desk, but the thought of work was defeating now. It was all very well to take refuge in the past and imagine a bright future, but in doing all of that she was ignoring the fundamental question: how had the affair started in the first place? She felt the familiar whooshing through her gut as the thoughts began to circle and enclose her. Because who the hell had she been kidding, thinking that something good was going to come from this disgusting mess? Surely she knew enough about life to know that wasn't going to happen, to know that it had to end badly. She felt her mind detach slightly from her body, so that she was both separate and part of herself, so she could both exist inside herself whilst hating every aspect of her being.

Come on, her mind taunted, you are nothing more than a selfish whore. There were no underlying motives. You did this for no other reason than you could. Admit it. Nancy groaned and lay her forehead on her desk. The thoughts had her now and they would spare her nothing.

Could it be possible that the offer of distraction from herself was all it had taken to make her turn her back on her whole life? And if that were true then what sort of person was she? Her neck was aching from the strange position she was in, sitting on her chair with her head on her desk, but she didn't move because the ache was better than the thoughts, although they still found the necessary pathways.

She didn't think it had been as base as sex either. It was true that she'd never had better sex, but she still slept with Robert, he made her come, it wasn't infrequent. And besides, she had gone to the flat that first time not knowing what the sex was going to be like. No, her betrayal had been mental and that was probably worse.

Howard had been like a bomb in her so-called perfect life, a life which up until then she had slightly sneered at, even found predictable and boring. Except surely that simply revealed a lack of imagination on her behalf. She could have made anything of the life she had both been given and created and yet she chose to spend most of it feeling sorry for herself, stuck in her own whirring mind. He had been like that pill she'd always claimed to want: one which just made everything bearable. Because if you set fire to enough things, if you shake yourself enough, if you hold your hand over the flame, if you make your heart beat faster, well, then the continual agitation stops feeling like fear and begins to feel like excitement.

In the beginning Nancy thought he had lived up to her expectations. She'd been enveloped, enraptured, entranced by him to such a degree it was like she'd taken a massive dose of Vicodin and all the rough edges of the world had been smoothed away. Even when she wasn't with him she felt like she was floating, like a better person, and she thought it couldn't be this simple – just love. Because that is what she'd thought she must feel for him; surely nothing else could make you feel this connected and at one with the world. And she was so much nicer, to Robert, Zara, her friends. As long as you didn't count Mary, who she couldn't bear to see, or even speak to, so she found herself ignoring her calls and making excuses not to meet.

But for the first few months even that guilt had been possible to suppress because Howard overrode everything. He'd made her feel ten feet tall, as if he gave her the power to do or be anything. We're different from normal people, he told her, and she chose to believe him. He devoured her, told her he ached for her, said he dreamt about her, begged her to leave Robert and start a new life with him. And some days she imagined that might be possible, saw a cabin in American wilderness in which they would lie under bearskins and fuck for sustenance. Some days no one else seemed to matter, they faded in her mind to mere outlines and she imagined she could live without them. Some days she really thought she might do it. Until she remembered everything she stood to lose.

Often it felt like she had to tell someone what was going on, almost as if it couldn't be real unless someone else knew about it. She wanted to share herself with the world, like there was too much inside her to contain. But mostly she wanted to tell people about what was happening to her because it just seemed like too much joy to keep secretly inside her.

Now, of course, Nancy desperately regretted telling Eleanor, the only person she had said anything to, and probably the stupidest person she could have confided in. But at the time she told Ellie she had managed to separate David and Howard so completely in her mind that it wasn't until she saw Eleanor's reaction that she remembered this betrayal was not just about Robert. Eleanor's disapproval was instantly palpable, but she reserved judgement by asking practical questions, wanting to know who he was and what she was going to do about it, which made Nancy realise that she'd forgotten what it was like to live in the black and white world she used to occupy, in which nothing seemed special or unusual. In the end, mainly to shut her up, Nancy told Eleanor two partial lies: she'd met him at a work thing and his name was David.

Nancy knew she didn't deserve Eleanor's sympathy, and

perhaps it wasn't even surprising that Eleanor was finding it hard to be kind now she'd crashed and burned, like predicted, but Nancy did wish her old friend could find it somewhere in her heart to wrap an arm around her shoulder now and then. Because this prolonged ending had been, was, terrible. Nancy stood from her desk and went into her bedroom to stand in front of her wardrobe and try to find the right thing to wear. She didn't want to look in any way seductive of course, but nor did she want to appear low and depressed. Howard read something into everything and she had to strike the perfect note tonight to get him to realise she was serious and to get him to let her go. Her hands ran absentmindedly over her clothes and they felt momentarily like falling leaves.

It had been, when all was said and done, a form of madness; a madness that had enveloped her physically and emotionally. Looking back she could hardly believe the things she'd done – letting him kiss her in parks and take her to restaurants where her friends might see them. Fucking him in the afternoons and not washing him away, so that Robert could have smelt him on her. Taking him into their bed when Robert was away on business and Zara was at Oxford.

Perhaps the worst of it though had been that she hadn't stopped him criticising Mary. She'd never agreed with or added to his laments, but she hadn't stopped him. She had instead listened, without comment, to his litany of criticism of one of her oldest friends. She'd let him say things about Mary which now made her skin crawl; like how disgusting he found her skinny body, or how boring she'd become since she'd had the kids and got totally obsessed with them, or how she didn't understand that he was a free thinker and sometimes needed space, or how she lived in a world filled with petty moral rules which didn't take creativity into account. Sometimes she had even found herself internally agreeing and wondering what had happened to Mary and why she let herself exist in such a small life. Someone had once told her that everything is a competition, but where last year she had thought she was winning, Nancy now knew how very close to losing she really was.

She decided on a pair of black trousers and a grey jumper with a white shirt underneath, but she felt defeated by the idea of make-up and doing her hair and so she just scraped it back into a ponytail and made do with a bit of mascara. She knew she looked rough, her skin sallow and her eyes ringed with bunged greying skin, but she also found she didn't care, which she knew wasn't a good sign. If she wasn't careful life could come to feel like a chore again and she would have to drag herself through daily tasks that shouldn't feel hard. Nancy had once asked Robert if he ever felt like that, but he'd looked at her with wide eyes and she'd known he hadn't and that the fault lay within her and not the outside world.

'The reason you feel dissatisfied with life is because you're not normal,' Howard had said to her once over dinner in a crowded Japanese restaurant in Soho. 'You're a goddess and should be treated accordingly.'

She'd laughed, even though the assessment had felt cathartic. 'What, I should lie on a sofa and be fed grapes?'

He'd run his foot up the inside of her calf under the table. 'Yes, partly. But not a sofa, you should be high up, above us all deciding our fates.'

Nancy had continued laughing, but something about his words had felt ominous and then she'd remembered how Mary always said that being a goddess in Greek mythology was always the worst role. How they were all either passive or being punished or raped or falling from grace. She wondered then at the casualness with which Howard had mentioned goddesses, when that was

Mary's world, and did that reference really not jolt him like it had her?

And then Mary was simply there, standing on the narrow table between them, except it was Mary from nearly thirty years before, and they were in their student house getting ready to go to a party, jostling in front of a mirror. 'The truth is,' Mary said as she outlined her lips in a coral red, 'I'm starting to realise that goddesses are only there to teach us lessons, and yet that's what little girls are taught they should want to be. I mean, we think of Medusa as this vicious monster, but she was punished by Athena for being *raped*. And Athena was born out of Zeus' head because he swallowed her pregnant mother. Because he was angry with her. Goddesses are a false myth. The definition of bloody suppression.'

'Down with goddesses,' Eleanor chanted from somewhere behind them, but Nancy remembered she hadn't known what to think, or what to believe, that in truth she still didn't know what to think or believe.

The taxi was late, which was maybe why she felt jittery, although she knew it wasn't. She sat back against the leather seats and watched the dark streets filled with people wrapped against the cold, hurrying home. Please, God, let it end tonight, she said to herself, like a mantra. Because the thought of this all continuing was too much, more than she could bear. She wasn't strong enough to field the phone calls any more or to keep hiding so much from Robert. If it continued, something would crack and her sordid, terrible secret would leak out into the world like an oil spill in the ocean.

Nancy felt a pain building in her chest and had to swallow down some tears. She simply could not imagine Robert's anger if he were to find out that the other man was Howard.

Robert had found the incriminating letter about a month ago now. They'd been in Sussex and had just finished decorating the Christmas tree, ready for Zara's return the following weekend. The night had been dark and blowing outside and Nancy had allowed herself a minute away from her problems as she'd sat in the warm glow of the fairy lights, the fire warming her legs, a glass of red in her hand. But then Robert walked into the room and she'd known something terrible had happened by the way he stumbled slightly and the glazed look in his eyes.

She'd immediately thought of Zara. 'What's wrong?'

He hadn't answered, instead coming to sit in the other chair by the fire, letting his head drop forward and his hands rest on his knees. She'd seen the letter then, the one that Howard had put through their front door only the day before, which she'd found on the mat when she'd come in from food shopping and it had made her retch in the downstairs loo, the thought of Robert coming home before she had. She'd read it and then stuffed it deep into her handbag, meaning to burn it or something, not wanting to trust it to the bin.

Robert was holding the letter between a thumb and one finger, as if it was contaminated, and she'd thought she was about to die. She should have been brave and said something, but she found she couldn't, as if she was pinned to the spot. 'I found this,' he said eventually. 'I was looking for the bloody Nurofen you always have in your bag and I found this.'

'Oh God, Robert, I am so sorry.'

He looked up at her and it seemed as if the jelly of his eyes was shaking. 'Do you want to tell me what's going on?' She found her only response was to start crying, her hands over her face. But he pulled them down. 'You're not going to get away with it that easily.'

He was right, but she still wanted him to make her feel better. 'It's over.'

'It sounds like he's not too happy about that.'

'He isn't.'

Robert looked down at the disgusting paper. 'No, because you two are above petty morality.'

She had to stifle a scream as she could not listen to Robert recite the awful words. 'Oh God, Robert, please don't.'

'How long has it been going on?'

'Not long, a couple of months.'

'Who is he?'

'No one, really. You don't know him.'

'How did you meet then?'

'Through work. It was a moment of madness, I regretted it as soon as it started.'

She sat very still and watched Robert's shoulders moving with his breathing. 'Do you love him?' His voice caught on the words, which gave her hope. It made Nancy realise how much she didn't want to lose her husband, how totally he was part of her, as if he existed in the marrow of her bones.

'Oh no, not at all, Robert. I promise you, never.'

'Then why?'

'I don't know. I think I was flattered or something stupid. Or maybe Zara leaving home affected me more than I admitted to myself.' She felt grubby for using their daughter as some pathetic excuse.

'Christ, I hate Zara not being around, but it hasn't made me want to fuck someone else.'

Nancy felt the tears building again. 'Are you going to leave me? Because I don't think I could bear it if you did. I think I would die.'

He laughed without mirth. 'Of course you wouldn't die. And I should leave you, but I expect I won't.'

The relief drained through her, leaving her feeling weak and shaky. 'It didn't have anything to do with us, I never thought about leaving you,' she lied. Although how she had ever even considered that was already so far beyond her powers of comprehension that those thoughts felt like they belonged to another person.

'What did I do so wrong?' He leant his head forward, his voice weak and low.

Nancy wanted desperately to kneel at his feet and take him in her arms but she didn't dare. 'Nothing. Don't be silly. You've always been amazing.'

'But then...?'

'It's me. I don't know what's wrong with me. I can't seem to be happy.'

He looked up at that and she saw the spark of recognition in his eyes. Keeping Robert might well involve admitting to being the person he'd always suspected her to be, but which she knew she wasn't. A tiny thread of anger shot through her, making her want to tell him that in many ways he had eroded her so much she'd been forced to do something this destructive. But he spoke first, 'You've always been like that. Always fought against making things easy.'

He was right, it wasn't just him, she had always been like that. He might have made it worse with his constant rightness, but he probably wasn't entirely to blame. 'I know. I don't know why.'

'I suppose I'm not the easiest person though. I want to understand you better, but I find it so hard. I mean, I look at you and all the things you've achieved and I just don't understand why you can't be happy.'

Nancy's stomach was an empty cave filled with stagnant water, which she could taste on her breath. 'Do you think there's something fundamentally wrong with me?'

'I don't know.' The admission was so bald she wanted to scream.

They sat in silence for a while and she thought about the time after Zara was born, her dissatisfaction with her lot all through Zara's school years, her annoyance at builders who were only making her a dream house, her desire for work which she never quite fulfilled, then getting a good job and finding it hard and stressful when it was really anything but. And now this. It was like taking a match and setting fire to her life. She heard herself gasp before she could stop herself.

But underneath all that there was also the knowledge that she wasn't wrong for wanting something different. Women in this world are still expected to conform, even though it doesn't seem like that any more. You can be many things in this life, but a dissatisfied woman is not one of them. What's wrong with you, men ask, as they push forwards, why aren't you happy back there, why isn't it enough? Pimps say it to their hookers in the same way rich men say it to their wives, in the same way bosses say it to their employees, in the same way fathers say to it mothers. Sometimes we just want something different.

Robert held out his hand, which she took, letting herself fall to the floor between his legs. He pulled her up so she was sitting on his lap, where she wrapped her arms around his neck and buried her face in his shoulder. All her thoughts of a minute before fell away. My God, she loved him, she could almost feel the force of it in her body. It was like they had been together for so long she had forgotten it, but the thought of losing him rampaged through her blood.

'I could never let you leave me,' he said from somewhere above her. 'I think I'd rather you died than left me.' They made love then by the fire and again in bed later and that had been the beginning of their desire, as if their bodies were the only places they could properly tell each other how they felt.

The next morning she did something she'd never done before and went to church on her own, out of some bizarre sense of penance. She stood in the cold, empty room and sung uplifting hymns with the four other people in attendance. She listened to the vicar's sermon on sin and redemption which seemed to have been written especially for her and was filled with a sense of purpose. She picked up one of the hand-drawn cards in the nave, dropped a five pound note into the honesty box and took it home, where she wrote a desperate note to Robert sitting at their kitchen table, before she even took off her coat: *I am sorry, Robert darling, forever and completely sorry. I don't mean to make you so sad and angry. I know I must try harder and I know how frustrating I am. I think I forgot back there all we are, all we always have been. Please be kind to me.*

She didn't know where Robert was, but the house seemed still and empty, so she took the card straight to his study. She knocked but there was no answer, so she went in and left the card on his desk. The letter was lying face up and she couldn't stop herself reading it again, which made her want to scrunch it into a little ball and throw it in the river that ran at the bottom of their garden. It seemed impossible that she had ever let this man into her life and she was washed through with embarrassment that Robert had had to read such pathetic words and think they were associated with her, but she also knew the letter now belonged to him to do with as he pleased.

Robert never mentioned the card to her, but that evening he asked her to sit with him while he worked, so Nancy took the Patricia Highsmith she was reading and sat in the chair next to him, looking up now and then at his steady profile lit by the light of his screen. The card and letter were nowhere to be seen and she was grateful for that. Grateful almost that all of this had happened, because it had exposed something in both her and Robert that felt precious, as if a seam of diamonds ran through their core.

Stuck in traffic in the back of the taxi, Nancy wondered if that's all love was: a deep, dark binding, but with a seam of pure wonder at its heart. For the first time in her life she knew with complete certainty that she didn't want to be Howard's goddess, but nor did she want to be Robert's flawed neurotic. With Robert, she saw now, it would be possible to exist in that middle ground, to just be herself, which was a wonderful, uplifting thought, despite the fact it had taken close to thirty years negotiation to get to this point. But the thorn in the side of it all was of course still Howard and all he could reveal about her. He could make being a goddess or a victim seem appealing, because he had the power to turn her into a demon.

She couldn't stop a moan leaking from her, which made the cabby look at her in the rear-view mirror. He would hate her if he knew what she'd done, everyone would. She wanted almost to lean forward and confess, as it still all seemed impossible to her, as if the last year really had been a magical myth filled with demons and goddesses. It had felt like nothing more than a story she'd been telling herself; one that had only become real when Howard started properly talking about walking out of his life, which had made everything crash down around her.

Yes, they'd spoken absently about running away to the other side of the world, but that was like talking about opening a tea shop in Devon, just one of those fantasies that gets you through dark nights. But as the summer had faded he'd started talking about feeling trapped, which had led on to him saying that he couldn't go on leading this double life, especially not when he felt like his real life was what he shared with her. It had made Nancy properly consider what she was actually doing. Because her first thought had been one of terror at the exposure, a deep desperate fear for no one to know. But if that had never been a possibility, then what they'd been doing was stupid and dangerous, mean and sordid.

Nancy looked out of the taxi window at a rain-slicked London and remembered Howard's pure anger when she'd told him it had to end, an anger that told her she'd misjudged him in some fundamental way. It had made her realise that she'd forgotten their affair was his story as well and he had every right to demand a different ending. That in fact it was also many other people's stories, their partners', their children's, even Eleanor's to some extent. It had implanted tentacles far and wide and everyone would have a different way of telling it, no one was the true protagonist and she was probably doomed.

'You fucking what!' he'd exploded almost as soon as the words had left her mouth and, even though the music in the pub they were in was loud, people still turned to look.

'I just can't take the guilt any more,' she'd said, which was only a small part of the truth. It was strange to think that had only been about eight weeks ago, around mid-November, the pub they were in already festooned with gaudy tinsel and flicking fairy lights which flashed against his pale face, making her feel sickened. Mary almost occupied her by then, to the point that she was sure she saw her most days, turning down street corners or jumping on buses, always just out of reach. She dreamt about her as well, most nights; sometimes Mary was righteously angry, but in others she was beaten and bloodied, holding her hands out desperately to Nancy.

'Guilt,' he spat at her. 'That hasn't seemed to bother you much this past year.'

Nancy clutched her hand round her gin to stop her tears. 'I know. But it has to stop now. I can't bear it.'

'What you can't bear is accepting who you are.' He took a gulp of his black pint and some of the froth caught on his beard. 'I can't believe you're saying this. I mean, I thought you were better than this.'

'I am better than this. That's why I'm ending it.'

But he waved that away. 'No, I mean better than letting society's petty morality get to you.'

She looked at him and momentarily saw a stranger. A very angry man in the place of the one who had held her and whispered to her, promising to make things better. 'But it's not petty. Morality is just another word for decency really, basic human decency. And we haven't behaved decently towards the people in our lives who deserve better than that.'

'Deserve better than.' He snorted. 'God, I hate that phrase. Nobody deserves anything, or haven't you learnt that by now? Life's inherently unfair and shit for most people and it's got nothing to do with karma or any other bollocks.'

'You know I'm not talking in a mystical sense. We have fucked over the people we love the most and they do deserve more than that.'

She saw his face soften and he leant forward over the table. 'Look, it's not surprising you might be getting cold feet now.'

'It's not cold feet.'

'I mean, we're getting to the stage where we're going to have to make a decision. And of course it's going to be messy and horrible for a while, but even a year from now it will be getting better. And we'll be together, which is what we both want.'

She felt a tightening across her chest that felt like proper fear. She looked at him and realised he was serious, he genuinely thought that what he'd just said was a possibility. She kept her voice calm. 'That is simply not going to happen. We would both lose everything. None of our children or friends would ever speak to us again. No one must ever know about this.' Although she regretted her words as soon as she spoke them because she saw his mouth twitch up into a smile; they both knew he had her over a barrel.

'I worship you. And I know you love me really.'

'I don't.'

'Come back with me. One last time.'

She shook her head. 'No, I don't want to.'

But she saw the glint in his eyes that told her who he really was. 'I insist.'

She wanted to put her hands over her head because it felt like the walls of the pub were falling. 'Are you saying if I don't fuck you you'll tell everyone?'

He shrugged. 'I want to help you. I want you to realise how much you love me. I want to love you out in the open.' He looked unhinged as he spoke, his face red and a sparkling sheen of sweat on his forehead.

'I don't think you do love me.'

His anger flashed to the surface, contorting his features for a moment. 'Don't tell me what I feel. What we have together is the real thing.'

'It's passion, nothing more.'

'It's not, it's true love, and you know it. You have to come back with me so I can prove it to you.'

She went back to the flat with him that evening and then cried in the shower afterwards, her whole body aching and tingling. But when she came out smelling of the lavender soap

Howard's friend always had, she promised him she would think about it because she didn't know how else she was going to get out of the flat. That terrible, humiliating situation went on for four horrific weeks, until the night Robert found the letter, which gave her enough courage to tell him she couldn't sleep with him any more. That if he didn't stop harassing her she would kill herself. It didn't even sound melodramatic when she said it to him over the phone because she knew it was true.

'If my choices now are that I have to go on sleeping with you or live in a world in which you've told everyone what we've done, then I choose death, either way.' She'd been sitting at her desk in her study, staring out at the sky which looked like a stretched white fabric, when she said the words, whispering because Zara had come back from university the night before. But she'd meant every word, because if that was her future then she would either have to scrape out her insides every time they met or all the people she loved would hate her. It was not a liveable life either way. She stood as she spoke and looked down out of the window. Her study was right at the top of the house, on the fourth floor, and it would be that easy. Climb on the desk, open the window and jump into oblivion.

Something about her tone must have communicated it succinctly because she heard him splutter. 'Don't say that. God, please.'

'You're killing me,' she said, very simply.

Then she heard him crying quietly down the line. 'I just love you so much. You're everything to me.'

'If that's true you have to let me go.'

She held her breath, waiting for his reply, which came eventually. 'I can't. It's not possible.'

*

211

Nancy was late by the time the taxi had negotiated its way through London's clogged roads, which she always imagined as a dying heart. Eleanor was already there, sitting at a table by the wall, scrolling down her phone. She looked annoyed from her tense posture so, even though Nancy needed the loo, she went straight to the table.

'I'm sorry. The traffic was a nightmare.'

Eleanor put her phone back in her bag. 'Don't worry.'

Nancy sat, while Eleanor poured her a glass of wine. The room felt too full, as if everyone's voices were ricocheting around her head. 'How are you?'

'Oh, you know, fine. I always forget how shit British winters are. There just isn't any light.'

'You're not thinking of going abroad again are you?'

'No, no. I feel too old for all that now. And the business is going well. And you know, it's good to be settled really. It's just that I miss it.'

'Of course you do.' Nancy sipped greedily at her wine. She felt desperately agitated and wasn't sure she could sit still for the time it was going to take to eat her food. She knew she was shifting too much in her seat, while Eleanor seemed so composed and still opposite her. 'Did you have a good birthday? I'm so sorry we couldn't come.'

'Are you OK?' Eleanor asked.

'Oh well, you know.' She heard her voice crack slightly and sipped again at her wine to smooth it back down.

'Is it David?'

Nancy nodded. 'He's still calling.'

'Fuck, Nance. This has been going on for too long.'

Nancy looked up and into her friend's face. Eleanor had always had such an open face. In fact her face had been what had attracted Nancy on that first night at university, made her call over to her even though they'd only met briefly at their orientation lecture. Maybe it was to do with the roundness of her cheeks, or the black bob she'd always had which sort of framed her features, or perhaps her short stature, which made her seem solid.

'I don't really know what to do any more. I wrote him a letter a couple of days ago but it just seemed to make him more angry. I've agreed to meet him after this to try to put an end to it once and for all.'

'But haven't you done that before?'

'Yes.'

'Do you want me to come?'

'Oh God, no.'

The waiter came over and Nancy realised she hadn't looked at the menu. She glanced at it but nothing looked appealing, in fact the thought of food was sickening.

'I'll just have one of your special salads. And another bottle of wine,' she said, feeling Eleanor staring at her.

'You've lost weight,' Eleanor said when the waiter had gone.

'I'm worrying it away.' Nancy tried to laugh.

'I know I've said it before, but don't you think it's time to get the police involved?'

'No. No, I can handle it.' And that was the terrifying thing. Nancy knew she was totally on her own with the situation because of the impossibility of anyone knowing what was going on. She couldn't even tell Eleanor that Robert had found the letter and knew about the affair because, if she did that, then there would be no barrier to her going to the police. And if she went to the police everything would come out and then there would be no point in anything ever again. It felt like all the possibilities and non-possibilities and lies and misrepresentations were whizzing round her brain, so she spent most of the time feeling dizzy. Sometimes, in the middle of the night it felt like she might have found a solution, but by morning it had always crumbled to nothing.

'I know you don't want Robert to find out,' Eleanor said, as if she'd read her mind. 'But he loves you so much, I think he'd forgive you.'

Nancy felt like her throat was closing in on itself and scratched at her raw skin. 'Please, Ellie. I really can't.'

'You look awful.' Eleanor's words sounded harsher than they needed to.

'I'm not sleeping at all.' Her heart raced as she spoke and she knew her mind and body were close to giving up with exhaustion. 'I feel . . .' She searched for the right word. 'I feel totally consumed by the guilt. Like I'll never be free of it. Like everyone can see right through me to what I've done. I should have a scarlet letter on my forehead or something.'

Eleanor sighed so Nancy knew she'd irritated her, again. 'You know you're not the first person to have had an affair, Nance. I don't know why you have to be so bloody melodramatic about it.'

Their food arrived and Nancy looked at Eleanor as the plates were set in front of them, hating her momentarily for her judgment. She wanted to tell her that she'd been conned by a man who was clearly a master manipulator, who got some sexual kick out of exerting power, who had as good as forced her to have sex with him five times since she'd told him it was over and that if he didn't leave her alone she planned to jump out of her study window. But naturally that was impossible and, anyway, she could have just not done it in the first place, so it was all her fault anyway.

'I don't think I'm being particularly melodramatic.' Nancy poured them both more wine, knowing she couldn't stomach even one lettuce leaf. 'It's a fucking horrid situation.'

'Yes, I know.' Eleanor forked another mouthful. 'But it was a choice. I mean, you didn't have to do it.'

'Haven't you ever had a moment of madness?'

'Yes, of course. But not when so many other people were involved.' Eleanor flushed and Nancy realised she was even more irritated than she seemed. 'I mean, I know you don't like to talk about it. But I take it he's married, probably has children?'

Nancy nodded. 'I do hate myself, if it makes you feel any better.'

'That's a stupid thing to say.'

She sat back, feeling like a naughty child.

'Aren't you going to eat?' Eleanor waved her fork at Nancy's untouched salad.

'I feel sick.'

'Oh God, this is insane.'

They sat in silence for a while, the time ticking down, neither of them clearly saying exactly what they were thinking. In the end Nancy spoke. 'I know I'm shit and melodramatic and irritating, you know, Els. And I know I got myself in to this dreadful mess. But I'm finding it really hard to get out of now.' All she wanted at that moment was for Eleanor to lean over and take her hand, something, anything to show she understood or wanted to help in some way.

But Eleanor started eating again, looking down at her plate. 'I don't know how I can help when everything I suggest you say no to. I mean, don't you feel angry with this David? Don't you want to get him in trouble, if that's what it takes? Don't you want to stand up for yourself a bit?'

But Nancy hadn't ever felt anger, apart from at herself, and even that was dissipated. The only emotion she felt with any regularity was fear. 'I don't know. I haven't really thought about it like that.'

Eleanor looked up, her eyes hard. 'You know, Nance, it's sort of always been like this. You always create problems where sometimes there aren't any. I think this affair has been a bit like that. Sort of manufacturing something dramatic and exciting. I'm starting to wonder how much you actually want to end it.'

'Really?' Nancy recognised this ugly version of herself too well and it sunk her further. Although of course Eleanor was wrong and she wanted nothing more than to be out of the situation, except she couldn't articulate that because it opened the door for too many unanswerable questions. 'But if that's true, why do I feel so guilty?'

'Because anyone would feel guilty.' Eleanor sat back and puffed out her cheeks. 'I mean, from where I'm sitting you have a pretty nice life. And you and Robert are good, really. I just don't understand why you did this.'

Nancy drank some more, holding the glass against her chest, not even pretending any more that she might eat something. A normal person, she thought, might feel anger at those words, but she accepted them, just as she accepted Howard's behaviour, because her fear overrode everything else. 'I haven't really got an answer. I wish I could explain it to myself.' Eleanor drummed her fingers on the table and Nancy wondered if she was boring her. 'You know, Robert isn't perfect either, like everyone seems to think.'

'Of course I don't think he's perfect. But he's not bad.'

'He is sometimes.' Nancy didn't really know where she was going with this conversation. He's been manipulative as well, she wanted to say. He's made it impossible for us to live in any other way than his version of life, which wasn't what I would have chosen at all. And he was being kind now and saying many of the right things, but it had taken too bloody long to get there. She knew her relationship had been no more undermining than most, in fact probably much less so, but still it felt unfair that she'd had to go to the end of the world to get him to see her, actually her, Nancy. 'Nobody knows what anyone's really like, behind closed doors.'

Eleanor snorted. 'What, like Howard really brings Mary tea in bed every morning. We might not know the ins and outs, but we have a pretty good idea, I'd say.' It was a shock to hear his name like that and it confused Nancy to the point at which she worried she might just admit everything, her exhaustion now so complete she didn't think she had the mental energy to do anything else.

But then her brain shifted as she looked across at her friend, and the desire to confess vanished as Nancy thought that Eleanor really didn't understand what it was like to live with someone for a very long time. How you knew each other so well that you could always be the most vile, most hateful version of yourself. How most couples never really moved on; how they found the other's weak point and then spent the next forty or so years picking at the same scabs.

'Look, I do love Robert,' she said finally. 'But, Els, you're being quite hard. I mean, maybe I'm just not as self-sufficient and sorted as you. In fact, I know I'm not. And that probably does make me pathetic, but I'm floundering a bit here.'

Eleanor's face didn't crack into the smile Nancy needed. 'I'm hardly self-sufficient and sorted. I doubt the choices I've made all the time. But also, I sort of think we all ultimately make the decisions we have to make, about the big things, I mean. I'm not sure you've ever owned your choices.'

Eleanor's words felt unnecessarily brutal and she nearly challenged her, but the words got lost in her guilt. 'Sometimes I don't think I've grown up properly, not fundamentally. You know that feeling you have as a teenager of not quite being able to believe that you have to do something? Well, I still have it about so many things. In a way I think that's why I've found Zara so hard over the years – I just couldn't accept that I was responsible for another human being.'

Eleanor's brow furrowed like she had a bad smell under her nose. 'Zara's great.'

'I know.' Nancy thought she didn't have the words to make herself understood. She also thought she'd made herself slightly revolting to Eleanor. Which also made her realise that she'd kept a fantasy right at the back of her brain, hidden even from herself, that if it all came out Eleanor would be shocked and angry, but ultimately she would understand and support her. This evening, however, was making it clear that if Eleanor did find out the truth she would never speak to her again. In fact, she would actively hate her. 'Look, I'm sorry,' Nancy said finally.

'You don't need to apologise to me.'

'Yes, but still.'

'You really need to get a handle on this, Nance. It's fucking exasperating being on the other side of it, watching you screw up like this.' Nancy nodded, her eyes filling with tears. 'I'd help you happily, but you seem intent on doing it all on your own.'

'I have to.'

'Well, whatever. I'm just saying you need to do something. At least tell David you're going to go to the police if he doesn't stop calling, even if you're not going to. And if he still doesn't stop then you really need to think about telling Robert and sorting it out. If you really want to end it then you can't go on living like this.'

Nancy's head felt heavy on her neck. 'I know. I will.' Except of course she wouldn't because she couldn't. There was so much about the situation she couldn't tell anyone and it made her feel as helpless as a stranded fish, dying silently on the shore. She looked at her watch and saw it was nine forty-five. 'Shit, I better go. I'm meeting him at ten.'

'OK. Don't worry about the bill, I'll get it.' Eleanor reached for her bag.

'Are you sure?'

'Yes, yes. Just sort out this mess, once and for all, please.'

Nancy stood and realised she was a bit wobbly on her feet, she must have drunk more than she'd thought. She looked down at the top of her friend's head as she rooted in her bag and felt a stab of love for this woman with whom she'd shared so many years. 'I'll call you tomorrow, let you know how it goes.' She willed Eleanor to look up and say something heartening, smile even.

But her head stayed down. 'Yes, great,' she said in to her bag, so Nancy turned and walked back out through the restaurant.

The temperature felt like it had dropped about ten degrees so Nancy pulled her coat more tightly around her, wrapping her arms around her waist. Her teeth were chattering and she wanted nothing more at that moment than to get in a cab, go home and climb into bed next to Robert. She hadn't eaten or slept properly in days and her mind was starting to lose its focus so she could almost feel it crumbling inside her head like wind-blown stone. No, she had to try one more time, she had to beg him to see sense. Perhaps if Howard looked into her defeated face he would realise what he was doing and let her go. She saw the orange light of a taxi and stuck out her hand.

The inside of the taxi was warm and she sat down gratefully, but as she reached out to shut the door she saw a flash of blond hair on a tall, lithe body and her heart leapt because the impression she'd had was of Robert. She flipped round in her seat, as the taxi began to move into the traffic, but the pavement was crowded and whoever it was had been swallowed up by the crowd. She turned back to the front but couldn't stop her heart hammering in her chest, fear breaking onto her skin in little beads of sweat which ran down her body inside her clothes.

She remembered how he'd checked again that afternoon where she was going. What if he'd come to see if she really was meeting Eleanor? What if he was following her now, checking she was on her way home? What if she led him straight to the extent of her crime? Nancy craned round in her seat again but the road behind her was filled with taxis, any one of which could contain Robert, or not.

Her phone buzzed: **I'm here. It's freezing. Do you want to meet in pub?** But she couldn't bear the thought of being seen in public with him, even if there was unlikely to be anyone there they knew, so she replied: **No, stay where you are. 10 mins away.**

She didn't know whom she had betrayed more: Robert, Mary, herself, their children, Eleanor. Everything felt like a jumbled mess inside her brain; as if their lives were a series of interconnecting pathways which crisscrossed each other, ever joined, always over-lapping. She could barely remember who they all were, or where they led to, or why they were even there in the first place. She knew only that she had ruined it all, that she had destroyed all those intricate and delicate lines, which had taken so many years to build, which had run with love, and which she had now poisoned with hate.

It felt colder still when she stepped out of the taxi, onto the dark back road leading to the patch of grass they'd taken to meeting on in the summer, which had felt like it belonged to them almost, in the way that lovers turn everything into something special. It was why she'd suggested meeting there, in the hope that it would remind him how things had been and how if he really did love her he had to help her now. Except it felt sinister in the dark, like a culmination of all the things you are told not to do as a woman. Fear wrapped itself around her like a cloak as she began to walk away from the light of the road, squeezing the life out of her so her breath came in sharp pants. The air was filling with ice that tickled her nose, her short breaths puffing out in front of her like a dragon, which is what Zara used to say when she was little. Her eyes moistened at the memory and in the blurring she saw the pinpricks of white already forming on the grass, promising a cleansing frost.

He was standing next to a bench they'd sat on quite a few times, often with their hands entwined and their mouths snatching kisses. He was dressed for the cold better than she was with gloves and scarf, but still he was stamping on the ground and banging his hands against his arms.

She drew level with him and they stared at each other for a few seconds, as if neither of them could believe quite what they were doing. There are no goddesses, she thought out of nowhere, and we are fools ever to think there are. Mary had been right all along, it was nothing but a false myth, the wrong story she had been chasing her whole life. She saw herself so clearly suddenly, a woman deified for the way she looked, which was nothing to do with her, searching for another way to be herself, and coming up with that most worn desire of all, centrality. And all the while life had sped past her, taking with it all the things that make us complete, all the little moments that make life worthwhile. She was not a goddess or a victim, she was just a normal woman, dazzled by bright lights, afraid of nothing more scary than herself. It was one of those revelations that could change a life, but she'd gone too far, fucked too deeply with her life ever again to have the luxury of thinking about change or renewal.

It was suddenly as clear as the ice that would settle that night that she had nowhere else to go with this, which made her know they couldn't go on pretending in any way any more.

'What's going on, Louise?' he asked, trying to reach for her.

'Don't call me that,' she snapped. 'I'm not Louise and you're not David. It's all been nothing more than a stupid fantasy. We've run away from who we are for too long now. I'm Nancy and you're Howard. We always have been, and, unluckily for us, we always will be.'

He didn't answer and the silence loomed over them. Her vision was pitted with white spots that spoke of an exhaustion so total she wanted to lie down on the cold path and give in to whatever wanted to take her. Everything suddenly seemed hopeless and she had been a fool to think there was a way out. There was no hiding from what she'd done and it seemed suddenly obvious that one way or another, everyone would soon know, which meant she was going to lose everything. She turned her head to look at the wall separating them from the freezing water of the Thames, but knew all at once that she didn't have the courage to jump, either over the wall or out of her study window. She was, in fact, weaker and more desperate than even she had realised and this filled her with a fear so deep it felt like a devil had crawled inside her.

Howard reached for her, but she stepped back, which made him grab desperately at her arm. She opened her mouth to tell him that it didn't matter any more, that nothing good was ever going to happen again. But, even as she registered the anger rampant in his eyes, she heard a crashing noise behind her and turned to see who else was coming, who else hated her enough to be on this freezing, desolate ground.

Someone or something was emerging out of the darkness of the path, their tread so loud it spoke of a recklessness that eroded safety. For a moment it could have been anyone, it could have been a ghost even, but then the figure materialised and she knew it was all over.

'Oh, God,' Nancy said. 'What are you doing here?'

# MARY

Mary nearly didn't answer her phone because she'd just walked into Howard's study and she really had to find the insurance documents. But when she pulled it out of her back pocket she saw it was Eleanor and she'd been trying to get hold of her for a couple of days because she'd sounded strange the last time they spoke and it wasn't like Ellie not to return phone calls.

'Hello, stranger,' she said, walking to the window where she looked out over the rows of small gardens below, everyone's allotted rectangle of green. It was a lovely day, with a bright sun that had attracted people outside. Her neighbours were having lunch in their garden, laughing at the somersaults their little girl was turning.

At first she couldn't work out what she was hearing, but then she realised Eleanor was crying in that totally abandoned way her children had done when they were little. 'Ellie,' she shouted into the phone. 'Ellie, what's happened?'

'I've finished things with Robert,' she gasped. 'And I feel awful. Like I don't know what to do.'

'Where are you?' Mary felt a rising fear building because Eleanor sounded so out of control.

'I'm driving.'

'Driving where?'

'Back from Sussex.'

'What?'

'I went to see Nancy.'

Mary put her hand to her forehead. She couldn't understand what was happening. 'Ellie, calm down, what are you talking about?'

She heard Eleanor take a breath down the line and when she next spoke her voice didn't have the same edge of hysteria, although she was still crying. 'I've really fucked up. I've felt mad this past week. I went to see Davide Boyette.'

'You what? As in the man who might have killed Nancy? What were you thinking?'

'I don't know. And then I had to go to Irena's funeral yesterday. It's all been too much.'

'Oh, Ellie, sweetheart.'

'I've started to wonder if Robert could have been involved in Nancy's death. Actually, I don't know what to think.'

'Robert?' Mary felt like she was having one of those conversations you have with toddlers in which nothing makes sense and everything is possible.

'And then I woke up this morning and I wanted to apologise to Nancy so much I drove to her grave, but Robert was there and we had this bizarre conversation. And I know we can't be together, but I love him.' Her last words sounded as if they were choking her.

'Ellie, you have to calm down,' Mary said, using a voice she reserved for when the girls were fighting. 'Listen to me, this is what you're going to do. You're going to pull off the motorway as soon as you can. Splash some water on your face and drink a cup of tea. Then when you're calm again you're going to drive straight here.' All she could hear was Eleanor snivelling, so she raised her voice. 'Are you hearing me, Ellie? Please do as I say because I am not fucking losing my two best friends in the same year and you are in no fit state to drive.'

'OK,' Ellie said, sounding now as if she was far away.

'I love you,' Mary said. 'We'll sort it out.'

She felt suddenly breathless, so sat at Howard's desk and leant back into his chair. The wall in front of her was covered with curling, yellowed notes and articles that he'd pinned up over the years and his desk was a mess of papers surrounding a decrepit Mac. It was absurd really that he'd always commandeered the small back bedroom like this, when Mimi and Maisie were long past the age at which they should still be sharing. She would sort the place out and reassign the room not just because it was starting to become obvious that Howard was unlikely to ever get better, but things had to change. Recently Mary had begun to feel like his illness had shone a light onto all the things about their marriage that she'd let slide, or pretended to herself didn't amount to anything much. But without Howard's constant emotional presence in her head she was starting to see quite how bad the last decade had been, quite how much it had undermined her, quite what she had let herself become.

She roused herself because, before Ellie arrived, she really needed to make a start at finding the insurance documents; there had to be some clause or something that protected them from what was going on with Howard. Maybe they could at least get his care funded or something, or help with the mortgage, anything really. She stood again and opened the window to let in the warm, soft air and the sound of children squealing, which still made her smile. She began with a search of the drawers, but there didn't seem to be any coherent system; most of it was his random thoughts, or copies of essays he'd written, or teaching schedules from years ago. She briefly scanned a few of the papers as she picked them up, but none of his writings appeared to serve any useful purpose, aside from as a record of his academic life, as if he expected people to still care in years to come. A lot of the essays had been published in obscure journals and periodicals with minute circulations and she wondered at the point of it, wondered more what she would do with it all. The thought made her sad, made her feel like so much of life was a waste, or a distraction, and that nothing really meant anything beyond human relationships. She laughed or shouted at the girls for all the reality shows they watched, but sitting at the desk, she thought maybe she'd got that wrong – maybe all they were doing was looking for what was real amongst the chaos of life.

The third drawer was stuck and she had to stand and jangle it, until it released with a jolt, thudding into her thigh. Papers spilled to the floor so she knelt to pick them up, but once there she saw a brown envelope which had clearly fallen down the back of the drawer and caused the jam. She leant into the dusty opening and pulled it out. There was nothing on the outside, but the inside felt bulky. She knew it wasn't the insurance documents but also that she had to know what it contained. Knew enough about life by then to know that whatever it was wasn't going to be good.

Mary pulled the thick wodge out of the envelope, a piece of paper wrapped around a bundle of mementos. She unfolded it carefully and let everything spill onto the desk: a jumble of receipts and ticket stubs, a pressed dandelion, a lock of blonde hair, a pencil drawing of a heart, a postcard of a reclining nude from the Tate, the wrapper of a chocolate bar, the first page of *A Tale of Two Cities* with the first line underlined torn from a book, the corner of a red silk scarf and a polaroid. Her vision jarred and her hands shook as she touched the back of the polaroid, it's black back raised and livid, like a bruise. She already knew what she was about to see could be her undoing, as her fingers flicked at the corner, daring her to turn it over. Except by then she had already seen Nancy's handwriting on the letter and thought that the words she was going to have to read would probably be worse.

She turned the polaroid, touching as little of the surface as she could and at first she couldn't work out what she was looking at, just a dark mass, maybe hills in twilight. But then she laughed at her naiveté because suddenly there Nancy was, splayed naked across a bed, her legs parted to reveal the red openness of her cunt, a word Mary wouldn't usually use, but which she knew to be totally correct, her stomach rounded behind and her face slightly lifted so you could see the desire rampant in her eyes.

Mary put the letter on top of the photograph and made her eyes focus.

David,

You have to stop contacting me. If you do love me like you say then please do this for me. You are beginning to scare me and I feel myself becoming ill with the worry. I thought spending time apart at Christmas might have given you a bit of perspective, but I see that hasn't happened and I am starting to feel desperate.

I have thought a lot recently, and this is what I have learnt about myself. I am a weak and selfish person. No one else I know would have begun an affair with the husband of one of her best friends. I search back through my memories and try to find a reason as to why I have done such a hideous thing, but nothing is clear, as if my whole mind is shrouded in fog. Can it be as primal as sex? Maybe, but there were many moments when I could have stopped you kissing me that first time and I cannot imagine why I didn't. I remember the thrill it gave me, I remember how you ran your hand up that slit in my dress and how it felt like I was on fire. But still I cannot remember why I let it happen.

I think that I have always been heading for destruction in one way or another. I have sabotaged my happiness for as long as I can remember. I don't know why I do this, but the one thing I do know for certain is that I have no life if I do not have the people I love in it. And these are the people I love: Robert, Zara, my mother, Eleanor and Mary. It's not a particularly long list, but it'll do for me.

If the truth were to come out about us all these people would quite rightly hate me and never speak to me again, which for me would feel like death. But above and beyond that I simply cannot bear to watch these people realise who I am, to see me for the disgusting vile stain I have become. Better by far that they never know and I can silently and completely hate myself for ever more, whilst trying with every fibre of my being to make things right for them.

You are right, by the way, you should leave Mary, whatever happens. I didn't realise it before, but you make her miserable and you are ruining her life. I was totally fooled by you, and I suppose she must have been as well. You should pack a bag and leave for good. It would be hard for her at first, but I will be there to make it all right.

It will always be difficult for a man to

understand what women mean to each other. You would be shocked at the intensity of our feelings.

It only shows me how far from natural human experience I have come that I cannot turn to my friends at this time.

I cannot do this any more.

Leave me in peace, please, I beg you, Louise.

Mary laid her hands over the top of the letter and tried to regulate her breathing, but it was too high in her chest and threatened to overwhelm her and leave her scrabbling on the floor with white pinpricks of light in her vision. She thought of Howard dribbling in his chair downstairs and she thought of Nancy under the ground and it was like a collision of horror in her head, like a ghastly reimagining of everything she thought she knew. She thought she was going to be sick and actually leant over the side of the desk and retched.

The dizziness refused to shift so she dropped her head forward into her hands. A low sound, like a cross between a groan and laugh, escaped her. And then she just felt impossibly stupid not to have connected the dots before now. Howard's devastating illness occurring at the same time as Nancy's death. The fact that she'd known he'd been having an affair in the year before Nancy died. And the name David, which truthfully hadn't even registered before this moment, but now it made complete sense: Howard David Smithson and Nancy Louise Hennessy. David and Louise, her husband and her friend.

She bundled the papers back together and stuffed them back in to the envelope, because she knew she needed time to think about this, knew this wasn't something that should be blurted out. As she pushed the envelope back into its hiding place she couldn't help thinking there was a certain cruel irony to finding out about Nancy in the same way she had found out about so many of Howard's affairs. So often she had been squatting on the kitchen floor removing tissues from pockets before stuffing the washing machine and out had tumbled receipts for restaurants she had never visited or single earrings that matched none of hers, once even a daisy chain. Before she had always scrunched them hard in to her hand and stuffed them deep into the bin. Mary was after all a Greek scholar and with this came the knowledge that even the gods are flawed. Except Nancy was of course different. Nancy required a vengeance worthy of the gods. At that moment she was sure if Nancy wasn't dead she would kill her herself.

As Mary took the stairs slowly on her wobbly legs she felt something loosen inside her, as if the feelings of propriety which had bound her before were unravelling. But this felt also like a filling, as if she was a balloon expanding with air, readying herself for take-off. She suspected that soon she would look down on her life from the height she was reaching and her concerns at keeping everything together would seem as illusory as a child's Lego set when seen from above. She knew she was about to stop caring in the way she had always done, knew she was about to admit defeat sometimes, incompetence often, frustration daily, fear hourly. It was a new sensation, but it wasn't altogether unpleasant. It had a ring of truth and liberation to it, which, Mary thought, had been missing from her life before this point.

Eleanor would be ringing on her door relatively soon and she longed for the absolution of telling her friend everything, but she realised that telling Eleanor would certainly mean involving Robert and the police, no doubt the newspapers. She physically shuddered at the thought of her children exposed in this way, not just to public scrutiny but to the knowledge of who their father really was. In the time it took her to reach the bottom of the stairs she knew with a steel cold clarity that she had to protect them above all else. That, even though it would answer questions for Robert and Eleanor they might never stop asking, no one could ever know what she had just discovered.

She watched Howard for a while from the door to the lounge, her arms crossed tight over her chest. He was sitting in the chair that had become his, his eyes fixed on a point in the distance, his fingers drumming against his knee. A line of spittle was stuck in his beard and his body had withered and shrunk.

She remembered that when Eleanor had arrived to tell her about Nancy, Howard had been upstairs in bed with what she'd then thought was a sick bug; how he had come home the night before after she'd gone to bed and she'd been woken by the sound of him retching over the toilet. She'd hauled herself out of bed automatically, her mothering instincts overtaking her tiredness and the penetrating cold to go and sit on the side of the bath and rub his back while he'd heaved and spluttered. She also remembered how she hadn't been unduly worried, how when they'd passed Marcus's room and she'd seen the open door and the unslept-in bed, she'd been more worried about where her son was than what was going on with Howard.

Mary walked into the room and round so that she was standing in front of Howard, but he didn't stop staring at whatever it was he could see.

'Howard.' Her voice sounded like a sharp bark and it pulled his attention to her. 'What happened to Nancy?'

'Nancy,' he repeated, but she saw the light momentarily turn back on in his eyes.

'Yes, Nancy.' She took a step closer and realised that, thin as she was, he was now thinner and for the first time in their marriage, she was stronger than him.

'Nancy?' He craned his gaze over her shoulder.

Mary wanted to ram her fist into his face, wanted to tear at his skin and shred his nerves. 'She never loved you,' she said instead, turning and leaving the room, his snivelling following her like she still cared.

The girls were both at various Saturday classes and she had no idea where Marcus was so she poured herself a large glass of wine and found a stale packet of cigarettes, which Howard had always kept on top of the cupboard by the window. She opened the back door, even though she didn't particularly want to feel the sun's warmth, and sat on the step. Her thoughts were totally at odds with the sounds of fun and laughter drifting across the fences, as if some lives never got shattered.

The wine and nicotine hit her bloodstream together and for a moment she felt all right. Mary was imbued with such a strong sense of responsibility to her children she knew this was a one off, that by the time Mimi and Maisie walked through the door, she would be normal, she would know what they were having for supper, she would be able to answer their questions, she would even manage a smile. She checked the time over her shoulder. She had three hours before then, three hours in which she was allowed to shake and squirm and try to put the pieces of her life into their new order.

For the first time in years she longed for her parents, which filled her with a deep loneliness, because she barely spoke to them any more. Howard had always found her family difficult and he didn't like to go there or have them to stay, something she'd let happen, because Howard was so good at spinning arguments that it had been easier to acquiesce. Besides, it was true, they hadn't liked him. Her father had even taken her to one side on her wedding day, with Marcus rounding out her stomach, as they'd stood in the front room having a photograph taken and told her there was no shame in being a single mother and the family would do all they could to help, which must have taken so much for him to say, it now made her want to cry. He'd leant in close as he'd spoken, so she'd been engulfed by the rich, spicy scent that clung to him always, as he told her she could move back home to Birmingham, even back to her girlhood bedroom with the crinkled pink coverlet. She remembered physically shivering at the thought, shivering when she'd looked at her sister, Naomi, with Terry and their three kids, all one road away from their parents. How she still shivered at the thought of that now, fool as she was.

She supposed she agreed with Nancy, there was something about Howard that defied reason, that made you do the things you knew you shouldn't. When he had first put his hand on the back of her neck, under her hair, as he stood over her desk, she had known all about his wife Penny and the rules of womanhood. She'd also known that it was a cliché, sleeping with her boss; that she might be jeopardising her dream job at UCL, fresh from her PhD, her head full of knowledge.

'You haven't read *The Divided Self*?' he'd said to her with such surprise on her first day working for him that she'd bought it in her lunch hour and spent the whole of the next weekend wading through it. She'd found it pretty flawed; the whole idea of being ontologically secure was surely a male fantasy. Women couldn't possibly afford to marry their personal and public personas, which must mean that all women were mad, which seemed a pretty persuasive view in society, when Mary thought about it.

When she'd taken Howard his coffee that Monday she told him about her weekend reading. He'd looked up from his desk and laughed, which made her feel like a silly schoolgirl trying to impress her teacher.

'What did you think?' he asked, which made her feel better, because he sounded like he was actually interested.

'I think it ignores some of the most basic aspects of human behaviour.'

He raised an eyebrow. 'Such as?'

'Surely we have to have a public and private face, or there would be anarchy.'

'Which would be a bad thing why?'

She felt impossibly parochial then, remembering all the ways she could shame her parents by saying all the things she thought or felt. 'Because –' she stammered over her words '– because then everyone would know how we feel all the time.' It wasn't exactly what she'd meant to say, but he was making her feel unsure of herself.

He laughed even louder this time, throwing his head back and revealing the open plain of his neck. 'That's a really interesting point. But I don't think you've understood Laing at all.' Mary felt her eyes smart because maybe she hadn't and she didn't want to seem stupid in front of Howard. 'He was revolutionary because he put the patient at the heart of our understanding. He made mental illness into a political issue because if we have to treat the individual rather than a symptom, then the state has responsibility not just for the treatment, but for the prevention.'

Mary nodded, her face now so hot she knew it must be cherry red. She had in fact sort of understood Howard's analysis of Laing, but she still didn't think it meant the concept wasn't ludicrous. She imagined instead a world in which people were free with their feelings and it seemed absurd. But then that was maybe because women thought more than men. She didn't yet know.

'Anyway,' Howard said, looking up at her with a much more

serious face. 'What is it that you feel personally that you wouldn't want, say, me to know?'

'Nothing,' Mary said, way too quickly, knocking her leg against the desk as she left the room.

The first time they'd slept together he'd taken her to the flat of a friend who spent half his year in America, at another university. By then he was going out of his way to make her feel special and as if he valued her opinion, so she had let him kiss her and lay her down on the bed and fuck her. Although let was the wrong word, because she longed for him in a way that made her tremble when he was nearby. She'd worried about all her responses to his touch, worried he would think she wasn't enjoying it, but it wasn't that, it was more that she didn't know how to act with him because it was so different from all those university fumbles. Afterwards, as they'd lain panting on the bed, looking up at the ferns, which bizarrely hung in woven pots above their heads, she'd felt an unfamiliar warmth spreading through her body which she wanted to feel again and again.

Besides, by then he was, without doubt, simply the most fascinating and extraordinary person she had ever met. How was it possible that she'd never read Marx or considered how inherently unfair society was? Howard said her father was part of the oppressed working class and that the rest of her family was slipping down the same hole. The fact that they were immigrants made things worse as they must continually feel like outsiders, which confused Mary who'd been born in Birmingham, her mother so British she had never actually left the country. But she didn't say that to Howard, as one point always led to another and by then he was talking about how he didn't blame them, as a fundamental aspect of oppression meant denying proper education the further down the social system one went. Her father, he claimed, was a classic example of a man who never thought about anything beyond putting food on the table and providing for his family, so became disengaged with politics and the best way to change his lot. Mary wasn't sure this was strictly true, or if her father wanted to change anything, but she found the more she exploited her ethnic, working-class credentials to Howard, the more he wanted to lie next to her.

'Doesn't Penny wonder where you are ever?' she asked one day, after they had been visiting the strange fern flat for about a month. She remembered very clearly the sense of falling she'd experienced, at the thought that Penny had the greater claim on him.

Howard blew smoke rings into the sex saturated air above their heads. 'Not really. There's always another lecture to write anyway.'

'I feel sorry for her.' Her photo sat on a shelf in Howard's office and it showed a sleek brunette, with large, sad eyes and a small smile.

'And that's one of the many reasons I'm falling in love with you,' Howard replied. 'Most women wouldn't be able to see past their jealousy.'

Mary felt turned inside out by his words. She tried to seem grown up by ignoring them. 'Do I have something to feel jealous about?'

Howard leaned over her to grind out his cigarette. 'No, not at all.' He kissed the top of her arm. 'You don't really want to do this, do you?'

'Do what?'

'Discuss Penny.' He looked directly at her as he spoke.

But she did so she went on. 'But, I mean, if you're here with me then you can't be happy with her, so why do you stay with her?'

He swallowed and she worried that she'd upset him, a feeling that fluttered in her stomach. 'I feel very disloyal telling you this, but she can't have children. Our marriage has been over for years really, but she's so sad and I can't make myself compound that by leaving. I've been a coward, I suppose.'

'Oh God, that's awful. You're not a coward.' But then another thought sprang into Mary's mind, one which she felt foolish for never having considered before. 'How old are you?'

'We both turn forty this year. It's made her feel like time is running out for a baby.'

She tried to process this information, as forty seemed impossibly old. She turned onto her side to look at him properly; his tall, lean body was very deceiving and maybe the beard hid other signs.

'How old are you then?' he asked.

'Twenty-eight.'

He reached over and stroked the side of her face. 'We probably shouldn't be doing this. But something about you makes me feel crazy, like none of the usual rules apply.'

She melted into his touch. 'I don't care about age.'

'Would your parents be OK with it?'

She loved that he was thinking in this way, as if they had a proper future together. 'Maybe. I don't know. My sister, Naomi, would actually probably be more shocked than my parents.'

'Mary and Naomi,' Howard said, tracing a finger down her cheek. 'They seem such incongruous names for girls like you.'

She looked for the first time at the brownness of her skin next to the whiteness of his and something about his assumptions smarted inside her. 'You know my mum's white, right? Her name's Sheila and she votes Conservative and works at Asda and goes to bingo on a Friday and really you'd be hard pushed to meet anyone more British than she is.'

'No, I just presumed...' He at least had the decency to blush.

'My dad's from Bangladesh. At least his parents moved over here when he was little, so he's always lived in Birmingham as well, really.'

'That must have been hard.'

'What?'

'Being mixed race growing up in the eighties.'

She laughed then. She had noticed that people always missed the point about what was really hard in life. Or they liked to look at you and think they understood things they couldn't possibly without talking to you. She thought out of nowhere how Ellie and Nancy were perhaps two of the only people she had ever known who had, from the very start, simply wanted to know her, as in what was in her head, not what she represented.

'Do you want children, Mary?' The question was strange and out of context, but she caught the vulnerability in his tone.

'I suppose I do.'

'Suppose?'

'Well, yes, I can't imagine my life without them. It's just they seem very hard work. Naomi's just had twins, so she's got three under five and when I went to visit her last it just seemed like fire fighting. And then I've got this friend, Nancy. She had a bit of breakdown earlier this year, before I met you, after her daughter was born. They said it was postnatal depression, but it sounded pretty terrifying and even though she's better and everything, I wouldn't say she's gone totally back to normal.'

He laughed. 'I can see how you might be ambivalent. Surely you must know someone who's happy with their children?' But Mary didn't and shook her head. 'It's our patriarchal society,' he said, stroking a finger across the rise of her breast. 'So few men understand what it means to have children. Not that long ago lots of men gave their partners a bit of cash once a week for housekeeping and spent the rest down the pub, and sometimes

I think wisps of that attitude still prevail. As a society we don't listen to mothers properly, or understand they still have separate desires.'

She was blown away by what he'd said, but his assessment didn't ring true of either Naomi or Nancy, and she felt the need to defend their choices. 'Terry and Robert are both really nice. I mean, Naomi and Terry don't have much money, but I think they share everything. And I guess Robert's a bit conventional. Nancy said he didn't want her to go back to work.'

Howard shrugged as if she'd proved his point. 'What does he do? I bet he's a banker or something.'

'Actually he's a human-rights lawyer.'

Howard lit another cigarette. 'Still slaving for the capitalist dollar. Money makes monsters out of men.'

'I'd hardly call Robert a monster.'

'You cannot work in the capitalist world and not be turned into a charlatan.'

She sat up, suddenly worried that the ferns above their heads might drop on them. She took the cigarette from Howard's fingers and sucked deeply on it, the intoxicating nicotine streaming through her blood and filling her head. She thought about the fact that both their lips had been wrapped around the same object and was filled with a sudden sense of daring glamour.

Howard looked at her through the smoke and his mouth twitched upwards into a smile. 'God, I love how imperfect you are.'

She felt herself wither slightly. 'That's what you like about me?'

He took the cigarette back. 'Absolutely. Perfect women are so bloody boring. Imperfections are such fun to iron out.' Then he leant up and kissed her again and her head swirled with all the things he was which were so different from everything she'd ever known.

That weekend she'd met Nancy at the National Gallery and after they'd looked at the Monets and the Gauguins, they sat in the café and had a cup of tea.

'I was wondering what had happened to you,' Nancy said as they looked out of the window at the river rolling by. 'You've gone off the radar recently and Ellie said she hadn't heard from you either.'

Mary felt herself blushing. 'I'm sorry. It's just work, you know what starting a new job's like.'

She should have known better than to try and hide herself from Nancy. 'God, Mary, have you got a new man?'

'No.' But she felt a desperate desire to release Howard from her mind, to give him a bit of reality. 'Well, actually, yes.'

Nancy shrieked, clamping her hand over her mouth. 'How exciting. You have to tell me everything and brighten up my drab existence.'

'Oh don't, Nance. I asked you out because I want to hear all your news.'

Nancy waved a hand in front of her face. 'Come on, I don't have any news unless you'd like to hear what shade of green Zara's shit was this morning. Or how Robert likes his eggs. Or the relative merits of painting our sitting room Sahara or sandy yellow, which surely must be the same bloody colours anyway.'

Mary laughed. 'I could do with some advice actually.'

'Go on.'

The words turned out to be hard to say. 'It's the professor I work for.'

Nancy beamed. 'How incredibly Laurentian.'

'Not really. He's twelve years older than me and five times as clever.'

'Don't be absurd.'

'And married.' Nancy didn't answer, so Mary looked up and saw she was shocked. 'Oh God, it's completely shit, isn't it?'

'It's not ideal.' Nancy picked up a lump of sugar from the bowl in the middle of the table and began turning it over in her fingers. 'Did you know he was married when it started?'

'Yes.'

'Well, at least that's something. But I mean, what about her?'

'Exactly.' Mary thought she might cry. 'He wants to leave her, but he feels really sorry for her because he's such a good man. She can't get pregnant, you see.'

Nancy flushed. 'Bloody hell. That's horrible. I almost think that's worse than if he just left her.'

As soon as Mary heard the words, she knew they were true so emphatically it was like she had already worked it out for herself, but they also made her realise something else distressing. 'I'm in love with him.'

'Christ. But do you think he'll ever leave his wife?'

'I have no idea.' A couple of tears popped from the side of her eyes and Nancy reached over the table and stroked her arm.

'Has he done this before?'

The question surprised Mary. She used the napkin to dab at her cheeks and saw the black smear of her mascara on its neat whiteness. 'I don't know. I wouldn't have thought so.'

'I think you should end it.' Mary looked up at her friend and saw a steeliness in her perfect face. 'I mean, I can totally see the attraction in shagging not only your boss, but also a clever professor. And, you know, maybe he hasn't done it before. But now he's done it once and that's not great. Nor's his reason for staying with his poor wife. And think about how she must feel. I mean, don't you think it's sort of our job as women to stick together against situations like this?'

A sob broke from Mary before she could check it and a lady at the next table turned to them and then away again very quickly. 'You're right. But life is just so much more complicated than what you should do, don't you find?'

Nancy laughed. 'Of course I find that. Christ, they had to put me in a funny farm because I found the reality of looking after Zara so bloody hard.' Mary thought momentarily of R.D. Laing. 'But the right thing to do is, well, usually the right thing to do for a good reason.'

'What if I can't?'

Nancy withdrew her hand. 'OK, I'm going to tell you something. I think there's some sort of secret women's code that means you're not meant to reveal all in case you put other women off marrying and procreating, but sod it. When you get married and have a baby and make a home a lot of it is completely fantastic. But a lot of it is also fucking awful. Living with someone else is mind-blowingly hard. I do not believe there's a couple out there who would call themselves completely happy. Nor do I believe there's a couple out there who haven't at some point thought about how much better it could be with someone else. But that's all a fallacy, because even if you jack in the one you've got and replace them with the younger, better model, they'll still sometimes do smelly shits or snore or say something you disagree with so fundamentally that you want to stab them. Most of us battle on, but some chose to fuck someone else and, quite frankly, those people are not to be trusted.'

The words succeeded in drying Mary's tears. 'Are you talking about you and Robert?'

'Yes, partly. But not just.'

'Do you think he's been unfaithful to you?'

Nancy shrugged. 'I doubt it. But that doesn't mean there haven't been nights when he's been late home that I haven't run through a hundred scenarios. When I haven't seen that as a pretty sane action on his part. I mean, our lives are so divided.'

'In what way?'

'In the way that he goes out to work all day and I stay at home. He leaves the house, goes to a bustling office, chats to interesting people, probably gets taken to a fancy lunch. Whilst I cook and clean and fold clothes, take Zara for a walk around the park and feel pleased when the postman delivers a parcel and we have to exchange pleasantries on the doorstep. And I'm not saying I have it so much worse than him or anything, it's just that there's lots of empty space in my day that I occupy by thinking. But it means when we do finally sit down together at night sometimes it's hard to find common ground. Because I don't care about his latest deal and he doesn't care that Zara and I saw a family of rabbits in the park.'

Mary felt one of her bad heads coming on, one of the ones that gripped her shoulders and squeezed out her brain. Tiny white flecks danced at the corner of her vision. 'Oh God, Nance, I've been so naive. Poor bloody Penny.'

'You're not the first and you won't be the last. And it doesn't make you a bad person.' She laughed. 'I sound like my bloody mother. Next I'll be telling you there are plenty more fish in the sea.'

Mary had mentally given Ellie a couple of hours in which to arrive, after their tearful phone conversation, but it took much longer. So long that by the time her little car pulled up outside the house, Mary was watching out for her from a window, envisaging horrible death crashes on the motorway, in which she had to wait hours to be told because she was only a friend. It had, however, given her time to make sure there was nothing in her demeanour that would give away the fact that pretty much her whole world had been shattered since they'd spoken.

But, as soon as she opened the door, she knew that Eleanor wasn't in a fit state to notice anything about her anyway. She looked completely rumpled, her eyes so red and swollen they could have been part of a medical experiment, her cheeks puffed, with blotches on her shirt that Mary thought were tears. She pulled her friend into her, hugging her close and making soothing noises, before leading her to the kitchen, where she sat her on a chair and made her a cup of sweet tea.

'Tell me everything,' she said, sitting next to her with her own cup of tea.

Eleanor's hands shook as she took a sip. 'Oh God, Mary, I've been such a fool.'

'Let's not do that now,' Mary said. 'Let's take it for granted we feel shit about ourselves.'

Eleanor looked up and half laughed. 'Sorry, right.' She rubbed at her sore eyes. 'Look, I know I shouldn't have started sleeping with Robert, whatever, I know that. It was completely stupid. But Irena dying has felt like a slap in the face because, and I know you think I'm being melodramatic, but I could have prevented it, or at least made it less bad, if I hadn't been so consumed by Robert that I couldn't think of anything else. The last week has made me really question myself and what I'm doing and that made me think I haven't made any effort to find out anything about Nancy's death and what sort of friend does that make me?'

'But the police—'

Eleanor waved that away. 'I know. But, anyway, I went to see Davide Boyette, which was very... well, very unsettling, I suppose.'

'In what way?' There was a chance, Mary supposed, that she had misunderstood something and got it all wrong.

'Well, I know he might be a consummate actor, but really I would say he wasn't the lover, that he barely knew her in fact. But still his life has been pretty devastated by the whole thing and that made me feel worse.'

Mary felt a bit lost. 'I don't understand what it's got to do with you though. I mean, you didn't accuse him, you just told the police the lover was called David.'

Eleanor fixed her with her eyes. 'There's something I haven't told you.'

'OK.' Mary thought of the brown envelope upstairs.

'I think Robert knew about Nancy's affair.'

'Didn't he say he did?'

'No, he said he suspected she was having one. He made me tell him the night she didn't come home, before we knew she was dead.' Mary saw Eleanor swallow and realised her friend had kept this secret inside her for a long time and she felt jealous of her ability to now release it. 'But I found a letter to Nancy from her lover in Robert's desk in Sussex.'

'What?' Mary tried to arrange her thoughts coherently. 'So, you do know who her lover was? Why on earth did you go to see Davide?'

But Eleanor shook her head. 'No, no. The letter wasn't signed, or dated for that matter, but it was obviously from the lover.'

'What did it say?'

'Oh, you know, actually it was quite strange. I took a photo of it on my phone.'

'Can I see it?' Mary could feel her heart in her throat.

'Yes, but that's not the point.' Eleanor flushed, which made Mary realise how trapped they both were in their own version of this hell.

Eleanor unhooked her bag from the back of her chair, but tantalisingly only held it on her lap. 'Don't you see, Mary? If Robert knew Nancy was having an affair before she died, then he lied to me and the police. And what would he have to gain from that? I mean, if Howard was killed and you had any scrap of information that might help find who did it, wouldn't you show the police?'

Mary shifted under the intensity of Eleanor's gaze. 'I suppose. I don't know. It would depend.'

'Depend on what?' Mary looked at her friend's searching gaze and thought Eleanor was really quite innocent, which was a strange thing to think about someone who'd seen and done the things she had. But there was a naivety to her she hadn't fully appreciated before, even after thirty years of friendship. She didn't, Mary realised, yet understand what happened when two people lived together for the length of a marriage. She didn't know what damage lay within the walls of every home, she didn't know the highs and lows hidden by curtains and behind closed doors. 'Maybe he found it after Nancy died?'

'Yes, I thought of that. But still, why wouldn't he have shown it to the police? And it was folded inside a card Nancy had written him in which she didn't sound like Nancy. It was a sorry card and she sounded so contrite. I think she could have only been saying sorry about the affair, which means he knew before she died.'

Mary decided not to ask why Eleanor was looking through Robert's desk, she after all understood. 'They were together for a long time,' she settled on.

Eleanor batted this away. 'But what if he didn't want the police to know the identity of the lover?'

Mary felt sick and wondered if her oldest friend was about

to confront her with a terrible truth she already knew. 'Why wouldn't he want that?'

Eleanor pushed her fringe back and Mary saw the sweat on her forehead. 'Because what if he knew the lover hadn't killed her? What if it served a purpose for him to keep the police chasing the lover because it, well, because it kept the attention off him?'

Mary felt as if she had developed a sudden head cold so that everything had gone thick and fuzzy. Eleanor clearly didn't know about Howard. She thought of him drooling in the other room and the letter and mementoes upstairs. She could end all this speculation by showing Mary the brown envelope and she desperately wanted to, but the children were always there. And also, what if she was wrong and Robert had known and Howard hadn't been responsible? She could barely catch hold of her skittering thoughts. 'You can't really think Robert had anything to do with it?'

'I don't know what I think.'

'Can I see the letter?'

Eleanor fished her phone out of her bag and scrolled through it, finally handing it to Mary. She used her shaking fingers to enlarge the screen and read words she could almost hear Howard saying, words she knew had been formed on the battered type-writer he kept on a shelf in his study, which she had even heard occasionally clacking away over the years. She wanted to spit at the word 'guilt' on the screen. Nancy was his perfect lady, and he had lied at ever pretending he wanted anything else. She nearly asked Eleanor to send her a copy, but she didn't need one, it was already seared on her brain.

Mary handed the phone back, her head overloaded. 'I don't think we're ever going to know the truth.'

The phone slipped from Eleanor's hand and she bent to pick

it up from the floor, so her voice was distorted when she spoke. 'Do you think I should tell the police?'

She had to think very quickly, but the answer was in the letter. 'No. Absolutely not. Imagine Zara reading that.' Or her own children.

'Yes, but if it was Robert, he should be punished.'

'It wasn't Robert, Ellie.' Her friend tipped her head, her brow furrowed. 'Come on, I can't imagine Robert hurting anyone, least of all Nancy. The reason he hasn't shown that letter to the police is because he's protecting Zara, it's obvious. No parent would want their child to read that about themselves, especially if it had been written by someone their mother had risked everything for.' She had no idea if what she was saying about Robert was true, but there were more important issues at stake. She couldn't help glancing at the door as she spoke, as if her anger and disgust could melt the walls between her and Howard.

Eleanor looked relieved. 'You're right. And I guess, just because Davide wasn't the lover, doesn't mean the lover didn't kill her. He certainly sounds crazy enough to have done something.'

'And, like you say, there are no names on the letter. Robert probably doesn't know who he is anyway.'

'But wouldn't Nancy have told him after he found out?'

Mary was once again shocked at Eleanor's innocence. She didn't think she had ever known the identity of any of Howard's conquests, at least until now. 'No, not necessarily.'

Mary felt like she was underwater. She shut her eyes for a second and it was almost as if she could see Howard ramming his fists into Nancy's perfect face and cracking her skull against the ground, his rage as potent as the river rushing beside them.

'It's just whoever did it really meant it,' Eleanor said, drawing her back into the room. 'I didn't tell you at the time because it was all so distressing and then Howard got ill, but when I saw her in the mortuary, she had marks on her face as well as the big head injury. I mean, it looked like she'd been hit, you know, like the person who did it wanted to hurt her.'

Mary looked down at her hands, trying to ground herself, but they had just become shapes she could barely believe in.

Eleanor was rubbing at a spot above her eyebrow. 'Irena said something to me once that I keep remembering at the moment. I don't know if I ever told you, but her husband died really horribly and suddenly when their children were still young, from an aggressive cancer. I asked her once how she'd coped and she said that bad things happen to people all the time and the trick is to remember that what seem like great catastrophes to you, are really just small sorrows in the big scheme of things.' Everything seemed big to Mary and she couldn't think of a way to answer, but Eleanor went on anyway. 'She said we tend to contain sadness within us, but when something good happens we want to share it with people. She said if you looked down at the world from the moon it would shine with light, not dark.'

Mary snorted. 'Christ, that sounds awful, all our shit killing us silently from within.'

'I don't think that's what she meant at all.' Eleanor's voice was harsh and Mary regretted what she'd said because it wasn't even what she meant, it was just hard to believe in anything good at this moment.

Eleanor went on. 'I think she meant we should learn to find comfort in the fact that everyone's got their own sadnesses. It's sort of like something Davide Boyette said actually, he said we've taken Nancy's death too seriously. I've mopped up after countless disasters and still I've let Nancy's death mean more to me than any of those. Maybe we haven't put her death in context, we've allowed it to overtake our lives.'

Mary felt rooted to the argument, as if there was the

possibility of a meaning if only she could see her way through it, around the myth and to the truth at the end. 'Irena's sorrow sounds like another word for guilt. You know that special guilt only women feel. Maybe, as women, we should stop fucking absorbing sorrow and shielding others from facing it?' Her words made her feel like a crash-test dummy, designed to absorb shock after shock, until the final break. Then it struck her, neatly and plainly. 'Maybe death is simply an act of equality.'

'What do you mean?'

'That nobody's special when it comes to death, so it's sort of like a levelling process.' She thought of Nancy and wished what she had said was true, wished she had simply dissolved to dust, her meaning blown away by the wind. Except of course it wasn't true, it would probably never in fact be true because Nancy's death had affected them all in ways they could never even have imagined.

As she fed Howard his supper that evening, Mary imagined ramming the spoon so far down his throat that his windpipe cracked. She imagined the sound as it broke and his desperate struggle for breath. How his eyes would widen and plead with her, how his hands would twitch and flail, how she would smile down on him.

But he didn't notice anything different. He opened his mouth for the mushy food and let some of it dribble out down his chin. When Mimi came in to ask for money for a school trip he didn't even turn in her direction, his attention instead directed at his finger, worrying the worn bit of material on the arm of his chair. She wanted to take his chin in her hand and force his neck round, to scream in his face that his daughter was speaking and to stop wasting time on memories of Nancy. But she didn't, she just told Mimi where her purse was and went on spooning the food.

The girls started arguing and she knew one of them would soon burst in to complain about the other, asking her to arbitrate. And all at once she knew she wasn't capable of that any more, as if what she'd discovered that day had rocked her world so totally she no longer knew how to function. Her heart thundered against her ribs and for a moment she thought she might swoon like a Victorian heroine at her husband's feet. But then she thought maybe that was what she'd been doing for the past twenty plus years anyway, a thought so revolting she gagged into the air.

She stood, taking Howard's bowl with her, even though he'd only eaten less than half. He flicked his attention to the vanishing food, but she ignored him, going into the kitchen where she flung the bowl in the sink. She stood in the middle of the room and surveyed her tattered kitchen, this ten-foot by ten-foot space in which she'd spent so much time. This space that had been both a refuge and a burden and she knew all of a sudden that what Howard and Nancy had done could ruin this all for her. It could eat into her soul and fill her with a bitterness that would take in everything she held dear, until eventually it would spit her out, probably ridden with disease, to a lonely, hostile future. But she knew just as suddenly that she would not let this happen. Nancy and Howard might have abandoned her, or worse, not been bothered enough by her to care, but she was better than them and she would rise above the shit they had created.

The cracked face of the clock above the door told her it was coming up on nine and, if she told the girls she had a headache, they would accept her having a bath and going to bed. In fact, they'd like it; they'd like the opportunity to watch people shouting at each other on the television, or to go to bed a bit late. Tonight she wouldn't text Marcus and ask him where he was, worrying over her phone all evening. Because he always appeared at some point in the night and, just for this evening, she wasn't going to wonder about him. She was going to exist only in these moments.

She ran the bath scalding hot, even though the evening still contained some of the warmth of the day, which she always did because Howard so rarely let them turn on the heating in winter. In the early years he had justified this by saying that Penny had taken him to the cleaners, a phrase he used so frequently that Mary often imagined her being turned in a giant washing machine. Now though she couldn't remember why this had continued and why they all had to continue suffering the cold. Howard, she realised, usually showered at the university, after using the gym, so rarely had to endure the chilblain-inducing bathroom.

She let her clothes fall where she stood, revealing herself in the mirror above the bath: her tiny, emaciated body with its slack, ruched skin. The sight was shocking; she thought she looked almost like she had melted, as if she was dissolving away, losing all her last reserves of fat and protection. She looked away from herself and stepped into the loving water, which enclosed her like a hug as she sank down. She submerged her head but kept her eyes open, so she was staring up at her ceiling through the water, her hair dancing around in the corners of her vision.

She laid her hands across her belly under the water, feeling along it to her jutting hipbones. It seemed incredible that it had expanded enough to grow her three amazing children. And that thought made her feel better, because she would marry Howard again, even with all she now knew, because of her children, the best, most amazing things ever to have happened to her.

*

She'd only missed one pill, after Penny rang Howard at work one day to say her mother had had a fall and she had to go to Surrey for the night. The friend with the ferns above his bed was away again and from the way Howard told her all this news it clearly had never entered his head that she would say no. They were alone in the small staff kitchen and he'd come right up behind her, pressing his body against hers and moving her hair from her neck so he could whisper into her ear; he ached for her, she turned him inside out, he only saw in colour when she was next to him. And it felt like she physically melted, her body responding to him so primally, she knew she would do anything for him.

It was strange that missing one pill equated to a blue line on a stick, and yet it also didn't entirely surprise Mary, as their love-making was so passionate it was sort of bound to create life. But she still felt very scared as she sat on her own in the staff toilets; she was way too young, her career only just started, unmarried, her parents' disapproval wafting down the motorway. The shock paralysed her for a while, almost as if not speaking about it would make it go away. So she told no one, not Eleanor, not Nancy, not even Howard. Until she saw a young woman who looked very like her dragging a small girl onto a bus in front of her, the girl twisting with anger. One day what was in her stomach would be a whole, living person with its own needs and wants, which she was going to have to meet, and she couldn't ignore the situation any longer.

Mary asked Howard if he would meet her in Hyde Park that Saturday, but he said it was difficult because they were having friends over for dinner and Penny always got in a bit of a state when that was happening. But unusually for her she insisted. They met on one of the bridges linking the walkways of the

Serpentine and of course he was late. Mary leant over the stone railings to look at the swans gliding on the water and, as she did so, felt a hard roundness in her belly unlike anything that had existed in her body before. She stayed very still, her weight still pressed against the stone, the alien sac just underneath her skin. She tried to imagine what was there, what the baby looked like, what parts of it identified it as human already, but she couldn't see it as anything other than a complete, already formed little baby. She put her hands between her stomach and the stone and knew with a nauseating shock she loved it already.

Howard suggested a cup of tea but she wanted to walk, in case she'd misjudged everything and she was left sitting alone at a table. He walked, she noticed, in large strides that paid no attention to her own and talked haphazardly about an article he was trying to write and how annoying Penny was being. She had begun to notice that he could sometimes become jerky and twitchy, something she had before only seen happening at work, and it made her scared that she could produce this reaction in him. Mrs Sodart, the department secretary, would sometimes shut the door to his office and tell everyone in hushed tones that Professor Smithson was not to be disturbed and they all knew what it meant.

She stopped finally, out of breath, with sweat on her forehead and after a few more steps he stopped as well and turned to look back at her. They had walked off the main path and were under a large tree.

'What are you doing?' He looked at his watch. 'I told Penny I was getting a book from work and I've got a list of insane food I'm meant to be buying.'

'I'm pregnant.' Mary held herself very still.

His face contorted and she was sure whitened underneath his beard. He looked round to see if anyone had heard and then retraced his steps towards her. 'You can't be. I mean, you're on the pill.'

She tried to swallow down her romantic fantasies about the moment. 'There was that night, when Penny went to her parents and I didn't have anything with me. I didn't think missing one pill would matter.' She didn't like the flicker in his eyes and the ground appeared to be swaying slightly underneath her. If only she didn't love it already, she thought, because she wasn't certain she could do it alone.

'My God.' He raked his hands through his hair in an almost comic gesture. 'How far gone are you?'

'About ten weeks, I think.'

'Ten weeks?' His voice rose in pitch. 'Why didn't you tell me before?'

'I don't know. It's been a lot to process.' Mary realised how stupid she sounded.

'There's still time to do something about it. I can ask around, it'll be fine.' He wasn't meeting her eye and he hadn't asked her how she felt.

'I don't want to do anything about it.' Mary felt heat rise to her cheeks and something like indignation spread through her chest.

He looked right at her then. 'You want to have it?'

She instinctively put her hand on her stomach. 'Yes.'

He looked like he was going to shout, but he calmed himself and took a final step towards her, taking her hands in his own. His voice was much softer when he spoke next. 'Mary, come on, think about it. How would you manage?'

She held his gaze. 'But I'd have you.' Really it was nothing more than a dare because suddenly she didn't expect him to be with her and it felt like she was free-falling.

He dropped her hands. 'But Penny, I mean, what would I tell her?'

'What are you doing with me? You can't be happy.' She felt as if she was in a bad film, where an unsuspecting woman is duped by a mean man, except the last few months had felt so far from that.

He turned to the side so he was looking out at the lake. 'My God, you don't understand anything, do you?' She had to bite down on her lip to stop her tears.

'I love you, Howard,' she whimpered, feeling the last vestiges of pride leave her.

But he turned back at that and pulled her into him. 'Oh, I'm sorry, I love you too.' He kissed the top of her head. 'We'll get through this. Everything will be OK, I promise.'

He said he would leave Penny, but my God, the time it took. Days, weeks, months passed in which her belly rounded, her back ached and her feet swelled. She only wanted to eat bread and jam. And still he said he was waiting for the right time. There is never going to be a right time, Nancy told her, you're going to have to accept that and tell your parents what's going on and make arrangements. Eleanor told her about places where the rent was cheap for single mothers and the living was communal to stop depression. And they both promised to help her as much as they could. Mary listened and nodded and thanked them, but really couldn't believe everything wasn't going to be all right. She felt the baby kicking now and could sometimes see the heel of its foot undulating her belly if she lay still in the bath.

He's a bastard, both women said to her on numerous occasions, but she couldn't agree with them. Because by then Howard had apologised so many times it was almost funny. He blamed his initial reaction on shock and his desire not to hurt Penny, which he also said he knew to be foolish and misplaced. He told her he loved her over and over and she was certain he did, she could feel it in the power of his embrace as they lay on the strange round bed his friend had recently installed in his flat; ultimately it felt like their love was enough to see them through.

Then one day he told her he'd found them a flat near the university, which he said he would live in with her and the baby, eventually, once he'd told Penny. He's got you right where he wants you, Eleanor told her, but Mary relaxed even further because no one else understood what her and Howard had. How everything for them was insular and different. Society, he told her, likes to set rules which we all have to conform to because then we're easier to control. But they were above all that, he assured her as he stroked his hand over her belly, which now looked like she had swallowed a football when she was naked. She felt almost dissolved when she was with him like that; she would have climbed inside him if she could have, happy to be carried around by him all day.

As Christmas approached, Howard decided he would tell Penny in the New Year, so she could have a final happy Christmas. By then Mary was six months pregnant and her options were to spend Christmas alone in London, or go home and tell her parents. Eleanor and Nancy told her she had to go home, she had to tell them. With Howard's help, she concocted a story that omitted Penny and told how he had to go and visit his sick parents. He somehow contrived to call her most evenings, once speaking to her father and telling him how much he loved his daughter and how excited he was for the baby. When she finally took the phone he said he couldn't bear to be apart from her and that every minute at Penny's parents was like watching a bad TV show. His real life, he said, hadn't started until he met her, and Mary felt as if her whole body was on fire.

Her parents didn't ask her if they planned to get married, which Mary loved them for, but she walked into the kitchen one morning to find her mother crying on her father's shoulder and knew what it would be about. On the coach back to London she thought it was probably nothing more than another thing they would never understand about her. Howard had been right when he'd called her an outsider, just wrong in what he thought that meant. It was lonely to be outside your family, even when that family loved you, because it made you wonder why you couldn't be happy with what had been given to you.

Two weeks after she returned to London Mary received a brown paper parcel in the post from her mother, which contained a knitted white blanket. She held the tiny, soft garment as she ate her toast and marmalade alone in the flat Howard was paying for and it was like she woke up, like a light went on, a light that illuminated the fact she had nothing to sustain a baby.

It was Nancy who she rang in a panic and Nancy who'd turned up the next day with a bag of clothes, a Moses basket and a small plastic bath. She'd also written a list of things to buy, like nappies and wipes and cotton wool and pads to put in her pants to catch the bleeding. And then Nancy had taken her to Mothercare when it became apparent that she wouldn't even be able to accomplish this simple task.

'My parents want us to get married,' she said to Howard as they ate their sandwiches on a bench the next day, which wasn't something they had actually said, but something that Mary knew would be true. But more than that, it was what she wanted, although she knew better than to expose her bourgeois sentiments to Howard.

He had begun to look tired, with purple circles beneath his eyes. 'We were probably stupid not to tell them about Penny when we had the chance.'

'How long does it take to get a divorce?'

He screwed his half-eaten sandwich into the paper it was wrapped in. 'Too long.'

One tear popped out of her eye before she could stop it and dropped onto the bread of her sandwich.

'God, what a bloody mess,' he said.

Except it seemed to do the trick because he came into work the next morning ashen-faced and told Mary he'd done it. He would be sleeping with her in the flat that night and for all the nights thereafter. He'd asked Penny for a divorce, he'd told her about the baby. The relief she felt was like liquid pouring out of her. She wanted to fall at his feet and thank him over and over again. She wanted to weep.

She went out at lunch and bought the ingredients for supper, splashing out on two pork chops as she knew they were Howard's favourite. But when she got back to the office he wasn't at his desk and Mrs Sodart and another assistant were whispering by the filing cabinet.

'Have you heard?' Mrs Sodart asked as Mary hung up her coat.

'Heard what?' Mary already knew it wasn't going to be good.

'Professor Smithson's wife tried to kill herself this morning. She jumped out of their bedroom window into the street.' The two women stared at Mary's stomach, the parentage of the baby an open secret in the office.

Mary sat down and the room turned. 'Is she dead?' She wasn't sure if the question was hopeful or not.

'No,' Mrs Sodart said. 'But she's broken her legs very badly and hurt her back. They're worried she might be paralysed.'

The pork chops went to waste as she couldn't stomach them and Howard didn't show up either at work or the flat for two days. Mrs Sodart kept her up to date with what was actually occurring: Penny wasn't paralysed, although she'd broken both legs badly; apparently she'd done it because he'd asked for a divorce; once she was discharged she was going to convalesce at her parents' home in Surrey; Howard hadn't left her bedside, even when her father turned up and called him all the names under the sun; another woman was apparently involved, the rumour was she was pregnant. Mary twisted her finger in the phone flex as Mrs Sodart imparted her news, her whole body pulsating with hot embarrassment that Howard should be ringing Mrs bloody Sodart and not her. But the crease between Mrs Sodart's eyebrows told her all she needed to know, like a line of disdain at the mess she had created.

On the third night he turned up at the flat just after nine when she'd given up hope, grey skinned and having lost weight, even in that amount of time. He had a bottle of whisky with him, which he drank out of a chipped porcelain cup as he told her he'd never expected Penny to do anything so bloody stupid. His hands shook as he raised the cup to his lips, but Mary also thought she saw a faint smile play at the corners of his mouth as he spoke. A woman had, after all, jumped out of a window for the love of him, something she understood entirely.

'I think you'll have to give up your job,' Howard said. 'Which you'd have to do soon anyway as I've been reading up on it all and attachment parenting seems like the best way forward.'

Mary was tempted to ask for some of his whisky. If she gave up work she would be an unmarried single mother without any means of supporting herself. But instead she asked, 'What's attachment parenting?'

'I'll give you a book about it.' Which Mary had noticed was often his answer to anything.

'And if I'm going to give up work, what will I do for money?'

'You've got me now,' he said, but his smile looked like the line of a faraway horizon.

'But we're not even married.'

'Don't worry, we'll sort it out. Now Penny knows about you and the baby she wants a quick divorce.'

The bath had grown cold around her, as if her memories had frozen the water, so Mary pulled herself out and dried herself with a scratchy towel. She changed into the worn tracksuit she slept in and then went back downstairs to deal with Howard. He was still in his chair and the room was cold and silent. She couldn't be bothered to wash him or even undress him and simply took his shoes off his feet. It made her wonder what she would have felt like if she'd discovered something like this when they were first married. She thought it probably would have killed her. But they were so far from those people now, nineteen years down a pitted, fractured line, in which she'd long ago learnt to harden her heart to him. Not that she would ever have expected a betrayal of this magnitude, although why she hadn't now seemed peculiar.

'Come on,' she said gruffly, 'it's bed time.'

His eyes wavered over her face and she thought he looked disappointed. She held out her hands and when he took them it made her shiver. She pulled him up and led him out to the toilet under the stairs, where he stood half in, half out of the door, as if his engine had broken.

'Go on, Howard. You need to pee cos I am not changing your sheets if you piss the bed again.' She wondered why she hadn't spoken to him like this before, wondered why she'd softened her voice and cajoled and reasoned with him, when clearly it made no difference to the way he felt. Besides, she didn't care any more.

'Oh for God's sake.' She noticed him flinch slightly, which pleased her. She manoeuvered herself around him and pulled him towards the toilet, where she unzipped his trousers and pulled his wizened, flaccid penis out of the gap. It felt soft and delicate and she wanted to yank it, maybe even pull it off him. 'Come on, Howard. Have a piss. I'm tired.'

He looked at her with scared, watery eyes and for a brief moment she felt sorry for him, but then she hated him even more for his ability to still make her feel anything. She held his gaze until she heard the steady stream of his urine hitting the water. She looked down and saw his trousers flecked with damp spots. It would only take a few days for him to smell like he was decaying, like those old men who shuffle on and off buses in tweed suits. She tucked his penis back inside his trousers and led him back to the front room and over to his bed against the far wall. He was much more placid tonight than usual, he didn't even stiffen as she removed his cardigan and pulled off his trousers, even when she lay him down without dressing him in pyjamas and left him alone in the dark without a kiss to his forehead. She should have behaved as if she didn't care years ago, she thought as she shut the door.

The girls were both absorbed in their phones, which she told them to turn off and then to go to sleep, but they all knew she was just going through the motions. Marcus's door was shut, which meant he must have come home; she knocked lightly and heard a muffled response. He was lying on his bed with an ashtray balanced on his chest and speakers wrapped around his head, which he removed when he saw her.

'Good day?' she asked.

'Yeah, not bad.' He never told her what he did with his time, but his eyes were always bloodshot. She knew that she needed to properly address whatever it was that was going on with her son. It had been nearly a year now of him switching from a quiet, calm boy to this parody of an unruly teenager who spoke in slang and wore his jeans too low. She wanted to grab hold of him and pull him back, but she wasn't sure where he was or where she wanted him to be.

'Are you going to be OK? For Monday, I mean?' He was meant to be starting his volunteering at Eleanor's then and she worried he wouldn't go.

'Yeah, I'm quite looking forward to it.' She felt her breath catch because it was like being given a glimpse of the old Marcus. 'You look done in.'

She nodded because she didn't trust herself to speak. She wanted to sit down next to her son and lay her head on his shoulder. To tell him about the letter and what it must mean, to apologise for making him live with a murderer. There had always been a bond between her and her children, which Mary thought of as a string attached between their hearts, so that she always knew what they were thinking, always felt whatever it was that was troubling them. She still loved Marcus as fiercely as the day he'd been born, which wasn't any more than she loved the girls, but was different because she'd always known they would never need her in the way he did. He wore his vulnerability like a layer of raw skin and yet she had failed to do the one thing that might have helped heal this.

'You should get some help with Dad,' he said.

'Maybe. I was thinking about getting a job. I mean, we're going to need the money soon.'

'It'd be good for you to get out of the house a bit anyway. It's miserable being stuck in here with him all day.'

Her muscles felt tired. 'Night, Marcus. Sleep tight.' She closed his door as she left, her heart bursting in her chest. The clarity that Howard's illness had given her about their marriage had extended also to their children and she was able to see more obviously now that he hadn't been a good father, especially not to Marcus. She couldn't yet work out why he hadn't been able to love them as she did, but she knew it had been damaging. She was beginning to think that she should have taken them away from him earlier and it worried her that perhaps she had sacrificed her son for her husband. It was a thought so terrible it felt as if she might die with regret.

Mary woke the next morning with fear pumping round her body. It was of course still possible that Eleanor could change her mind and take the letter she had found at Robert's to the police and, if she did, they could maybe connect it to Howard's typewriter. She got up and, because it was Sunday, was able to leave the house before any of the children woke up. She drove the typewriter to the local dump, wrapped in an old sheet, stuffed down into the bottom of a black bin liner and covered over with the contents of her bin. A man at the dump asked her if she wanted a hand but she said no because she knew how much she was going to enjoy feeling the weight of the bag pulling against her arm as she launched it into the massive metal container. She heard it clunk as it hit the bottom and she peered over the edge to see how innocuous it looked, surrounded by the detritus of other people's lives. More rubbish she knew would be thrown on top of it today and then one of the big lorries would come to collect the container and the whole lot would be taken to be incinerated at one of the council sites which people protested against. The typewriter would end up as no more than fragments, inhaled probably by some poor child who lived on an estate too close to the rubbish-disposal facilities, as she thought they called them now.

As she drove home she cried because it hadn't all been bad,

how could it have been? Reeling across her mind was the evidence of them all standing on windy beaches, at the doors of caravans, even in their own back garden. Birthday candles being blown out, first days at school in oversized uniforms, Christmas hats worn askew.

When she arrived home she went straight to the photo albums and there they were, her and Howard, smiling in almost all the photos; in one they were even holding hands, standing in front of the sofa in the sitting room. She remembered Mimi taking it on a camera she'd been given for a birthday, how she'd made them pose, moving and constructing them into her approximation of a happy couple. She remembered how enthusiastically Howard had taken her hand, how he'd laughed at Mimi, how he'd turned to her afterwards and said, 'There's no mistaking she's your daughter, is there?' Mary tried to hear the malice in the words now but realised they weren't there.

In the caravan she both remembered and saw petrified behind the plastic cover, Howard had divided the space with an old sheet so he could make love to her every night after the children had fallen asleep. She remembered the taste of salt on his skin and beer on his tongue and how when they'd been packing up to go home he'd wrapped his arm around her waist and said, 'This is how it always should be.' But, also they'd had that terrible argument on that holiday, in strained hushed voices to avoid waking the children, in which he'd told her she was like one of those oranges which look so good on the outside, which even smell good as you dig into them, but are really shrivelled and tasteless inside, so each segment feels like sand on your tongue.

'Why would you say that?' she'd asked, tears popping in to her eyes.

'Because you seemed so fun and carefree when we met, like you were going to go out into the world and do something.

But now you're just this drudge, always nagging me and asking things of me.'

'I just said that I thought the MOT has run out on the car and we should check it before we drive home.' Although in the open the words did sound bland, except also, also they were necessary and if something did happen and the MOT was out of date, which meant they weren't insured, she knew Howard would blame her. And also, also, she might be a drudge, but she had become one washing the floors in his house, cooking for his children. She couldn't believe now that she hadn't shouted those words into his face.

And if she was going to be really honest with her memories, then she couldn't any more turn her mind away from the past decade and all those nights she had waited for him to come home, knowing that when he did he would be imbued with the stench of another woman. How, when he was in the process of becoming infatuated, he would be rude and dismissive to her and the children. How he would strut round the house filled with his secret knowledge that someone else found him irresistible, asking himself why on earth his family couldn't appreciate his greatness.

Worse than all that though was that he hadn't been a good father, something she could admit to now it was all about to end. She supposed he'd been all right with the girls, uninterested but sometimes affectionate and less likely to scream and shout at them. But his treatment of Marcus had often verged on spiteful. He'd never hit him or anything like that, but a seam of disdain ran through all his dealings with the boy. Over the years Mary had learnt to put herself between them, metaphorically speaking, trying to deflect Howard's anger onto her, which often worked. Although he also saw through what she was doing most of the time, telling her she was pathetic and no wonder Marcus was such a sissy mummy's boy.

She wondered now if Howard had ever really wanted children. Maybe he'd lied from the very beginning and the reason he and Penny hadn't had them wasn't because they couldn't, but because they hadn't wanted to. Mary was sure that he had loved her in the beginning, but now that she'd had to live through so many of his infatuations, she thought he probably always felt that way at the start of any new affair. Howard liked the thrill of beginnings, that unreal moment of falling in love, not the mundanity of everyday life or a comfortable love that had to acknowledge flaws. He was a man imbued with a sense of his own greatness, who didn't want to see his imperfections reflected in the dissatisfactions of another.

It seemed obvious now that if she hadn't become pregnant he would have got bored eventually and stayed with Penny, which would have probably suited him better. Because what she thought now was that Howard was a narcissist and that made it impossible for him to love anyone else, including his own children, as much as he loved himself.

'All you do is fucking nag,' he said to her on more than one occasion when she'd tried to pin him down to a time or remind him of a commitment. 'I can't operate in your boring world of routine,' he'd shout, 'it's bad for my head.' And so Mary would go again to parents' evenings alone or walk home from the shops with plastic bags digging into her wrists so that the pain became almost transcendental, at times believing him, almost allowing herself to think that she shouldn't bother him with minutiae, that she made too much of a fuss.

Perhaps that was the worst thing Howard had done to her. Made her believe that her needs and concerns were small and petty, when really they were what kept their family alive and functioning. He had insisted on the ability to remove himself from the drudgery, as if he were so special and she was so ordinary. As if all the things she was added up to so much less than all the things he was.

Mary's grief ambushed her over the next few days and she was surprised to find that it was centred around Nancy, not Howard. She felt an overpoweringly crushing sensation that Nancy could have cared for her so little, after all the things they'd shared and all the things they knew about each other. Meeting Nancy and Ellie at university had been the start of what Mary always thought of as her real life. It wasn't that she'd been unhappy before, but there had been this huge great part of her that had almost felt like a dirty secret, so she'd find herself hiding her books under her bed or saying she was meeting friends when really she was going to the library. Then she'd gone to university in a gable-topped town and on the first night there'd been a knock on the door and a short, round girl had been standing there with her hand extended in front of her, telling her they were neighbours. And Mary could clearly remember thinking, I'm getting friends out of this deal as well?

They'd gone to some Freshers' party that night, which had been held in a long room with trestle tables along the walls and a bar in the far corner, which served local beers and cheap vodka. Eleanor seemed to know a few people already, telling Mary that she'd been to a meet-and-greet day for her course, which annoyingly wasn't Classics but English. Mary had missed her own meet and greet, but Eleanor was careful to include her in all the conversations and introduce her to everyone.

Mary spotted Nancy before they spoke, standing in a corner of the room like a beacon, as if light shone out of her. She was tall and rail thin, with her straight blonde hair falling either side of her face, her eyes made comically huge by black eyeliner flicking along her lashes and cheekbones that jutted out of her face like an accusation. She stood with one hip tilted upwards and an arm slung lazily across her middle, which she raised now and then to take a sip of drink. She was chatting to a red-faced boy who kept on flicking his floppy fringe, and she seemed to Mary like how she'd always imagined Athena to look.

Amazingly Nancy called out to them as they passed, or at least to Eleanor, who went over to her as if there was nothing strange in the most intoxicating person in the room wanting to speak to you. The boy had been quickly dispatched and then it had been the three of them, standing in their corner, and Eleanor had said something funny, which made them all laugh and somehow that had been that. Life cemented around them, fortifying them into a unit, wrapping them in safety that felt like cashmere. They sat up late talking, they planned their futures, honed their ambitions, fantasised about love, revelled in secret dreams, imagined important lives. They held each other's hands as they stepped into the world, they made each other feel as if things were going to be all right.

Mary revisited the letter again and again, devouring every word and trying to see beyond the paltriness of their meanings. There were times when she found a shred of comfort in there – how Nancy called her one of her best friends, how she clearly felt disgust at herself, how she urged Howard to do the right thing and leave, how she said she would be around to pick up the pieces. Mary fantasised about this life sometimes; the thought of Howard on the other side of the world, her own heart broken, Nancy not only still alive but rescuing her, making her realise how much better off she was without him. How she would emerge from it all a stronger, better woman, her and Nancy's friendship strengthened beyond measure.

Ultimately, however, it was easier to see the worst version of Nancy on that page. Oh, the melodrama of calling herself a vile stain and the blatant stab at poeticness when she wrote how far she had come from normal human emotion. But the line which really grated was 'if you love me as much as you say' because not only did it hint at all the things Howard must have promised and all the promises Nancy had absorbed, it also revealed a woman totally at one with her loveliness. She hated Nancy for this self-belief.

She tried to remember times with Nancy in the year or so before she died, when she must have been fucking Howard and still managing to look her in the eye. Except the truth was she'd barely seen Nancy in the year before her death. Mary supposed she'd been absorbed with the kids and the daily grind of never having quite enough money and suspected most of the time she'd been too tired to notice Nancy's absence, or even to miss her. She did remember calling Nancy once, she thought it was the summer before she died, because she'd wanted some of her friend's energy and grace in her life. But she remembered also the excuses Nancy had made; how she'd shifted and prevaricated and dissembled to get out of the lunch Mary had suggested.

Of course she'd seen her. It would have been impossible for that not to have happened. There had definitely been a trip to the theatre to see the play a woman from university had directed, with Eleanor as well. Mary could remember the look of concentration on Nancy's face as she'd read the programme and how she'd almost thrown it on the floor afterwards and banged on about how everyone else had done so well and what a bloody failure she was. They'd had to cajole and reassure her and tell her she was wonderful, which sort of ruined the evening and made Mary angry on the bus home because who the fuck felt good about themselves anyway?

They'd also been out for a couple of drinks, but she realised always with Eleanor. She couldn't, in fact, remember a time she'd been alone with Nancy at all in the year before she died. It was now obvious why, but that didn't make her feel any better because it fundamentally meant that Nancy had chosen Howard over her.

One day she remembered with what felt like an electric shock that they'd gone to Robert and Nancy's annual bonfire night party together only the year before, just a couple of months before Nancy had died, when she must have been fucking Howard. Howard was usually unconcerned by her social arrangements, but she remembered now how he'd made a point of asking her if they'd been invited, which she'd found strange at the time, but not enough to really consider. She tried to conjure details from the night and thought she saw a tension on Nancy's face, a furtive glance or two between her and Howard. But it was impossible to tell if her memories were real or if she'd painted over them with what she now knew. She certainly hadn't come back from that night and thought anything remotely like what was going on. Memory, she realised, was meaningless without context.

Except there was a memory that went with that night which didn't need any context. She had tried to smother it down in the way she had become so adept at, but now it refused to lie still. Howard had drunk too much at the party, which was unlike him, so she'd gone straight upstairs when they got home, surprised that he followed almost right behind her. He had walked in from the bathroom as she was half undressed, pulling her leg out of her jeans, so she was only wearing underwear when she stood up. He had come over to her as she straightened and stood behind her, placing his hands on either side of her arms and turning her to face the full-length mirror on the front of their wardrobe.

They had stood like that for a moment, both of them looking at each other in the half light of their bedroom, their images distorted by the dust on the mirror. Howard had bobbed his head and, for a fleeting second, Mary had thought he was going to kiss her shoulder and all up the side of her neck. Her body flexed, an old muscle memory moving under her skin, because it had been so long since he'd touched her like that.

'Look at you,' Howard had said, but his hissing tone warned her this was not going to be a romantic moment. She dipped her head to the floor, but he put his fingers around her chin and pushed it back up, so she had to look at herself, at her grey underwear, her pubes snaking out of her pants, her puckered stomach, her protruding bones. 'How the fuck have you let yourself get like this?' Howard whispered. 'How can you expect anyone to love you looking like this?'

She'd whimpered then. 'Howard, please.'

He let go of her chin, but she could still feel the pressure on her jaw. Then in one swift movement he snaked his hand under the front of her bra and yanked so it snapped off her body. He dropped it listlessly to the floor, then brought his hand to her left breast, cupping it gently. It looked like a used teabag, her nipple huge, but her skin like a scrunched piece of wax paper. He put his thumb and forefinger either side of her breast and pinched, so hard that tears darted to her eyes. But then he took both his hands off her body, turning his back on her and leaving the room, so all she was left with was the sound of her hitched breathing, not sure if it had even happened.

Mary had always been a walker, but as the memories of her marriage began to surface, refusing to be silenced any more, she took herself off for long walks round Kensal Green cemetery, which had always been her favourite place in London. She would stride down the green roads, with their dripping trees, past the thousands of souls, each with their own story to tell, hoping that reason would settle over her restless thoughts.

Once, aged about fifteen, a man had stopped Mary on the towpath near to where she used to walk along Birmingham's long canal. He'd engaged her in polite but transparent conversation, and she'd answered in the way she'd been taught to do. From her vantage point in the present, she saw his yellow teeth and large tongue, knew what his hand was really doing in his trousers, noticed the grease of his hair, the desperation in his voice. Back then it hadn't been until she'd said that she really must get home and he'd grabbed her arm, telling her not to be silly, that she'd felt afraid.

She remembered looking at him in silence, her face passive as she ran through her options. He reacted first though, pulling roughly on her arm so she followed him exactly where he led. She knew there was a turning in a few yards that led up a bank and onto a patch of waste ground and she knew that was where they were going. She even knew how she would look after he had finished, bloodied and bruised, possibly totally broken, but still she let him lead her, still she stumbled on behind.

They'd only been steps from the turning when a dog barked into view, making both of them jump. A man followed, walking purposefully towards them. 'Fuck,' the greasy man said, dropping her arm and running up the turning Mary had known he would take. The man with the dog smiled as she passed and it was only after this that she had started running.

Over time the terror shifted its focus from the man to herself. She had seen something in herself that day which frightened her more than all the blows and worse he could have rained down on her. She saw as clear as day her own passivity, her own complicity in her destruction. She could not even be sure, had he gone on holding her arm and had the dog man reached them, that she would have cried out or struggled to free herself. She seemed instead totally accepting of her destiny, totally at the will of something else entirely. As Mary strode through the streets of the dead in the cemetery she realised she was still that girl, still that passive, still that incapable.

Howard had killed Nancy.

Mary had known it as soon as she'd read the letter but it had taken a while for her brain to properly assimilate the fact. And he had obviously done it because she wanted to leave him. She doubted Howard had ever been left before in his life; he was always the one to end affairs, walk out of marriages, trample over families. And his illness, she realised, was an extension of the whole thing. Probably he hadn't known how much he loved Nancy until she was gone and now his brain couldn't compute living without her, which was something Mary knew he wouldn't feel if she had been the one to die. He had no doubt, in retrospect, killed the wrong woman.

She still fed and washed him every day, but she didn't speak to him. His eyes now followed her as she walked round the room in a way they never had before and she enjoyed not returning his gaze. But it wasn't enough. It was pathetic really; as pathetic as everything else which had gone into their sorry marriage.

She wondered constantly and obsessively at why she'd let her life continue in the way it had done. She would never believe that what they'd felt for each other at the beginning hadn't been the real thing, but she also knew that life had changed them somehow, that responsibility and pressure and money and debt had penetrated into them and that for way too long now things between them had been woeful. What she was also starting to admit to herself, however, was that how they operated wasn't normal, that most people didn't live with the level of disdain and disgust Howard showed her. She knew that every couple argued and hurt each other, but they were also tender and cared about each other. Mary thought it was time to admit that everything good had been eroded from their relationship, like a flood that washes away not just houses and cars, but also trees and soil, leaving a ground ravaged and destroyed.

Things had really started to go wrong after Mimi's birth, and she was now fifteen, which meant this had all been going on for far too long. The birth had coincided with Howard being passed over for a promotion he felt to be rightfully his, which established a deep morbid melancholy in which he constantly obsessed about his age. He started to judge everything in terms of how long he had left alive, once he even came back from the dentist and said he had told him not to bother to clean his teeth because there was no point in trying to make them look nice when his face was disintegrating around them. Mary used to feel a fear in the pit of her stomach when he spoke like that, looking at her fledgling family. She would try to drag him out of the crisis with soothing words, tender touches and funny stories about the children, but nothing worked. Eventually everything became a numbers game: how many more elections would he vote in, how many more passports would he renew, how many places did he have left to visit, how many more books would he read.

It was around that time that she'd first started to field tearful phone calls from young women, who lied badly, but well enough for a new mother to gloss over. And then she'd become accidentally pregnant with Maisie so quickly, which had lowered him into an even fouler mood, as if everything that had ever gone wrong with him was her fault.

Maisie's birth had been mere weeks away when Mary had

answered a knock on the door one cold Sunday evening to see a young girl standing on her doorstep, wet from the rain that was falling, or the tears she was crying, it was hard to be sure. They had both appeared shocked to see each other, but the girl had managed to ask for Howard, who had looked equally shocked when Mary called him. He'd ushered the girl into the sitting room and closed the door, not even looking back at Mary as he did so, a hard, tense expression on his face. She'd heard the whimpering and pleading through the door, but not the content, although it wasn't hard to guess at.

The girl finally left after about an hour, when Mary was bathing Marcus and trying to stop Mimi from screaming. She expected Howard to appear and offer some form of explanation, however lame, but he never did, so she had to wade through the whole of bedtime simmering with anxiety. Howard barely even looked up when she finally found him in the sitting room and she had to ask him what was going on, standing over him as he read an article on political tribes.

'Nothing,' he said. 'She's one of my students.'

'I gathered that.'

'She got the wrong end of the stick.'

'Please don't treat me like I'm stupid.' She was trying to keep her cool because she'd read that it was bad for the baby if she got too het up. Maisie started to kick her anyway.

He looked up at her, slowly, and half smiled. 'I don't know what you expect, Mary. The only way you seem to be able to extract any meaning from the world is by having children. I've been beginning to wonder if you have some sort of mental condition. And it's not exactly attractive.'

She instinctively placed her hands on her huge, taut belly. 'Who is she?'

He snorted. 'As if I'd tell you that.'

Mary had left the room then and gone and stood in the kitchen. She didn't think she had ever felt more alone or desperate in her life, as if she'd been stranded on an island, as if all the things she'd so carefully constructed had fallen. She wanted to grab hold of something solid, but there were only the kitchen counters, covered in the dirty pots and pans from their dinner.

And then she had three children under five, she hadn't worked in five years, her family was far away in more than just a physical sense, and she would have done anything to keep him close. After that a fear of upsetting the children at vulnerable ages had certainly come in to play, then a sense that she had nowhere else to go and no way of making proper money after a decade out of work. And, if she was completely truthful, a sense of convention and not wanting to show that bloody private face of Laing's, which had got her in to the mess in the first place. But it had all dropped away now and she felt ready not to care any more. It was interesting that if she were to say exactly what she felt now, or if she acted as she pleased, she would be considered mad, Laing could even be used in her treatment. And yet, how she was feeling and thinking was surely the sanest she'd ever been.

He must, she thought, have hated her all this time. All those times she had taken as tenderness he must have really been laughing at her. Because there had been tender times. They'd made love, they'd laughed at funny stories together, she'd sometimes typed up his articles and essays, they'd discussed politics over flickering candles, they'd raised their eyes at each other over their children's heads. Yes, there'd been long stretches of time that had felt like living alone in a barren desert, but there had been more than a handful of good. She couldn't begin to understand why he had bothered, unless he was such a sadist he'd revelled in wrong footing her.

*

Mary still had a few friends who worked at various universities in London and she told them she was on the lookout for a job, anything, however menial it seemed. Getting out of the house would no doubt help, but she would still have to come home to Howard every night and breathe the same contaminated air as him. She could, she supposed, leave him, although that was also a ludicrous idea as he had nowhere to go and was incapable anyway. She toyed with the idea of selling the house and using some of the money to put him in a home, but then she wouldn't be able to afford anywhere big enough for her and the kids and, quite frankly, she didn't see why they should suffer because of her bad choices.

Fundamentally she also couldn't bear that Howard wasn't going to be punished. And she knew she meant this as much for herself as she did for Nancy. Some might say his present state was punishment enough, but the problem with that was he had chosen that state. It was of his own making and she couldn't help looking at it as his choice. It would be so typical of bloody Howard to commit a crime and then think he should devise his own punishment, a punishment that condemned her as much as him.

In the end the only thing she could think to do was to kill him. She'd got them all into this mess and it was up to her to get them out. Also, Nancy needed avenging, and this could never happen in a conventional sense because then everything would have to come out and her children would have to live with the fact that their father was a murderer. She would never forgive her friend, but she would avenge her, and in doing so she would punish a guilty man and free herself. A bit like birth and death, no one was going to help her and nor should they.

She lay in bed night after night trying to work out the best way to do it. The easiest would be to simply hold a pillow over his emaciated face. If she slipped him a sleeping pill then she doubted he would even struggle, but if he did he was so weak now it wouldn't matter. Except it would be a very obvious murder with only one suspect and she was certainly not going to serve any more time for fucking Howard.

A fall down the stairs would be satisfying, with all the accompanying blood and mess, but what if he didn't die, but just became paralysed and even more dependent? Then there couldn't be a second accident and she really would be stuck with him forever.

Poison was too detectable and she had no idea where she would get any. She could fake a burglary and stab him, which had a certain poetic justice to it when you considered what he'd done to Nancy, but it would maybe be too suspicious for that to have happened to two people in her life and probably the police would investigate. And if they did find out maybe they'd then wonder if she'd been responsible for Nancy's death as well which, you could argue, she had been. Because, if Howard hadn't been married to her, then maybe Nancy would have agreed to run away with him and he wouldn't have had to kill her to stop her leaving him.

She guessed the only option was an overdose.

It was slightly easier to be not exactly nice to Howard, but at least tolerant, after she'd decided to kill him. She devised a plan, which she set in motion by going to see the GP. She told him that Howard was complaining about pains in his legs, but she didn't know if she could give him painkillers with all the medication he was on. The GP said he should come and give Howard a check, but that a few painkillers weren't going to do him any harm.

Mary bought a packet on the way home. She thought she'd

read about long-term painkiller poisoning, but she didn't know how effective it was or how long it took. She knew she couldn't google the information, even from an internet café, because everything was traceable everywhere now. The only thing really to do was to somehow get him to take an overdose. But not until she was as sure as she could be that she wasn't going to be blamed.

She took the packet of pills into the lounge with her, not even bothering to remove her jacket. The days had recently begun to shorten ever so slightly and on the walk back from the surgery she had noticed the first chill in the air, which trailed after her as she walked across the room. Howard looked up at her as he always did now, his eyes rounded like a baby animal, and it made her want to laugh, how easy it was to get him to notice her after all.

'I've got you the pills for your leg,' she said as she approached, holding her nerve like she really could wrap it around her.

'My leg?' He looked down at the delicate structures resting on the chair. When he looked back up his brow was creased.

She sighed. 'Yes, your leg. You said it hurt.'

'Did I?'

She felt suddenly hot, so she had to remove her jacket and lay it on the sofa. But with her back turned to her husband she reminded herself of all he had done. 'Come on, Howard, you've been crying out at night. I keep having to come down. The doctor says these pills will make it better.'

'I did?' But she could hear the softening of his tone and the beginning of acceptance. He was after all totally self-obsessed and would enjoy thinking about an ailment.

She picked up his beaker, which was thankfully half full. 'Hold out your hand.' He did as he was told and she popped two of the soft, red pills onto his palm, noticing the dirt that had collected under his fingernails. 'Swallow them down,' she said softly and he did as he was told, drinking from the beaker so she could see his Adam's apple bobbing up and down.

She suspected that she could get him to take the whole packet right then. She imagined popping the pills into his hand and watching him swallow them one by one. How he wouldn't question her and how easy it would be and she longed for it to be over and done with. But she held back because she had to protect her children, which meant protecting herself.

By the time the doctor visited they had their routine in place. He was a well-meaning young man, who came by on a darkening evening that reminded her of the coming winter, with a slanting rain battering the windows. Mary had washed Howard the night before, combing out his tatty beard and wrapped him in a thick cardigan and fluffy socks. She'd put an electric heater by his legs and some lavender oil in a burner on a shelf.

'So, I hear you're having some trouble with your leg,' the doctor said, kneeling down in front of Howard.

Howard looked over his head to Mary. 'My leg hurts,' he said.

'So your wife says. Perhaps you can show me where.'

Howard kept his panic-laden eyes on Mary. 'It hurts,' he repeated.

'You won't get much more than that,' Mary said. 'Sometimes I don't even know if the pain is real.' It was like a game of dare.

'Do you mind if I touch your leg, Mr Smithson?' Howard shook his head so the doctor felt along the bones, squeezing at the knee joint and flexing the ankle back and forth. Mary wanted to laugh, it was all so outrageous.

'Well, there doesn't seem to be anything obviously wrong,' the doctor said, standing back up. He turned to Mary. 'How have the painkillers been working?'

'They do seem to calm him.' She looked over his shoulder

at Howard as if she cared. Humans are so stupid, she remembered Howard saying on more than one occasion, our brains are susceptible to almost any suggestion. She wished she had remembered that particular lesson before.

'I think it's useful for you not to question the origin of the pain,' the doctor was saying. 'If they calm him and if they stop the pain, for whatever reason, then I don't see any harm in continuing giving them to him.'

'But he asks for them every day.' Mary let her voice sound worn down with worry.

'As long as you don't exceed the dose, that's fine.' He smiled at her and she knew he felt sorry for her.

They walked back in to the hall together and she shut the door so Howard was blocked from view.

'How are you coping?' the doctor asked as they stood in the hallway.

'Oh, OK, you know.'

'It's very important you look after yourself, Mrs Smithson. Your life has changed immeasurably in the last year and it's a lot to deal with.'

Mary couldn't help the corners of her mouth from twitching, because the doctor had no idea of the changes she'd had to absorb. 'I just feel so sorry for him.'

'Yes, but we don't want you getting ill.'

'I was thinking about getting a part time job. I mean, we need the money, but also, just getting out of the house for a bit.'

He nodded vigorously. 'I would say that is absolutely essential. There are lots of organisations that can help you with care and the like. We have to rely more and more on charities as our funding is so tight, but the help is still there. I can help you find it.'

'Thank you.'

'And I know you don't want to think about it yet, but we do need to start to consider the long-term situation. Your husband has had a complete, catastrophic breakdown. People do of course recover, but things never go back to how they were. Sometimes, not even close.'

Mary dipped her eyes and her head jolted because the thought of Howard getting better was too awful to consider. But the doctor misread her and put a hand on her arm. 'I'm sorry, I know you know all this. We'll take things slowly.'

She nodded as she opened the door to the strange rain that almost felt monsoon-like and smiled as the doctor waved from her broken gate. Then she shut the door and leant back against it, taking in deep breaths. It was so hard to tell if she was doing the right thing. Sometimes she forgot who she was even avenging. Did she even care about Nancy any more? She looked over at the closed door of Howard's room and her hatred and anger at him bubbled and curdled, cementing her resolve.

The next day she got a phone call from a friend at UCL who said someone in her department was looking for an admin assistant and this would be perfect because the professor was a Greek scholar. The woman, Thea Brackenbury, called that afternoon and Mary arranged to go and see her the next day. Not so long ago Mary would have been intimidated by Thea, imagining someone with such a name perfectly positioned to study the gods, but now she didn't give it a second thought. She left Howard alone in the end, locking him into the sitting room so he couldn't cause too much damage, but sure he wouldn't move anyway. Then she took the tube to Warren Street and emerged into a sea of people living very different lives to hers.

Just being in the building felt a little like coming home, as if someone had laid a hand over her restless brain. She imagined her days spent in this place, communing with the gods again and finding hidden treasures buried within other people's words. It seemed in fact incredible that she had denied herself access to this part of herself for so long. Except, as she waited on the soft chair outside Thea's office, she thought it had more been Howard's choice than hers. He had wanted her to stay at home with the children, he had refused to help pay for childcare, he had told her there wasn't room for two academics in one marriage.

'Seriously, Mary, who's going to employ you?' he'd say to her whenever she raised the subject. 'You didn't exactly have a stellar career before you got pregnant and you've not got much to offer. I mean, you can't really even keep on top of a house, so I don't know how you think you'll manage in an office.'

As she breathed in the rarefied air of the university she wondered what his motives had been, because they'd certainly needed the money. She supposed it kept her vulnerable and easier to control, but she thought it had probably simply been practical for Howard to keep her away from his work. Academia was a small world and, had she worked in the field, she would no doubt have encountered rumours about him. She wondered suddenly if the things she knew about him, like the weeping girls, or the disciplinary committee he'd been forced to address five years earlier for his aggressive attitude to colleagues, were just the tip of the iceberg. She saw herself suddenly like a ghost moving about her own life, not fully participating because it was all too dangerous. Because what woman lets girls turn up on their doorstep or simply accepts their husband's aggression both at work and home? It had been very wrong of her to ignore these things, to allow them to become the days of her life. She sat up slightly straighter, shot through with the realisation that Howard had a deep disdain for humanity.

Her mind shifted and recalibrated and, for the first time ever, she saw Howard as the fucked-up one in their relationship. Maybe he had never been this lofty fighter for justice, railing against an unfair system, using his mind for good. Maybe he'd just always been a man so angry with the world that he saw people as commodities whom he could bend and break to fit in with his life. And she had let him get away with this, when really she should have installed her own discipline years ago. Or maybe she should have just got angry herself. Her skin tingled with the idea.

Thea was charming and kind, her eyes expressive and generous. She was worried that the work was a bit beneath Mary, but also said her research assistant was looking to move on so there would be an opportunity to change things around in a bit. They laughed about aspects of a text Thea was struggling with at that moment and talked about papers she'd published and Mary knew the job was hers before Thea offered it to her. She was going away in a few days for a month on a lecture tour of America, she said, and then there was the hell of Christmas, so would Mary be OK to start in the new year?

In the new year Nancy would have been dead for a year and Mary would have known about her and Howard for nearly six months. There was a certain symmetry to it all, she thought as she accepted the offer; it would be the right time for Howard to be dead and life to feel totally different. She saw a tantalising glimpse of a freedom that had always eluded her and the thought was breathtaking but also unreal, so she felt like she would probably never actually arrive there.

On the tube going home Mary's anger with both herself and Howard started to intensify. Yes, the children had always been the most important thing to her, but that shouldn't have meant that she had to sacrifice everything which made her who she was as well. The two states were not incompatible and yet Howard had made her believe that they were. She looked around the carriage at the harried faces there and thought that other people organised their lives so that one person wasn't forgotten. Because that was what Howard had done – he had forgotten she was a person with needs and desires as well. She had let herself live a life that women had chained themselves to railings to avoid, a life that was meant to have vanished, but actually still existed terrifyingly in too many homes. They all thought society was so fair and liberal now, but what people didn't talk about was how it still often operated along the same old debasing lines for so many women. Howard had, she realised, as the tube scrunched to a halt in a dark tunnel, made her completely dependent on him – both financially and emotionally.

Her new found anger bubbled in her veins and with it came a clarity of thought she didn't think she'd experienced for years. The truth was Howard had used money as a weapon for at least a decade now. Whenever she had brought up the idea of getting a job he had ranted about the cost of childcare, then when the children had gone to school he'd told her she was unemployable. They'd never had a joint bank account, instead he'd handed out cash, which was never quite enough, always chiding her at her inability to budget, as he called it. The house shrivelled around them, they never went anywhere and the children had second-hand everything. In the past few years, before his illness, she thought he'd even started to imply that she was the one to blame for it all, as she was the one who'd wanted three children and not to go back to work, as if she spent her days lying on the couch eating grapes.

In another life she thought she might have been Thea, with her kind eyes and her lecture tour of America. Except she also knew she wouldn't have swapped the children for that, or for anything. She hadn't asked Thea about her family, but Mary hadn't got the sense of anyone living in her life. Women, she realised, had to choose in a way men didn't.

Her head began to ache as the tube jolted and the air heated up with the collected sighs of the passengers. Her brain felt soggy and confused, which brought with it a fluttering panic that took hold of her heart, making it jump in her chest. She had no real option other than to kill her children's father; she was going to remove him from their lives and, in doing so, was going to fundamentally alter their stories. And she would never be able to tell them what she had done or why it was the best thing. They would grieve for him and she would comfort them, when she had been the cause of their pain.

She didn't think they loved him, not really and completely like the four of them loved each other. Marcus certainly didn't, in fact he had frequently told her so, although he hadn't lately, not since Howard had become ill. And the girls were ambivalent. They loved him in an abstract way, in the same way one loves a family pet. His illness hadn't rained down on them, it hadn't affected them in the way it would have done if it was her dribbling in the chair. They made him cups of tea and occasionally sat with him and chatted on about their days, but he didn't leave a mark of sadness on them.

Their lives would be no different if she let him live. It wouldn't stop them from going out into the world and living their lives, it wouldn't make anything better or brighter for them. Perhaps, in fact, his death might even release them in some way, especially Marcus. Mary had found him leaning against the lounge doorway just the night before. She'd put her hand on the small of his back and when he'd turned she'd been surprised to see tears in his eyes.

'Are you all right?' she'd asked.

'Yes.'

'It's OK to be sad.'

He shook his head. 'It's not so much that I'm sad about what he is now, more that I never got the chance to find out what he was really like before.'

She thought it an odd thing to say. 'You know what he was like.' They both let the statement hang in the air because they both could only have been thinking about all the arguments and shouting, all the slammed doors and tiptoeing past the study in case they disturbed him.

'I don't know,' Marcus said, scratching absentmindedly at the side of his face. 'I'm starting to wonder if anyone is just like one thing. Do you think you ever really know anyone, Mum?'

Naturally she thought of Nancy. 'No, I suppose not.' But then she thought of Eleanor. 'Although with lots of people I think you have a pretty good idea.'

'I hope so. It's too frightening to think that we're all alone in our heads and no one's ever going to get in.'

She reached up and ruffled his hair in a gesture designed to hide the flip of fear in her stomach. 'Oh don't worry, someone will get in all right.' She'd even offered up a silent prayer to Venus as she made her way to the kitchen, because when it came down to it that's all she wanted for her children, that they found a kind, generous love.

She stood shakily as the tube made the final uphill climb to her stop. The truth was Marcus was terrifyingly right. She was going to kill his father and he would never for an iota of a second think that was possible. Goodness, before the letter, she would never have thought that possible. And that was perhaps more frightening than the fact we never know others, the fact that we never know ourselves.

Mary walked from the station to her house, the roads so much quieter than where she'd just been, and wondered if what she was going to do had been caused more by her never knowing Nancy, or never knowing herself. She was beginning to find it easy to accept that Howard had betrayed her so terribly, but almost impossible to think this of Nancy. The thought of that friendship being fake was more than she could bear.

As her feet trod the dirty pavements, past the never-ending building works gentrifying her area, she tried to remember something that would prove Nancy's love. And because she had just been thinking about her son, her brain offered up the large bunch of flowers Nancy sent after Marcus was born. They had arrived the day after she came home from the hospital, proceeding Howard into the room and making her heart soar, because they weren't a slap-dash purchase, but a bunch of flowers chosen with care and consideration just for her, wonderful in all their bright intensity and heady scent, two things she still loved like a hangover from her childhood. She'd looked at her husband holding them as her son sucked on her breast and thought that she had never felt happier, that they were now a unit, unbreakable and complete.

But Howard had surprised her by chucking the flowers onto the bed, causing at least one stem to break.

'From your capitalist friend,' he said with a sneer. He'd seemed slightly disorientated since the birth, which she'd put down to a combination of the tiredness and excitement she was feeling, which did make everything seem a bit unreal. But his eyes were glassy and his mouth was set hard.

'What are you talking about, Howard?'

'I mean, look at them,' he said. 'They must have cost a fortune.'

'Are they from Nancy?'

He snorted. 'Who else.'

'Can you put them in a vase?' She tried not to cry because

his reaction didn't seem like him at all. 'I expect she was just trying to be nice.'

There had been a catch to her voice which had at least returned him somewhat to himself because he'd fetched a vase and put the flowers on the chest of drawers by the window where she watched them wilt and die over the next few days. Howard had always been exorcised by Nancy, she thought now. If she had been quicker she might have recognised the fascination buried in his annoyance, but she'd been stupid enough to take it all at face value, to sometimes even agree with his criticisms.

Howard, she thought as she let herself in to her house. Howard, the killer of dreams, the opposite of love, the dagger in my heart, the thorn in my side, the layer of traps, the king of selfishness, the never-ending warrior, the man who now must die.

Unlike most other people in her life, Eleanor hadn't been lying and she really did return from Yemen after four weeks. The relief Mary felt at seeing her was physical, like something drained through her when she opened the door to her at the end of a dour October that was so warm she would sometimes wake in the morning and think they were at the start of spring, contributing to her sense of unreality.

They went into the kitchen and Mary couldn't stop looking at her funny, squat friend, with her severe hair and button eyes. Travelling never changed Ellie, Mary thought. It elongated and slimmed and tanned most people, but not Ellie, she remained constant wherever you put her.

They sat at the wooden kitchen table and ate bowls of steaming curry whilst the girls came and went and asked questions and looked at photos on Ellie's phone. Mary felt her shoulders droop for the first time in so long that her eyes also felt heavy and she wanted to sleep, but she also didn't want to miss a moment.

'I still haven't said hello to Howard,' Eleanor said when they were finally alone.

'There's no point.'

'Really? But, I'd like to.'

'You never liked him anyway.' She couldn't bear to think of Ellie feeling sorry for him, but saw the shock register on her friend's face.

'There's a difference between that and wishing him ill.' Which Mary thought was an ironic thing for Eleanor to say, as she would wish him nothing but ill if she knew what he'd done to Nancy.

Mary stood up. 'Come on then.'

They went in to the lounge together, but Howard was asleep, his head lolling against his chest and his spine rounded out. She felt Eleanor start and looked at her in time to register the shock on her face. She put her finger to her lips and they tiptoed back out, shutting the door behind them.

'Oh God,' Eleanor said when they were sitting back down. 'Shit, Mary.'

'I know.'

'I didn't realise it had got so bad. He's worse than when I went away. Do they have any more idea what it is?'

'They're calling it this random bi-polar thing. But really it's a massive, catastrophic breakdown.'

'But why? I mean, I know that's a stupid thing to ask, but—'

'It's impossible to say.' Mary longed to fetch the brown envelope and share it with her friend, longed for the companionship so much she worried she wouldn't be able to stop herself. Although recently she'd begun to wonder if Howard hadn't always been heading this way, Nancy simply being the final crack. She had noticed how lots of his colleagues had seemed unsurprised by what had happened to him, how many of them made coded references to his moods and temper. It almost made her feel better, that it hadn't just been her, like she'd always thought.

'Can he still speak? I mean, does he know you?' Eleanor asked.

'He can speak, but he doesn't much, and when he does he doesn't make much sense. He knows me, yes, but I'm not sure that's a good thing.'

Eleanor reached across the table and enfolded Mary's hand in her own. 'Are you doing this all alone?'

'Well the kids are here.'

'No, you know what I mean.'

Mary was crying before she really realised what was happening. Great, big fat tears that rolled off her face and splashed on the kitchen table. They clogged her throat and filled her mouth and blurred her vision. She felt Eleanor draw her chair closer and wrap her arms around her and realised it had been so long since another human had held her close. It was possible that the last time it had happened had been when they'd sat like this after Nancy.

'You need to get some help. There must be some available,' Eleanor said.

Mary pulled out of the embrace and wiped her eyes with the back of her hand. 'The doctor's looking in to it. But there isn't much, there's no money left in any of the budgets.'

'But there must be something.'

'Come on, Els, you of all people know there's too much need and not enough money.'

'Christ.' Eleanor tucked her hair behind her ears. 'What a fucking shitty year.'

'At least it's got to get better.' Mary thought of the silver packets of red pills waiting in her bedside drawer. Again the urge to tell Eleanor flooded her so completely she had to physically put her hand over her mouth to stop the words spilling out.

'Things often get worse before they get better,' Eleanor said, which made Mary feel bad about going on about her problems. 'How are you feeling about Robert now?'

'I should probably call him, but I can't face it.' She sighed. 'Everything has felt so weird this last year, like Nancy put a spell on us all or something.'

Mary snorted and felt Eleanor look askance at her. She'd forgotten that she would have to spend the rest of her life deifying Nancy's memory if she didn't tell anyone. 'Sorry. I know you really cared about Robert.'

'I think I loved him actually.'

'Oh, Els, that was never going to work though, was it?' Mary looked at her friend's neat face as she spoke and saw the wince of pain from her words. 'It's not because he didn't care about you, but it was all too raw and you were too close to Nancy.'

'I know, I know, but—'

'You loved him, so.'

Eleanor nodded, biting down on her bottom lip.

'Love's shitty,' Mary said.

'Do you still love Howard?'

'No.' They sat silently for a while, but then Mary spoke again. 'It isn't just his illness. It's more that I've had time to look at him from outside, almost, if that makes sense. I've done a lot of thinking about our marriage over the past few months and it doesn't make for pretty memories.'

'I'm glad you don't love him any more. He never deserved your love.'

Mary smiled at the fierceness of her friend's protection. 'I should have listened to you years ago and left him.'

'And I should have listened to you about Robert. But we never do, do we? I mean, love sort of trumps everything, doesn't it? It makes you mad.'

'Well, apart from death. Love doesn't trump death.'

'But it makes you just as mad.'

Mary laughed and for the first time in ages she felt a glimpse of genuine happiness, because of course Eleanor was right and her words went in some way to absolving Nancy. Or at least not absolving her, but maybe explaining her a bit; maybe making her betrayal slightly less wounding.

'At least we can love each other safely,' Eleanor said.

There was the noise of a key turning in the front door and they both turned to see Marcus. He came straight into the kitchen.

'I've been hearing such great things about you from Lucy and Tom,' Eleanor said as soon as he was in the room.

'I'm really enjoying it,' Marcus said. 'Thank you, you know, for ...'

'You don't have to thank me every time you see me. I should be thanking you really. In fact, I know now isn't the time to talk about it, but we were thinking maybe we should make it official and pay you a bit of money.'

'Really?'

Mary's heart contracted at the tone of her son's voice, an excitement there she didn't think she'd heard since childhood.

'I'm coming into the office tomorrow so let's all discuss it then.'

'Thank you,' Mary said when Marcus went upstairs.

'Please, you've got to stop thanking me. He's great.'

'Yes, but ...' It was always the little things, Mary thought, things that someone outside of you might not notice, but which the people who loved you knew made the biggest difference.

'How do you feel about Robert's, you know, involvement in Nancy's death now?' Mary asked as lightly as she could because she was scared that Eleanor wouldn't let that go.

'I don't really know,' Eleanor said. 'I mean, I'm not sure he could have done anything to Nancy. And I think you're probably right, he could easily not be sharing that letter to protect Zara, which I guess is the important thing now. But I'm also sure it wasn't Davide Boyette. Although, of course, like we said, just because he wasn't the lover doesn't mean the lover didn't kill her. But his life has clearly been fucked by it all. In fact so many peoples have been. It's all such a mess.'

'Good old Nancy,' Mary said before she could check herself.

'What do you mean?'

Mary found she couldn't force the word 'nothing' out of her mouth. 'I don't know, just that she behaved pretty selfishly when you think about it all, don't you think?'

There was a moment of recognition in Eleanor's face, but she swallowed it back down. 'I think it was all typically Nancy.'

'Well, yes, that's sort of what I mean. We've all always danced to her tune, haven't we?'

'I don't know—'

'I mean, even telling you about the affair and not me. And obviously all that lying to Robert.'

Mary could feel her face heating up and when she looked over Eleanor was looking at her with a crease between her eyebrows. 'I think Nancy was one of those people who sort of came as she was, if you know what I mean.'

'Yes, I do, but that's irritating in itself. I mean, how often are you uncompromisingly yourself?' Eleanor smiled. 'I don't think I ever am and yet Nancy thought it was her right to be whatever she wanted to be at all times, fuck the rest of us.'

'Funnily Davide said much the same. I mean, obviously he

didn't know Nancy, but he said something about how we put people like Nancy at the centre of life. He said we make too much of some lives and deaths, when really shouldn't we see everything as the same?'

Mary felt the hairs on her body rise up out of their pores. 'I think there's a lot to that.'

'A lot has happened to you this past year.' A faint blush washed Eleanor's cheeks. 'I mean, some would say what's happened to you is worse than what happened to Nancy, but still that's not the central story, is it?'

Mary shook her head, worried suddenly that she was going to shout the truth so loudly everyone would hear.

After Eleanor left Mary went in to check on Howard and was surprised to see he was awake, but hadn't called out for her. She switched on the sidelights, sparing them the hell of the overhead light, which she'd taken to using, almost like an interrogation on Howard without the questions. Her hand brushed the silver framed photograph of their wedding day as she withdrew it from under the lampshade and she picked it up and looked into their faces. Howard's smile was small and forced underneath his beard and her face was so rounded out by a pregnancy which was going to end only seventy-two hours after the shutter snapped that her cheeks almost sparkled and her features had dwindled to nothing.

No one should get married looking like that, she thought, as she marvelled at the size of her stomach under the material – because you could barely call it a dress – she had worn. She remembered the pinch from her shoes that day, the tightness across her stomach, the ache in her back, the sweat on her brow and in her armpits.

She could barely remember any more why she had insisted

on it. Her parents probably preferred the fact that she wasn't going to be an unmarried, single mother, but they also wouldn't have minded that much if she had been. They were so used to her difference by then, had accepted her incessant reading, her Greek gods, her getting into Oxford, her living in London. They were proud of her and her eccentricity, as they termed it, and the baby wouldn't have seemed that different to all the other things. No, she knew the answer: it had been to tether Howard to her, to claim him, to stamp him with her scent.

She took the photo over to Howard and sat down next to him, on the stool she had put there to make feeding him easier. 'Do you remember this?' She hadn't expected anything, but he moved his hand slowly, brushing it along the glass, over both their faces. 'Did you ever even want to marry me? Would you rather have stayed with Penny?'

His brow wrinkled; maybe he didn't even remember who Penny was. Mary momentarily imagined her stretched out on a yacht, laughing at them.

'Why did you kill Nancy, Howard?' She sounded angry even to her own ears.

'Nancy's dead,' he said, and then started crying. He let the photo fall to the floor, but it didn't break. Mary picked it up and sat with it face down on her lap.

'She's dead because you killed her.'

Howard was making a strange sound, almost like a keening; snot was dripping out of his nose, which he wiped on the sleeve of his jumper.

'Did you love her?' Mary felt her heart hard and fast beneath her ribs.

'Yes.' He looked straight at her.

'She didn't love you. She loved me.' She knew it was pathetic, this bargaining over a dead woman, but it seemed important.

She looked at Howard and thought he was a condemned man. She wondered if the letter in the brown envelope had condemned Nancy, or if it had bought her a bit more time. She thought about how the man with the dog on the towpath had chosen exactly the right time to go on his walk as far as she was concerned, how Penny's mother had fallen down the steps at the perfect moment for Marcus to be conceived. Sometimes life and death were nothing more than accidents of timing. But sometimes they required planning, sometimes you had to play God or nothing ever changed.

Howard put his hands over his face and his shoulders began to shake. She thought of the red pills and it calmed the urge she had to go into the kitchen and find the sharpest knife they owned. She had it all planned out. In the middle of the night she would come downstairs and wake him up and start giving him pills for his leg, as she had done every night for the past few weeks, even though really he had never once cried out for her. Except this time she wouldn't stop. She knew he would take them, but she wasn't sure if he would know what he was doing. Then in the morning she would pretend she had accidentally left the packet next to his bed and he had taken an overdose.

It was just she couldn't work out when this was going to happen. She would wake in the mornings convinced that today would be the day, but as the time passed she would lose her nerve, weighed down with what it meant to wilfully take another life, even if that life had as good as taken yours. The gods, she knew, would be laughing at her spinelessness.

A few days later Mary received a strange text from Robert asking her to the annual bonfire night party that he and Nancy had always held. Their house sat in a large oval of similarly proud houses, all of which enclosed a beautiful communal garden. The residents held a joint bonfire night party, to which outsiders were invited, like serfs to the castle, and Nancy had always included her and Ellie.

'Can you believe he says it will be a good opportunity to banish ghosts?' Eleanor spluttered when Mary rang her to see if she'd got the text as well. 'I mean, it hasn't even been a year.'

Mary though quite liked the thought of that. 'Well, he's got to move on sometime. I think it's positive.'

'And just asking me like that, on a group text.'

'He's being conciliatory. He didn't have to ask either of us really. And you did make it clear that you didn't want a relationship with him.'

'I know. But—'

'Anyway, I'm going.' Mary knew already how pleasant it would be to stand in Nancy's house, without Howard, watching Robert banishing his bloody ghosts. It might even dampen the fiery anger, which now raged constantly inside her. 'Please come.'

Eleanor sighed. 'Yes, of course I will.'


Marcus agreed to sit with Howard on the night, so she fed him early and got him into bed with the radio turned up.

'I'm going to Nancy's house,' she said, as she straightened herself from tucking him in.

His eyes flickered to her. 'Nancy?'

'Yes, you remember. Nancy, my best friend, who you were sleeping with all last year and then killed because she decided she didn't like you any more.'

His face crumpled in a strange way, almost like it was folding in on itself, like in fact how she imagined it would look if you saw a house being swallowed by a sinkhole. She turned her back on him and stalked out of the room because still she couldn't bear to see the devastation Nancy wreaked in him.

Eleanor was waiting outside Notting Hill tube and they walked down the hill together, through roads that had become a parody of themselves, past shops that sold goods more expensive than the entire contents of her house. There was a vulgarity to it that she thought now Nancy had loved and which she bet Socialist Howard had embraced. Only a few nights before she had gone through all the mementos in the brown envelope, trying to find the courage to turn her anger into actual murderous rage, and found a restaurant receipt so exorbitant it could have fed their whole family for a week. It was in fact more money than Howard gave her to do just that every week.

Nancy's house was lit up and they could see people in the windows, sipping on drinks and chatting.

'Christ,' Eleanor said. 'It's a fucking party.'

The door was open so they made their way in and downstairs to the huge knocked-through kitchen, where the majority of the noise was coming from. There were probably twenty or so people in the room, a few friends and work colleagues of Robert's whom they'd met before, and Zara by the stove ladling out chilli. Robert spotted them immediately and came over, reddening as he approached.

He kissed them both on the cheeks and Mary could feel Eleanor stiffen beside her. 'I'm so glad you both came,' he stuttered. 'It wouldn't have been the same without you here.'

'I wouldn't have missed it,' Mary replied, entirely truthfully.

'It might seem a bit strange,' he said and Mary knew that even though he was looking at her he was talking to Eleanor. 'But Zara and I discussed it and we thought Nancy would have liked it. She always loved bonfire night and this party. And the thought of just the two of us sitting here and feeling sad seemed awful.'

'No, it's the right thing to do,' Eleanor said. Robert allowed himself to look at her then and Mary thought the tension between them was like watching ice form on a pond

'Anyway,' Robert said. 'I think you know most people.'

'I can see Dido,' Mary said, waving at the sleek woman Robert had worked with for so long that they'd met her at lots of parties.

'Get some food and then I'll introduce you to everyone else,' he said, his blush now extending up into his hairline.

Zara was effusive with her greetings and it was obvious that she'd drunk too much red wine because her lips were stained. Her and Eleanor started an intricate discussion about a book she was studying and Mary let her eyes wander around the room she knew so well. It seemed completely different without Nancy in it, as if her presence had somehow held everything in place, so that now everything drifted, not sure where to land.

After a while the group made their way outside towards the massive bonfire in the centre of the garden, which Mary remembered Nancy complaining about. Something to do with how it was the only thing Robert ever got really animated about, how he collected wood and spent several Sundays helping to build the pyre. She couldn't now remember why that had been a problem; it was a beautiful structure, the orange flames weaving through it, the air filled with the thick scent of wood smoke.

The first firework whizzed into the sky, closely followed by another and another. They all tipped their heads back and watched as colours fizzed above their heads, splattering the sky like a crime scene. And for a moment she allowed herself to believe that the world as they knew it had ended and there really were dragons up there, about to impart a new order.

Eleanor nudged her in the ribs. 'Mary, look,' she whispered, gesturing over to the right of them.

Mary squinted, but couldn't make out what she was looking at, there were too many people and she could taste gunpowder in her throat, which she loved because it made everything seem old and like it meant something.

'There,' Eleanor hissed. 'Robert.'

Mary followed the way her friend was pointing and then she saw, silhouetted against the fire, Robert with his hand pressed into the small of a woman's back. 'Is that Dido?' she whispered to Eleanor.

'Yes. What the fuck?'

'It might be nothing. They're old friends.' Except it didn't look like nothing. It looked like a proprietorial gesture.

'My God,' Eleanor said.

Mary turned to her and couldn't see if she had gone red or if the fire had dyed her that way. 'It's OK,' she said. 'Something like that's bound to happen sometime. Remember everything we said about how it couldn't have worked with you.'

But Eleanor surprised her by smiling, even attempting a little laugh. And then Zara was there, linking her arms through both of theirs in just the way Nancy would have done if Howard hadn't ruined everything. She felt sad then, and maybe a little drunk. There were too many loud pops and bangs and the fire was very hot and it was hard to understand why things had turned out the way they had.

She told Eleanor and Zara she needed the loo and made her way back into the house, where she drank a glass of water, standing by the sink. But then she did need the loo, except the one in the basement was locked, so she made her way upstairs. The door to the drawing room was open and something like nostalgia, because she doubted she would ever come back here, made her walk in and stand inside the yellow room. She walked towards the long bookcase, drawn by the photos leaning against some of the books, knowing before she reached them who she would see. And there Nancy was, smiling out at her, as if nothing had changed.

She was drawn mostly to a photo in a simple wooden frame of Nancy with her arm around Zara aged about ten, dressed in a football kit, a medal round her neck. Nancy was wearing a white t-shirt with jeans and trainers, her long arm bronzed and her smile turned out to the camera. Mary reached out and took it off the shelf, holding it closer to her face, feeling it tickling some hidden part of her brain, some memory not quite at the surface. Then she heard Nancy speaking, saying something about how it was a shame that Zara and Marcus hadn't got into football at the same time, how they could have formed the first ever gender neutral team and how it had made them both laugh.

She looked at Zara again in the picture – yes, she must have been about ten, she'd won some league or something two years in a row and then grew breasts and got her period and stopped playing, which had made Nancy furious, enough to rail at the unfeasibility of being a woman in this world on a number of occasions. Marcus, on the other hand, hadn't shown any interest in football at all as a child and had suddenly got into it at, what, thirteen, just as Zara was stopping? That was it, wasn't it? Her brain was trying to tell her something to do with Marcus and football and Nancy?

The truth is that nothing stays buried forever. Everything eventually works its way up through the cold, hard ground. She must have always known what she had just realised since the day she found the brown envelope, but somehow hidden this knowledge from herself, although now it sliced through her brain, cold and hard. A memory so complete began to play inside her mind, the grainy images projecting onto her white skull.

It wasn't a memory tinged with Nancy's death, but it was recent, from not the summer that had just gone, but the one before that. Mary was lying in the garden with the girls, on their thin stretch of patchy grass with old towels under them and lemonade in a jug, watching aeroplanes streak across the blue sky, talking about where they would go if they could. And she had let herself have a moment of pleasure at having got to at least that point; she remembered the feeling almost like a physical sensation, spreading through her body like treacle.

She had been aware that Howard had taken up with someone new for a while by then. All the usual signs had been there encapsulated within his distraction and agitation at them, his constantly working late, his clipped tone when he spoke to her. But somehow, perversely, she hadn't felt as affected by it as usual and this had been part of her pleasure, as if her learning to accept Howard's infidelities meant something. She'd told herself that she knew how it all went; the girl would be appealing for a few months, then he would tire of her, there might be a few ugly phone calls which she would pretend not to hear, his mood would dip, then substantially improve. And while it was happening they would be given a reprieve from him because he'd be around less.

My God, you were actually that stupid, Mary said to herself as she stood holding Nancy's photograph, like a god looking down from Mount Olympus. Because now her knowledge about this moment was omnipotent, which meant she knew she had every reason to dread what had been happening, and no pleasure could ever come from the situation. Because now she could see that this new, other woman had been Nancy.

'Mum,' Marcus said, only in her memory, except the power of what she was remembering meant it reverberated around the room.

She'd raised herself up on one elbow and squinted at him, framed by the kitchen door. 'Oh, hi, when did you get back?'

'Just.'

'You OK?' Even from Nancy's sitting room Mary could hear the catch in her voice, because she'd always known her boy too well, known his mood from the slant of his shoulder or the set of his chin.

'Yup.' But he stayed standing just inside the kitchen door, his football balanced against his hip.

She stood up. 'I'm going to get the biscuits, girls,' she said, although they weren't really listening.

Inside was dark after the sun and little spots danced before her eyes. 'Was football good?' she asked as she went to the cupboard to get biscuits she didn't want.

'There's something I need to tell you, Mum.'

She turned, her heart thudding against her ribs, her mind awash with bad things that could have happened to him. 'What?'

'I saw Dad.' He kicked his foot against the table leg and wouldn't meet her eye.

'In the park?'

'Yeah.'

'But I thought he was giving that lecture.' She couldn't believe she still believed his lies.

Marcus looked up finally and he had tears in his eyes. 'He was with ... well, he was with ...'

Mary's throat felt dry. 'I'm sure the lecture just got cancelled or something.'

'No, Mum. I mean, I saw him kissing her.'

She looked instinctively into the garden. 'Oh God, Marcus, don't tell the girls.'

His eyes dried suddenly. 'You knew?'

'No. At least, maybe.'

'Maybe?' The word sounded disgusting repeated by him. 'So you do know?'

'It's complicated.'

His eyes withered her and in the look she felt something die. 'How can you let them make such a fool of you?'

She reached for him but he jerked away. 'Marcus, please, you don't understand.'

'Don't,' he said as he walked out of the room. 'You're the one who doesn't understand.'

She ran in to the hall after him. 'Marcus, we need to talk about this.'

'Don't worry,' he said from the top of the stairs. 'I won't say anything to the girls.'

He never really spoke to her again, or so it felt like. And with every day she felt him slip further and further from her grasp. The first night he didn't come home she was literally sick with worry, her hand on the receiver all night, debating whether or not to call the police. But by the tenth time she slept through the night. She smelt cigarettes on his clothes and found vodka bottles and little plastic pouches under his bed. College called to say he'd missed lessons and Howard refused to discuss it.

'Oh God,' Mary said out loud. She had to put a hand onto the bookcase to stop herself from falling as the time line fell sickeningly in to place. She checked back through her memory trying to see her children's faces, to date them, and yes, it had been that summer when things had started to go wrong with Marcus, when he'd started obliterating himself with drink and drugs, staying out so late days merged together, discarding the child he had been. And now she knew why. Her son hadn't just seen his father with another woman, he'd seen him with one of his mother's best friends, his godmother for fuck sake, and his mother had told him she was OK with it. It must have toppled everything he thought he knew, upended his entire world.

The ball of anger, which she had been gestating for a while

now, suddenly exploded, so she felt it leach into her stomach and pool out through all her organs. She felt lost within it, as if nothing had prepared her to feel like this. She had grown children inside her, she had loved, she had nurtured, she had cared. As a girl she had been taught to do all these things, people had assured her it was in her genes, but no one had prepared her for this, as they might have done a boy. Her eyes darted around the room and her hands twitched at her side; she felt like a Fury.

'You fucking bitch,' she said to Nancy, looking down at the photo. But then it felt as if it was burning her hands so she turned and threw it against the far wall, where it shattered and splintered.

Her feet felt uncertain as she left, as if there was a cushion of air between her and the ground. All she knew was that she had to speak to Marcus and that she hated Howard with every fibre of her being.

The house was dark and quiet by the time she got home, but there was a line of light creeping out from under Marcus's door, so she knocked and he called for her to come in. He was lying on his bed, with a laptop balanced on his chest, watching something that was flickering on the screen.

'Did you have a good time?' he asked.

Mary pulled out the chair that sat unused by his desk and sat down heavily. She'd already had this conversation with him a hundred times on the tube and she needed to know how it ended. 'Not really. I have to ask you something.'

He shut the lid of his laptop and sat up. 'What?'

'Do you remember a day not last summer, but the one before? Before Dad got ill and Nancy died. I was in the garden with the girls and you came back from football and told me you'd seen Dad kissing another woman in the park?'

She watched her son pale before her eyes, like a cartoon. 'Why are you asking that?'

'Please, Marcus, do you remember it?'

'Of course I do.'

Mary folded her hands together in her lap and they felt small. 'That woman was Nancy, wasn't it?'

His eyes narrowed. 'You know it was.'

And, oh God, there it was, she hadn't been mistaken. Her own son had thought that she had chosen to protect her friend over him. 'No, Marcus, I didn't know, not then.'

The features on his face flickered. 'But you said, I mean, you said you knew.'

'I knew, or at least I suspected, Dad was having an affair. I didn't know it was with Nancy.' She watched something like relief pass upwards through her son's body, her beautiful boy who was only just an adult, who had been bullied by his father all his life and then thought his mother so pathetic that she would sacrifice him for her life. 'Marcus, I would never have tolerated that. I know I'm pathetic, but I'm not that laughable.'

'I don't think you're pathetic.'

'Well, you should, because I am, or at least I was. I let Dad treat me like shit for years. And you. God, I should have left him years ago and taken you three away from him and I am so fucking sorry and angry with myself that I didn't.'

Marcus started to cry, so she went and sat next to him, pulling his strange awkward body, overgrown like a sapling, towards her. 'It's not your fault,' he said into her shoulder.

'I should have spoken to you that day, but the truth is I couldn't explain how we lived to myself, let alone you. Marcus, you have to believe that I love you and the girls more than anything. I sort of thought Dad could be separate from us, but I can see now what a nonsense that is.'

He pulled away from her and he looked so like a little boy, with his red eyes and mussy hair, that her heart contracted. It felt almost as if he was a newborn baby again and with that thought came a memory: that moment just after giving birth when you feel all-powerful, as if you are capable of absolutely anything, as if you hold the answer to the whole of creation inside you. Mary had forgotten that feeling along the way, but it was back now and she wouldn't ever forget it again.

'If you didn't know then about Nancy, how do you now?' he asked.

'I found a letter from her to Dad a couple of months ago. A letter she must have written before she died, which made it obvious that her and Dad were having an affair.' He nodded. 'Marcus, did you ever talk to Dad about having seen him and Nancy?'

He shifted on the bed. 'Yes, after I spoke to you that summer. But he got really angry with me.'

'But I don't understand, that means he thought I knew?'

Marcus shook his head. 'No, I didn't say I'd spoken to you because he went into one of his rants. He said I mustn't talk to you about it because it would upset you and I didn't want to be responsible for that. I thought he meant you didn't like talking about it, which is why I never mentioned it to you again, but I guess he meant that he didn't want me to tell you.'

Mary whimpered. 'Oh Marcus.' A small shake had built up inside her, but she tried to hold herself together. In a bit she would deal with the fact that Howard had lied to their son and involved him in a terrible situation to save his own skin. She did not feel spineless any more and by morning the gods would have stopped laughing at her. 'When you saw them together in the park, that was the summer before she died, wasn't it? It was the school holidays, so August?' Marcus nodded again. 'And they looked happy?'

He reddened. 'Yeah. I mean, they were kissing. Lying on the grass. They were acting like teenagers, it was gross.'

'But in this letter I found she was clearly trying to end it. And she was dead by the January, so things must have gone wrong.' Mary felt hot, despite the fact that the radiators had switched themselves off, so took off her jacket.

Marcus leant forward. 'I know there was all that stuff about the lover maybe being the killer in the press, but I don't think it was Dad, Mum. Seriously, you mustn't think that. The lover thing was just an easy angle, I'm sure of it.'

'Oh God.' Her vision pitted as her fury rose.

'Are you going to say anything to the police now? About Dad and Nancy, I mean?' His voice was shaking with emotion.

'No. I wasn't ever going to because I wanted to protect you and the girls from it all. But then tonight I worked out you knew anyway and I've been a fool.'

'You haven't been a fool, Mum. Dad was the fool.'

She nodded, because of course he was right. 'I don't think we should say anything to the police or anyone about this, Marcus. I don't want the girls to know, or to have to deal with that knowledge about their father. And I don't think I care about what happened to Nancy any more.' He nodded as well. 'I'll get rid of the letter.' She stood up, her body stiff, but her mind lucid. 'I think we should both get some sleep now.' But she couldn't make herself leave without saying words that meant something. 'I can't tell you how sorry I am, Marcus. I should have spoken to you that day. I really let you down and I am so proud at how you've handled it all.'

'Oh God, Mum, please.' Marcus began to cry then, in a bleak way that made her fearful. 'I'm really scared.'

She hurried back to him and sat next to him, pulling him into her. 'What do you mean? Scared of what?'

He turned his face into her shoulder so she felt her shirt becoming wet. His voice was muffled when he spoke. 'I know what happened, Mum. To Nancy, I mean.'

The world stopped entirely for a moment, so that nothing existed outside of the two of them, a light pulsating in the corner of Mary's vision. But then everything rammed back into full Technicolor focus, the sound turned right back up so she was aware of every atom of her son, weeping beside her. 'I don't understand,' she said as calmly as she could. 'What do you mean?'

He pulled away from her and tried to breathe deeply but it got stuck around his chest, so he swiped at his red eyes. 'You were right, when I thought you knew about Dad and Nancy it made me so angry with you, like I'd got everything wrong.'

Mary reached over and grabbed desperately at her son's hands.

'I spoke to Dad about it a couple more times after I spoke to you, but he always gave me the same shit about how I didn't understand and how I mustn't talk to you because it upset you so much. And then I'd look at you and you seemed so, I don't know, defeated, and I started to realise that it wasn't so much you letting them get away with it as you having no choice. And then I realised I was angry at the wrong person and it made me want to make things better for you.'

'Oh, Marcus.' She had to accept that her son had seen the worst version of her, had lived for too many years with a mother who was just a shadow. But she was not that woman any more and there was still plenty of time for him to see who she really was.

He nodded, once, quickly. 'I got it into my head that I had to get rid of Dad. I thought if I could persuade him to leave then things would get better and we could get on with our lives.

Especially after last Christmas. Do you remember how shit it was?'

'Of course.' Mary's head was suddenly filled with the shouting and the rages, the slamming doors, the thrown china. She knew now that Howard must have been desperate at the thought of Nancy leaving him, but at the time it had just seemed like more of the same, more of his moods, more of his inconsistency. More of his bloody anger. She wondered how long it would have taken her to find her own anger if it hadn't been for Nancy and, momentarily, she felt grateful to her friend.

Marcus swallowed. 'I had this idea to confront them both and tell them to just leave us alone. I thought if Nancy knew I knew it might change things somehow.'

He let out a sob, but then pulled it back into himself.

'The night she died you told me Dad was working late so I did find your iPhone, but he really was at work, so I thought if I went there I could follow him or something, or catch them together. I waited outside till about nineish and then he came out and I was able to follow him to the river in Hammersmith. Nancy turned up about ten and I watched them for a bit. They looked like they were having an argument and Dad was grabbing at her. But in the end I couldn't work out what I was waiting for so I just went over and confronted them.'

Mary wanted to shut her eyes against what she was hearing, it all seemed at once too real and completely unlikely. 'What did they say?'

'Dad just went on about how he was going to tell you and it would all work itself out. But Nancy really lost it. She kept going on and on about what an amazing person you are and how much she loved you and it totally freaked me out, Mum.'

And despite everything Mary wanted to scrabble back through time to hear Nancy say those exact words. 'Go on.'

'She started apologising to me and even though I kept telling her to shut up she kept going. And then she tried to hug me and, I didn't mean to hit her, but I sort of jumped when she touched me and my hand shot out and I felt it connect with her face. But I think Dad thought I'd meant to hit her or something cos he went for me. I saw him pull his fist back to punch me, but as it came towards me Nancy stepped in front of me and he hit her instead, on the side of her jaw.'

Mary rubbed Marcus's arm, like she used to do when he'd fallen as a toddler. There hadn't been enough time between now and then, there would never be enough time. 'It's OK, Marcus,' she soothed.

He looked up at her words.

'Then I lunged at Dad and I don't really know who was hitting who, but Nancy was trying to stop me. She was pulling at me and trying to wrap her arms around me and I didn't want her there. I just wanted them both to go away, so I pushed her. I didn't mean to hurt her, I just wanted her to get off me, but she was so thin, it was like pushing a twig, like nothing. She fell so hard.'

He put his hands up round his face.

'Oh, Mum, the sound she made when she landed. Like this giant thwack so I was surprised people couldn't hear it from across the river. And then she was just lying there, totally still, with this little circle of blood around her head like a halo. Dad started screaming and crying and I tried to help, but he pushed me away. I've always known Dad hated me, but when he looked at me that night it was all right there in his eyes, all the terrible things he's always thought I am. I just ran after that, round and round until I was so tired I had to come home. I thought I was going to wake up the next morning and Dad would go to the police and that would be that, but of course he's been too sick to do anything since then and I don't know what to think now. I probably deserve to be punished, but I'm also so scared.'

They sat silently for a while. Mary felt her anger like an electric current, its power sparking through her body. 'Marcus,' she said, in a voice that made him look at her. 'You have to know that none of this is your fault. You do understand that, don't you?'

She wasn't sure yet whose fault it was. Maybe it was nobody's fault. Maybe the fault of death was not the biggest crime that had been committed here.

'But I pushed her, Mum. If it hadn't been for me she wouldn't have died.'

'No, that's not true.' Mary remembered the letter and silently thanked Nancy for helping her even now. 'Nancy was always heading for destruction one way or another. And Dad might not have administered the final blow, but all this was his responsibility. You are the last person who deserves to be punished in this mess and I promise you I will do absolutely everything in my power to make sure that never happens.'

'But what if you can't, Mum?'

'I can,' she answered. 'I love you very much, Marcus.'

He reddened. 'I love you too, Mum.'

She would go through it all again for Marcus, Mimi and Maisie, which was the second time in recent months she'd had that thought. But it was time now and what she had to do was very clear.

After watching Marcus fall asleep, stroking the hair off his face as she had done when he was small, Mary went first to Howard's desk and retrieved the envelope. She took it to her bedroom, where she laid on the bed, fully clothed, with it clutched to her chest. She didn't bother to turn on the lights or shut the curtains. Her blood raged in her veins and her breathing came hard and fast so she could almost imagine herself like a dragon, breathing fire. She lay like that for over an hour, allowing her thoughts to settle in her brain, her hatred and anger solidifying into a hard mass.

When she could move again she took the letter out of the envelope and read it by the light of her phone, letting the words wash into her. Nancy, she realised as she read, had always been fooled by the goddess myth, not ever understanding how constrictive it is. Beauty and adoration are such hard crosses to bear, and she wished now she'd helped Nancy sooner, wished she'd noticed her friend struggling. But life pulls and pushes, dropping endless barriers in the way, so before you know it someone you used to see every day becomes someone you speak hurriedly to once a month. For the first time since she'd found the envelope Mary felt sadness at Nancy's death, felt that itching disbelief that she was never going to see her again. One day she imagined thinking of her fondly, of remembering her and not what she had done. Eleanor was right, no one existed inside great dramas, and Nancy's mistake had been in conflating her feelings for something larger.

No, the person who had fucked around with her life for way too long was Howard. Howard, who thought it all right to infect their whole house with his moods. Howard, who disregarded his children, who liked to belittle those he claimed to love. Who had taken her best friend from her, then lied and cheated their son into disregarding his feelings to protect his own. When all was said and done he was nothing more than a sadist.

She waited until the house was completely silent, lulled by the regularity of sleeping breath, then got up and drew her curtains. She changed into her nighttime tracksuit and covered her feet with thick socks. Then she collected the pills from the drawer of her bedside table and picked up the envelope before tiptoeing downstairs.

She went first to the kitchen where she found the matches without turning on any lights. Then she stood by the sink and burnt the contents of the brown envelope one by one, all Nancy and Howard's memories disintegrating to nothing but black embers. She saved the letter for last, holding it by one corner and lighting the other, watching the fire creep up with its blue light, over each and every word, obliterating everything they had ever said. When she was finished she ran the tap and watched the soot disappear down the drain, imagining it washing through the junk of her pipes and into the sewers, becoming nothing before it was even washed out to the sea. Then she collected up the used matches and threw them in the bin, replacing the box by the cooker and filling a glass with water.

The box of pills felt rounded against Mary's leg as she opened the door to Howard's room. He didn't stir when she shut the door behind her, so she walked over to his bed, where he lay on his back with his mouth open and his eyes sunken in his face. My God, she hated him. She could kill him with her bare hands wrapped around his throat, squeezing his paltry life out of him. Except of course she mustn't give in to such tantalising temptation; she must not leave any room for doubt about how and why he had died.

Mary put her hand onto Howard's bony shoulder and shook it, watching the sleep leave his body and his brain start to fire. He blinked open his eyes, looking up at her. She thought this is what the gods must have felt like when they brought down their judgements; they didn't feel any sentiment, they were perfectly happy to enact their revenges, often in the cruellest of ways. Anyway, they had gone so far past the point of sentiment, her and Howard, this was all that was left. He had dangled her life over a ravine for years now, pretending that he was the only thing holding her up, when she now knew that had never been the case.

*You're such a bloody strong woman*, she remembered Nancy saying to her from somewhere in the past, and the memory was almost enough to knock her off balance. She hadn't felt strong for so long now it was an almost unreal sensation.

'Sit up,' she said to Howard and he did as he was told, scrabbling with the covers.

'Your leg hurts.' She handed him two pills on the palm of her hand and the glass of water.

He dutifully took them, as all their hours of practice meant he would, so then she popped out two more and he swallowed those, then two more. She wished there was a more painful way of doing it.

She popped two more and held them out to him. 'No.' He turned his face away.

She used her fingers pinched around his chin to turn him back to her. 'I know what you did to Marcus. And Nancy. And me.'

'Not Marcus,' he said.

The words shocked her. 'Not Marcus what?'

He stared back at her in the dark, the whites of his eyes shining but she couldn't tell what he meant. His lips were trembling and they caught at her heart despite everything. She let her head fall forward so her shoulders felt like a deep valley in her back and all she could do was moan, because if she couldn't do it now then there was no hope and her anger would be her undoing.

But the position she was in felt too defeatist, so she forced her head back up and looked into his haunted eyes and the features of his face she knew too well, all hiding the mess of his brain, the terrible things he had done for so many years now. Her hands shook as she brought the pills between them. 'I can't do this any more, Howard. I don't know what you want from me, what you've ever wanted in fact. But I do know this. I know that if you don't die I will sell the house and leave you alone on the street because I will not be this person any more.'

He nodded at the pills then and held out his hand. She straightened, not sure any more where right began and wrong ended. But he nodded again and pointed at the packet. She hovered it over his hand and pushed the back of the silver foil so another pill dropped, then another, on and on until she'd lost count and he folded his hand over on his own inevitability.

He smiled at her before emptying them into his mouth, a sly smile which made her feel like she'd done what he wanted anyway, that he'd manipulated her right up to the end. She willed herself to hold his stare for once, to not buckle under his pressure, to let him know that she would not regret this.

But then he grimaced and the pills looked like they were sticking to his throat, which made his eyes bulge slightly. And, despite everything, a part of her wanted to stick her fingers down his throat and force the poison from his system. A part of her panicked with the knowledge that she would never see him again. A part of her wanted nothing to change because even when things are going to change for the better, it is still scary. Her tears came unbidden, dropping down her front.

But he simply lay down and turned his face to the wall so she was left looking only at his bony back curved under his pyjamas. 'It's OK,' he said to the wall.

Her tears dried at his words, a strange calmness overtaking her. 'Thank you,' she said finally.

*

Mary woke with a start just before 5 a.m., surprised that she had slept at all. She knew immediately what she'd done only a few hours before, but the knowledge wasn't accompanied with the complete dread she'd expected. She searched her soul for feelings of disgust and remorse, but they weren't there. It didn't seem like something momentous, just another task in the long line of tasks she had performed. Even her anger had softened, so it no longer felt hard or dangerous inside her, but more like something she had absorbed for strength.

She dressed slowly and deliberately – a pair of worn jeans, a rumpled shirt with a navy sweatshirt over the top and large woollen socks. The day outside her window looked like night still, with a dark sky and the first spots of rain on the window. She pulled her hair into a low bun and smeared her face with an inexpensive moisturiser which did little for her dry skin. Her nails were long and misshapen and she had to resist the urge to file them. It was imperative that she find Howard, she could not forgive herself if one of the children did, although realistically she had hours before they woke.

She opened the door to her bedroom and tried to gauge if the house felt any different, if it was lighter somehow, but there was nothing in the atmosphere giving anything away. It was, she supposed, possible that Howard wasn't dead. If anyone could survive an overdose she felt sure it would be him. The thought was enough to propel her down the stairs and to his door, to take the round handle and turn it slowly, cautiously, feeling the seconds pass between knowing and not knowing.

It was still as dark as night outside, but the light from the hallway was enough for her to see that he was lying on his back, but not whether his chest was rising or falling. She stepped forward and the room felt cold, like it was filled with an absence, which made her heart speed. She flicked on the light, scared suddenly of being alone in the dark with him. It was obvious when she came level to the bed that he was dead. His skin had greyed and his body already looked stiff and unnatural. His eyes were closed, but she knew there was nothing behind them and his lips were parted but there was no sense of moisture or breath on them. She pulled the covers down slowly and opened his pyjama top, revealing his emaciated, immobile chest. She didn't want to touch him, but knew she had to, except when she did she pulled back instantly because his skin felt cold and waxy and she hadn't expected it to be this final, not so soon.

She took a step backwards and heard a little cry escape from her mouth, as her vision blurred over with tears. Her reaction was perverse, but she couldn't stop it; her shock was visceral and deep and came from a part of her she hadn't even known existed. But it also felt good that she remained, that Howard hadn't obliterated her, or knocked out the fundamental things that made her who she was. Perhaps everyone had been wrong and anger didn't ruin a woman, perhaps it made them stronger.

She made herself focus, taking the empty pill packet from the side and wrapping Howard's hands around it. She had to account for all eventualities and there was a chance they would take fingerprints. Obviously hers would be there, but his needed to be as well. It felt very strange holding his hand this way and the magical moments of his death the night before flooded her.

She went to the kitchen to make the call, her fingers shaking against the keys as she punched in the three numbers she'd never used before. Her voice, even to her own ears, sounded small and scared as she recited her address against the catch in her words. They would be there in about thirty minutes, the operator told her, before asking again if she was absolutely sure he was dead.

The kitchen felt hollow so she put on the kettle for something to do, but then couldn't face even making a cup of tea. She should probably wake the kids before the noise of the ambulance did, but it was like when they were little again and every minute alone felt precious. Her head spun suddenly and she leant forward over the kitchen table, taking in deep breaths. This was it, this was the moment she had been waiting for, this was in fact her doing, but now it was here it felt terrifying and she didn't know if she was strong enough.

The door opened behind her so she turned and saw Marcus framed in the kitchen door, his hair mussed from sleep.

'What's all the noise?' he asked.

'Oh sweetheart, shut the door.'

He did as she said, sitting at the kitchen table. 'What's going on?'

She sat next to him and folded her hands over his, not sure that any of this was real. 'I'm so sorry to have to tell you this. Dad died last night.'

His face contracted, as if hit. 'What? But how?'

'His leg was hurting so I took in the painkillers, but I left them by his bed by mistake, and I think he must have taken an overdose.'

Marcus put his hands over his face, but she could see the tears falling from underneath them as his shoulders shook like in a bad film.

'Oh, Marcus, I'm sorry.' She pulled his hands away from his face, but his eyes refused to meet hers. 'I know it must be a terrible shock,' she tried, because she hated how he'd never been able to resolve his relationship with his father. 'Dad was never going to get better. In some ways he's done the right thing.'

He stopped crying then and looked back at her. Mary thought they could only be thinking the same thing. 'We're not going to tell anyone about that night, Marcus. There's no point. You have your whole life ahead of you and you're a kind, good person. What happened with Nancy has nothing to do with you really.'

'If I'd known Dad was going to die, maybe...' He stopped and she couldn't work out what he was trying to say. 'But Dad made his own choices, didn't he? We weren't responsible for the things he did?'

'No, of course we weren't.'

'You know, doing this job for Ellie has made me think that we're all here for a short time and then we're not. I'm going to try to remember only the good things he did.' She could see tears trembling in his eyes.

Mary nodded, her own eyes full. 'I'll try to do the same.' Marcus was right, part of allowing anger in also meant you had to know when to let it go. She would remember Howard's turned back and his low voice telling her what she was doing was OK.

'You know, Marcus, I don't think Dad would have ever gone to the police. It must have been him who got rid of Nancy's phone and money and made it look like it could have been a mugging. He must have been protecting you.'

Marcus shrugged. 'I guess. You shouldn't feel guilty, Mum.' Marcus's eyes were searching, as if they wanted to peel back her skin. 'I mean about leaving the painkillers.'

She looked at her son, trying to work out what he meant, because he must suspect what she had done, although it was better if they never said it. She had promised to protect him and the girls always and that is what she had done, what she would continue to do until the last breath left her body.

'No, really. It's totally understandable. It was never your fault, any of it.'

She smiled at her son, still not sure if they were talking about the same thing. 'Nor was it yours.'

'It'll be OK,' he said, and she chose to believe him, her son, a man as unlike her husband as it was possible to be, which was something, which had to be something good she'd done. They had the tools to get over this, she thought, because they loved each other, because they knew what that meant, because that had to trump all the hate Howard had inflicted on them for so long.

The girls were vocally upset, but she'd expected that. They wanted to see him and they wept over him, but she thought it was more about them than him. Marcus hung back and she thought he looked young and scared. He didn't want to go into the room and he sat on the stairs, raking his hands through his hair, his eyes wide and jumpy.

By the time the ambulance arrived Maisie had made them all sweet tea and their eyes were red, so Mary thought they looked as much like a grieving family as it was possible to look. The paramedics confirmed death and she told them the same rehearsed story and they patted her hands and told her it wasn't her fault and that caring for someone sick is exhausting and it was such an easy mistake to make. Then the police came and offered more sympathy and drank more tea. They sat at her kitchen table and didn't even ask if Howard had been depressed because it was all so obvious. And it wasn't hard to cry because she felt sad, not just for Howard's death, but for their scrap heap of a marriage and all the things they'd done to each other over the years.

There wasn't any sense of justification in what she'd done, but nor did she feel terribly guilty. Instead she felt a sense of disbelief that either of them had let it go on for so long. She remembered the way Howard had held out his hand for the pills the night before and how he'd told her it was OK and she'd thanked him after he took them. She thought those few minutes were perhaps the kindest and most human act either had ever performed for the other.

Then Mary thought of Eleanor and even though it was still early she knew she could call.

Eleanor answered groggily. 'Mary. Are you OK?'

'Howard's dead.' As she spoke she looked out over their small garden, her eyes drawn to the few stubborn leaves still clinging to their one tree.

'What! Oh my God, is that why you left without saying goodbye last night?'

'No, no. He died in the night.'

'Shit. How?'

'It's my fault.' The words tasted delicious and there was a moment when she could have simply told the truth. 'He was complaining about his leg in the middle of the night and I gave him a painkiller, but I was really tired and I must have left the packet next to his bed and he's taken an overdose.'

'Oh God, Mary, I'm so sorry. But that is not your fault.'

'I feel very strange.' And she did, a bit like she was floating.

'Who's with you?'

'Well the kids are here and the paramedics have been. I couldn't think of anyone else to call but you.'

'I'm getting dressed. I'll be there in half an hour.'


When Eleanor arrived she held Mary for a very long time, so Mary felt as if she could almost give in to the feeling of having her tired muscles entirely supported. But in the end they disengaged and went and sat in the kitchen. It was a strange thought to have at that moment, but Mary noticed that Eleanor looked luminous, as if she'd covered herself in gold or something. Howard was still in the other room and everything seemed unreal.

'I was thinking,' Eleanor said. 'And it might be too early to say this and I'm sorry if it is, but you know it's for the best, don't you?'

'I know.' Mary looked at the tea in her mug vibrating quietly with the thrum of the house.

'It wasn't a life he was living and he was stopping you living one as well. It could have gone on and on for years and that would have been terrible.'

'I still feel weird.'

Eleanor took her hand across the table. 'Of course you do, sweetheart.'

'I've got a job.' She didn't know why she'd said that and laughed apologetically. 'It's definitely not the time to say that.'

Eleanor waved her away. 'It's the perfect time.'

'I don't know why I didn't mention it before now. I got it a while ago.' Except she did know why – she knew that everything had eclipsed her before this moment. But the thought of Thea, whom she had only met once, was wonderfully uplifting.

'Oh, Mary,' Eleanor said, 'you're going to be so fine.'

Life suddenly seemed like a road ahead, which made her realise she'd only ever looked one or two paces in front of her before now. It was an exciting and fresh feeling, a bit like spring, which seemed like the wrong emotion when your husband's corpse was lying in the next room.

She had killed Howard. That was the plain and simple fact and she wondered if that made her no better than him, when all was said and done. She worried suddenly that the knowledge of this or just the action itself would curdle inside her. But it didn't feel that way, it felt more like a liberation and she imagined a time, years from now, where she would tell the story of Howard's death and forget that it wasn't entirely true. She saw all of a sudden that there is never a simple fact when it comes to death.

'You look different,' she said to Eleanor.

Eleanor brushed her fingers along her lips, almost as if she was kissing herself. 'I feel different. I don't know, something about seeing Robert last night. Maybe he was right and there were ghosts that were ready to be banished.'

'I don't suppose life has really worked out how any of us thought it would.'

'I don't think it does for anyone. And for the first time I'm OK with that.' Eleanor smiled with her flashing eyes. 'When I had supper with Nancy the night she died, she kept going on and on about how guilty she felt. And I remember feeling almost pleased that she thought that, I remember thinking that she was guilty, that out of the three of us she was always the one who fucked up and made a meal out of everything. And it made me feel really annoyed with her. So annoyed, that I let her go off into the night to meet that stupid man, without even saying something kind to her, or giving her a smile. Which of course I've felt guilty about ever since. And then there was that thing with Robert, which just compounded how I felt. But what's the point of all this fucking guilt? It doesn't matter. It's not possible to always get it right.'

Mary desperately wanted to tell Eleanor the truth about what had happened to Nancy, but she would protect her children to the end of time. Her and Eleanor would both have to live with their versions of Nancy's story. Marcus had told her earlier that Nancy had thought she was amazing and she could imagine that. As the years passed those would be the sort of memories her and Eleanor would share about their friend, that was the most important story here.

Eleanor reached down and pulled her bag up from the floor, she rummaged around until she pulled out a tiny wooden box, which she put in the middle of the table. The wood was so light that for a moment Mary thought it was painted gold and that maybe some of it had transferred itself to Eleanor and she really was flecked with gold dust, but then she saw it was just smoothed so it almost looked polished, as if it had been touched many, many times. There were words on the lid, which she craned forward to read, but they were in another language.

'You Are Loved,' Eleanor said behind her, so she looked back at her friend and saw the tears sparkling in her eyes.

'Irena left me this box,' Eleanor said. 'She told me that we have a responsibility to those who love us. That being loved makes us precious and that means we have to take care of ourselves. I think you and I, Nancy as well, we're good at loving, but not so good at being loved. But that means we're missing something important, we're taking on too much of the bad responsibility and not enough of the good and that's not right.'

Mary looked over at her wonderful friend and understood, for maybe the first time ever, that they knew each other so completely they didn't have to pretend they'd got it right. They didn't have to lament the people they never became or wonder at what might have been. They understood the words each other said, and knew each other's stories. Their strengths lay in their weaknesses, and she wished she had worked that out in time to save Nancy.

It felt like her heart had swelled slightly, as if blown by a breeze. 'I love you, Ellie,' she said, simply.

'I love you too,' Eleanor replied and closed her hand around the tiny box. If her skin had turned to gold then her eyes now looked like diamonds. 'And you know how they say bad luck comes in threes?' Mary nodded. 'Well, that's Nancy, Irena and now Howard.'

Mary puffed out her cheeks because something still didn't feel entirely right to her. She shook her head and it was as if she had dislodged a feeling, or a thought, maybe even a memory. She smiled up at her friend. 'You know what, Ellie, maybe we don't have to see life like that any more. Maybe the things that happen to us have nothing to do with luck or fault or responsibility. I think that could be what Irena was trying to tell you.'

Eleanor nodded. 'I've been thinking about that as well recently and I think you're right. I think she was telling me to live my life without always thinking I was getting it wrong or worrying about everybody else.'

'Robert didn't kill Nancy, Els.'

Eleanor looked straight at her then. 'Yes,' she answered. And they didn't have to say any more.

'You know what I'd like to do,' Mary said, sucking back her tears. 'I'd like to put all our sorrows and guilt into your box, where they can live with the love and not feel like the most important thing. For the first time in my life I don't mind the mess of that. I don't feel like I have to make it right. I don't mind being imperfect.'

Eleanor looked momentarily jolted, but then she smiled deeply, the lines around her eyes creasing upwards. 'Oh yes,' she said, 'that's the best idea I've heard in a long time. Maybe we can be imperfect women together.'

The doorbell sounded and Eleanor made to stand, but Mary waved her down. She knew it would be the people who had come to take Howard away and she wanted to be the one to let them in and close the door behind them.

Nothing had worked out the way they'd thought it would when they'd met as three young women all those years before, Mary thought as she walked down the hall. But what she had learnt was that it didn't matter because there is always the possibility of new chapters in everyone's stories. It seemed suddenly clear that Irena was right: we do have a responsibility to take care of ourselves, to feel precious, despite our failings. Because that is how you learn there is no such thing as perfect.

The sun must have come out because a shaft of bright light was shining through the glass in the door. She stepped into it and it warmed her right through.

# Acknowledgements

This book is unashamedly about women and, in many parts, female friendship. I am so lucky to work with many incredible women and also to have lots of amazing female friends, without whom my days would be considerably duller and less easy to navigate.

Books are such a collaborative process and it is not hyperbole to say that nothing would exist without so many others than the person who writes the book. So, my heartfelt thanks to all these people:

My agent, Lizzy Kremer, who pushed me to write this story after I faltered a few times at the beginning and lost my nerve. And who is an amazing champion and help, editorially and practically, and everything in between. Thanks also to the whole team at David Higham, including Maddelena Cavaciuti, who is a fantastic reader, Nicky Lund who can turn words in to pictures and Alice Howe and her wonderful translation team who send books around the world.

I am incredibly lucky to be published by the wonderful and innovative team at Orion, especially my editor Francesca Pathak, who has been such a brilliant and enthusiastic champion of this book. Massive thanks as well to Debbie Holmes for the beautiful and striking cover design.

This book is dedicated to my five oldest friends, some of whom I've known since before I even reached double figures. But I have also made many wonderful and lifelong friends through working and being a mother, all of whom are the most inspiring, strong and funny people. Thank you Amy, Bryony, Emma, Sophie, Clare, Cherry, Moya, Eve, Lizzie, Dorothy, Kate and Laura.

Thanks as ever to my parents, Lindy and David, my numerous siblings, all their partners and children.

And, finally, but never least, to my husband Jamie and children, Oscar, Violet and Edith, without whom nothing would mean anything.

# Credits

Araminta Hall and Orion Fiction would like to thank everyone at Orion who worked on the publication of *Perfect Strangers* in the UK.

**Editorial**
Francesca Pathak
Lucy Frederick

**Copy editor**
Joanne Gledhill

**Proof reader**
Linda Joyce

**Audio**
Paul Stark
Amber Bates

**Contracts**
Anne Goddard
Paul Bulos
Jake Alderson

**Publicity**
Francesca Pearce

**Design**
Debbie Holmes
Joanna Ridley
Nick May

**Editorial Management**
Charlie Panayiotou
Jane Hughes
Alice Davis

**Finance**
Jasdip Nandra
Afeera Ahmed
Elizabeth Beaumont
Sue Baker

**Production**
Hannah Cox

**Marketing**
Katie Moss
Jennifer Hope

## Sales

Jen Wilson
Esther Waters
Victoria Laws
Rachael Hum
Ellie Kyrke-Smith
Frances Doyle
Georgina Cutler

## Operations

Jo Jacobs
Sharon Willis
Lisa Pryde
Lucy Brem

Don't miss Araminta Hall's new dark, compelling mystery:

# BROKEN WATER

Coming January 2022

Turn the page for an early sneak preview...

'Fail we may, sail we must.'

*Irish sailing proverb*

# WEDNESDAY

# Lily

The funnels were surely too big. They were easily the biggest manmade things Lily had ever seen and they made her feel like she was floating, even more so than normal. They could in fact be bigger than the terrible, dreary hills she had to stare at out of one of the hundreds of windows at home, hills which only moved between the dankest of colour spectrums, from forest green to granite grey to coal black, only allowing a sprinkling of violet purple on the rare occasions the sun shone. Like the hills, the funnels were also imposingly dark, all four of them standing so straight and true as if there was nothing to worry about.

Lily turned her attention back to the room and focused on Henry, absorbed in his newspaper. She imagined telling him what the funnels made her feel like and the look of scorn he would give her, if he even acknowledged her words. She looked instead at what he was reading, but there on the front page was a replica of the ship she'd just been staring at through the window. The sensation of the two ships, of herself soon to be in one of them, made her feel dizzy, like she was going to have one of her turns, but she forced herself away from the edge, desperate not to annoy Henry more than was necessary.

She concentrated instead on the laughter coming from the next table; two women and a man, excitedly discussing the crossing they were about to make, as if there were things to look forward to. Their voices were cut from glass and tinkled across the china, the toast, the kipper bones, the scraped bowls of porridge and cold cups of tea that had constituted their breakfast.

Lily's gaze involuntarily strayed back to the window, out of habit from home, but she forced them downwards, away from the ship and into the street. It looked like a river of people streaming below, a palpable sense of adventure rising from them like steam, which tickled at the glass. One of the women on the next table laughed again and Lily wished she could share in the joy around her, but all she could feel was a deep, lacerating fear, which speeded her heart and slicked her skin with sweat. And it wasn't really anything to do with the funnels looking too big; it was more because her life was joyless and loveless and graceless and had been for far too long. She folded her hands protectively over her raised skirt, wishing for things she could barely believe in.

Her mind tipped and swayed but she forced it to steady by holding on to the thought that they were finally going home, or at least back to her home. Once there she was certain things would get better; her nerves would calm and the prospect of the baby wouldn't terrify her like a nightmare constantly stalking her thoughts. And, if she still felt this daily terror at home, perhaps there was some way she could refuse to board a ship back to England. She would appeal to May in some way, beg her for help, cling to her if necessary.

Henry snapped his newspaper so it made the sound of a whip and Lily jumped in her seat. He allowed their eyes to meet for the briefest of seconds, although that was all it needed.

'Are you ready?' She asked, trying to pull her mouth upwards.

He looked pointedly at her untouched egg, the yellow yolk congealed against the side of the shell like blood, which made her wonder how she'd forgotten to eat again. He snorted his derision and stood, so she followed, knocking into the table which made the china clink together.

'For God's sake,' he growled under his breath and Lily saw one of the laughing ladies glance quickly over at them, so she worried that she would have dampened her happy day.

Henry strode before her through the dining room with all the confidence of his birth right, while she trailed in his wake. A few people glanced up as they passed, but she doubted any of them knew him because they were strangely not staying in the smartest hotel, where his set would be. She supposed some of the women might recognise him from the society pages, not that she knew when he'd last been in them as she'd long ago stopped trying to track her husband's progress through the gossip columns.

Becky was in their bedroom trying on Lily's blue hat when they opened the door. She pulled it off her head too hastily, so her hair snagged and her cheeks flushed as she caught Lily's eye through the glass.

'You really should not touch my things, Becky,' she made herself say, the words sticking in her throat.

Becky bobbed her head. 'Sorry, Ma'am. I was just finishing off your packing. It was all a mess when I came in.'

'My wife always leaves everything in a mess,' Henry said, which made tears smart to Lily's eyes.

At almost her first society party in London, when she was still a fresh-faced, rosy-cheeked new bride, straining with love and passion, an older American woman, a duchess no less, had taken Lily to one side. 'You look like you are in love,' she'd said, in a voice which had reminded Lily so much of her mother's rich Southern drawl she'd longed pathetically for the woman far away across a long ocean.

'Why thank you. We are very happy,' Lily had replied, looking over at her new husband as he chatted to a group of men. He looked so fine, in his smart clothes with his thick moustache, that she found it easier to forget his greying hair and short stature.

'Well, be careful,' Consuelo Vanderbilt, as Lily, as every aspiring American girl would have known her to be, said, 'I have come to learn that the British upper-class male spends their formative years being hugged and kissed only by working-class maids and nannies, a taste which never leaves them.'

Lily turned to the tiny, delicate woman standing next to her, but all she saw in her eyes was a flashing knowledge. 'Ours is a love match. Henry, Fitz, has been the perfect gentleman.' She hated having to call her husband by the nickname everyone used in London. His second name was Fitzherbert, but she thought the diminutive made him sound insubstantial, like a cracker or a firework, which everyone knew shone brightly for only a few seconds before extinguishing entirely.

Consuelo raised an eyebrow in a perfect arch. 'At least we knew what we were doing in my day. I mean, there was no pretence then, you swapped your millions of dollars for a title and thought it fair until you arrived on this wet island. I cannot believe you girls failed to learn our lessons.' She popped open her tiny, tortoiseshell bag and handed Lily a thick, embossed card imprinted with her name and address. 'You know Fitz was almost bankrupt before he met you.'

But Lily didn't see how that was possible, with his smart London house and the castle they were going to visit in Northumberland in just a few days. His tailored suits, his gold watches, the beautiful ring he'd given her, the fine wines he liked to drink, the private railcar he'd hired to take them back to Newport to speak to her father.

'I think you must be mistaken,' she stammered.

Consuelo had leaned in closer so Lily could smell the violets on her breath. 'It's time to grow up, Lily, dear. You have to create your own life over here, you have to fight for it, because if you don't it will consume you whole. Not that you have to do it alone, there are people who will be your friends if you let them. And, believe me, you will need them.'

Becky had been her friend once, her dearest friend, in fact. The person she'd confided in when writing to May had seemed like too much of an admission of failure, the person she'd laughed with when nothing was funny, the person she'd sat with on cold nights when home seemed a million miles away. The person who'd listened and held and comforted her.

'Organise the cases, Becky,' Henry said. 'Lady Elsworth and I will walk to the ship. Also, tell Dr Henderson to make his own way there.'

'Yes, Sir.'

Lily tried to catch Becky's eye as she hurried from the room, but she kept her head determinedly low.

'Have you taken all your medicine this morning?' Henry asked, as he gathered up his papers.

'Yes.'

'I'm so bored of reminding you.'

'But I never forget.'

He snorted, which made Lily wonder if she really had taken it. She tried to remember the sensation of mixing two drops from the glass bottle in to her water that morning and found it impossible to tell if it had happened or not, if what she was remembering was from this morning or from all the other mornings she'd done the same thing. Her heart began to race, but then Henry was making for the door, and Lily knew it would irritate him too much to find the bottle in the case, so she simply followed him out into the crowded streets.

They were very noisy and bright, which filled up too much of her mind, so it felt hard to fully believe in what she was doing, as if there were a veil in front of her face. She wanted to cover her ears and shut her eyes, but knew it would anger Henry, so concentrated on her feet on the ground, on placing one in front of the other. In that way she could move without too much consequence, without feeling like she was part of anything larger.

The quayside was even busier than the streets and the atmosphere was heavy with activity, the scents of sweat, smoke and rose mingling in an acrid mess that made her lift a handkerchief to her nose. She forced herself to glance up at the ship towering over the scene, but the hugeness spun her head so she had to immediately look back down, knowing that when she felt this way she had to take every second as it came. She forced her attention to the tiny buttons on the back of her gloves, made her mind wonder at the delicacy it would have taken to sew them, imagined the women bent over tables spending days at this work.

It worked to get her to the bottom of a wooden gangplank where people were filing up onto the ship, white ropes on either side to keep them safe. They had to stop and wait their turn which she knew would irritate Henry and, sure enough, he huffed dramatically behind her. She turned and saw him looking up and over at a metal gangplank high above them, crossing over from a large metal structure, on which she could see people ambling serenely, looking down at the crowds below. It was an ornate, beautiful contraption, clearly the First Class entrance and it made everything feel wrong because before today there would have been no scenario Lily could have imagined in which they weren't up there. Henry's face was red and contorted and she knew how slighted he would feel to be beneath, in every sense of the word. The unlikelihood of what they were doing knocked in to her again so she couldn't catch her breath for a moment.

Her turn had come to ascend the much inferior structure which would transport them to the similarly inferior part of the ship and all she could do was step up. She held on to the thick rope as soon as she could, enjoying feeling its heft, as if it could support her. Henry was close behind, his hand in the small of her back, and she had a sudden desperate desire to turn and run because it would be like this for the next week, this feeling of being enclosed and trapped, with no hope of escape.

Henry pushed into her back, the pressure mounting, even though she couldn't move any faster because there was a line of people in front of her. She tried to turn to him but, before she could, he gave her a sharp shove and she fell forward, knocking in to the man in front, who had to grab on to the rope to stop himself falling in to the woman in front of him. He turned, his face moving from anger to concern when he saw Lily.

'My apologies, Sir,' Henry said from behind her. 'My wife is often unsteady on her feet.'

'It's quite alright,' the man replied, his cheeks reddening. 'I hope you're not hurt, Madam?'

Lily shook her head, her throat clogging with tears. But the man had turned and was already taking larger strides to catch up with his companions in front of him, who were all looking down at Lily, pity smearing their faces.

The baby was quiet in her stomach, so she thought it was safe and, it was true, she was often unsteady. And she must have been mistaken because, even though Henry had never needed much of a reason to hurt her, there was no way he would have endangered the baby by pushing her on purpose. He'd told her too many times that a baby was all he wanted and her pregnancy had certainly been the most fervent wish for all the years they'd been married. Before this year she'd long given up hope at the thought she would be able to do this for him, long accepted her uselessness as her body failed and faltered so, when the unlikely conception came, she found she couldn't quite believe in it, couldn't quite make herself even desire what lay at the end of the nine months.

'Come on, then,' Henry said behind her and Lily had to make her feet move again because there was simply no other option.

**Don't miss the rest of Lily's story in *Broken Water* –**

**Coming January 2022**